THE AWAKENING OF THE HALO

The Awakening of the Halo
Copyright © 2017 Shea Swain

Warning: The Awakening of the Halo is for 18 years and older.

ISBN-13: 978-1548762537
ISBN-10: 1548762539

Cover Designed: Sanja Balan of Sanja's Covers
Edited: Pam Howard
Proofreader: D. Swain, Kim Bey, Kelly Bey-Borden
Format: Shea Swain

Other Books Written By:

Shea Swain
The Pulse of Provocative Romance

What Lilly Wants
previously known as Lascivious
An Erotic Novella

INVIDIOUS Betrayal
A Full-Length Paranormal-Sci Romance

ABSOLVE
A Short Romantic New Adult Drama

The Changing of the Seasons
Winter's Icy Heart
A Taste of Spring
Contemporary Romance

Chained to the Devil's Son
A Full-Length Dark Romance

The Binding of the Halo Series
Four Full-Length Paranormal Romance Series
The Binding of the Halo Book I
The Awakening of the Halo Book II
The Descent of the Halo III
The Battle for the Halo IIII
&
The Coesen-Origins

Heaven on Hell Island
A Contemporary Romance with Sci-fi undertones

Dedicated to my inspirations…
Sonserae
Daniel III
Daniel IV
Cianne

Prologue
October 12th

Bored almost to the point of changing her nail polish a third time, Tranae decided she may as well see what was going on outside. She walked out of her bedroom, jogged down the stairs, and left her house.

Tranae glanced at Cianne's house before looking down the road to where their street intersected with a main thoroughfare. The smell of burnt rubber and the unmistakable chatter of curious spectators filled the air as she approached the intersection of Roland Road and Ridgeview Park Lane. She lazily strolled along the sidewalk, her attention split between the gathered spectators and the text message she was sending her best friend about all the commotion she was missing.

At the end of the street, several police cruisers, three emergency vehicles, and at least one hell of a wreck littered the impassable junction.

"I wonder what happened?" Tranae asked herself. She let the hand that held her cell phone fall to her side as she slid her way through the group of spectators to get a better look.

A car accident wasn't much of a surprise at this particular intersection, but the several loud popping sounds that she heard following the crash tugged at her curiosity. Tranae didn't care for the macabre but the crash, the strange sounds, and the large number of people she saw walking by her house were enough to spark her interest.

This was so much more exciting than changing her nail color. Due to her current parental imposed imprisonment, she couldn't go to the spa to get them professionally done.

Tranae peered over the police barrier, taking note of all the police, emergency medical techs, and firemen. "So reckless," she said, dragging the words out. "Someone must be hurt bad."

"Looks like it," someone close by offered.

Tranae didn't look to see who spoke. Her attention was focused on the metallic silver car sitting just inside the police barrier, with its roof caved in due to a large palm tree resting on top of it. The car looked familiar.

The make and model is kind of popular, she told herself to dismiss her fears. There's no reason to stress. Still. Tranae scanned the scene from left to right, trying to see through the emergency workers who were huddled together in groups.

"It looks pretty bad."

Tranae looked at the man who spoke. She eased past him.

"Excuse me," the man sneered as he stepped aside, "no need to be rude."

Tranae paid the man no mind because her attention was directed beyond a huddled group of EMT's where there was another vehicle. It was totaled and it was a vehicle she was certain she recognized, despite the damage. Tranae's stomach knotted, curiosity making way for panic. She hurried around the length of the barrier, closer to where the huddled EMT's were frantically working. She needed to see who it was they were working on.

"I've got a pulse over here," a female paramedic yelled out.

In a state of utter panic, Tranae fixed her eyes on the female paramedic. When the paramedic jumped up, allowing a gap in the huddle, Tranae saw what she feared most. The scream that rose from her lungs caused everyone within earshot to look her way.

Chapter One

Present
About Four Months Earlier
June 2

Tristan parked the borrowed truck under a large tree at the end of the busy street. He looked at the dashboard and noted that it was a quarter after one. The sun, which looked to be at a high point in the afternoon sky, wasn't able to penetrate the tree's shade. But it was still about 90 degrees under the leaves.

It was a hot day but it was business as usual on the city block filled with vendors, residents, and children. For Tristan, the heat was never an issue, and just like the people around him, he had business to take care of.

He reached for the bag on the passenger seat and pulled out a bottle of water. He had about an hour before his meeting so he decided to look in on an old friend whose apartment was in clear view from where he sat.

As Tristan began to drink his water, he saw his friend's image appear in the rear-view mirror. He watched Jason Cruz, also known as JC, walk right by the truck Tristan sat in, turning every so often to glance over his shoulder.

Tristan made no attempt to move or hide that he was there, watching. He drank his water as JC strolled across the street and continued down to the far end of the block. He saw JC look around again before stepping into an apartment building, sure that JC didn't see him.

Jason hadn't seen him this time or the two other times he sat parked in the very same spot. "You seemed spooked," Tristan said in a low hiss to no one. "Being spooked should be the least of your worries Jason."

It was only two and a half weeks since Tristan saved Cianne from the hell JC and his friends put her through to extort a large sum of money from him; two and half weeks since she was left alone to defend herself from a pack of feral dogs that he had to kill with his bare hands to save her. It was two and a half weeks since he found out Cianne had supernatural abilities and had somehow inadvertently given him the strength and speed necessary to protect her.

JC should be on edge. He, along with his buddy, Nicklaus Carter, a college student Cianne once tutored, had literally gotten away with kidnapping and murder. The third accomplice, Peter Walter, a.k.a. Cook, a name given to him by Cianne for the home cooked meals he brought her when they held her captive, realized early on that the kidnapping for ransom scheme was wrong. For five days Cook secretly made sure Cianne ate properly; and in the end, he tried to help her escape but lost his life in the process.

The police have nothing to link JC or Nick to Peter or the crime other than they knew one another, but Tristan knew they were guilty. "Cook" had botched the kidnapping for Nick and JC so one of them shot and killed him.

Tristan was so damn thankful to Peter for helping Cianne and the baby she carried inside of her. My baby. She would never be the same because of them and if something had happened to her as a result of their actions…

"Shit," he cursed at the thought.

Tristan put the top back on his water. He dismissed all thoughts of Cianne's mortality. She and the baby survived their ordeal. It was time to look ahead. He would do whatever it took to keep them safe. There were just a few loose ends to tie-up. He focused on the apartment building JC went into.

◉

Cianne nervously glanced at her father. They both sat on an elegant sofa in a home that was bigger than Tristan's.

"What am I supposed to call her?" Cianne let her eyes wander around the large room again. This time she moved her eyes over each item slowly, to appreciate all the intricate details that she may have missed before. Beautiful pictures and tapestries adorned the walls, while wood carvings and figurines were displayed on tables and shelves. She wanted to stand and examine each piece but she wasn't bold enough to do so. Her eyes moved from a tall statue of a female standing upright with a bucket on her hip, to the wide sliding doors that led to the large stone patio.

The doors were closed.

"She will tell you what she wants you to call her," Joseph said, sounding indifferent. He looked at his wrist watch.

It was a quarter after one. Cianne knew because she glanced at his watch too. They had arrived fifteen minutes ago and he seemed more anxious than she was.

Cianne looked up to find her father watching her. He was most likely waiting for her to tell him that she changed her mind about meeting Vivian. Looking into his eyes right now, she knew he wouldn't protest if she did decide she wanted to just leave.

To both of their surprise, Cianne settled further back on the sofa. She was neither scared nor tempted to run. It wasn't just about her anymore. She needed answers that could only come from her maternal grandmother, who she was told had passed away before she was born.

A few weeks ago, the news of her grandmother's existence would have been a huge shock to her. But she was forced to accept that anything was possible, considering all that happened to her recently. An unplanned pregnancy; being kidnapped and held for ransom; and being attacked by wild dogs certainly changed her thoughts of what was possible. If that wasn't enough, she also talked to her deceased mother during a visit to the past, made possible by Time Weaving. All that, coupled with the realization that her visions and Time Weaving were not freak accidents of birth, but were instead inherited from her mother, was a whole lot to swallow.

The thought of her mother, who she thought of as perfect in every way, passing some cursed gene on to her was unsettling; and while Cianne never even entertained the possibility, she had no choice now but to accept it as fact.

What she found difficult to accept was that Tristan was somehow a part of this world or group. Whatever it was. Cianne didn't press him to explain how he was able to rescue her because she didn't think she could handle what he might tell her. She saw him rip those dogs apart with his bare hands that night he came for her. She witnessed the speed at which he moved. Cianne saw him as a boy in a fragmented memory.

Tristan was different, just like she was.

What if he knew for years about her and what she could do? Did he pursue her with such determination because Vivian ordered him to get close enough to spy on her? As she asked herself these questions another question came to her. If she confirmed that Tristan *was* aware of her and only got close to her for those reasons, how would it change her feelings for him? She pushed the questions out of her head and tried to relax.

"So," Cianne sighed after a few moments of silence, "she's some kind of Queen?"

"That's what I'm told," Joseph said with a frown.

A Queen?

Cianne thought of her grandmother, the queen, entering the room. Her stomach churned as she again focused on thoughts of meeting the woman. She wondered if it would be a formal entrance; was she expected to bow? Her concerns over what to call Vivian came back to the forefront, Queen

Vivian or Grandma? She could be safe and call her Queen Grandma.

Cianne gave that thought a little laugh. It felt good to laugh again.

"I hoped you would accept my invitation," a statuesque woman said as she walked into the room. She wore a long gray wrap-around dress that fit her lovely figure perfectly. Her hair was pulled back in a bun and her makeup looked as if it was applied by professionals.

Cianne watched as her father stood up and kissed the woman lightly on the cheek.

"Joseph, you look well," Vivian smirked.

"You look lovely as always Vivian," he said. A strained smile appeared on his face.

"My dear," Vivian said the smiled brightly at Cianne, "you are a true vision."

Cianne watched her grandmother from the moment she entered the room, and now looked up at Vivian as she stood in front of her. She hesitated but then stood and accepted the light kiss Vivian placed on her cheek. Cianne waited until Vivian was seated in a beautiful chair, which made her look like royalty, before sitting back down on the sofa.

"And the impressive Tristan, will he be joining us?" Vivian asked.

"He had some things to attend to," Joseph answered before Cianne could.

Vivian looked from Cianne to Joseph. The look Vivian and Joseph shared was neither hateful nor kind, but it was a *look* nonetheless. Vivian then looked back to Cianne. "He does have a lot of responsibilities for such a young man. How does he manage?"

Cianne didn't know what she meant by the statement. Tristan was as carefree as anyone she knew. A bit confused, she looked at her father.

"He seems capable." Joseph stood, exhaling as he did. "This is a lovely property you have here. I think I will take a look around your garden, if that's all right with you?"

Cianne could hear the agitation in his tone.

"It belongs to a close family friend who has graciously let me use it as needed," Vivian said plainly.

Cianne saw a faint smile on her father's face as he turned to walk toward the glass door leading to the patio. She looked at her grandmother, a beautiful woman seated across from her, thinking again that she looked familiar. It suddenly dawned on Cianne that this was the same lady standing in the crowd at her graduation ceremony a couple of days ago.

"So…" Vivian started after Joseph left out and shut the door. "How are you feeling?"

"Better." Cianne didn't really know how to sum up what she felt. If she was to be honest, she would tell everyone that she once loved the dark and now she feared it. That she was now frightened to be in small spaces and that she hated being in a room with the door shut. If she told them that the only time that she really felt safe was when Tristan was with her, everyone would give her that look. The "I feel so sorry for you" look.

No, she thought, *saying good or better was what people really wanted to hear*.

"Good. How is Dr. Reginald working out for you?" Vivian asked. Her eyes moved to the large glass pitcher sitting on a table in front of Cianne.

She was the one who referred the baby doctor?

It made sense now. Her father told her Dr. Reginald was highly recommended, so Cianne switched doctors and began seeing her immediately. "We've only seen her once, but she seems nice. I'm sort of disappointed that she doesn't believe in modern technology but I thank you for referring her."

"She's a little old-fashioned but a very skilled doctor; and she will be available to you twenty-four hours a day, so if you need to call her do so." Vivian stood. "Would you like something to drink?"

Cianne shook her head. She watched Vivian walk over to the table and pour water into the glass from the pitcher. The water swirled inside the glass as Vivian poured. When Vivian returned to her seat, Cianne asked the question that had been driving her crazy.

"Did you make Tristan the way he is?"

Vivian raised a brow. "Tristan hasn't explained it to you?"

"He asked me to come here, told me that you would explain everything."

"And you accepted that?" Vivian questioned.

"He accepts everything I say without explanation. I feel he deserves the same from me," Cianne said as she looked at Vivian.

Vivian nodded as she took a sip of water. "No, I didn't make him the way he is. But I will explain how he became the way he is after I give you a crash course about your people."

Cianne didn't speak; she was excited at the prospect of finally getting some answers, but at the same time she wasn't sure what to expect or what was expected of her. She decided to keep her thoughts and feelings to herself until she received more information. She looked at Vivian with an expression as if to say "continue".

"We are the descendants of a great nation of people called the Coesen (Coe-sin). We are basically human but our DNA has been altered, giving us the ability to do things that an average human cannot." Vivian sat back in her chair. "Coesen are born with these abilities but in some, the ability remains dormant. These Coesen are still an important part of our nation. They still carry our genes and our mark. When mated with another Coesen, a child with abilities can still be produced."

"There are four tribes and each tribe has an elder who represents them. These representatives collectively are called 'The Council of Four'. In no particular order, the tribes are Quende (Key-in-day), which is ruled by Chandra. The Gedgi

(Ged-gee), is ruled by Brenna, who is the youngest of our lot due to her mother's early passing. The Bode (Boe-dee) is ruled by Eldra and then there is the Arkean (Are-key-an), which is our tribe that I rule. I am also the Sovereign of all four tribes." She paused as if to see if Cianne had any questions. Vivian continued speaking. "This is our mark." She leaned forward and turned her head to the side, exposing her neck.

Cianne's eyes grew wide as she stared at the mark just behind Vivian's left ear. It was in the exact same place as Cianne's birthmark but it was different. Vivian's mark was the upper left portion of a circle, like a large piece of pie.

"The members of each tribe are born with a distinctive mark. This is one way to tell what tribe they're from. Think of a circle cut through the middle into four slightly uneven segments. The Arkean mark is the upper left segment, and is the largest of the birthmarks. The Bode's birthmark is the upper right segment of the circle and it is the second largest. Quende, is the lower right and Gedgi is the lower left segment and the smallest. If laid together the marks would make a complete circle like your inner circle." Vivian clasped her hands together. "You were the first to be born with a complete circle. You are also the only one of us who has ever had a thin outer ring that encompasses the inner mark."

Cianne realized she was touching her birthmark. She shifted in her seat as she placed her hand back in her lap.

"Our abilities manifest at the time of puberty. Most of us are born with a single ability. A very small percentage of us are born with two. Only one child in our entire existence has manifested power before the age of eleven and she was also born with more than two abilities. This Coesen was prophesied to have untold power." Vivian looked sympathetic for a fraction of a second. "I and the other members of The Four had to suppress her abilities because they were too much for a child to handle."

Cianne felt every beat of her heart and she swallowed as she shook her head. "Me?" she asked.

"Yes," Vivian confirmed. "I understand what I am telling you is shocking, but I must ask that you permit me to go on without interruption."

Cianne rubbed her hand over her belly. She had to know, no matter how unsettling all this was.

Vivian began again when Cianne nodded. "When our ability manifests sometimes a gift of sorts, a power, will transmit to another Coesen. The result is a Protector who is very strong and very fast, though the extent of the Protector's power is determined by the strength of the Coesen who transmitted the power to them. These Protectors are connected to that Coesen, who is now their ward, and they will do whatever it takes to keep their ward safe. This is possible because a Protector can sense when their ward is in danger and is able to locate them at any given moment. With training, the Protector will be capable of defending their ward and will lay down their lives to protect them if need be."

"So, Tristan is a Coesen, and my Protector," Cianne surmised.

"Tristan is your Protector but he is not a Coesen," Vivian amended. "We don't exactly know what qualities The Source requires of a Coesen who is chosen as a Protector. We do know that the transfer happens around the time of conversion, when a Coesen's power manifests. It is a process we have tried to influence," she said, as she grimaced, "but it's something we can't manipulate. We still do not know who will be chosen or why. All we know is that as a Protector, Tristan feels an overwhelming desire to protect you even if doing so means his life. Do you remember your zoo trip when you were eight years old?"

Cianne nodded her head, yes.

"Do you remember anything after that?"

Cianne thought of the memories her mother tried to help her recover. The zoo trip was there but everything after was still cloudy. She remembered that she didn't return to that school and she heard her parents arguing for the very first time, but many things were unclear.

"No, not everything," Cianne admitted.

"It may be a side effect of your abilities being suppressed," Vivian told her.

Suppressed, Cianne laughed to herself, *someone should inform the visions.*

She gave Vivian a vacant look but continued searching her memory for something else, anything else, that happened to her just after the zoo trip. Scattered memories flashed through her mind then the haze cleared and she focused as a latent memory came to her. Cianne remembered watching her mother, Kayla, as she stood in a large room a few feet away. She seemed anxious as she spoke to a woman. Both of them looked at Cianne as they spoke, and a loving smile was displayed on the woman's face. Cianne felt an impulse to go to her but the woman held up her hand, motioning for her to stay where she was.

The memory faded just as Cianne realized that the woman she saw in her past, standing between her and her mother was Vivian. Cianne touched her temple, hoping to ease the pounding inside her head as she looked at Vivian who was watching her.

"Is something wrong?" Vivian asked, a concerned look on her face.

"No," Cianne said immediately, resuming her calm display. The memory she had was vague, but it showed her that at one time she was familiar with and felt something for Vivian. As she thought about this, Cianne closed her eyes. "Ok, I 'manifested' early and Tristan is my Protector." She fisted her hands that rested on her lap. "Why did you abandon me when my mother died? Why wasn't I told any of this stuff? My entire life I thought I was alone, that I was the only one dealing with these strange *powers*." As she finished this outburst of emotion, Cianne realized that she wasn't following her plan. *So much for calm and collected,* she thought, feeling a bit sheepish.

"Because of who and what you are, we decided that you needed to be kept safe. Only, we could not agree as to how. So, your mother convinced me that the only real way to do this was to hide you among average people and raise you as a normal child. I helped her disappear with you. As a result, I maintained limited contact with her and you until the zoo incident. Then all contact had to stop to keep you safe."

To keep me safe, Cianne thought.

"Safe from what?" she asked.

Vivian took a deep breath. "You are unique even to us. Your mother, as a young adult, was unhappy with our traditions and refused to comply. She wanted to be "normal" even if it was only for a short time. She threatened that if I didn't give her time to live a normal life, she would disappear forever. Your mother was very gifted and it wouldn't have been much of a problem for her to make her threat a reality. So, I made the mistake of making a deal with her. I allowed her to go to a college with average humans and live without my interference for an agreed upon time.

"During this time, Kayla met your father. She chose what she thought was love, and not allegiance," Vivian said then paused. She looked as if she was trying to remove a bad taste from her mouth. "You needed to be protected because of who your father was. He was an enemy to our people and wanted for murder. We were actively hunting him when your mother was deceived by his charm. She loved a lie, and you were the product of that lie."

The product of a lie.

It took a moment for the harsh cold sting of her words to sink into Cianne's consciousness. She sighed as she looked at the sweaty glass of water on the table next to Vivian. A few of the melting ice cubes shifted inside making a low clattering noise. There was no point in getting angry, not when she needed to know more to keep her baby safe. Cianne focused on her grandmother again.

"So, I had to be protected from him or from your people?"

"*He* is dead. But our people…" Vivian sighed. "Kayla did the unforgivable, Zaria. We have laws just like any other society and she broke them. Some of our people wanted revenge for your father's crimes and they wanted your mother and her unborn child's blood as payment. We knew that you were special before you were born. The Augur, Oma, foretold that you were the Halo, the complete circle, and that you would be very important to our people. Because of that, yours and your mother's lives were spared. Your mother and I decided you had to be hidden from the radicals of our nation, those who are visible as well as those who are hidden, until you were old enough to understand your role and could control your abilities. But your abilities manifested early and we had no choice but to suppress them. You were to be reunited with me when you turned eighteen," Vivian told her. "And that is why I am here now."

A prophecy…great! *These people are mad.*

"So, you thought I would just go with you?" Cianne asked. "Leave my father and my friends when I turned eighteen to be some princess to people who want me dead? All because you believe I'm some kind of Halo."

"You *are* the Halo," Vivian said confidently.

Chapter Two

Cianne didn't miss a beat. "I hate to break it to you but I'm not what you people think I am. I don't have super powers. All I have is headaches and a few visions here and there. They're nothing spectacular, I can assure you."

"Once your abilities are unbound, you will be the Halo," Vivian said. "There are a few more things we must discuss." Vivian held her hand up to stop Cianne from speaking further. "We have been able to conceal our existence for so long because we follow a few simple rules. We do not bring attention to ourselves or make our abilities known to the human, or what we refer to as the Middling, world. We do not obstruct Middling laws or the natural course of their will unless it is to keep ourselves anonymous. We do not interfere in any part of their personal lives. And we only breed with our own. While there have been instances where these rules were tested, we handle any offense with swift justice."

Vivian lifted the glass to her mouth and took a drink. "There are a few other laws which are common sense so I won't get into those right now, but there is one other law that you should know. There must never, under any circumstances, be an intimate relationship between a Coesen and their Protector. You have given Tristan the speed and strength to protect you but your feelings for each other will surely hinder his ability to do so. We have previously witnessed the results of such a union and it almost caused the extinction of our people."

Cianne narrowed her eyes as Vivian's stare bore into her. *She must be kidding. To sit here and tell me I must follow…* She had to stop herself from laughing hysterically. "You can't be serious. You expected me to follow a law I had no knowledge of!" she shrieked.

"Let me explain the reason for this law. The first affair between a Protector and their ward ended with the death of the ward and two others. That Protector was cursed, and his actions still haunt us to this day. The second union resulted in the death of the ward and the mass murder of almost an entire tribe."

"Those other couples aren't us," Cianne interrupted boldly.

Vivian sighed. "There are several similarities between your situation and the last couple I mentioned. The Protector who committed all those atrocities was a Middling until his ward transmitted to him. He was the first and only Middling who was chosen by the Source until Tristan. That Protector also fell in love with a princess of our people which is similar to your situation. Personal feelings such as love or hate can interfere with a Protector's judgment." Vivian placed her glass down and looked to the sliding glass door as Joseph entered the room. She cleared her throat and looked at Cianne, "It is forbidden for you to be in a relationship with him."

Cianne didn't look at her father when he entered the room and walked over to sit next to her. Fighting to maintain control of her emotions, her attention was on Vivian. "Leave Tristan," she said accusingly, "and would you have me get rid of the baby too?"

"I would never, nor did I tell your mother to terminate her pregnancy. The child carries my blood as well. I would prefer that you mated with the Tandot victor and conceived, but what's done is done." Vivian looked at Cianne's belly. "There is something else you should know. You were thinking of an abortion, correct?"

Cianne tensed, and she could feel the heat rush to her face. She knew that her father and Tristan were aware of her brief lapse of judgment but had no idea this woman, who was for all intents and purposes a stranger, also knew. She was ashamed that she even considered it, but to have everyone know…

"My royal line of Arkean women can only bear one child. We aren't sure why, but if that child passes away, some of us have been able to conceive again…but some have not."

"One child…," Cianne said slowly. The thought of her sitting in front of that clinic, planning to end her pregnancy, maybe even ending the possibility that she could ever become a mother, made her stomach queasy. She swallowed, hoping to ease back the sickness. "So, I may only be able to have one child, and he will be different like me."

"She will," Vivian responded.

"She or he," Cianne corrected. Her comment sounded more like an unsure question rather than a statement.

"The odds of you having a boy are very slim. There have been no males born in the Arkean line in centuries," Vivian said with finality. She crossed her legs.

"Oh," Cianne said. She thought of Tristan. All his talk of a boy in the last few days was endearing. Now she had to burst his bubble and tell him that they were having a girl. "All of this is crazy." She turned to her father. "How could you think that I would be ok with this?" Cianne asked angrily.

"It is crazy to you because you were not raised in our world," Vivian said.

"Kayla wanted a normal life for you Cianne. That's why we hid the truth from you. She wanted you to have a choice." Joseph took her hand in his. "We all agreed that when you turned eighteen, Vivian would come and give you the option to go with her to learn your abilities or stay with me and live a normal life."

"That is not what we agreed, Joseph. We agreed that, at eighteen she would be unbound and would come to live with me and learn our ways," Vivian corrected harshly. She looked to Cianne. "Granted, your establishment of a relationship with Tristan wasn't factored into the equation. We assumed you would date before you reached 18, but we didn't foresee all of this." She held her palms in front of her. "The Coesen gentleman who won the Tandot and was to mate is very handsome and we were convinced that you would like him and maybe someday grow to love him."

Cianne gave Vivian a blank look. She couldn't believe she was hearing what she was hearing. They already found her a mate. *A mate*…like she was a mindless animal to breed out.

"Your strength was a surprise as well," Vivian continued. "Your abilities seem to be unbinding without our assistance. We became aware of this because of Tristan's show of strength and speed. His abilities should not have manifested until yours were released, but despite that, he is already as strong and fast as some of our seasoned Protectors." She looked at Joseph, "If I had known of him," she turned to face Cianne, "or that you were having headaches and nightmares, I would have come sooner." Vivian sat down the glass and stood.

"You said that I may only be able to bear one child," Cianne said as she pulled her hand free of her father's, "If I had ended the pregnancy or I refused to go with you, how would you have kept your bloodline going?"

Vivian walked over to a large statue that stood near the patio door. When she turned around to face Cianne she had a hard look on her face that suggested Cianne didn't want to know the answer to her question.

"What we need to concern ourselves with now is your relationship with Tristan."

"Are we in any danger? Will your people come after us?" Cianne asked. For the first time during their conversation, panic washed over her.

Vivian seemed to be thinking over the question. Cianne glanced over at her father and imagined what he was thinking. The look he gave her grandmother was one of pure disgust. If she had to guess what he was thinking she would bet he was wishing Vivian choked on what he would say was her venomous tongue. She studied his face. He looked so much older and tired these days. Cianne suddenly felt sad for him. He was just like Tristan, recruited into this life for the love of a woman.

Vivian cleared her throat, causing Cianne to focus on her again. "Your union will infuriate some, while others will pledge their allegiance to you just because you're the Halo. The rest will fear you because you will be more powerful than anyone we've ever encountered." Vivian walked slowly over to the chair she had been sitting in. She ran her fingers over the wood backing and looked down as if she were thinking something wicked. "Although," she said looking up, "you can release him. Strip him of his Protector abilities,"

"Release him?" Cianne asked as she stood. "I can release Tristan?"

"Yes," Vivian said with a smile, "you can."

"I think you should talk to Tristan first." Joseph spoke up as he stood.

Vivian walked slowly toward Cianne but kept her attention on the silver tray that sat on the coffee table. "That's cute Joseph; you're loyal to the boy." She looked at Joseph as she sat the glass down on the tray. "Don't worry, she will have time to run it by him. We would need to restore her full power before she could release him."

"How do you restore me then?" Cianne asked anxiously.

"It will not be as dangerous as it was to inhibit you, I'm certain. It took all four of us to bind you and still it wasn't easy." Vivian looked down at her hands.

Cianne looked at the solemn expression on Vivian's face and suspected there was a story behind her words, but she didn't ask what that story was.

Vivian looked up. "We will need to wait until you give birth of course."

"Why? Would it hurt the baby?" Cianne asked. She put her hand on her stomach instinctively.

"There is no way to tell; we've never had to restore a Coesen's abilities who happened to be pregnant at the time. Also, it never took all four of us to bind one either, until you." Vivian watched Cianne for a few seconds. "You look tired. I think that you have heard enough for one day Zaria, you need your rest."

"What do I do now?" Cianne asked. She felt helpless, lost.

"I will teach you all you need to know. Tristan, being a Protector and because he already has knowledge of us, will need to be taught our ways and laws as well. I would very much like to get to know you again Zaria." Vivian looked back at her.

Cianne needed some air. Whoever said that the truth will set you free was lying. She looked at Vivian then to her father. "I just need some fresh air."

"Of course, you do. You are in a very fragile state and I apologize that all of this had to be forced upon you like this. I had planned to explain it all to you gradually," Vivian said. She walked over to the door that led to the patio. She extended her arm and opened the sliding glass.

Cianne stepped over the track of the door with her head low. As she lifted her other foot over the track she paused, then placed her foot back down inside the house.

"I think Zaria is a nice enough name and I understand it was my name at one time, but I prefer Cianne." Cianne then stepped through the door. She didn't wait for confirmation, she just shut the door.

All she could do now was think through everything Vivian told her. The truth in this case was much stranger than fiction, and what did she do to Tristan? He was sentenced to all this because of her. Cianne intended to sit on the patio but decided she didn't want to see either her father or Vivian right now. They were both guilty in her eyes. They were keepers of secrets that, if she was told from the start, Tristan could have been spared this reality.

She walked down a couple flights of stone steps to a huge pool and a pool house. She stayed on the path, walking slowly, stopping briefly to look back at the house. A thought came to her. Tristan was her Protector and they are connected somehow. It was now clear Vivian hadn't planted him in her life but what if what they felt for each other was only a symptom of their connection?

Cianne felt a chill run through her body. She took a deep breath and began to walk again.

The path led to a large and beautiful garden bordered by large trees such that the garden could not be seen from the house. She relaxed a little, knowing that she couldn't be seen by her father's worrying gaze or Vivian's uncomfortable stare. She stayed on the pebbled path as she walked past patches of flowers and hedges until she came to the center of the garden.

In the center stood a large stone fountain inside a circle of stone pavement. Four benches evenly spaced apart bordered the fountain. Cianne walked into the circle to sit on one of the benches. As she moved closer she saw two people, a man and a woman, sitting on a bench on the other side of the fountain. She stopped moving forward, then something happened that she didn't expect. The two strangers both stood as straight as soldiers.

"Hello," Cianne said, a little taken back. Neither of them moved. They just stood in silence; one with her head lowered, the other staring right at her. The young woman seemed somewhat surprised and maybe ashamed but the male's expression was harder for Cianne to read. He looked both captivated and at ease.

"I'm sorry for intruding," Cianne apologized. She was just about to turn around when the young woman spoke.

"Please," the young woman said, with her head still lowered. "You must never apologize."

Cianne lowered her gaze to see the face of the young women with the lovely French accent. *Is this Zeta, the young woman who helped Tristan find me*? "Zeta?" she asked.

"I am, Zeta," the young woman raised her head and smiled.

Cianne smiled as she moved toward Zeta. Forgetting that Zeta was wounded in the incident, Cianne hugged her tightly. Zeta let out a low grunt, both surprised by the gesture and apparently still very sore. Cianne quickly released her, "Sorry," she said, as she let her go. "I'm eternally grateful and will always be in your debt for what you've done for me."

Zeta looked at Cianne then she looked over to the young man who stood beside to her, as if waiting for something. He nodded when their eyes met. She looked back to Cianne and said, "Your safety is reward enough." Then she bowed her head again.

Cianne thought it strange that Zeta kept bowing to her, but then quickly remembered that Zeta and the gentleman next to her were with Vivian. They were Coesen.

The gentleman cleared his throat quietly, but loud enough for Cianne and Zeta to hear.

"Forgive me," Zeta said to the young man standing next to her. "This is, Whodai (Who-day) Tam. He is a Royal from the Bode tribe."

Whodai stepped closer to Cianne. His eyes locked onto hers as he lowered his head and gently took her hand in his then lightly kissed it. Cianne felt her skin tingle beneath his warm lips; her face burned. When he let her hand slide from his, she wondered why she hadn't pulled her hand away.

"It is nice to finally meet you Zaria. You are even more exquisite than I was led to believe," he said. Each word was pronounced with perfect enunciation, and his British accent drizzled out every syllable like warm caramel.

She was blushing again. Cianne had been complimented before, more than she cared to admit. To her, being recognized for her appearance was natural, she was used to it. She dismissed the way guys looked at her without a single thought of it later. But the way Whodai was looking at her now would definitely leave an impression. Even when his lips touched her hand, her skin tingled with the contact. Only one other person ever caused a similar reaction in her. And the way Whodai looked at her and spoke to her made her feel important, as if she deserved his compliments.

"Excuse me," Zeta said. She began to back away.

Cianne pulled her gaze from Whodai. "I was hoping you would sit with me," she said, looking back at Zeta.

Whodai bowed. "Then I will excuse myself." When Cianne looked back at him he was returning her gaze. "I hope to have an audience with you again Zaria, sometime soon." His smooth full lips stretched across perfect white teeth, and turned up at the corners into a beautiful smile. Cianne held his gaze until he turned away. "Zeta," he said, his voice crisp.

Zeta bowed.

Whodai slowly walked down the path that led from the garden to the house.

"Would you prefer to sit in the shade?" Zeta asked.

Cianne, who was watching Whodai walk away, turned to Zeta. "Um," she said. Caught off guard by her reaction to Whodai, she lost her train of thought for a moment. "Um, no," she said, "here will be fine." Cianne preferred to be in as much light as possible nowadays.

Cianne waited for Zeta to take a seat on the bench, but Zeta simply stood there with her head slightly lowered. Cianne sighed, this princess stuff was something she wasn't ever going to get used to. She hated any and all situations where a person might feel obligated or unequal in any way.

Nevertheless, Cianne sat down first and once she was seated, Zeta took a seat next to her. She looked at Zeta for moment before speaking; she had a feeling that Zeta wouldn't speak unless she was spoken to first. This gave Cianne a few moments to compare what she thought Zeta looked like from Tristan's description versus the real image.

Zeta was small in frame and height. She maybe stood about 5'4" tall; a caramel colored beauty with prominent eyes that attracted attention. Her hair was pulled back tightly just as Tristan described. Cianne felt he was accurate in his description. Zeta was very pretty and looked very delicate just as he said.

"It was very brave of you to go with Tristan, not knowing what you had to face."

Zeta looked confused for a second then smiled. "It is not necessary to thank me. Being of use to you in any way is a privilege that many of us can only hope for," Zeta said.

"Us?" Cianne questioned.

"Protectors," Zeta explained.

"Oh right." Cianne's smile twisted. The Coesen-Protector thing was going to take some getting used to as well. "Are you my grandmother's—I mean Vivian's—protector then?"

"No. My ward is named Philippe. He is in France. I am currently serving my second year of rotation," Zeta told her.

Cianne didn't want to seem completely ignorant but she had no idea what Zeta meant and her face showed it.

"I will be happy to explain." Zeta paused, as if waiting for permission to continue.

Once Cianne realized this she said, "Please, if you don't mind."

Zeta nodded. "Every Coesen is required to enlist their Protector for rotation. The Council of Four's safety is more important than any other Coesen's, so to guarantee their safety and the safety of our general populous, the tribes have put in place a service rotation. Every Protector is mandated to serve at least three years as a Sentry Guard or a Royal Guard, if requirements are fulfilled, to The Council of Four. The Guard is what you would call our law officers. Each of the Four has at least two Royal Guards along with their own Protector assigned to them. Sentry Guards police each province. Our Sovereign…she makes due with only one Royal Guard and her Protector."

"So, your…person is left unprotected for those three years?"

"Not completely. Some have their own abilities that can be used to protect them. Others may choose to live at a safe house for that time. Or like Philippe," Zeta said, "they can just go on with everyday life as usual. It's a personal decision."

"Zeta," Cianne said then looked down. "Can I ask you something personal?"

"Yes, you may ask anything." Zeta replied with an excitement that suggested she *really meant anything*.

Cianne looked over at the stiff but perfect posture of the girl who sat next to her. Zeta looked like she was no more than a junior in high school. "Do you like being a Protector? Would you rather live a normal life rather than a life of service?" Cianne looked Zeta in the eyes when she posed this question to her.

"Yes, I love being in the Protector." Zeta smiled for the first time. "You see, for me it is an honor and a duty. I am a child of the Gedgi tribe. I have family members who have abilities and some who do not. Before one is selected as a Protector, he or she usually doesn't have any abilities." Her voice was enthusiastic. "So, we all rejoice if chosen to be a Protector. Having a Protector is a great honor as well. Not all Coesen have enough power to be granted a Protector." Zeta paused before speaking again. "Tristan is a natural."

Cianne sighed. "It is different for him. Tristan isn't a part of this surreptitious nation of the Coesen. He was a regular guy until he met me."

"Yes, it is unheard of for a Middling to be selected as a Protector, but he was selected for a reason. No one knows what The Source looks for in the person it chooses. Whatever the qualities, Tristan has them." Zeta's face became softer as she spoke.

"I understand." Cianne forced a smile. She liked Zeta very much and knew at that instant that she wanted to be a friend to her. "I worry about his safety, not to mention all these rules and laws, and now to know that we're breaking a law simply by being together..."

"Do not upset yourself, Soahn (Soh-on)."

"Soahn?" Cianne asked.

"It is a title of respect for royals," Zeta said as she looked at Cianne. "You will know everything there is to know about our people and the way everything works. Our Sovereign will be instructing you herself. Everything will work out."

"Fun times." Cianne said sarcastically.

"She is a strong, fair, and intelligent leader." Zeta seemed almost defensive.

"I'm sure she is," Cianne said almost immediately. "Zeta, I think we are going to be good friends. That being the case, my friends call me Cianne."

Zeta smiled again, a genuine beautiful smile. "I will call you Cianne if it is your instruction for me to do so."

Jason Cruz couldn't fight the urge to look through one of the smudged rectangle glass windows of the closed door in his apartment building's small lobby. If ever a person felt that they were being followed he did right now.

He looked down the sidewalk that was bustling with people. The street he lived on was always busy, but he never had the feeling he had now. Today, he couldn't shake the feeling that he was being watched, or worse, followed.

Hiding behind the lobby door, he watched as a tall man walked across the street, toward his building. The way the man turned his head from side to side, as if searching for someone, made Jason's stomach quiver. As JC watched the man stop just in front of his stoop, still looking around, he thought about what brought him to this point.

He could say peer pressure had been the motivator. Nick, his best friend, had convinced him to help with kidnapping that girl. Nick had been angry ever since the girl blew him off. But JC knew that peer pressure from his friend wasn't the real reason for him joining the caper. The truth was he did it because of the money.

JC continued to watch the man, and the feeling that he was being followed was almost solidified until he noticed a woman step in front of the assumed stalker. The man and his female companion began walking together after a quick greeting.

JC relaxed a little.

He eventually climbed the three flights of stairs to get to his apartment. He glanced down the hall to his left then to his right before opening his door. He saw no one, but that eerie feeling was still with him. He had this feeling ever since he left the police station last week.

Quickly shutting the heavy door behind him, he locked the deadbolt tight. He then rubbed his groin, reliving the pain he felt that day in the police station when Tristan Bertram attacked him. He rested on the door for a moment before walking a few steps to sit on his sofa. He pulled his phone out of his pocket, noting it was one thirty in the afternoon, and dialed. The phone rang five times before the other end picked up. He patiently waited for the voicemail to beep so he could leave a message.

"Yeah Nick, this is JC. I'm getting out of here for a little while. Maybe go stay with my father in Cali for a few days. Get at me when you get this message."

He closed the cell phone and laid it on the seat next to him then reached for the remote that sat on a small table in front of him. He flicked on the television. After twenty minutes or so of surfing through the channels, his eyes became heavy and he dozed in and out of sleep.

A car crashing into something and the sound of a loud explosion that followed echoed through the tiny apartment. JC woke suddenly and he jolted to a sitting position on the sofa. He rubbed his head as he focused on the television screen that was broadcasting a film that was in the middle of a high-speed action scene.

Once he understood where the noise came from he chuckled with relief. He looked at the cable box above the television to see what time it was. Only twenty minutes passed since he last looked at the time.

Wiping his mouth with the side of his hand, JC sat back on the sofa. Then he suddenly pushed to his feet. The sound on the television wasn't that loud before he fell asleep; he never listened to the TV loud because of his neighbors. He frantically looked through the sofa for the remote but it was nowhere to be found.

Something in the corner of the room caught his eye. Whipping around, JC looked over to the small dinette set to the side of the small kitchen. He wasn't alone.

Chapter Three

The sound coming from the television was low but still loud enough for Cianne to hear it. The show that was on was of no consequence because she wasn't really watching it. She hadn't watched much television lately. Though Cianne blankly stared at the television screen, she didn't see the bright pixels that made up the picture, but it was necessary that it stayed on.

It was on for the same reason she left her CD's playing through the night. She needed the background noise. The sounds made her feel like she wasn't alone, although at present she wasn't the only one in the house. Without the white noise, there is only quiet darkness, and inside that darkness is the sound of dogs barking and death.

"Buttercup," Joseph called as he came down the stairs.

Cianne blinked her dry eyes. "Hmmm," she said.

Her father sat on the edge of the sofa near her feet. "Can you please reconsider?"

She took a deep breath. "I'm not crazy. Crazy things just seem to happen to me." She sat up. "I just need to deal with things my own way that's all. Besides, our family has too many skeletons in the closet for me to see a shrink."

"You aren't getting much sleep and you're afraid of your own shadow. You're not taking care of yourself," he told her.

She sighed as she looked up at him, "I'm not afraid, I'm just careful. I need to be, with the baby to worry about." She knew that using the baby as an excuse wasn't going to work.

"I made you an appointment for two this afternoon. I think you should talk to someone not connected to uh, well, all of us. Tristan will stay with you. All I'm asking is that you try it out."

"You're in cahoots with my father?" Cianne looked over at Tristan who was sitting quietly at the bar for over an hour. The look he gave her was one that told her he was watching her for a while, long enough to observe that she zoned out again.

"I think you could benefit from seeing a therapist," Tristan finally said, breaking the silence and her stare. "Everyone I know has seen a therapist at some point in their life. My parents even sent me to one when I got kicked out of the first two private schools."

Cianne sighed. "Fine, if doing this will get you both off my back," she snapped.

"We should leave now then." Tristan looked at his watch.

***What's** the point*? Cianne thought as she sat quietly in the passenger seat of Tristan's newly repaired truck. She turned her body toward him and tugged at the seatbelt to loosen its grip around her midsection. Then she leaned her head against the headrest and looked at him.

It was only a week since she spoke to her grandmother and learned what she was, what Tristan was, and about the connection they shared. As she watched him, she couldn't shake the thought that the connection they shared was the reason he loved her. She shared with him everything Vivian told her later that evening when he stopped by the house. She asked him how he felt about her now and his role in it all.

Tristan gave her a typical Tristan response. He flashed "her" smile and said, "I think what I've always thought. That we were made for each other."

It isn't normal. How he doesn't freak out or ask a million questions about what we've learned in the past few weeks. Or even just turn tail and run.

The look on her face that day must have been one of shock when Tristan had calmly added, "Most people go through their entire life without knowing what they're on this earth for. I am one of the lucky ones who know; I've known ever since the day I first saw you at the county fair that I was born to love and protect you. Call it fate or whatever you'd like. It's simple." His expression was one of unwavering determination. "I can live with any and everything that comes my way as long as you're with me."

That day she wanted nothing more than to believe that his love was genuine, and not driven by their relationship as Protector and ward. Only, as they drove to the man who was trained to pick her mind apart, she knew she couldn't lie to herself about avoiding talk of the kidnapping, or her fears about her relationship for very long.

"You're making the right decision." Tristan looked over at her and winked.

Cianne felt his hand on her leg. She smiled and placed her hand on his.

She wasn't just questioning whether their feelings for each other were genuine and not just a symptom of their bond; the fact that she was responsible for his "special" attachment ate at her as well.

He slowly slid his hand from under hers and placed it back on the steering wheel. She watched him for the rest of their ride.

The receptionist was a pleasant looking middle-aged lady who smiled as she spoke every word. Tristan apologized for them being ten minutes late but the receptionist smiled and assured them that it was no problem.

"The doctor has no appointments after you," she told them. "He will be here in just a moment. In the meantime, I have some forms for you to fill out." The receptionist handed Cianne a clipboard and a pen and then instructed them to sit down.

The clipboard contained a questionnaire, and Cianne filled it out, grateful for the distraction.

"Nice office," Tristan said eventually.

Cianne gave him scornful look.

"Are you angry with me?"

He was trying to make her feel comfortable but she was still feeling some resentment about him taking her father's side instead of hers. "I'm trying to be," she said, grimacing. "But I don't think I could ever really be angry with you," she admitted.

"Cianne Baxter?" An average looking man about the age of 40 walked into the office through the same door they had come in. He smiled and extended his hand, "I'm Dr. Garrison."

Tristan stood instantly but Cianne looked up at the doctor before standing. When her eyes met the doctor's, a sharp pain stabbed at her temples, and she shut her eyes. "THERAPIST" in bold large letters flashed in her mind. She tilted her head and rubbed her right temple.

"What's wrong?" Tristan was kneeling in front of her.

"Are you alright?" Dr. Garrison asked.

"Everything is fine," she said, opening her eyes.

The pain stabbed at her again and the word "THERAPIST" flashed in her mind as it had before when she looked at the doctor. She clenched her teeth and tried to force the sudden headache away. *Yeah…he's a therapist*, she told herself. Just like that, the pain stopped.

"Hello," Cianne said, as she plastered a smiled on her face. She stood and reached around Tristan to grab the relaxed hand the doctor offered her.

Tristan watched her closely as she interacted with Dr. Garrison. When he focused on the doctor, Cianne could tell he was sizing the physician up. There was really nothing about him that stood out other than the nice quality of clothing he wore. He was an average size man with an average face, with a bit of gray sprinkled in his hair on his head and chin. Dr. Garrison looked harmless enough and she assumed Tristan thought the same as she did because he would have told her so, mentally of course. His manners were impeccable.

Dr. Garrison turned to Tristan and smiled big. "You must be Tristan." He extended his hand.

Tristan gripped the doctor's hand and shook it firmly while looking straight into his eyes. Dr. Garrison sort of smiled, clearly understanding what Tristan wanted to put across. Cianne covered her mouth as she used a cough to veil her giggle.

"Well Ms. Baxter," he pulled his hand from Tristan's, "if you would follow me." Dr. Garrison rubbed his hand briefly, as he walked over to the door and held it open.

Cianne hesitated. She hadn't really considered the fact that she would need to be alone with the doctor. She turned her head to peer at Tristan.

A faint feeling of fear that wasn't his own, brushed Tristan's mind. This was mild compared to the night he found Cianne in the abandoned school. That night he received a full dose of her fear that lit a rage in him he could barely control. Now, he was simply aware that she was uncomfortable.

"There is a sitting room just outside my office. You would be closer," the doctor told Tristan, "right outside my office in fact."

They followed Dr. Garrison to a door opposite the reception area doors. They entered another small sitting area, where Tristan took Cianne's hands in his and held them to his chest. "I will be here the entire time," he promised her. He lightly kissed her lips.

Cianne frowned but she followed the doctor into his office anyway.

It was a big office that looked the way one would think a shrink's office would look. There were lots of books lining the walls in large heavy-looking bookcases. There was one large wooden desk with papers covering almost every inch of it, a computer monitor, and a keyboard, but most of it was buried. Three long windows were right behind the desk. The partially open shades let in some of the hot summer day's sun. A sofa and two chairs sat to the right of her and there was a long table in between them.

Cianne looked to the doctor to see where he wanted her to sit.

"The sofa will be fine," he said. Dr. Garrison softly closed the door behind him then walked over and sat in one of the chairs that faced her.

Cianne hadn't heard the door shut but when she looked over her shoulder to measure how far away the door was from where she sat, she panicked. This was number one on her mental checklist of precautions—know your exits and make sure all doors are open.

"Ci, is everything ok?"

Dr. Garrison looked to her then the door. He got to his feet, walked to the door and opened it.

"Thank you," Cianne said *"Everything's fine, Tristan"* she transferred.

Maybe she did need to be here.

Dr. Garrison reached for the clipboard Cianne still held, and when she handed it over he sat back down and took less than a minute to read over her brief medical history. "Sea-Ann, am I saying it right?"

"Sahy-an," she corrected.

"Alright, Cianne, do you prefer all doors to stay open when you're in a room," the doctor asked, "or just when you are in a room with a stranger?"

Lie, Cianne thought. Instead, she replied with, "I prefer all doors to stay open whenever Tristan isn't in the room with me." She opted for the truth.

"Is there anyone else you feel safe around?" Dr. Garrison opened a pad and began jotting down some words.

"I feel safe with my father," Cianne said then paused, "and, Vivian." Vivian's name had just sort of came out, but truthfully, the woman made her feel safe.

"And Vivian is?" the doctor asked.

"She is my mother's mother."

"Your grandmother." He raised his left brow. "Why do you refer to your grandmother as your mother's mother?"

Cianne pulled the bottom corner of her lip into her mouth. "We aren't that close." She began to rub her thumb in her palm.

"How's your relationship with your parents, Cianne?"

"My father and I get along very well. When my mother died, he raised me all by himself. He's wonderful." Cianne smiled but couldn't help but feel like his questions were some kind of test.

"What about your relationship with his parents?"

"Um." She rubbed her hand more. "They don't really deal with me. He and my mother started dating after I was born. He adopted me but his parents didn't really like that he married a ready-made family. They're pretty old fashioned."

"And your biological father?"

"I've never met him." Cianne shrugged. She hoped he would be satisfied with just that.

"Mr. Baxter told me the circumstances of your recent ordeal. Would you like to tell me what happened?"

"I was taken and locked in an abandoned building for a few days. Then I came home. That's it." She scraped her teeth across her lip.

"You don't sound too angry about what happened," he said.

"Should I be?" She tilted her head as she spoke.

"Anger can be healthy if expressed properly." He stood and walked over to his desk. When he returned, he handed Cianne a softball before sitting back in his chair.

"You want me to use a stress ball?" Cianne laughed but still she inspected the little round black ball in her hand. She playfully began to squeeze it.

"Whenever you feel afraid or scared, take a deep breath and try squeezing it. When you release the breath, release the tension on the ball. It's no cure but it may take your mind off your fear long enough for you to reevaluate the situation." He paused. "I understand that no one was charged with your abduction?"

Cianne stopped squeezing the ball. "There wasn't enough evidence to charge them. I didn't see their faces, and they wore gloves the entire time. None of them ever spoke." She placed the ball on the sofa next to her then said, "except one guy."

Cianne saw herself in the room with the file cabinets again.

"Does the fact that you couldn't identify his voice upset you?"

"I can identify his voice," Cianne said confidently. "It's just that they haven't been able to find him to put him in a voice lineup." She watched as his pen moved over the pad again.

"Did you explain that to the detective assigned to your case?"

"Recognizing a voice wouldn't be enough to convict anyway." She felt a sudden urge to vomit. Touching her belly, she looked around the room for a garbage can in case she couldn't make it to the restroom. Just above the small over-flowing garbage can, she saw a glass candy jar on the desk.

"Is there something wrong?" the doctor asked, seeing the look on her face.

"May I?" she pointed to the candy jar.

"Sure." Dr. Garrison stood and picked up the dish containing clear wrapped blue candy from his desk and walked it over to her. He held it out in front of her. Once she took one out, he placed the dish on the table close to her and returned to his seat.

"I'm over the morning sickness but my stomach gets a little sour every so often." She opened the hard candy and put it in her mouth.

"Oh." he focused on her stomach then looked at the clipboard again.

"I can still fit into my clothes for now," she said happily.

"Well, that's good." He smiled. "Some of the medications we prescribe may not be good for pregnant women. Just to confirm the information on your questionnaire, how far along are you?"

"Seventeen weeks."

"So, the gentleman in the waiting room is your…?"

"My boyfriend," she said then smiled.

Tristan looked at the magazine rack attached to the wall across from him for a third time. He finally stood, and as he reached for a sports magazine, he saw a baby magazine and picked that up instead. He skimmed through the pages, focusing on one every so often until he found an article that looked interesting to him. When the outer door opened, he lifted his gaze from the worn-out pages of the magazine and looked up.

"You're here to tell me that you connected Nick and his buddy to the kidnapping," Tristan said. He closed the magazine and placed it on the chair next to him.

"Not quite Mr. Bertram," Det. Malone said. "May I have a word with you please?"

Tristan stood, stepped around the detective and into the hallway. He scooted by an officer who he recognized from the police station—Perkins was his name—and continued down the hall until he came to the entrance area of the building.

When he reached an unoccupied area, he turned to face the detective and officer Perkins.

"Mr. Bertram where were you on Tuesday of last week about three pm?" Detective Malone took a pack of gum from his breast pocket. He held it out to the officer, then to Tristan.

"No thanks." Tristan leaned against a column next to Malone. "Now, the question is where was I last week?" Tristan raised his eyebrow, placed his index finger on his chin and pretended to think.

Officer Perkins let out a soft chuckle and shrugged when Malone looked in his direction.

"This is serious Mr. Bertram. I need to know where you were Tuesday of last week." Malone placed a piece of gum in his mouth and began to chew.

"Nicklaus got run over by a truck fitting my truck's description huh?" Tristan grinned.

"Not exactly," Malone said. "One of Nick's friends Jason Cruz, also known as JC, was found murdered in his apartment yesterday." Detective Malone began to chew. He looked over-worked and underpaid. It was the same look that detective movies seemed to play up, but true in Malone's case apparently. "Where were you Tuesday?"

Tristan's smile was shameless and it grew bigger when he spoke. "If he was found yesterday then why do you need to know where I was Tuesday? That was," he said, pretending to count on his fingers, "six days ago. You don't actually want me to try and remember what I was doing six days ago?"

"He was found yesterday but he's been dead since Tuesday, so if you could try and remember that would be helpful," Malone said politely. He continued to chew the gum quietly.

"Alright." Tristan looked into the detective's eyes. "On Tuesday," he said, his smile was radiant, "I took a long drive."

"Anyone with you?" Malone asked. He looked at Officer Perkins.

"No." Tristan stood straight when he noticed Dr. Garrison's lobby door open. "I was alone." He watched as Cianne and Dr. Garrison stepped into the hall. Tristan's face lost all the humor he displayed just a few seconds before.

"Could you come to the station with us? There are a few more questions I would like to ask you." Malone followed Tristan's gaze.

"Not right now but I can be there in about an hour or so," Tristan said, as he looked at the detective then back down the hall. He tilted his head and gave the doctor an imploring look as Cianne turned her gaze toward them.

Malone looked back to Tristan. "I'll see you in about an hour then." He motioned for the officer, signaling that they were done.

Tristan watched them leave the lobby before he turned back to the hallway. It was empty. He quickly walked back to Dr. Garrison's office. Tristan could see Cianne inside. She sat in one of the chairs in the waiting area they sat in when they first arrived. She looked up from another clipboard full of forms when he tapped the glass. He could see the questions forming in her eyes. He gave her a slight smile before she turned her attention back to the clipboard.

"Ms. Baxter is filling out some more paperwork," Dr. Garrison said quietly. Tristan turned around to face him. "Is everything all right?"

"It's nothing really," Tristan said. "Thank you for keeping her occupied while I spoke to the detective. I don't want her to stress out." Tristan looked over his shoulder. Cianne was standing at the receptionist desk now.

"I agree," the doctor said.

Cianne stepped into the hallway. "All done?" she asked as she smiled at Dr. Garrison.

"Yes, and I will see you next Monday at the same time," Dr. Garrison smiled. He gave them a little wave before disappearing into his office.

"Why was Detective Malone here?" Cianne asked as soon as Dr. Garrison closed the door.

"He wants to talk to me." Tristan pulled her close and wrapped his arms around her waist. "So, how was it?"

"I lived," she smiled, as she raised her hand and rubbed his arms.

"Which is a good thing." He kissed her cheek. "And how is my little girl doing?" Tristan thought back to a few days before, when Cianne relayed the news that she would most likely having a girl. His response was that he would be just as happy to have a daughter. That put a smile on her face. "What?" Tristan asked. The questioning look she was giving him made him a little curious.

"It's nothing really." Cianne slid her hand down his arms and crossed in front of him in an attempt to move past him.

Tristan held her in place and drew his brows together.

"It's just that you're too good to be true. It's kind of scary."

Chapter Four

Four months in the Near Future
October 12th

"**O**fficer Perkins?" Detective Malone glanced over his shoulder. He sighed as he stood from the crouched position he was in. He shook his head and took one more look at the body that lay at his feet. "Shit…" he cursed several more times. "Officer Perkins?" Malone called out louder but the officer didn't answer.

Perkins just stood there with his eyes wide and his mouth slightly open. Det. Malone stepped in front of the man, blocking his view.

"Officer, let's try and get this situation under control. I know you must have worked scenes worse than this in New Jersey." Malone hit the officer on the shoulder before walking away to speak to another detective.

When Malone looked back at Perkins again he realized that the officer hadn't moved an inch. After realizing Perkins was mesmerized by the bloody nightmarish scene that lay before him, Detective Malone leaned in front of Officer Perkins and looked into his frozen eyes.

"Get him outta here," Det. Malone said to another officer who was passing by.

"I've got a pulse over here," a paramedic yelled.

Malone glanced at the paramedic as she stood but was distracted by a young woman who stood just beyond the barrier with the gathering crowd. She was screaming at the top of her lungs.

Present

As he drove her home, Tristan thought over the comment Cianne made at Dr. Garrison's office. He half listened to her hum with the radio as he tried to figure out what she meant. Her words replayed in his head several times as he moved smoothly through traffic.

She said that he was too good to be true, and it was scary sometimes.

He told himself that she didn't mean anything by it, *really*.

He listened carefully last week when Cianne came back from Vivian's and explained how there was something that connected them, like a force of energy that ultimately drew them to each other. She said the energy was something so strong that it may be responsible for their feelings for each other; that what they felt may not be real love but could instead be a reaction to the strong connection they shared.

He consoled her as she wept, and listened while she dissected their relationship like a science experiment turned romance. Tristan had listened quietly even though seeing her tears made him feel like a jagged knife was repeatedly cutting into his flesh then being ripped out.

He was aware that there was an energy that connected them, but he felt that all it did was connect them. It didn't make him fall in love with her. Besides, if the connection that a Coesen and their Protectors shared could produce those types of feelings, there would be a lot more love affairs between them besides the three now on record.

Tristan thought he had laid all her fears to rest that day. But as he glanced over at her while he waited for the traffic light to change, he could tell she was still having doubts.

"Are you ignoring me?" Cianne asked. She turned her legs to face him, pulling the seatbelt out a little then adjusting her position.

"Did you say something?" Tristan asked, glancing at her then to the road again.

"I asked you the same question twice." She stared at him.

Tristan pulled the car in front of her house and looked at her. "I'm sorry," he said, "I was somewhere else. What was the question?"

"What did the detective want?"

"One of the guys we suspect had something to do with your abduction is dead," he told her.

One *of the guys we suspect had something to do with your abduction is dead,* Cianne repeated in her head. He just told her that one of the suspects in her case was dead. But Tristan said it in such a matter-of-fact manner that he could have just as easily said he wanted no pickles on his burger. Sensing nothing in his demeanor that would give away his thoughts on the matter, she figured she would just ask him what she was burning to know.

"Was he murdered?"

"Yes."

"And they want to speak to you?" she asked.

"Yes." He put the truck in park then turned to face her.

Why? Did they think he… Cianne felt nauseous.

She searched his eyes for an answer to the questions that worried her but as usual, he gave nothing away. So, Cianne unbuckled her seatbelt and pushed the door open. Before she stepped out of the truck, she turned back and gave him a chaste kiss on the lips.

Cianne looked into his eyes again and asked, "Will you be coming back here tonight, after you're finished at the police station, or will you be going straight home?"

"I'll be coming back here," Tristan told her.

Cianne nodded then turned away as she climbed out of the truck. She heard the passenger side window being rolled down, and felt his eyes on her.

"Ci, I love you," Tristan called out to her.

She said nothing, nor did she look back at him.

Tristan slouched in a cold metal chair next to a small metal table, inside a small gray room. He sat perfectly still and didn't make a sound. A small part of him enjoyed sitting in this room. He always wanted to see if an interrogation room was as intimidating as TV led him to believe.

On the cop shows a lone suspect was led into a small room very similar to the one he sat in. After a few minutes of the suspect stewing, nervous jittering, and self-talk, a detective would enter and convince the suspect that telling the truth would ease their suffering soul. In the end, the detective left with a confession.

Thing was, he'd seen his fair share of interrogation spaces and could honestly say that authority figures never really frightened him. Authority figures received their power from titles they were given, and the threat of punishment for breaching a list of restrictions that were usually common knowledge. If you knew the potential punishment, you knew your limit. Tristan also believed that you shouldn't do the crime if you can't do the time—either that or be able to convince a judge and jury of your peers that you are innocent.

In any case the process of interrogation, to him, was useless.

Even still, he had never been in an actual police interrogation room before.

Alibi, he thought, just as the door opened.

"So, Mr. Bertram," Detective Malone said as he entered the room, "I'm going to get right to it. Where were you Tuesday between the hours of 1 to 4 p.m.?"

"I told you already. I was taking a drive."

"And there is no one to verify that?" Malone asked.

"Don't think so." Tristan frowned, then shrugged as the detective's gaze bore down on him; but he maintained the eye contact without flinching.

Detective Malone flung several photos on the table in front of Tristan as he sat in the only other chair in the room. "The person that did this was very angry."

"Looks that way," Tristan said, pushing the photos across the table without really looking at them.

"Didn't you have a run in with JC before, at his university? You broke a few of his ribs," Malone stated.

"Yes," Tristan answered. "He and his friend attacked me."

"You roughed him up a few months ago so I have to wonder if your suspicion that he was involved in kidnapping your girlfriend would upset you enough to kill him." Malone pushed the photos in front of Tristan again.

It took only a few moments for Tristan to review each photo. "This one," Tristan said as he handed Malone one of the pictures, "just might be my favorite."

Malone looked at Tristan the way his father did when he was being a smartass. The kind of look that said, "You better take this seriously or else." Or else—one of the great empty threats of all time.

Det. Malone looked at the photo briefly before placing it with the rest on the table. "Look, I understand what you are going through—"

"Do you?" Tristan's eyes narrowed and his jaw tightened as he leaned forward, placing his hands on the table. "So, the woman you love was kidnapped and left for dog food?" he asked angrily. "No? You know nothing of what I am going through. The thing is though," he said, his face softened, "I can tell you how I feel so you can understand. I would love to see Nicklaus and all his accomplice dead. The world would be a better place without them in it. So, if you can put a person in jail for wishful thinking, then I'm your man." He raised a brow. "But, that is all I'm guilty of, wishful thinking. I'm guessing you don't have any evidence linking me to this because you're showing me these pictures to get a rise out of me." Tristan stood up. "There are only a few things that interest me enough to warrant a reaction. So, if you don't have any more questions I'll be on my way."

"I have two more questions," Malone said as he stood. "Have you taken any self-defense classes, boxing, or martial arts of any kind?"

"I'm pretty sure you already know the answer to that. You're a smart man and I know you've done your research. You had two questions?" Tristan asked.

"The night you found Cianne," Malone said, "how did you fight off all those dogs with only a bite and a few scratches to show?"

"All those years of martial arts and boxing classes finally paid off," Tristan said with a shrug, "or, if you're the religious type, you could go with a higher power was looking out for me."

"You killed over six feral dogs with your bare hands. You could be a very skilled fighter or it could have been luck," Malone said sarcastically, "But was it luck that killed the dogs you didn't touch, and every dog in a five-block radius of that abandoned school?"

Tristan looked at the detective with a stoic gaze. The man was trying to piece together the events of that night. Tristan knew he would give nothing away during their talk unless he wanted to and he didn't. It was apparent that Malone wasn't able to make sense of so many things that it was eating a hole in him, hence the long pissing contest they were currently engaging in. A pissing contest Malone would surely lose.

Tristan kept up the android-like stare until his opponent cursed under his breath. He watched the detective walk around the small table toward him. Malone was a medium built man with short black hair and brown determined eyes. He seemed like a stand-up kind of guy. If they met under any other circumstances Malone could have been someone Tristan might have wanted to know. He liked the detective.

"You said two questions detective," Tristan said.

After another brief stare down, Malone opened the door and led Tristan through the police station toward the elevators. The detective stopped at a desk to speak to Officer Perkins. Tristan continued to the elevators. He felt the officer's eyes on him but didn't make eye contact.

"Be careful what you wish for," Malone said to him.

Tristan smiled with a shrug then hit the down button for the elevator.

Cianne knew her father would have to return to work eventually. Working from home was taking a toll on his company and him, though he would never admit to the latter. He decided today, a Saturday, would be the day. Most people would probably opt to return on a Monday but he'd been home over a month.

It had been nice having him around the house again.

It was also nice to finally know why he was gone so much during the weeks before her birthday and kidnapping. He explained to her that he was traveling so much at that time because he was trying to talk Vivian into giving her more time with him. When he failed to change her grandmother's mind about taking her, he began talking to a lawyer who specialized in family law.

Her father was awesome, and to show a small fraction of her appreciation, Cianne woke up early and saw to it that he had a hot breakfast before he headed off to work.

She tried to dismiss her anxiety about being alone for the first time in a long time, and all she could think of was being prepared. This was an opportunity to prove to herself that she could be alone. That she didn't need help.

A part of her still thought she didn't need a therapist but a small part of her did. The only way she would convince herself and the people who cared about her that she could handle what happened, was to get back in the swing of things. So, when her father drove off for work, Cianne locked the front door, passing her first test. She made sure that every door inside the house was left wide open.

Baby steps, she reminded herself with a sigh as she leaned on the door.

"I'm close, if you need me," Tristan transferred.

She heard Tristan in her head the moment her father pulled onto the road.

"I know," she eventually transferred back.

Cianne smiled as she climbed the stairs and entered her room. She knew Tristan wouldn't be far away. He was someone she could depend on before, but now that they knew he was her Protector, he didn't feel a need to hide or feel ashamed about his protective nature.

Proud of herself for how calm she was, Cianne took comfort that in an hour or so she would be out having fun with her friends. Today was going to be like old times, before everything changed. Before she knew she was Zaria, the supernatural princess. Before she got pregnant, and before the kidnapping.

Cianne sat down at her desk in front of her computer. She toggled from one screen that streamed music to another that was dedicated to social networking. Amazingly she felt relaxed. She really didn't know how she would react to being alone. Of course, she knew she wouldn't completely freak but the truth was, her being who she was, anything could happen. What she did know was that she could no longer hold her father or Tristan hostage to her fears anymore.

She also knew that she needed to keep her fears in check. She didn't want Tristan running to her side just to stomp a little spider because she was frightened. According to Vivian, their bond seemed to be much stronger than other Coesen-Protector pairings. When she experienced a small dose of fear it felt much worse than it should, to him.

Their pairing was also unique when it came to mental communication. Telepathy was something that the Coesen hadn't been able to do in a very long time. It could be an annoying ability, and Cianne wasn't shy about sharing that she thought so.

She checked her emails before shutting her computer down then reached for the baby book Tranae brought her, 'How Your Baby Will Grow.' She smoothed her fingers over the title before opening the cover and finding the section she needed.

The baby was now a little over five inches long, and the genitals were developing. Cianne read the three paragraphs that described what she should expect, then she closed the book after flipping the pages to see what her baby would look like in a few weeks. When she looked at the clock, it read 10:45.

"Alright little one," she said as she rubbed her belly, "time to go."

Outside, it was hot. Southwest summers could be brutal but they were worth it because the winters were so mild. If Cianne had to choose a favorite season it would be summer hands down. Warm weather and the sun gave her skin a beautiful bronze glow that some women paid lots of money to get, and to be honest the heat never really bothered her like it did some people.

Cianne stepped onto her front porch but didn't close the door behind her. Standing still, she closed her eyes and inhaled. The summer air was heavy with a dash of fresh cut grass to compliment the morning. She walked over to her porch glider, sat down, and gently pushed off with her feet into a rhythmic sway as she waited. She closed her eyes and focused on the soothing motion.

"You look amazing."

Cianne opened her eyes. Tristan was leaning on the stair rail in front of her. *Did I fall asleep?* She glanced over at his truck that she hadn't heard pull up.

"Thank you." She smiled. As she stood, Cianne dismissed the fact that she fell asleep. "But are you still going to think so in another month? I am starting to get my baby bump, so I'm guessing no." Cianne rubbed her lower belly.

His brows crinkled and he frowned. "Just kidding," he grinned, "has she moved yet?" He held out a hand to help Cianne down the porch steps.

"Not yet, but remember the obstetrician said it can happen any time now." Cianne placed her hand on his chest and met his gaze. His amazing soft blue eyes were fixed on her.

Just a few months ago she would have turned away from him to avoid conversation for fear of revealing her darkest secret, her abilities. Now she depended on his unfaltering attention, his strength, his beauty—inside and out, and his encouraging words to keep her sane.

"You are so beautiful," she said softly. Only she hadn't meant to speak her thoughts.

Tristan frowned at her then lowered his head and covered her lips with his.

"Oh," she said. Cianne pulled away and looked up at him, her eyes wide with surprise.

"What?" Tristan asked. He put his hands out near her waist as if he planned to catch her if she fell back.

Cianne grabbed his hand and placed it on her abdomen. Nothing happened for a few seconds then…

Tristan swiftly pulled his hand away and looked into her eyes. He reached for her again but hesitated, then slowly moved his hand toward her stomach, looking from her eyes to her belly. When his hand made contact, Cianne exhaled.

She felt a long smooth movement as if the baby was tracing Tristan's palm.

"I feel her," he said with enthusiasm. Tristan squatted in front of Cianne and kissed her stomach where his hand had been.

"Tristan!" Cianne blushed, looking around. She bent and pulled him up. "Please don't start talking to her. Every time you do, you go on and on. We're going to be late if you start now."

"I was just going to say one thing," he said as he chuckled.

"You can tell her when we get back. Besides we are a little hungry." She looked down at her belly then to him.

"Alright, but you will let me sing to her later?"

Cianne laughed, "Sing if you must. Quietly," she added with a whisper. Singing was not one of the things he was good at and apparently, no one ever told him.

"You know my hearing has gotten more sensitive, right? I heard that." Tristan smiled. He straightened to his full height, jumped up and over the few porch steps and pulled the front door closed.

"Would you like to drive?" he asked as he locked her front door.

Tristan lifted his gaze from the doorknob, swiftly turned his head around, and looked across the street. With lightning speed, he moved in front of Cianne. He placed his hands on her waist and leaned into her.

Cianne looked at him as if he lost his mind

"I need you to stay calm," he said close to her ear. He leaned back to look at her.

Cianne sucked in air as if she was going to speak, but before she said a word she stiffened. Her fear punched into his gut as the barking came close enough for her to hear. He watched her lively eyes take on a vacant, darker look as she stood frozen in front of him. He traced his hands down her arms to find her hands. When he did find them, they were balled into tight fists at her side.

"Ci," Tristan said her name softly. He heard the dog and its owner just before they were in normal hearing range. He wasn't focused due to his excitement of the baby moving. He wished he had more than just seconds before the dog and its owner came running up the sidewalk on the opposite side of the street. If he heard them coming sooner he could have gotten her to the car.

"The dog is on a leash and with its owner." He slowly moved his head so she could see them. Across the street, a woman was holding onto a chain that was attached to a small beagle trotting in front of her.

"Relax before…" Tristan stopped before he said too much. He watched Cianne as she took a deep breath then relaxed her hands.

Cianne's brows creased. "Before what?" she demanded.

Tristan exhaled. He never told her about the dogs, the ones at the abandoned school he didn't kill, but who mysteriously died anyway. She passed out that awful night and didn't know that part, and he didn't feel it was something she needed to know. Because she didn't pay much attention to television after the kidnapping, she knew nothing of the news reports about what everyone referred to as the 'Dog Day Mystery'.

"I'll tell you later," he said as he forced smiled, "I promise."

Cianne gave him a look of concern. "That's not fair, and it's not going to work this time. What is it Tristan?"

"You don't want to be late, do you?" He gently moved her toward his truck. "I'll drive." He helped her into her seat and closed the door. He quickly walked over to the driver's side and got into the vehicle. "I promise to explain everything later."

He buckled his seatbelt and started the engine.

Dinner conversation flowed nicely for everyone except Cianne. She listened halfheartedly as the others spoke of things that would normally interest her. But they were things that didn't seem so important to her anymore. Her life was different now and she was too preoccupied with thoughts of what Tristan was keeping from her to have fun.

"Come on Cianne. I want you to enjoy yourself." Tristan gave her a half pleading smile.

"I will try." She raised a brow. "I'll try *if you talk with your mouth and not your mind. Otherwise, I might make the mistake of replying out loud to a question you asked mentally."* Cianne waited for him to agree mentally but he just nodded.

"Would you like a refill?" the waitress asked as she stepped to their table. She shamelessly focused her gaze on Brian and Tristan only.

"Ladies?" Brian asked them with a grin. He was clearly aware of the waitress' blatant flirting.

Tranae gave the waitress a hateful look. Cianne placed her hand on Tranae's lap under the table. This was one way Cianne let Tranae know that whatever the situation, it wasn't that serious.

The waitresses at this particular sports bar seemed to be infatuated with Brian and Tristan, and it wasn't a closely held secret. The guy's glasses were refilled before they were halfway empty and napkins were brought over to the table more than once, without anyone asking. Staff members, women of course, walked by repeatedly even though walking by their table added a few extra steps to their destination. Tranae didn't seem to see the humor of it all and her patience was visibly wearing thin.

"We're good," Cianne said.

The waitress didn't move. She waited for a response from one of the boys. Cianne felt it when Tranae started tapping her foot. She knew her friend was about to say something rude but Tristan spoke up first.

"No thank you," Tristan said to the girl, "We'd like the check."

"That one has a serious crush," Cianne said after the waitress left.

"That doesn't bother you?" Tranae asked, pointing in the direction the waitress went, her tone curt.

"If you think back a few months that could easily have been one of us. Look at them," Cianne said. She looked across the table at their dates. Brian sat watching Tranae with a big smile on his face and Tristan was drinking from his glass, trying to hide his smile.

Tranae rolled her eyes. "I don't remember drooling."

"Keep telling yourself that," Brian said then chuckled.

Cianne felt Tranae jerk and her leg move. She assumed Tranae kicked Brian because he grunted a curse.

Cianne laughed as she slowly got to her feet. Tristan was at her side before she could completely stand, offering his assistance. "Please Tristan," she begged, "I can still stand on my own, for now anyway. I'm just going to the bathroom."

Tristan took a step back. He glanced over at Tranae and their eyes met.

"Um, I'll go with." Tranae said jumping up. "I don't need to be here when that chick comes back or I may be making an appearance on the local news tonight."

When Cianne came out of the bathroom stall, Tranae was sitting on a bench next to the door. Cianne washed and dried her hands and was ready to join the guys but when she realized Tranae wasn't going to stand, she joined her on the bench.

Tranae smiled. "How are you feeling mama?"

"I feel fine Tranae," Cianne said as she tossed the paper towel in the can next to her. She saw disbelief in Tranae's expression. "Really, I'm fine."

Tranae placed her hand on Cianne's little bump. "And our baby?" she asked.

"Perfect as far as I know, my doctor is sort of old school."

"You should get another doctor, Cianne." Tranae frowned. "Is she pushing that natural birth stuff down your throat?"

"As a matter of fact, she is but I don't mind. Vivian says she's a really good doctor and she's delivered lots of babies that are…" Cianne took a deep breath. "Babies like me. So, I trust her."

"How is that going, your grandmother and you? Are you guys getting along? Did she invite you to join her coven?"

"That's not funny, Tranae." Cianne didn't tell Tranae what she learned from Vivian, but her friend wasn't ignorant either. Her best friend figured long ago Cianne's abilities were inherited, and though her assumption was spot on, Cianne had no intentions of confirming it. That didn't mean Tranae wouldn't keep digging. The coven comment wasn't far from the mark either, but it wasn't nice.

"I was just kidding," Tranae said, grimacing.

Cianne tried to find the right words. "I really haven't seen her since our first meeting." Cianne frowned. "I've been trying to work out some things in my head first. Plus, I'm not real sure I want to be a part of her 'family' just yet."

"Working out things about Tristan, right?" Tranae asked.

"Mainly, but there are other things I have to figure out too."

"You used to talk to me about everything, Cianne. I miss that. I miss us. You know you can tell me anything." Tranae took Cianne's hands and held them to her chest.

"I know. It's just that everything just got complicated so fast and some things are too sensitive to share even with you," Cianne said. "I'm sorry I haven't been a good friend lately."

"Stop that. You've been through a lot and don't you dare think that you haven't been a good friend." Tranae hugged Cianne tightly.

They parted. "Our friendship means so much to me, Tranae. I promise when things settle I'll be my old self."

"**I** think they may have fallen in." Brian said, as he leaned against the wall in the restaurant lobby.

"They're talking, that's all," Tristan said. He looked in the direction of the bathroom and noticed two of the waitresses who waited their table and one he hadn't met, watching him. When he waved, the waitress he didn't know blushed and turned away with a squeal. The other two giggled as they waved back.

"You are going to get yourself into trouble playing with those girls." Brian shook his head as he watched the exchange.

"It's harmless." Tristan turned toward Brian and said, "Ci and the baby are my life."

"Did you ask her yet?"

Tristan grimaced and looked away for a moment. He slouched over and peered down at his feet. "She isn't ready to be a wife," he said when he raised his head and his eyes met Brian's.

"She wouldn't be *a* wife. She'd be *your* wife," Brian's said as his eyes narrowed.

Tristan spun his keys around his finger and caught them. He spun and caught the keys a few more times before Brian spoke again.

"She said no?"

"It's not as simple as yes or no," Tristan said. He stood up straight when he heard the bathroom door open and Cianne sigh. "Here they come."

Brian looked in the direction of the bathroom and seemingly saw nothing. He leaned his head to the side but he would have to see past several patrons and around a corner to see them. He looked back at Tristan and was about to say something but looked again and saw their dates turning the corner.

Brian looked at Tranae. "I thought we were going to have to send someone in after y'all."

Tranae cut her eyes at him and mouthed the words, "smart ass."

Tristan quickly walked over to the restaurant door and opened it for Cianne and Tranae.

"Wait," Tranae said, backing up, "can't we figure out what we're doing next, before we go out in that heat. It's hell on earth out there."

Tristan held the door for a couple to enter then released the door and stepped back inside the cool restaurant. He realized then that he didn't notice before how hot it was out. He looked to the couple who just stepped inside the restaurant. The woman was busy tapping her face with a napkin and the man's shirt was wet in the front and under the arms.

He looked over at Cianne. She didn't look over-heated or even irritated by the heat at any point during their time outdoors.

"What do you say, Tristan?" Brian looked at him.

Tristan looked to Brian, realizing he missed something else.

Brian laughed. "Man, you already got the girl. You'd think all that staring stuff would have stopped by now."

"I can't help it," Tristan said, winking at Cianne, "she's just so beautiful."

Cianne blushed as she walked over to him. Tristan opened his arms to embrace her.

"I guess you don't care as long as you're both together, so bowling it is." Brian shook his head.

"How about, we go bowling?" Tristan teased.

"Good idea, Tristan," Tranae said, then laughed.

Brian cursed.

"Brian and I have been practicing." Tranae gave Brian a little smile.

"Really?" Tristan said, sounding suspicious.

Brian pushed the door open and led the way outside. The rest of them followed. "Want to make a small wager?" Brian asked. They walked the few steps to their cars. Brian opened his car door for Tranae.

It smelled like a setup. "What do you have in mind?" Tristan asked. Cianne climbed into the passenger seat of the truck when Tristan opened the door then reached over and started the engine.

"The usual." Brian's smile widened.

"Deal," Tristan accepted. They shook hands then Tristan walked around the back of his truck to get to the driver's side door and got inside.

The bowling alley wasn't too busy when they arrived. Probably because it was so damn hot. Cianne didn't have a pool but if she did, she'd probably be swimming instead of making her friends brave the heat for a few hours of bowling.

Brian paid before Tristan was able to. Cianne noticed his grin as they walked toward the lanes. *Boys*, she thought. They had their choice of over a dozen empty lanes so they chose one that was closer to the middle, and paired up as couples.

"The balls aren't too heavy for you?" Brian asked. He sat down beside Cianne.

"Nope," she said then lifted a ball, "see, this one is fine." She watched Tristan pick up a ball and toss it down the lane.

Strike!

Brian winced at Tristan's good luck, or skill, and then turned his attention was back to Cianne. "Good," he said. "You shouldn't be doing any heavy lifting." He looked over at Tristan again. "He's a good guy you know."

Cianne knew it was only a matter of time before Brian approached her about Tristan's proposal. This was Tristan's best friend and it was apparent how much they cared for each another. She expected the "treat my man good" talk sooner but with so much going on, it had to wait. Until today apparently.

She glanced at Tristan then back to Brian. "He is," Cianne said.

Where Tristan stood, he shouldn't be able to hear what she and Brian were saying but his hearing was improving daily. Tristan moved toward her and Brian, and from the look on his face, she was certain he could hear them.

"*Don't*," she transferred.

Tristan stopped a few feet away. He nodded and gave her a look that seemed like an apology. Then he looked down at his pocket. Cianne watched as he pulled his cell phone out and looked at the number.

"I need to take this," Tristan said as he walked past them. He swiftly moved toward the wall of doors that led to the outside of the bowling alley.

Tranae walked over to them and stood near Brian. "Your turn!"

"Do you love him?" Brian asked.

"Brian!" Tranae gasped. She crossed in front of him and sat down next to Cianne. "Please don't—"

"It's ok Tranae." Cianne turned her attention back to Brian. "You know I do, but you don't understand why I didn't accept the engagement ring he offered me?"

"Tristan asked you to marry him?" Tranae stood. "And you didn't tell me?"

"I haven't told you because I didn't want anyone influencing my decision." Cianne's eyes were still on Brian. "I didn't say yes, *because* I love him. I don't want him to think he has to marry me because of..." She touched her stomach. "Tristan had a very bright future that didn't include being a husband and a father this soon. I'm sure his parents would agree."

"A far as Tristan is concerned, you are his future and he's felt that way for a long time. I told him he was crazy when he asked me to fly with him to California the weekend after your birthday to buy that ring. And you know what he told me? He said that he knew he was doing the right thing. He knew for a long time, he said." Brian looked at the door that Tristan had exited. When neither of them saw Tristan, he continued. "Tristan's been trying to find the right time to ask you. He planned to ask you when we all went to Houston, that way you guys would be engaged before you two left for college."

"He got the ring right after her birthday?" Tranae whispered, as she turned her doe eyes on Cianne.

"Yeah," Brian said then paused, "before he found out about the baby."

Cianne didn't see that coming. The baby wasn't what influenced Tristan. But, before she could celebrate that new information, there still was the bonding thing they shared. Their feelings may just be an illusion. If that was the case, she wouldn't want him locked into a marriage with someone he never truly loved.

"Another thing," Brian said as he stood up, "you can stop worrying about Tristan's parents and what they want." He rolled the bowling ball in his hands. "I know you love him, Cianne, so I'm going to tell you…" Brian noticed Tranae's gaze shoot past him. He stopped talking and turned to see Tristan coming toward them.

All three of them watched Tristan as he approached.

"What's wrong? Do you feel ok?" Tristan asked, taking long strides, cutting many steps down to three. He kneeled in front of Cianne. She lowered her gaze until they were eye level.

Cianne cleared her throat. "Fine, I feel fine," she said as she shook her head. Though, she wasn't fine. But, she hadn't been shooting fear spears his way so she figured he would relax. He did.

"Well, you looked upset." Tristan sat next to Cianne and placed his hand on her leg. "Whose turn is it?"

Brian swallowed the words he planned to say but he looked to Cianne and nodded his head. She figured it was his way of silently telling her that they would continue later.

"It's my turn," Brian slapped his palm on the bowling ball.

She expected to be told by Tristan's best friend that she was making a mistake by not saying yes to his proposal, but the revelation that he bought the ring before he knew about the baby was…well… a development.

Tristan leaned in and kissed Cianne on the cheek. "Are you sure you're fine?"

Cianne looked into his eyes. "I'm fine." She forced a smile. "But, I can't promise you I'll be fine later if we lose and I have to wash Brian's underwear." She patted his hand. "So, go up there and keep an eye on him," she said, playfully as she faked enthusiasm.

Tristan gave her a determined grin then jumped to his feet.

Chapter Five

In downtown West Hills, the large clock, built into a towering structure across the street from the bus stop where a teenager sat, read 9:25 pm. The boy looked up at the clock repeatedly, thinking that time was creeping by only to piss him off.

He reached for his backpack on the metal bench behind him. Throwing the bag over his back, he stood and slid his hands inside the pockets of his loose-fitting jeans. Frowning, he cursed quietly then began to pace the length of the shelter several times before he focused on the car that pulled up to the curve.

"You're out here kind of late. Is everything alright?" A male voice came from inside the vehicle. The speaker's face was shaded from view.

Standing only a few feet away from the dark blue sports car, the boy shifted from one foot to the other. He pulled his attention from the sports car and looked around, giving the sense that he was uneasy. His voice cracked when he spoke. "I didn't do anything. All I'm doing is waiting for the bus."

"Young man, I wasn't accusing you of anything," the man called from the driver's seat. "It's just that this area isn't too safe at night. Also, I'm certain this bus has stopped running for the night. You may want to call your parents."

The boy looked down. "My…my parents?" he stuttered. He took a step back.

"Would you like to use my phone?" The light from the street lamp caught the silver phone and caused it to shine as the man extended his arm.

The boy seemed to think it over for a few seconds. Then he walked over to the shiny blue car. He bent over and looked inside at the man and then the phone in the man's hand. "No thanks," he winced. "I'll just sit here and wait until the bus comes."

The man looked at the boy long enough to make the average person feel uncomfortable but the boy didn't seem to notice, and if he had he didn't seem to care. "How about I drive you home?" the man said finally. "I don't feel comfortable leaving you out here to the elements."

"I don't need a ride home," the boy snapped then seemed to calm. "I'm headed east."

"I see," said the man. He looked away from the boy and out his front windshield. "You see that building over there?" The man pointed to a tall building that rose above the others around it. "That is where I live. If you want to," he said as his gaze fell back to the boy, "you can sleep on my sofa, and in the morning, you can get the bus when they start running again. My sofa is much softer than that bench there."

The boy looked at the man in the car then back to the metal bench inside the bus shelter.

"You don't need to be scared," the man said.

The man smiled, showing what the boy thought to be thousands of dollars of dental work.

"I'm not," the boy said, rubbing his hands on his jeans. He looked into the car and at the man a few seconds more before opening the unlocked passenger door and slumping into the warm leather seat.

"What's your name?" the man smiled.

"Turner," the boy said. He placed his bag on the floor by his feet and shut the car door.

"Nice to meet you Turner, my name is Donald Garrison." Donald extended his hand.

Turner noticed that Donald was still smiling and wondered if he knew how creepy his smile was, but shook his hand anyway.

"Buckle up, Turner."

Turner pulled the belt over his chest/waist and clicked it as the car pulled off. He looked out the window at the bus stop again before it was completely out of sight.

"Would you like to call your parents?" Donald asked again, "They may be still awake."

"My parents are dead," Turner said, with no emotion.

"I'm sorry to hear that, is there someone else you could call?"

Turner, still looking through the window, shook his head no. He turned from the window and looked straight ahead through the front windshield. He felt Donald's eyes on him every few seconds yet he wasn't bothered by it at all.

Once the car was parked in the underground parking lot, Turner followed Donald to a fancy building. The doorman never looked up from his magazine as they passed the security desk but he did speak.

"Good evening Dr. Garrison."

Donald didn't reply as he quickly led the boy to the elevator. When they got off on the eighth floor, Donald led the way down an elegant hallway to his door. He led Turner inside and placed his briefcase on a wooden bench.

"Wow," Turner said, as he walked into the living room. "You have a lot of video games." He walked over to the large television that was hanging on the wall. Underneath it, were two game consoles, four controllers and lots of games. The boy picked up several game cases.

"You can play them if you like." Donald walked to the kitchen that was located directly across from the living room. "Are you hungry Turner?"

Turner saw Donald's face peek out between floating wall cabinets and a breakfast bar that separated the kitchen and the living room. It seemed that no walls separated any of the rooms in the living area except for the bathroom located by the door.

"I could eat," Turner said. He sat on the floor with several games spread out in front of him. He looked over the couch at Donald who was standing in the kitchen smiling. Turner turned his focus back to the games.

Donald had a hard time turning his focus back to the task he was performing. He glanced at Turner several times during the drive here but he realized now he hadn't gotten the full scope of the boy's beauty.

He let his gaze take in the boy's dirty blond hair framing his smooth angled face. The boy's skin wasn't like the average teen, covered with acne and marks. His skin was flawless and had such a healthy glow. Turner's features were strong and pronounced, yet symmetrical. But Turner's eyes were the most alluring gems but Donald couldn't shake the feeling he'd seen eyes like them before. He shook his head, trying to shake away his thoughts, and began separating the food.

A few minutes later Donald carried two warm plates over to the dining room that sat off to the side of the kitchen and placed them on the table. He saw that Turner was looking through the books on one of his large bookcases.

"So, how old are you Turner?" Donald asked as he walked back into the kitchen. He pulled two glasses from a wall cabinet and placed them on the counter.

"I'll be seventeen in four months," Turner said. He stopped looking through the books and walked over to the table. He sat down in front of one of the plates and began eating the food that was in front of him. "This is good," he mumbled.

"Leftovers from a dinner party I hosted. What would you like to drink, water or cola?"

"Cola please," Turner said, as he took several more bites.

Donald put ice in both glasses before pouring cola in one and water in the other. He then opened a drawer and pulled out a little brown box. He briefly looked over to see what Turner was doing. When he saw that Turner was more focused on eating than on him, Donald opened the box and took out a small thin folded piece of paper.

He unfolded the paper and peered down at the white powder contained in it. He quickly poured a little powder into the glass that had the cola in it and stirred the contents with a spoon. A little powder spilled onto the counter so Donald nervously brushed it off with the palm of his hand before walking the glasses to the dining table. He placed the cola in front of Turner. He placed the water next to his plate.

"Thank you," Turner said. He pulled the cola closer to him. "I got a little hungry while waiting for the bus, I guess." He had eaten most of his food.

"I can see that." Donald smiled. He picked up his fork and began to eat. After a few bites, he took a sip of his water. "Would you like to talk about why you were at the bus stop? Are you in some kind of trouble?"

Turner lifted his head and gave Donald a curious look.

"I'm sorry, Turner. You see, I am a doctor and it is hard at times to leave work at work." He lifted his glass slowly as he observed his guest. To Donald, Turner seemed to be a little mature in his demeanor, like a kid who had to grow up too quickly.

"You work in a hospital?"

"No, I'm not that kind of doctor. I'm a therapist. I listen to and try to help people with what they see as their problems." Donald leaned back in his chair.

"Do you treat any famous people?" Turner asked excitedly.

Donald liked that the boy was interested but he didn't know or treat anyone famous, not even someone that knew someone famous. In fact, the closest person to a celebrity that he treated was Cianne Baxter, whose kidnapping story appeared on television.

"Not really, but I am treating someone who was in the news recently." Donald smiled when he saw a flash of excitement in Turner's eyes. He continued. "She was in the news for a few days. I think she may have even made the national news." That's when it hit Donald. He *had* seen those same blue-green eyes before.

"What's her name?" Turner innocently questioned.

"I'm sorry, Turner. I cannot tell you that." Donald watched the boy's smile fade.

Turner placed his fork on his plate and picked up the glass of cola. He looked at Donald, who was watching him closely. Turner smiled. It wasn't really a friendly smile, but more of a sly one. Then he put the glass to his lips and tipped it a bit. Without taking a sip, he slowly pulled it away and held it a few inches from his mouth.

"What did you put in my drink?" Turner asked. He straightened himself in the dining chair and gently jiggled the glass in small circles.

"Excuse me?" Donald choked. He wiped his mouth with his napkin and looked at the boy sitting next to him. The piercing gaze of Turner's eyes—eyes Donald felt had seen much more than they should have—looked back at him. "I'm sorry?" he asked nervously. Donald took another drink of water from his glass. "I don't believe I heard you."

"Sure, you did, Dr. Garrison. I know that you put something in the drink I have in my hand." Turner looked at Donald's arm, his voice stronger, surer. "There is still a little powder there on the sleeve of your very nice shirt." Turner motioned to the sleeve. "You have great taste doctor. Is that shirt a Canali?" Turner grinned as he waited for a response.

Seconds passed as Donald Garrison looked at Turner with wide eyes and with shock evident in his face. A sick feeling rose in Donald's gut as he watched the young man.

"Your shirt, is it a Canali?"

"Yes," Donald managed to say, "it's a Canali."

"I can respect a man who appreciates nice things. Although, you doctor, do not deserve respect, do you?" Turner took a long drink of the spiked soda. "I was a little worried that I may not have been your *type*." He emphasized the word type. "But a boy could hope, right? And wouldn't you know it, I am." Turner took another long drink. "So," he said as he placed the empty glass on the table, "What were your plans for me? Were you going to look but not touch and uh…take care of yourself? Or were you going to throw caution to the wind and do what your heart desires and then throw me out with the garbage and hope my body wouldn't be found for weeks?"

Sweat beaded up on Donald's forehead, and slowly dripped down his face. He absently dabbed at it with his napkin while his breathing grew louder and his chest noticeably heaved up and down.

"I can assure you that what you've done to all those boys in the last ten years, no matter how foul, is of no consequence to me," Turner said plainly. "So, would you please calm down Dr. Garrison, I don't want you to… Damn it," Turner hissed.

Turner sighed as he looked at the doctor, who just a few moments before was sitting up in the chair, but now was slumped over in it, unconscious.

Chapter Six

Cianne couldn't place the soft musical score that drifted out of the car speakers, but she knew she heard it before. *From a movie maybe*, she thought as she shifted in the seat. She would have been able to figure it out if a number of things weren't occupying her thoughts at the moment. She wanted to know what Brian was going to tell her earlier today when they were at the bowling alley. She wanted to ask him but couldn't seem to get him alone.

After the initial phone call at the bowling alley, Tristan turned off his cell phone, possibly feeling guilty because it was their first night out in weeks. From the moment he returned from taking that call, he didn't leave her side. Now, sitting in the car next to Tristan, who usually garnered all her attention when they were together, all Cianne could think about were the things Brian told her, and the things he didn't.

Tristan intended to propose in Houston. He wanted her before all this madness.

The madness…

Cianne shifted in the seat again, uneasily recalling how she pulled him into her life of madness.

The dramatic climax of the music brought her back to the moment at hand. Cianne tried to relax and listen to the music as Tristan drove. Their destination…she shifted again, was his house. He convinced her to sleep over his house tonight, and it *had* taken some convincing.

Since the end of April, Cianne stopped coming over when his parents were home.

It was Mrs. Bertram's idea, or more like request, for her to sleep over tonight. Tristan's mother wanted to spend Sunday morning with them, to talk about the pregnancy, no doubt.

Cianne dreaded the meeting. The two families didn't have a sit down yet. She avoided this discussion as long as she could, so she reluctantly accepted the invitation.

She used to enjoy spending time at Tristan's house. His mother was pleasant and welcoming. Celia, Martha, and Ben were like family. They all made her feel welcome. All of them except for Mr. Bertram, who was the reason Cianne began to avoid the Bertram residence.

She told Tristan that it was the pregnancy and all the discomforts that came along with it. But the truth was, she got the impression that Mr. Bertram didn't care for her very much. The night Tristan was surprised to find her asleep in his bed was the first time in over a month that she set foot in his house.

Cianne sighed as she performed her newly-acquired car ritual again. She pulled the seatbelt away from her body and let it retract slowly back across her chest and belly to get comfortable. She closed her eyes, and the memory of the day she realized that Tristan's father wasn't her biggest fan forced itself through the other worries she accumulated since then.

It was before the kidnapping and Vivian's sudden arrival in West Hills. She remembered the day because, hell, how would she forget it? It was April 30th, while Cianne was hanging out at Tristan's house. Tristan told her he had some important calls that he needed to make. He didn't elaborate so Cianne hadn't pressed him about them. He often traveled and made private calls for various reasons.

She assumed he was preparing for life after high school. Job interviews, internships, or things like that were her best guess. All she knew was that he needed to go right home after school that particular day. Cianne drove him to school that day and had no issues with taking him home. Tristan knew how much she liked Celia, Martha and Benjamin, and she assured him that she wouldn't be bored. As soon as they got to the house that day, Tristan quickly kissed her and went straight to his office next to his bedroom.

The Past
April 30th

Cianne went to the kitchen to say hello to Celia but the sassy cook wasn't there. Then she remembered that Celia's shift started later. Cianne grabbed a bottle of water and went to see if she could find Martha, who actually lived on the property. It didn't take Cianne long to find Martha, who had an addiction to the daytime soaps.

The short thin middle-aged woman was in the theater/hearth room vacuuming the carpet, but her attention was focused on the gigantic flat screen television hanging over the fireplace. Cianne waved hello and Martha turned the vacuum off.

"Hey sweetie," Martha said. She swung the cord out of her way and gave Cianne a hug.

"Hi Martha." Cianne smiled. "How's everything going today?" Cianne stood in front of the tall unused fireplace.

"Well," Martha said, "Jackson is falling for Marie, and she knows that he is the real father of her sister's baby. I can't stand Marie's sister but there are other men out there."

Cianne giggled.

"Oh, you meant with me." Martha laughed. "I'm doing well. Thanks for asking."

"I have some free time if you need some help." Cianne helped the staff out from time to time. The bonus was getting to know them better. Cianne talked to Martha about everything going on with her, and Martha would let her know about the soaps. They talked about almost everything, except the personal and private business of the Bertram's of course. It was the perfect arrangement. Plus, Cianne was used to having Martha, Benjamin and Celia in her life. They were the aunties and uncle she never had, and she enjoyed spending time with them.

"I could use some help in the laundry room," Martha said, as she pushed a button on the vacuum and the cord retracted. Martha turned off the television then led the way past the kitchen and across the main hall to the laundry room. She placed the vacuum in its appropriate spot and the two began to do the rest of the laundry. All Martha would let Cianne do was the folding, so she knew exactly what to do and where everything went.

By 1:00 p.m. all the laundry was folded. Martha told Cianne she had to clean Tristan's parent's room and that Cianne could help by putting their dry cleaning in their closet. Cianne and Martha carried the dry cleaning to the bedroom. Then Martha left Cianne in Mrs. Bertram's closet while she went into the bathroom and began cleaning it.

Cianne heard when Martha turned on the radio and closed the door. It was a signal to the Bertram's that she was in the room cleaning. With Martha busy, Cianne began hanging up Mrs. Bertram's dry cleaning.

After a few minutes in the closet, Cianne was startled when she heard the bedroom door close. When she peeked out of the closet door she saw Mr. Bertram walking toward her. Cianne backed away from the closet door, pushing it a little so she could not be seen if he glanced in.

Tristan had warned her to never let his father see her helping the staff. So, she went further in and hid, having no good reasons for why she was in the room if she got caught.

She heard Mr. Bertram open his closet which was directly across from his wife's closet. Cianne could also hear that he was on the phone. *This is so messed up*, she thought as she pulled her cell phone from her pocket.

First, Cianne muted the sound then she began keying a text, but stopped. She could hear Mr. Bertram talking, and she thought that she heard her name. Cianne decided that she was mistaken and that it was flat out rude to listen to his call. Never the nosey type, she lifted her phone to the light coming through the opening in the closet door and began keying the message again. But before she hit the send button, she heard her name again, clearly this time. Cianne moved closer and listened behind the door.

"Yes," Mr. Bertram said, "I don't know. Who knows where names come from these days? This Cianne, she's a very attractive girl. She could have even been one of those models or teen stars if she had the right start."

Cianne leaned closer to the door but backed away when she saw a shadow move past the crack. He was back in the bedroom and must have sat on the bed or a chair because she heard him sigh with relief as if he was tired.

"Exactly," he agreed with the person on the other end of the cell phone. "Let me get these shoes off. I feel like I ran a marathon," he complained.

Cianne heard the shoes hit the floor. She crouched closer to the door.

"As I was saying, I just hope he isn't serious about this girl." He paused again. "Being attractive just isn't good enough these days," he said firmly as if defending himself. "Tristan deserves more than a pretty face. He is a part of a legacy and…" he stopped. "She could be. But there are a lot fewer diamonds in the rough nowadays." He paused again. "You know I'm not racist, besides I don't know what ethnicity she is anyway. I think her father is black so her mother could be white or something else." There was a brief silence again then he spoke, "No, I just think it's easier if the rich stick with the rich. Then there's no issue of money. If the working class didn't train these daughters of theirs to be gold digging femme fatales, and taught them the importance of hard work, their economy would be in a better state." He laughed. "All I am saying to you is that I need you to look into her for me. He has been dating her for a few months and she already has her claws in the boy."

Cianne stood quietly, trying to hold in her anger and her tears. She could still hear the muted sounds of music coming from the bathroom. Martha most likely had no idea Mr. Bertram was even in the house yet.

"The same fee," he said, "three days then, alright. Thank you."

Cianne looked at her cell phone through eyes blurred by her tears and pushed the send button. Within seconds she could hear Tristan knocking on the bedroom door and Mr. Bertram saying for him to come in. Tristan made up some excuse to get his father out of the room—something about a video conference call, and that he needed his father to say hello or something. Cianne didn't care what excuse he used to get his father out of the room. She just wanted out of the closet, and most of all, out of their house.

When it was clear, she crept out of the closet and out of the room. Cianne went to the powder room next to the front door, and stayed there for several minutes, ignoring the text messages from Tristan who wanted to know where she disappeared to. When she finally composed herself, she went back to the kitchen where she found Celia who was whispering to Martha.

"Did he see you?" Martha whispered to her.

"No," Cianne said, "I was in the closet." Cianne gave a half smile as she waved to Celia.

Celia held her gaze a moment, long enough to see the redness in her eyes.

She lowered her head. "I'm uh, going to go hang out upstairs," Cianne said. She spun on her heels and walked out of the kitchen to the stairs. She quickly climbed the steps before Mr. Bertram decided to come down them. She didn't want to see him or for him to see her. Once in Tristan's room Cianne went straight to the bathroom and silently cried again.

When Tristan finally came into the room, her face was clean and she was lying on his bed. She told him that she wasn't feeling well and that she wanted to go home.

Present

"**Are** you feeling ok?" Tristan asked. The engine was off and they were sitting inside his garage. Tristan reclined in his seat and turned toward her.

"I'm fine," she answered, "and the baby is fine too." She figured she might as well say it before he asked. "We're just a little tired."

"Yeah, I figured. I've been sitting here for about ten minutes watching you sleep. I didn't want to wake you, but we're here."

Cianne unfastened her seat belt. The passenger door swung open before she could touch the handle. Tristan had positioned his seat upright and was out of the car and opening the door for her before her seatbelt had retracted.

"You shouldn't move like that here." Cianne gave him a disapproving look.

"I doubt if anyone's awake." He reached into the car, lifting her easily. He cradled her in his arms.

Cianne closed the car door before wrapping her arms around his neck. She brushed her lips across his jaw, smiling when she felt him shiver and sigh from a mere touch from her. It was nice knowing how she affected him. She buried her head into his neck and found herself sighing as well because being close to Tristan, feeling his strong body so close to hers, was her dream coming true over and over again. She knew that no matter how his feelings for her were generated, she loved him with all she was.

"Listen to you trying to protect the family secret."

Cianne lifted her head. "I'm not interested in the Coesen or their secrets," she scowled. "I just want you safe. You embraced what I am and what's happened to you and that's fine but you need to be careful. Nothing in the world is perfect and I fear the Coesen are more flawed than our government. Us…we are all I care about."

"I know you worry, Ci," he said as he grimaced, "but you really don't have to. I admit that I enjoy the training and learning about your people but it's more than that. I feel…" He paused, then said, "I can't explain it."

Cianne nuzzled her face into his neck. He didn't have to explain. She knew he loved the image of the Coesen that Zeta laid out for him. And she didn't blame Zeta, but she knew that it was only an image. Plus, she herself felt some kind of relief when she came in contact with the Coesen, like a heavy burden had been lifted. The feeling was similar to the one she had when she kissed Tristan that first time. Like it was where she was supposed to be. As if she had purpose, a home.

But she had issues with the Coesen. Some of them wanted her and her mother dead. They were willing to kill a child to satisfy her father's debts. They most likely still wanted her dead. Would they want to kill Tristan and their child as well? She flinched at the thought.

Tristan must have felt her fear because he held her tighter.

"You're wrong you know," he said, walking through the dark garage.

She lifted her head. Her brows creased together.

"You said nothing in this world is perfect. You're wrong. You are."

She didn't know what to say to that. She hardly saw herself as anything but flawed, and with this prophecy hanging over her head…

That she was some Halo…

She winced at the thought but forced herself to smile before he noticed. She touched his face, letting her thumb brush over the barely noticeable scar that led from his ear to under his chin. She wondered how he got it. When he moved his head into her touch, she gazed into his beautiful blue eyes and Tristan slowly moved forward and kissed her softly.

He was the one to pull away first. "Do we need a snack?" he asked as he opened the door that led from the garage into the utility room of the house.

"No. I... We just want a warm shower and you holding us in your soft bed," Cianne said in a low exhausted voice.

Tristan lifted Cianne up in his arms. "*Just relax*," he transferred. He carried her through the house and up the stairs to his room as if she weighed nothing. He used his foot to close his door. Without turning on any lights he took her into the bathroom and placed her on the black chaise next to the tub.

His eyesight was almost as good in the dark as it was in the daylight so he had no problem seeing everything clearly, but he didn't know if Cianne's eyes were the same. Not knowing if she could see, he lit several candles before going to the tub and tapping a button for warm water to fill it.

"Shower," she moaned when he turned on the bath faucet.

He kicked off his shoes. "You don't need to be on your feet a second longer." He heard her sigh and knew she needed no further convincing.

"I've never noticed it before but you really like black," Cianne said, as she unbuttoned her shirt.

"Black is my safe haven for when I can't choose a color." He held his hand under the chrome faucet to see if it the water was warm enough. Tristan flicked his wet hand over the full tub and walked over to Cianne. He helped her take off her shirt and when his eyes swept over her exposed bra, a low hiss escaped his mouth.

He willed back his urges to touch her, to take her.

After assisting her with undressing, Tristan carried her to the tub and gently placed her into the waiting warm water. After she settled in he went to the linen shelf and grabbed a wash cloth and two large matching towels and returned to the tub.

Sitting on the floor next to the beautiful claw footed tub, he folded one of the towels and placed it on the edge of the tub so Cianne could relax her head on it. She submerged herself underwater completely before slowly rising and wiping the water from her face with her hand, reminding him of a beautiful cover girl on location at some beach. Then she rested her head and neck on the towel he placed on the edge of the tub for her.

Tristan let Cianne soak for a while before he washed her hair. He took his time washing her body, driving his desires back with every stroke. To him it was an honor to bathe his queen and he wanted to worship every inch of her no matter the pain it caused him.

He hadn't touched her in a sexual way since right after her kidnapping. While the experience was the most erotic and earth-shattering night he'd ever had, her control had been lost in the rapture of their pleasure. The end result was a release of power that had shaken the very ground beneath them.

To his dismay, Cianne decided that it would be safer if they waited until the baby was born before having sex again. The pained look on her face had told him she feared for his safety as well. He'd agreed out of concern for her and the baby, thus suffering with every glance at her. Her mere presence drove him lust crazy but she or the baby could have been seriously injured and their safety was all that mattered.

When he was done washing her he rinsed her thoroughly then carried her to the chaise where he patted her dry before helping her into a long silk night coral tank top with matching panties.

Cianne didn't notice all the beautiful teal shopping bags that lined the room until Tristan pulled out the beautiful coral colored silk top and underwear. "Are all those for me?" she asked, sounding more exhausted than she expected.

"Yes," he told her, as he dried her hair with the towel. His strong hands massaged her scalp, relaxing her more.

Cianne watched Tristan walk to the long floating sink and look into one of three smaller bags, undoubtedly from the same shop, and take out a hair brush. If she looked at it closely she would see her name engraved in the beautifully hand-crafted silver brush.

She sat fully relaxed from the warm bath and half asleep as Tristan gently brushed her long dark hair until it was free of all tangles. Then he tied her long locks in a loose knot, just like he had seen her do so many times before.

"Not perfect, but I'm learning." He smiled.

"It takes lots of practice," she slurred. She sat on the chaise while he blew out all but one of the candles.

"Let's get you to bed," he said, lifting her again.

Cianne wrapped her arms around his neck. "I could easily get used to this," she said, sleepily.

"That's my intention," Tristan carried her to the bed and pulled the sheets down. Then he gently placed her on his bed and covered her with the top sheet.

Cianne stretched out her arms and legs. She loved the feel of nice linens after a bath or shower. She purred like a cat that was completely satisfied with life. She reached for Tristan and pulled him down next to her. Cianne turned over on her side, allowing Tristan to lay his arm over her, and quickly fell into a deep sleep.

Cianne rolled over in the bed. With her eyes still closed, she extended her arm over the space next to her. When she didn't feel Tristan, she opened her eyes, squinting as she tried to get adjusted to the sunlight filling the room. She looked at the side of the bed Tristan should have slept on, and saw that it was undisturbed.

Pushing the sheet off, she scooted to the edge of the bed. The baby moved beneath her skin so she looked to her belly and rubbed. "I'm hungry too little one," she said.

Cianne looked up to see if Tristan was in the sitting room beyond the columns separating the bedroom area from the sitting area. What she saw was something she would have never imagined in all her dreams. The large sitting area where the television and furniture once sat was now a beautiful nursery.

"Oh…My…God," Cianne said as she stood up. She must have stood a little too quickly because she felt a stab of pain shoot through her stomach that made her sit back down. She sat holding her belly for a moment before getting up again, slowly this time.

She walked between two of the large white columns which were adorned with long sheer white fabric stretching from the ceiling to the floor. She moved her fingers over the fabric as she walked down the three stairs that rounded the length of the room. Once in the sitting room she stood still, not knowing what to view first.

In the center of the room was a round black wooden crib with white lace bedding and canopy. On either side of the crib were black wooden gliders with matching foot stools that had the whitest of white cushions. Next to one of the gliders sat a long black side table that had baby magazines and a lamp placed on it. A changing table filled with diapers and baby care products like lotions, oils, etc. was what she focused on next. Beside it were several beautiful pink bags filled with baby supplies. There was a six-drawer chest to her right with all the drawers slightly open, revealing clothing neatly packed inside. And right beside her stood a tall black bookcase filled with children's books and teddy bears. Cianne noticed an envelope on the bookcase that had her name on it. She took the envelope down and opened it.

Cianne,

At my age, foolishness is always a curse and rarely is it replaced with sensible thinking. I know I have been a fool not to see what my son had already known. Forgive me for my unfriendly and appalling behavior and accept this as a beginning to a new start.

Yours truly,

Grandfather to be, Leslie D. Bertram

Cianne's fought back tears as she folded the card and held it to her chest. *Maybe things are going to work out after all*, she thought.

Her heart drummed with excitement as she walked over to the crib and touched the frame. The crib, heck the entire room, was breathtaking. She looked over to the bathroom door.

Tristan, she thought, as she walked up the three steps, across the length of the bedroom section and into the bathroom.

Tristan wasn't there but all the bags from last night were still lined against the wall. Cianne went over to the bags and lifted one and read the logo, "Precious Bundles".

Inside the bags were maternity clothing, as well as shoes and personal items. She quickly went through her morning routine and chose some of the new items to wear. When she was done dressing in one of the new outfits, she made the bed and decided that she needed to eat.

She could smell the food cooking as she opened the bedroom door. Cianne walked down the stairs and into the kitchen. She was so hungry at this point that the baby was kicking her repeatedly.

"Good morning, I hope you're hungry," Mrs. Bertram said, looking at Cianne in the doorway. Her smile was all class and elegance as she stood over the kitchen table holding a plate of pancakes and sausage. As she placed the plate on the table Mrs. Bertram looked over to Cianne who was still standing in the entryway to the kitchen. Her smile widened. "Well don't just stand there sweetheart," she said, as she walked over to the refrigerator. "Feed my grandchild."

"Good morning," Cianne said in a low cautious voice. She stood there for a few more seconds before going to sit at the table. Mrs. Bertram brought her a large glass of orange juice once she was seated. Cianne looked up at Tristan's mother as she sat the juice in front of her. Mrs. Bertram was beautiful and refined; she hardly seemed like the type who cooked. Cianne watched her with amazement for a short while, before the smells coming from the table began to nudge at her.

"Tristan is cleaning up. He will be joining us shortly." Mrs. Bertram kissed her on the head then spun around and walked back over to the stove. "Go ahead sweetie," she urged, "You don't need to wait for him. I made your favorite, blueberry pancakes."

Cianne thought she was in the twilight zone. First Mr. Bertram's gift to her, and now Mrs. Bertram was cooking breakfast, or cooking at all for that matter. Cianne was sure she had fallen asleep and awakened in a dream. A wonderful dream.

Mrs. Bertram came over and sat down across from her. She had a coffee cup in her hand and was about to take a sip, but stopped. "So, how do you like the nursery Leslie put together?"

"It's lovely," Cianne said with a big smile. She picked up the fork by her plate. "Is Mr. Bertram here? I'd like to thank him."

"He isn't, but I can give you his number later. It took him three days to put all that stuff together." She took a sip of her coffee, "I told him to get Benjamin or Tristan to help, but he wanted to do it all by himself. You know how the Bertram men can be when they get an idea in their heads. Still, I'll have Tristan check to make certain everything is sturdy."

Cianne watched Mrs. Bertram speak while she cut a section of blueberry pancakes with her fork and placed it in her mouth. Her taste buds went wild with delight. "These are very good," Cianne said.

"Well they should be," Mrs. Bertram said, "I hope you don't mind but I called your father and asked him if you had any favorite foods, and he gave me the recipe."

"Oh no, I don't mind. I haven't had blueberry hotcakes in a long time," she said. Cianne was saddened by that truth but immediately cheered up when she saw Tristan enter the kitchen. He smiled as he walked over to her and kissed her on the forehead.

"How did you sleep?" he asked.

"Fine," she answered. "*I would have slept better if you were there next to me.*"

Tristan watched her as he walked over and kissed his mother. "I slept in the guest room," he said out loud, "I thought you would be more comfortable if you had the bed to yourself." He cut his eyes, "*I thought you didn't like it when we conversed mentally.*"

"*I missed you, but I don't think your mom wants to hear that,*" she transmitted.

"I missed you too," he said, "I didn't sleep well at all knowing you were here but I couldn't hold you; it drove me crazy."

Cianne looked at him with a shocked expression on her face. Her cheeks were probably bright red.

"I think we are past that sweetie," Mrs. Bertram said then laughed. "Way past that." She looked to Cianne's belly. "Don't get all red in the face on my account." Mrs. Bertram stood and went to get Tristan a plate.

Tristan sat next to Cianne. "Did you like your surprise?"

"Loved it," Cianne said joyfully. She was also happy that he changed the subject.

"Whenever you're ready we can go shopping and get what you want for the baby's nursery at your house," he said. He took the plate his mother passed him and filled it with food. "I had an account set up for you but the card hasn't arrived yet.

For now, I'll give you one of mine if you'd rather go shopping with Tranae."

"Or me," his mother said, sounding excited.

Cianne brows drew together and she frowned. "Why did you open an account for me?"

They both gave her the "why not?" look. Then his mother answered, "You and the baby will be well cared for, Cianne. You are a part of our family now." She sipped her coffee. "I know things have been really hectic," Mrs. Bertram started, "but have you two talked about your plans yet? Like living arrangements, college, marriage?" She looked from Cianne to Tristan.

Cianne didn't know how to refuse the line of credit they planned on giving her but this clearly wasn't the time for that. She would talk to Tristan later about it. She focused on the question at hand

"We haven't really had the time—"

"Not yet," Cianne interrupted Tristan, "but I was hoping we could today." Cianne looked at him. Mrs. Bertram stood and walked over to the coffee machine and began to fill her cup.

"We don't have to make any decisions right away," Tristan said, as he looked over at Cianne.

Cianne sighed. "We really do."

"You have been through a lot in the last few weeks," Tristan said. "You shouldn't be rushed into making any decision right now. You can take as long as you need."

"He's right you know," Mrs. Bertram said, as she leaned on the counter. "You can take all the time you need." Mrs. Bertram held the mug to her lips.

"Before," Cianne said, "when it was just college I had to decide on, I was trying to convince myself it was ok to leave home. Now with a baby on the way, I'm not sure I want to leave."

Tristan moved his hand under her hair and placed it on the back of her neck. He caressed her neck gently. "No one is asking you to. We have time to figure all of this out. I don't want you stressing over this now." Tristan moved closer to her, "I am not the only one who can feel your anxiety," he whispered, kissing her on the cheek.

It was true. Tristan could feel her anxiety. It was another undocumented symptom of their connection. He was told by Zeta that no other Protector has felt anything other than their Coesen's fear. Because Cianne was like "Coesen 2.0" and Tristan being her Protector, their connection seems to be stronger than others. He sensed her fear which he described as feeling like a painless or muted awareness kind of like white noise but he also sensed minute versions of all her feelings. Even her never-ending morning sickness seemed to transfer over to him. It was like sympathetic daddy illness in High Definition.

Cianne wasn't too happy about any of it.

"Let's talk about something easier then. Did you two discuss what you are going to name the baby yet?" Mrs. Bertram asked, trying to lighten the atmosphere. She obviously planned for a happy, worry free morning.

Cianne looked over to Tristan. Naming the baby had never come up before. To most mothers-to-be, naming the baby was one of the most important things to do, just after the shock or joy of learning they were pregnant. Granted, a name may not get picked until the last minute but many would have had some choices by now. How could she forget something so basic?

"We haven't really talked about it," she admitted.

Mrs. Bertram walked over to the breakfast bar and opened a drawer with a bounce in her step. She placed her coffee mug on the counter in front of her and pulled out a pen and a piece of paper. She leaned over the counter and scribbled on the pad, making sure the pen had ink. "Now this is something I can help with," she said with excitement.

She wanted to be included, Cianne realized at that moment.

"Now let's see. If it's a girl, do you want her name to be something new and original, or something classic? You can even name her after a loved one. What was your mother's name?" she asked, as she lifted the coffee mug.

"Her name was Kayla. Kayla Baxter," Cianne said, smiling.

"Kayla Baxter," Mrs. Bertram repeated as if she heard the name before. "Kayla Baxter." She said it slower.

"Would you like to name her after your mother?" Tristan asked after wiping his mouth with a lovely cloth napkin.

"I really haven't thought about it." Cianne grimaced, then said, "I think that we should…"

Both Cianne and Tristan quickly turned their attention to a loud crash that echoed through the kitchen. Mrs. Bertram stood in silence as she blankly stared at them. Her coffee mug had shattered into pieces, spilling coffee all over the floor and on her feet. Tristan immediately got up and went to his mother's side.

"Mom," he said as he backed her away from the puddle of coffee and broken porcelain. "What's wrong?"

Cianne took a towel from the drawer and was about to bend over and wipe up the coffee.

"No," Tristan said, almost yelling. "I will get it up," he said quieter. "You help my mother."

Cianne was a little taken aback by his tone, he never yelled. She gave him a confused look but walked toward his mother anyway, to see if she was alright.

Mrs. Bertram shook her head frantically, "No, I am fine. She looked at Cianne who was standing in front of her now. "I didn't have a good grip on the mug, that's all."

She looked into Cianne's eyes as she slowly backed away from her. She hadn't noticed them before, those amazing eyes. "No," she waved her hands in front of her, signaling Cianne not to come closer. "I need to freshen up a little." She hastily turned and walked out of the kitchen.

A few seconds later Mrs. Bertram entered her bedroom and shut her door, locking it to ensure she would have complete privacy. Leaning against the door, she tried to relax, to calm herself.

"It's probably nothing. "Could it be her? That name pairing could be more common these days," she told herself.

Mrs. Bertram pushed herself off the door and went to her closet. On the floor behind some shoes she never wore, was a green box. She pulled the box from its resting place. It was almost four years since she last laid hands on it during the move to West Hills. Another six years since she had actually seen the contents inside.

Mrs. Bertram carried the box to her bed and sat down. She placed it on her lap and pulled the top off. A long white envelope sat at the top of a folded pile of papers. Mrs. Bertram's name in large letters was centered in the middle of the envelope. She turned it around in her hand and lifted the flap. Gently she pulled out a letter and unfolded it. Without reading the letter, she looked at the name of its sender.

Closing her eyes, Mrs. Bertram dropped her hands to her side, still clutching the letter in her hand.

Tristan wiped the remaining coffee off the bottom of the breakfast bar's cabinet door. He took another look at the kitchen floor for pieces of the mug that he may have missed.

"I think you got all of it," Cianne said.

Tristan had asked her to sit at the table while he cleaned the floor. He was thankful she listened.

"I'll be right back. I need to make sure she didn't cut her hand." he told Cianne. But as he turned to leave the kitchen he saw his mother standing a few feet from him. She held the green box in her hand.

His mother stepped into the kitchen and walked toward him. She took him gently by the arm and led him to the table.

"Are you alright mom?" he asked her.

"I've always believed in fate," she said, looking at both of them, "but I've never before seen undisputed proof." She looked down at Cianne, who was watching her with an intense stare. "Sit down Tristan." He did as he was told. "I don't really know why I saved all this stuff." She paused and seemed lost in thought for a moment. Then she sat and placed the box on the table in front of her and covered it with her thin manicured hands as she sat. "Maybe I was to save it for this particular moment. I don't know."

"Mom?" Tristan sounded worried.

"The whole thing seems like a dream when I think about it now. I don't know," she said, thinking back. Mrs. Bertram took a breath before she began. "Tristan, you were about nine years old…"

Chapter Seven
Ten Years Earlier

Parking in the school bus lane was really not a good idea especially when it was so close to the end of the school day. But Kayla Baxter pulled into the bus loop and parked her car there anyway. She took off her seatbelt and looked through her passenger side window at the large green double doors that were the main entrance to the elementary school.

Grabbing the strap to her oversized handbag, Kayla threw it over her shoulder and reached for the driver side door handle. With one foot outside of the car on the ground and the other still in the car she paused when she heard her mobile phone ring.

"Hello," she said, into the large phone. She pulled her foot back into the car and closed the door.

"Kayla," the caller said, "It's Vivian. I have spoken to Cassius; he will have all the documents you need with him. I hope North Dakota is alright."

Kayla knew who it was and thought it was funny how she and her mother talked so little that Vivian felt the need to say her name. "Hey, I did say anywhere," Kayla replied, trying to sound upbeat.

"Is there anything else you need to tell me or need me to do?" Vivian asked.

"Nothing's coming to mind at the moment," Kayla said. "Vivian, I really appreciate everything you and the Council have done and what you're doing for us."

"You're my daughter, Kayla," Vivian said without feeling. "You don't need to thank me." Neither woman spoke for an uncomfortable moment. "How is she doing?" Vivian asked finally.

"She remembers little of the zoo trip and nothing of the binding ritual but I guess that's a good thing. She's more upset because she has to leave her friends. She doesn't care that their parents have restricted them from spending time with her. Anyway, she's really excited about her new name."

"So, she hasn't exhibited any more of her abilities?" Vivian asked. There was a hint of concern in her tone.

"No. Nothing," Kayla said with relief. "But I still don't feel comfortable just leaving like this without—"

Vivian cut her off, "You have nothing to worry about, Kayla. The odds of her transmitting to someone during that…" She paused as if searching for the right words. "That little spark of power at the zoo is very minimal. A Coesen needs to be at a hundred percent power to transfer, and she hasn't shown any signs that the binding didn't work. Don't worry yourself; you have enough to worry about."

"Please thank the Council for me. I know that it was hard for them to put aside their feelings about me to do this for her," Kayla said quietly.

Vivian sighed. "They didn't do it for you, Kayla. They did it because your daughter bears the mark."

Kayla swallowed the sting she felt from her mother's words. "Vivian," she said, opening the car door again, "Whatever the case, thank you." She hung up the mobile phone without waiting for a reply.

The Council of Four hated her and still, she didn't care.

Being inside the main office of any school always made Kayla feel very uncomfortable, and this one was no different. Maybe it was because she associated the office with being in trouble. Or it could have been that all school offices seemed unusually small to her, and with people coming in and out, she felt they were overly crowded. She hated the desks of school office personnel. They were often overly decorated. They always contained too many pencils, pens and personal items. The staff would even resort to using coffee mugs as pen holders with pictures of their cats or children on them. But what she disliked the most about being in Fairfield Elementary office was Ms. Peters.

Ms. Peters was the main secretary for Fairfield Elementary School and she made it her goal to know as much as she could about everyone's personal business. She got most of her gossip by giving away just a little bit of her own private business. That made the person she spoke to feel somewhat comfortable enough to share their own business. Most of the time these unsuspecting parents would tell their business or the business of someone they knew, just to make Ms. Peters feel better about her situation.

It was a trap Kayla had seen a lot of the parents fall into over the years.

Kayla hated even listening to Ms. Peters, and usually made every effort to avoid her. But today was different. Ms. Peters had the paperwork she needed to officially withdraw her daughter from school. It was easy to create fake papers to get her child into another school with a different name, but she actually needed to make sure that her daughter was withdrawn properly. She didn't want to raise any more red flags, just in case someone came snooping around. Kayla waited at the long wooden counter that separated her from the six cluttered desks of the school staff.

"Has anyone helped you yet?" a short round woman asked.

Kayla smiled. "I'm here to see Ms. Peters."

"She'll be right back," another woman said, peeking over her cream-colored computer monitor. "She's in the back on an important call, but she should be out in a few minutes." The lady cleared her throat before returning to her typing.

Kayla could only imagine what was so important about the call.

"Hello Mrs. Baxter," a nasally Ms. Peters called out. It had taken only five minutes for her to come out of the back room.

"Hello Ms. Peters." Kayla summoned a smile for the woman.

"We are going to miss your little girl so much. Where is it you guys are moving to?" Ms. Peters asked. She held a large document folder in her hand.

"I'm not actually sure what school she'll be going to yet." Kayla held her hand out.

Ms. Peters gave her a questioning grin. "You know we can just transfer these papers to the school district you're moving to. All I need is your new address." She lowered the folder.

Thank you," Kayla said firmly, "but I can handle it." Kayla reached for the packet. Ms. Peters, looking a little disappointed, handed over the brown folder. Kayla took the folder and turned to walk away.

"Oh, Mrs. Baxter," Ms. Peters called in a singing drawl, "before you go."

Kayla stopped. She rolled her eyes before turning around. "Yes?" she asked, a little too cheerfully.

"I almost forgot to tell you," Ms. Peters started. "The Northridge Hospital in Keen County just contacted us. It seems they have a kid there who apparently has fallen ill with some unknown virus. They are getting in touch with anyone who could have come in contact with him. They want to know if any of our students have fallen ill. How is your little angel doing? I know she maybe wasn't feeling good before that horrible accident. At least, that's what Derek Ross's mother said. Mrs. Ross says your Angel had some kind of fit just before."

Kayla knew Derek's mother. She also knew that Mrs. Ross gossiped just as much as Ms. Peters, and she was certain they knew it was much more than a fit. She disregarded the inquiry, "Keen County is over 40 miles away. Why would they need to know if one of our children is ill?" Kayla walked back to the counter.

"Well," Ms. Peters said with a huge smile. She knew Kayla was interested now. "Apparently because the little boy was at the same zoo we went to on our field trip last week. He's really sick." She leaned in closer to Kayla, "I have a friend who has a cousin that works at Northridge. She says the boy is in isolation. They don't go in his room without rubber gloves and face masks."

"Did they say what was wrong with him?" Kayla asked.

"No one knows," Ms. Peters said, straightening her posture. "But my friend's cousin said that all he does is draw pictures. That's when he isn't screaming like someone's killing him, which is most of the time, she says." Ms. Peters looked over her shoulder then leaned in closer again, "You would think that they would know what was wrong with the boy; his parents are loaded I hear, and are sparing no expense for his care." Ms. Peters backed away some. "I was wondering myself if that little boy was spooked by the same thing that spooked your little one that day. Did she ever tell you what spooked her?"

"Poor kid," Kayla said, again refusing to answer the question, "I hope he gets better soon."

Kayla turned and swiftly left the office. She jogged to her car, her mind racing. She was just in time too, because the yellow buses were pulling into the loop. Kayla started the engine and pulled off. She pulled into traffic and took the on-ramp, heading for Keen County.

Kayla tried to convince herself that she was overreacting. That the sick boy was just suffering from some normal illness and it had nothing to do with her daughter or the Coesen, but she needed to be sure.

After she found a parking spot, Kayla calmed herself and entered the hospital through the main doors. She needed to see the boy but it wasn't going to be easy. Several options fluttered through her mind about how she could do that without being noticed.

She looked around and beelined to the first person dressed like a staff member. "Excuse me, could you tell me where the children's ward is?" Kayla politely asked a woman in a lab coat.

"Sure. Follow this hall to the elevators and go to the 4th floor. When you get off, make a right. The doors will be right in front of you," the woman explained.

"Thank you," Kayla said. She followed the directions just as the woman said. The children's ward was behind a large set of double doors. A set of locked double doors, she realized when she got there.

Kayla sat down in the waiting area and watched as a woman with balloons pushed the button on the wall next to the doors. A voice came through an intercom and the woman was asking what room and her name. The woman gave her answers and the doors unlocked and swung open. Kayla hurried over. Her plan was to piggyback the woman as she walked through the doors.

"Hello," a melodic voice came from behind her.

Kayla reluctantly turned around. Just as she did, the double doors closed behind her. With disappointment, she looked at the person who had spoken to her. A handsome man with a long white lab coat was standing a few feet away.

"Hello," he said again.

She hoped her face didn't show her irritation. She could almost hear Vivian telling her to smile and to stand up straight. "Hi," Kayla said. She smiled at the man but turned back to the closed doors.

"Can I help you?" he asked, leaning around to meet her eyes.

"Uh," she said, glancing over her shoulder. She moved an inch forward, giving them more space. "I don't think so."

"Are you sure?" he asked. The next words he spoke were not English, and if anyone had passed by at that time they would have heard what sounded like a mixture of several languages. What he said translated to, "I am Kevin Bannerman from the Gedgi lineage. You are Arkean, correct?"

Relief washed over Kayla and she responded in the same dialect. "My name is Kayla." She thought it best to leave out her last name. Her hand went to the small birthmark on her neck just behind her ear. She forgot that her newly cut short hair was no longer covering the mark. She would need to cover it with makeup from now on, especially before leaving the house.

"Nice to meet you Kayla," he said in English. "I usually don't speak our native tongue but you never know if the mark is a tattoo or not. Everyone seems to be marking themselves these days." He held his hand out. Kayla took it and shook. "So, is there something I can do for you, Kayla?" His smile and demeanor were calming.

She thought for a moment. If he could help her get into the ward, she may be able to get into the boy's room. "Well I have to see a patient through those doors," she said, pointing to them, "but I don't know his name or what he looks like."

"I would like to help you," he said. "I really would, but you are going to have to give me a little bit more than that." He smiled.

He was flirting with her. She gave him points for his handsome face and pleasant smile. But her heart belonged to another and always would. Not to mention the little issue of her being married to a nice man who didn't have her heart but he had her respect and devotion.

"I'm here as an ambassador to our Sovereign. We have been informed that a Middling boy may be in the midst of Cycling."

"How did that happen?" he asked. The playful tone was replaced by a serious one.

Kayla liked people who knew when to switch gears and could do it so easily.

"We aren't really sure," she admitted.

"If it is possible, which I don't know if it is, but if so…" he said then paused, "there's no way to treat him." He stepped around her and let the box on the wall next to the doors read his badge. He let Kayla pass through the doors ahead of him.

She moved through the doors and stepped to the side so she could walk with him. He quickly led her to the nurse's station.

"Hello Dr. Bannerman," a nurse said, smiling big. She walked around the desk and stood next to him—intimately close to him, but only for a moment, then she moved to allow some distance. She was a fair skinned beauty with neat shoulder length dreadlocks and beautiful deep-set brown eyes.

"Hello Darlene." He smiled at her.

"Is there something I can help you with, doctor?" Another nurse who was sitting behind the nurse's station asked.

The smile on her plump face was even bigger. Kayla looked at the doctor. He was handsome, but they were shameless. She would have thought the flirting was funny if she hadn't been so worried.

"You can Sally," he said to the nurse who was sitting behind the desk. "I need to know if you have anyone on this floor who has an uncontrollable fever with unexplainable fits of pain."

"Funny you should ask," Sally said. "There's a kid in room 407 with just that. Would you like me to call his doctor?"

"Who is his doctor?" Dr. Bannerman asked as he leaned on the top of the counter closer to the plump nurse.

"Dr. Metzger," the dreadlock beauty next to him answered first.

"Darlene," the plump nurse said; a hint of irritation could be heard in her tone, "don't you need to get back to your floor and do your rounds?"

"Actually," Darlene started, "I'm on my lunch break." She shot the plump nurse a dirty look.

"**No**," Dr. Bannerman said to them, "**contacting Dr. Metzger won't be necessary. Hand me his chart please**?" He said to Sally, holding her gaze. The plump nurse stared into his eyes for a moment. Without saying a word, she stood and went to the files. When she handed the doctor the file she blinked slowly, then smiled at him. "Thank you," he smiled back, holding her gaze for a moment. He turned toward Kayla, pointing down the hall to room 407.

"Anyone with the boy?" Bannerman asked.

"His father usually sits with him throughout the day. He rarely leaves the kid's side since he was admitted but," Sally tilted her head, "he's not here, the mom is."

"Thanks, Sally, I'll be back in a bit."

"I'll walk you to his room," Nurse Darlene said to Dr. Bannerman.

Kayla followed them down the hall. The nurse flirted shamelessly while they walked slowly to the room. This gave Kayla a few seconds to figure out what she was going to say to the kid's parents.

"Wait for me here," Dr. Bannerman told the nurse.

"Sure," she said, as she flipped her hair off her shoulder.

Kayla looked at the name on the door. It read Bertram.

Dr. Bannerman gave the door a few short taps and then opened it. Kayla followed him inside. The room was like any other hospital room except for the scent that filled it. It was a clean fresh scent. She liked it. Kayla breathed in the nice scent as she looked around the private room that was clearly at one point a double occupancy room. The doctor peeked around the privacy curtain and announced himself.

In a bed in the center of the room, a boy not much older than her daughter lay under a number of disheveled sheets. His hair was wet, possibly from the fever, and it clung to his skin. He looked as if he was sleeping.

"He just passed out right before you knocked," a woman's voice informed them.

Kayla looked to the reclining chair over near the window. That part of the room was not as brightly lit as the rest of the room, so Kayla didn't see the woman until she stood and turned the light on. Dr. Bannerman was already at the boy's side, examining him.

"Are you a specialist? Did Dr. Metzger send for you?" The woman asked.

"Dr. Metzger didn't send me but I can help your son," he said to her. "I am familiar with this kind of illness." He regarded at the woman. "My name is Dr. Bannerman."

"I'm Tristan's mother. Your colleagues haven't had much success. We've made plans to take Tristan to Johns Hopkins Hospital in Maryland." Mrs. Bertram folded the blanket she had in her hands. She neatly placed it on the recliner and walked over to the bed, on the opposite side from where Kayla and the doctor stood. She extended her hand over her son as if she was going to wipe his hair from his brow but Dr. Bannerman reached over and took her hand in his. The woman was startled at first, but relaxed when he began speaking.

"Mrs. Bertram," Dr. Bannerman said. He looked Mrs. Bertram directly in the eyes as he held her hand and said, "I am going to try to help your son, but I need you to stay quiet."

The faint tingling brushed against Kayla's mind as he spoke those words.

Dr. Bannerman then looked at Kayla. "It looks as though he's in the middle of the second cycle."

"Can you treat him?" Kayla asked quietly. His tone seemed different when he spoke to her versus when he'd just spoken to Mrs. Bertram.

"I don't know," he admitted. The doctor let go of Mrs. Bertram's hands and picked up the boy's chart again. "According to his chart he's been here for a week and a half. His symptoms would suggest that what usually takes our bodies three days to complete is going to take his body about three weeks, a week per cycle. His body isn't made for this kind of stress. He should have succumbed days ago."

Kayla felt sick. She looked down, then at the boy's mother. Mrs. Bertram's eyes were open but it appeared that she hadn't heard a word they said. The woman didn't move an inch even though Bannerman just said that her son should have passed away last week.

Then it dawned on her. "You are a Wheddler!" Kayla said. "You're one of the few Coesen with the ability of mind control!" The revelation was almost too good to be true. "It seems that the stars are lining up in my favor." But the question in her mind was, why? Kayla looked at the boy again. "I need to touch him."

"Mrs. Bertram," Dr. Bannerman wheedled, holding the woman's gaze. He took her hands in his again. "I would like you to sit down in that chair over there. You will not hear, see, or move until I speak your name."

When he released Mrs. Bertram's hands, she walked over to the chair like a robot and sat down.

Kayla ambled closer to the bed. She wanted to get a good look at the boy. As she came close enough to see him, she noticed the collection of drawings on the side table. She picked up several of the pictures. Each drawing was different but they all shared a common theme. All the drawings were related to her daughter.

A few were very accurate drawings of her daughter's birthmark, which the boy couldn't have seen because Kayla made certain it was hidden under makeup every day. The others were crude drawings of a little girl with peach-toned skin, long plaits, and green-blue eyes.

Confusion flooded her mind. Kayla placed the drawings back on the nightstand and sat on the edge of the bed next to the boy's arm. His chest moved up and down slowly, almost peacefully.

"He is only going to be out like that for a few more minutes before the pain begins again." Dr. Bannerman told her as he placed the clipboard back.

Kayla raised her hand. "I just need a moment." She gently wiped the sweat from the boy's forehead with the tips of her fingers. "You're a very handsome little boy," she said softly. "I'm just going to touch you for only a second."

Kayla moved his hospital gown to the side a bit and placed her hand directly on the boy's shoulder, and closed her eyes. Her heartbeat slowed down to match the pace of his. It only took a few seconds for her to see what she needed to see. A little noise escaped her mouth as she opened her eyes and grabbed a piece of tissue from the nightstand and held it to her nose. She wiped the blood away quickly and put the tissue in her pocket before the doctor could see.

"We need to treat him," she said hastily, looking from the boy to Dr. Bannerman. "Is there anything you can give to comfort him?"

"This isn't like treating one of us. No Middling could possibly survive a cycling. The inside of his body is basically being destroyed and rebuilt," Dr. Bannerman told her.

Kayla faced him with a determined look. "One already has," Kayla said confidently. "And he will too."

Dr. Bannerman looked surprised by the information but didn't let it distract him. He thought for a moment. "I may have something," he said, "It will make the cycles more tolerable, but he will still experience some pain." Then he looked a little concerned. "It could kill him. We have never given it to a Middling before."

"He survives this, I saw it. That means you helped him. He's strong enough," she said giving him that confident look again.

Dr. Bannerman agreed with a nod of his head. "I've known a Seer or two, So I'll trust you're telling me the truth." Bannerman quickly left the room.

Kayla stood and went into the washroom. She wet a cloth with cold water from the faucet and walked back to the boy's bed. She sat down and gently washed his sweaty face and neck. Kayla looked over to the boy's mother who was still seated in the chair she been told to sit in.

She had met several Wheddlers but she knew that Kevin Bannerman must be one of the stronger ones, because the woman was still under his control even though he wasn't in the room.

It wasn't long before Dr. Bannerman returned and walked over to the bed. "I've weakened this a great deal," he said. He took out an alcohol pad and wiped the boys arm. Then he injected a clear fluid into him.

"How long will it be, before it takes effect?" Kayla asked.

"Almost instantly," he replied. "He won't be able to get out of bed until the 3rd cycle begins, but he will feel a lot better very soon." He walked the needle over the sharps container and put it in. "How much do you want her to know?" He motioned at Mrs. Bertram.

"Very little," Kayla said to him. Their laws were clear and she couldn't ask Bannerman to break any 'more' by telling the boy's mother what was happening to him. She looked at the boy again before standing up.

He hadn't moved at all. She knew he was still alive only because she could see the quiet steady movement of his chest. Kayla walked over to Mrs. Bertram and kneeled in front of her. She looked over and gave the go ahead to the doctor.

"Mrs. Bertram," Dr. Bannerman wheedled, "I want you to listen carefully to the woman in front of you."

Mrs. Bertram slowly looked from the doctor to Kayla.

"My name is Kayla Baxter and my daughter has the same illness your son has. I have come here today to offer my support. You and I spoke for over an hour and decided that it would be a good idea to introduce our children when your son is feeling better." Kayla paused then said, "You will find my name and number on the side table next to his drawings."

Dr. Bannerman walked over to Mrs. Bertram. Kayla stood and went to stand by the nightstand with the drawings. While Dr. Bannerman gave Mrs. Bertram some instructions, Kayla wrote her name and number on a piece of paper and placed it on top of the pile of drawings. When Kayla looked up, Mrs. Bertram was sitting quietly, reading a book. Dr. Bannerman motioned to Kayla that they were done.

As the two exited the room they noticed Nurse Darlene speaking to a man a few feet down the hall. His back was turned to them so he didn't see them leave the room.

"Thank you for your help, Dr. Bannerman," Kayla said quietly as they walked around a large partition that separated some of the rooms. She stopped him. "But I need to ask something more of you. This boy is special and will need to be kept secret. He will also have to be watched closely over the next few weeks and will need a permanent physician who knows what he is. Are you able to do this and not speak of him or what he is to anyone except me?"

Dr. Bannerman looked at Kayla and smiled. "You have an honest face, but you know that."

Kayla gave him a crooked smile. He was making it really hard to be serious. She liked that, it made her a little more at ease.

He cleared his throat and made a serious face, a playful serious face that is. "I will not breathe a single word to anyone, not even the Queen herself."

Kayla winced a bit inside at that.

Dr. Bannerman continued, "You can count on me. Besides, having the opportunity to record this kid's progress has guaranteed my cooperation. This is evolution at its finest. I'll insist that Tristan's case is handed over to me," he said with a grin.

They began walking again and soon they reached the nurse's station. The doctor handed the chart to Nurse Sally who was standing beside the area where files were stored. Kayla watched her put the chart back without looking at it. Then Kayla and the doctor walked back through the double doors they had entered.

Once they reached the outer area, Kayla turned to him. "Thank you again. If you hadn't taken the time to speak to me, I don't know how I would have helped him."

"I'm glad I was of some use but it was Darlene really. She spotted you when you asked a doctor for directions downstairs. She recognized you instantly, Soahn," he smiled.

Of course, he knows me, Kayla thought as she he walked her to the elevators.

"I am honored to have had the opportunity to assist you." He looked at her and smiled. Dr. Bannerman turned and pressed the elevator button for the ground floor.

"And I thought she was just a girl with a crush," Kayla teased as they stepped into the elevator. "Your Protector is very believable."

"She's a very good actress," Dr. Bannerman smiled. "She has to pretend to be enamored of me to explain all the times she pops up when I'm around."

"Are you sure she's pretending?"

"Oh yes," he said confidently. "I'm not Darlene's type," he said then chuckled, "but, I'm certain you are."

"Oh," Kayla said, then smiled. The elevator stopped its descent.

"I'm certain you don't want me calling the palace, so how will I contact you if something arises?" he asked quietly. He held the elevator door for her, not intending to get out.

Kayla laughed. "She doesn't live in a palace. I'll contact you. Thank you again." Kayla said as she walked away. She knew she would never see Dr. Bannerman again, because according to her daughter, she had no future. But from what she saw of the boy's future, and Cianne's, she had to adjust her upcoming plans.

"Looks like sunny Arizona instead of North Dakota," she said as she headed for her vehicle.

Present Day

"You were released from the hospital a few days later. The doctors said they had never seen anything like it before. It was a miracle." Mrs. Bertram reached over and placed her hand on Tristan's. "You were so sick baby. They didn't think you were going to survive, and when the bruising started…" She paused to hold in her sobs.

Mrs. Bertram continued after a moment, "Everyone was really scared for you. Then Dr. Bannerman came along," she said then looked at Cianne, "and I met your mother. She heard about Tristan being ill and felt compelled to come and see him because you had the same illness." She looked back to Tristan and then to Cianne again. "She and I talked for a while that day. It felt as if we were old friends by the time she left."

Mrs. Bertram opened the box that she had placed on the table. From inside the box she pulled out a number of papers that she passed to Tristan. She waited until Tristan looked through the drawings and handed them to Cianne.

Cianne looked over each drawing slowly. There were drawings of her birthmark in various sizes. The other drawings were of a little tan-skinned girl with long pigtails and green-blue eyes. Cianne looked over at Tristan before placing his drawings on the table in front of her. She was at a loss for words.

"Your mother called the day Tristan was released from the hospital. She wanted to know how he was doing. I told her that he was feeling a lot better. We talked about getting together for lunch but your mother told me that she was in the middle of a move. She never mentioned where she was moving, and I didn't want to pry. But I recall she did say that she had set up everything in one city but had to change locations at the last minute. Because of this, she was very busy and she wouldn't be able to make a commitment to meet up just yet." Mrs. Bertram sighed. "Imagine my surprise when I was told that you and your mother had come to our home for a visit a few days after we spoke. I was out that day, so your mother left this for me."

Cianne reached for the letter in Mrs. Bertram's hand. She looked at Tristan, who was looking at the letter.

"Would you like me to read it to you?" Tristan asked her. His eyes were still focused on the letter.

"No," she said to him, hoping that he couldn't feel all the emotions flowing through her. Cianne held the letter for several more seconds. She opened the envelope gently, as if it was an old and priceless document that needed to be unfolded with care. She read it out loud.

Dear Melanie,

I am sorry we missed you. I should have called first but it was a spur of the moment decision to visit you and Tristan today. It's too bad that we didn't get to set up a play date before we moved but I will call once we are settled to plan a proper visit. I hope Tristan is doing well and I will call you soon.

Sincerely,
Kayla Baxter

Cianne placed the letter carefully on the table and stood up. The sound of the chair screeching back as she stood broke the silence in the room. Tristan began to stand, but Cianne held her hand up to stop him. He sank back in his chair and watched her leave the kitchen.

An hour passed before Cianne heard Tristan open the double doors leading to the patio. She lay on a lounge chair near the pool, and had been watching the light that danced and reflected off the blue tinted water when Tristan stood over her. Cianne acknowledged him with a half-smile, then looked back to the water. He took a seat on the edge of the lounger she was lying on.

"You told me you were going to tell me why you wanted me to be calm yesterday, when the dog passed by." Cianne didn't look up.

Tristan sighed and rubbed his head. "I can't be sure, but on the night I came for you at the abandoned school, you passed out right when the second wave of dogs came to attack me. Those dogs didn't live long enough to reach me though. They died seconds before you went out." He looked at her but she didn't meet his gaze. "That's not all. I was told that every canine for two miles died around that same time."

"And you think I did that?" she asked. She was looking at him now. His silence gave her his answer.

He watched her as if he expected tears. But she didn't cry, she just looked at him then back at the pool.

After a few minutes of silence, she asked, "What did you tell your mother just now?"

"I really didn't have to tell her much," he answered. He moved a few inches down the lounger to sit closer to her feet. Tristan slipped off her sandals and began to massage her feet. "She thinks your mother was one of God's earthly angels sent to save me."

"Angel?" Cianne repeated. "And you think that's best?" Cianne moved her feet away from his hands. He turned to look at her but she refused to meet his gaze.

"I think that it is safer to not give an explanation. My mother coming up with her own idea of what happened saves me from telling her an elaborate lie. She is probably in there right now looking for biblical names for our baby."

His hands moved toward her feet again. She moved them a second time.

"She's more worried about how what she told us is affecting you." He tilted his head to see her eyes. "So, how is it affecting you?"

As if he couldn't feel it.

Cianne looked away from the water and back to the house. Her mother knew back then that Tristan was her Protector and had kept it a secret. Cianne wanted to know why, but all she could think about was all the suffering he went through at such a young age. She replayed the zoo incident in her mind a hundred times after her mother brought her memories to the surface.

Yet, memories were still locked inside. Memories of that day and several days after. Over the recent weeks, Cianne started to accept that she passed on her curse on to him at some point, but she was comforted by the knowledge that she could take it from him. Now she had to live with the knowledge of how he suffered, and almost died, because of her.

"I cannot express how sorry I am for what you've been through. I didn't know what was happening to me back then, or that I was capable of transmitting…" She shook her head. "Whatever it was that I transmitted to you. If I had known, I would have never... I knew after you saved me from the dogs, that you were at the zoo with me years ago, and I didn't tell you."

"I don't remember any of it," he said sternly, "and to be honest I would go through it all again just so we end up right here. I was able to be there for you when you needed me the most. You can't know how good that makes me feel, Ci." He cleared his throat. "Look, I know you have been struggling with the reality of me being your Protector. I also know that our relationship is forbidden and that you can choose to release me."

Cianne's eyes widened. She had no idea that he knew she could release him. She sat up and placed her bare feet on the stone patio. "You know that I can release you?" Cianne asked him softly as she looked in his eyes. He nodded. "But you never said anything to me about it."

He continued, "The Coesen's history is very important to me, and I know that every Coesen is required to know it. Even though I'm not one of you, I am your Protector. That being so, I am held to the same laws. I've been reading the Annals, the recorded history of the Coesen. I didn't want to make the decision you have to make any harder than it already is, by giving my opinion." Tristan moved to the top of the lounger and laid back, pulling Cianne to his chest.

"What do you want?" she asked him, pleadingly. Cianne let his arm cover her shoulder.

He looked down at her head that rested beneath his chin. He kissed her hair as his finger swirled circles on her shoulder. "I want what every man wants, to protect his family. You being a hybrid Coesen and me being just a Middling will be a big disadvantage for you. All anyone would need to do to hurt you is get to me."

Cianne looked up at him, her face showing her confusion. She had heard Vivian and Zeta say the word when referring to him. "A Middling means what it means in English, ordinary," he said, then smiled. "The Coesen refers to an average person without special abilities as a Middling." He continued, "If I become a Middling again, average, I can't protect you, our daughter, or myself from any supernatural attack. But you also have to also consider what will happen to us if you choose to allow me to remain your Protector."

"All I want is for you, me and our baby to be safe."

"That's all I want," he said.

Cianne and Tristan relaxed in silence for the next twenty minutes, then he spoke. "Your mother knew I was your Protector and she didn't tell Vivian," he said. "She wanted me to Protect you."

Cianne didn't respond to his statement. She lay on him for a while longer before she realized how hot it was getting. "I don't sweat but it seems I'm sweating all over your shirt," she said. Cianne sat up. The doctor mentioned that her body would go through some changes.

"I'm sure it's mostly my sweat," he said, as he took off his shirt.

She never saw him sweat before either. *Always the Protector.*

Tristan stood, pulling her up with him. He walked them over to the edge of the pool. Then he kneeled down and hopped in.

"Come on in and get cooled off." He held his hand up for her to grab.

"I can't get this outfit wet, your mother just brought this." She swatted his hand away.

"You *could* take it off." Tristan raised a brow in challenge.

"You'd like that." Cianne lifted the dress up in her hand so her knees were exposed and sat down on the edge of the pool, lowering her legs and feet into the cool water.

Tristan stood in between her legs and lifted his chin. She bowed her head and met his lips with hers. The kiss was gentle and sweet. His hands rested on her waist and a jolt of passion shot through her. As she surrendered to his touch, she felt herself being lifted and placed down into the cool water.

Chapter Eight

Cianne sat quietly on the sofa in Dr. Garrison's office as she flipped the pages of a random magazine she found on the table in the waiting room. She glanced at her watch and noted the time. It was three minutes to two.

When she looked up, her attention fell on the hard candies over on the doctor's desk. She frowned, remembering that the desk was a cluttered mess before. She looked around the office, noticing that everything was neat.

Dr. Garrison entered the room, causing Cianne to jerk her attention his way. He smiled a smile that lit up his face and made her smile back. He held her gaze for several intense seconds, as if he didn't want to turn away, but then he looked away abruptly.

"Hello Cianne," he said as he started to close the door. He stopped, looked up as if he'd forgotten something, then pulled the door open a few inches before walking over to his desk. He picked up a folder and the glass bowl of hard blue candies before sitting in his chair across from the couch Cianne sat on. He extended the dish of candies for her to take one.

"Thank you," she said, as she reached for a hard candy.

He placed the dish in front of her just as he had last Monday. "How was your week Ms. Baxter?" the doctor asked as he briefly looked through the folder in his hands.

She was intrigued by the behavior he displayed since he entered the room. At first, he seemed almost happy to see her, now he seemed indifferent.

Cianne didn't answer the question, which caused Dr. Garrison to look up at her. Their eyes met and neither turned away. She only met him once before but he seemed different now. Even the reminders jumping in her head about him being a THERAPIST were silent.

Cianne curled her mouth into a smile then spoke. "Do you really want to know or are you just being polite?"

"I really would like to know," he smiled back. He placed the folder on the table that sat between them.

"I had a really nice week. How was your week?' Cianne asked, sounding a bit more playful than she wanted to, most likely because she felt more comfortable. She twisted the wrapped candy in her hands.

"Do you really want to know or are you being polite?" He smiled.

"I *really* want to know," Cianne said then laughed.

"Well," he said, "I had sort of a difficult week to be honest. I expected things to go a certain way but they didn't."

"Would you like to talk about it?" she asked.

"Yes. As a matter of fact, I would, but not right now. I want to try something first." He looked at his office door then to Cianne. "I know that you are a very smart young woman. I also know that there are a lot of things going on in your life right now that have caused you a lot of sleepless nights. I feel that you just need someone to talk to who isn't requiring anything of you." He smiled. "So, for you, I feel that our sessions should be more casual. Everything we discuss will of course be completely between you and me. I am not interested in dissecting and diagnosing you." Dr. Garrison leaned forward and picked up the file that sat on the table between them. "This is your file." He handed it to her.

Cianne looked at her doctor as if he'd lost his mind. Therapy was something new for her but she was pretty sure this wasn't how it worked unless, unless Dr. Garrison was one of those spiritual doctors. But she didn't get that spiritual vibe from him on their first visit.

She lowered her gaze to look at the file, then she looked back to her doctor before picking it up. Cianne read her name on the side tab before opening the file. She quickly read over the notes that Dr. Garrison had written about her. It contained some basic information about her and some personal stuff. Cianne closed the file.

"Usually, these files are filled to overflowing," he referred to the file in her hand, "with lots of notes and medical terms, but as I said, I don't think you need that." He reached for the file. Cianne placed it in his hands. Dr. Garrison stood up and walked over to his desk. He took the loose papers out of the file and inserted them into the paper shredder beside the desk. When he returned to the chair he placed the open, empty folder on the table between them again.

"So," Cianne said, "what do we do now?"

"Let's talk," he said. "I will ask you a question and if you answer it, you can ask me one. If there is something you don't want to answer, just say so. We'll do this until we are comfortable with just talking. Eventually I hope that we will just be two people meeting twice a week to talk. How does that sound?"

"Fine," Cianne said, her voice sounding a little unsure. "But we meet once a week."

"I think we will do twice a week for now," he said absently.

"You're the doctor, right?" Cianne smiled.

"That's what they tell me," he said, then chuckled. "So, would you like to go first?"

"Alright," she said, "Why was your week so difficult?"

He grinned. "Ok. Going straight for the jugular, I like that. Let's see, well I ran into someone who wanted something that I wasn't able to give. That person was very persistent and would not accept no for an answer; he didn't even give me the option to say no. Things got a little physical and ultimately I think that our disagreement may have hurt our budding friendship."

"That was vague," Cianne told him.

"I am only being vague because the situation is sort of work related." He told her. "My turn then?" he asked. Cianne nodded her head in agreement. "What is it that you stress about the most and why?"

Cianne didn't need to think about the answer to this question. "Tristan," she said quickly. "He's asked me to marry him, but I couldn't say yes."

"You couldn't or wouldn't?" he asked.

"I can't say yes," she said. "There are several reasons why."

Dr. Garrison leaned forward. "Does he hurt you?"

Cianne couldn't resist smiling at the doctor's intense stare. Obviously, he didn't like domestic violence. His concern was sweet. "Tristan would never do anything to hurt me."

He relaxed in the chair. "Good."

"It's complicated," she told him.

"Do you love him and does he love you?"

"I love him so much that I can see that he will be better without me." Cianne sighed. "In the short time that we've been a couple, I've managed to turn his entire world upside down, literally."

"Does he know you feel this way?" Dr. Garrison asked.

"I haven't told him yet," she said.

"I see," Dr. Garrison said. "Have you considered that Tristan may be happy with the way his life is turning out? That he loves you and wants a life with you, whatever that life will be?" He looked at Cianne and smiled. "If you love him and you know without a doubt that he loves you, then what's the problem?"

"It's not that simple."

"Isn't it?" Dr. Garrison said. "Don't fool yourself into believing that he would be better off without you. People so often make the mistake of thinking they know what is best for someone else but in truth they haven't got a clue. I can bet that being without you would be much worse. I would also wager that his concern is only for your wellbeing." He smiled. "To be honest with you, and I will always be honest with you, Cianne, Tristan seems to be well adjusted. Let him decide for himself what he wants and what he doesn't. This is going to sound cliché, but my advice for you is to follow your heart. If a decision is an easy one, then it probably isn't that important."

"Follow my heart," she repeated. Her mother had said the same thing.

It was easy to sit here and just talk to Dr. Garrison, easier than she initially expected it to be.

"Are you married, doctor?"

"Not presently." he said. "My lifestyle is a little unorthodox. I'm thinking about getting a dog though."

Cianne's face lost all its color. The sudden appearance of Tristan standing in the doorway pulled Dr. Garrison's attention away from her. Tristan looked to the doctor then to Cianne.

"Sorry," Tristan said. He was speaking to Dr. Garrison but was looking at Cianne. "I just wanted to check on Cianne, to see if everything was alright."

"Everything's fine," Cianne said, looking over her shoulder at Tristan. *"You can't pop in here every time I get scared Tristan."*

Tristan backed out of the doorway, leaving the door open a crack as he did. *"I'm sorry Ci. It's just that I can feel it so much stronger lately. Like it's more concentrated now. I just need a little time to get a handle on it that's all."*

"I apologize. Tristan likes to check on me from time to time." Cianne turned back around to face Dr. Garrison.

"You don't have to apologize. I think it's natural that he would be a little jumpy. You've both been through a lot. Though…" he said, then paused for a few seconds. "Never mind," Dr. Garrison said. He reached for the candy dish and picked up a blue mint.

"What?" Cianne asked.

"I don't know," he said. "It just seemed like Mr. Bertram came in at the exact time I mentioned that I was thinking about getting a dog. I saw your face then, and you looked terrified." He opened the mint and placed it in his mouth. "Like he…"

Dr. Garrison laughed. "Don't mind me Ms. Baxter. I'm just an old man who's been told on more than one occasion that I need a therapist myself. You are a lucky young lady to have a young man who is so *protective* of you." Dr. Garrison smiled again. "So, you don't care for dogs?" He folded the wrapper several times before placing it on the table next to the dish.

Cianne noticed his emphasis on the word protective. She gave the doctor a questioning look, but when he just returned the look she began to question her reasons for thinking he knew anything about the Coesen.

How could he?

She dismissed her suspicions. When he said the word dog again she didn't tense up. She just tapped her finger on the arm of the chair. How was she to keep all the Coesen stuff from Dr. Garrison if things like what just happened, happened. And with him asking her things that will cause a reaction like the dog questions, it was going to be hard.

"Actually," she said, "I get to ask the next question." The doctor conceded with a gentlemanly flip of his hand. Cianne continued, "Do you think that this, what you're trying to do, is really going to help me?"

A look appeared on his face, a look of sincerity. Then he smiled a smile that made his dimples reach from his jawbone to his eyes and said, "I'd stake my life on it."

For the rest of her session Dr. Garrison asked Cianne questions about her friends and her relationship with Tristan. He seemed to realize how at peace she was when she spoke of

Tristan and that she was happy to answer most of the questions he asked her about him. Tristan was a subject she liked and felt comfortable speaking about. By the time the session was over, Cianne felt that Dr. Garrison knew just about everything Cianne knew regarding Tristan Bertram.

June 28th

The sweet smell of flowers filled Cianne's nose as she walked by the rose bushes and toward the pool house. A couple of bees tangled in a tussle over a flower, buzzing near her ears, causing her to stop walking to allow them passage.

She closed her eyes and listened. An assortment of sounds played around her like a summer concert. A warm light breeze blew her loosely curled tresses so that her long hair lifted off the middle of her back like a flag billowing in the wind. The birds sang, the insects hummed, and cool water sprayed from the sprinklers onto the fresh cut lawn with several drops catching her legs.

Cianne opened her eyes and looked around her. She loved life and all its complex beauty again. She felt like anything was possible as she continued down the path. Not that all her problems were solved because of a few sessions of therapy, but she felt like things were definitely becoming clearer. After five sessions, Cianne almost felt like herself again.

Today, Dr. Garrison made her realize something that she'd been fighting for so long. That she would always and forever love Tristan. There was something else too. Four sessions ago, when she watched Dr. Garrison shred her file, she didn't believe he wasn't going to analyze and diagnose her but she was wrong.

Dr. Garrison only wanted to talk; there was no judgment, no requirements. She realized that she liked talking to someone who was impartial. Everyone around her seemed to want what was best for her, to keep her safe even if that meant going against what she wanted. Dr. Garrison only wanted to know what she wanted.

The stone path Cianne was walking on rounded the side of the Estate's main house and led to a pool house that had been transformed into a gym/sparring area for Tristan's training. Since Tristan was her Protector, he needed to be trained to protect her effectively. So, Tristan trained for hours every day with Zeta, sparring and learning to perfect numerous fighting styles.

In addition, Vivian trained him mentally. A Protector had to be strong in mind as well as body. They need to know when to react and when not to. They have to process a situation and recognize a threat by taking in everything around them all within a matter of seconds. To the Coesen, being a Protector was a way of life and they took it very seriously, and so did Tristan.

Cianne saw the pool house come into view. The French doors were wide open, most likely to let the natural afternoon breeze flow freely into the building to cool it down. She walked down a few more steps before she was able to see Tristan and Zeta. They were sparring but it looked like a martial arts dance.

Why isn't the floor padded?

Tristan's gray tank top was soaked through with his sweat. His head was completely wet but he looked sprightly, as if he had just awakened from an eight-hour nap. Zeta, who trained with him the entire time, looked as if she was in an air-conditioned room instead of outside in the sweltering heat.

Cianne watched them from the steps. When Zeta grabbed Tristan from behind and bent his arm in an awkward way, Cianne grimaced. That slight sense of dread she felt caused him to turn in her direction. The little distraction pulled his attention away for a moment but it was long enough for Zeta to kick his feet from under him and at the same time slam her open palm against the back of his shoulder. It was the shoulder of the arm she held behind his back, and it was knocked out of its socket.

Cianne heard him grunt, then curse. She covered her mouth to muffle her gasp.

Zeta reached down for him while saying something Cianne couldn't hear. On his knees with his forehead pressed to the marble floor, Tristan raised his uninjured arm and shook his head.

He was in pain and Cianne wanted to help him. Before Cianne could move toward the pool house, she heard him in her head.

"Relax buttercup, I'm fine," he calmly assured her.

Then in a swift movement, he slammed his injured shoulder into the marble, got to his feet just as quickly, and rolled his shoulders as if shaking the injury off like it never happened. Zeta smiled with approval as Tristan squared off with her again.

"He is doing well, Zeta tells me." Vivian said just as Cianne stepped onto the shaded patio.

Cianne turned quickly in the direction the voice had come from. She didn't realize anyone was on the patio and was startled, but only for a split second.

"He's becoming better at sensing your fears as well. He also learns quickly." Vivian motioned for Cianne to look down toward the pool house. Cianne saw Zeta lying on the floor and Tristan standing on the steps that led to the patio where she was standing. He was looking in her direction. "You put your opponent down first then sort out the rest."

"Just startled by Vivian." Cianne smiled.

Tristan winked and in a blink of an eye was standing over Zeta and helping her to her feet. Cianne took a seat next to Vivian on the patio. She watched as Vivian poured her a glass of tea and placed some fresh fruit next to the glass for her. They sat there in silence for a few minutes before Vivian spoke again.

"You did that thing just now, the telepathy." Vivian said.

"*Mm-huh*," Cianne admitted.

"Remarkable," Vivian smiled. "I cannot tell you how much easier it would be for me to be able to communicate with Cassius like that. It's just remarkable." She took off her sun shades and looked at Cianne. "He tells me he can not only feel your fear but has been feeling some of your other emotions as well."

"I think it's just pregnancy sympathy 2.0. He may feel a little more than most because of our connection of course but it'll probably pass," Cianne said.

"Of course it will," Vivian said but her raised brows said that she clearly didn't agree.

Cianne looked at her lovely grandmother who was now smiling at her. Grandmother was such a weird word for Vivian. She wasn't your average grandmother. Grandmothers were not usually so magnificently beautiful with the body of a twenty-five-year-old model.

"Tristan is relentless when it comes to his training." Vivian placed her sun shades on the table and took a sip of her tea.

"I'm going to marry him," Cianne blurted out in a whisper. She looked at Vivian and braced herself for the fireworks that were about to ensue. At the same time, she was shocked that she actually said it. She'd been told that someone had won her hand in a Tandot competition. She knew from past discussions that a Coesen Princess was expected to marry the victor. She just didn't know what Vivian expected. "I've known since the day he first kissed me that I would never deny him anything for too long."

"He studies hard as well. His mind is like a sponge," Vivian said as if she hadn't heard what Cianne said.

"I don't mean any disrespect. I just didn't know how to tell you without just, well, telling you." Cianne watched for any change in Vivian's expression.

Vivian glanced at Cianne then she turned her attention back to the pool house where Zeta and Tristan were still sparring. "It is a matter that I've already resigned myself to my dear."

Cianne frowned. "Is it so awful?"

"No," Vivian said without emotion.

"My mother knew I transmitted to him when I was eight years old. She knew and she went to see him." Cianne looked for some sort of change in Vivian's composed manner; a shocked expression or a few choice words, but Vivian said nothing. "I know I would have her blessing."

Vivian sipped her tea then placed her glass on the table and looked at Cianne. "My daughter liked to do things the hard way. That was her nature. It was something I learned to accept a long time ago," Vivian said plainly. Her face was still as serene as it was when Cianne first walked onto the porch.

"I've also decided that he will remain my Protector." Cianne used the same conviction for these words as well. "I want to be your granddaughter but that's all. I don't want to rule anyone. I just want what's best for us as a family and to live a normal life. Well, as normal as we can. I hope that you will still want to be in my life but I don't want to be anything other than Cianne."

Vivian faced the pool house and continued to watch the sparring match that was going on. Several minutes passed without a response from her. Cianne was worried and hurt. Vivian was her grandmother and although they hadn't known each other that long, she felt a connection between them.

Cianne sat forward. She needed to excuse herself before she started crying. Damn pregnancy emotional roller coaster!

"There are so many things I would have done differently if given a second chance." Vivian looked at Cianne, who was just about to stand up. Cianne relaxed back in her seat. "But a Queen should never admit such a thing Cianne. To do so would suggest regret, and regret of one's actions instills doubt and doubt spawns weakness," Vivian said. She looked to the pool house again. "Your mother…she was more like her father. Gaither was a good man, kind and gentle just like

Kayla. She took his passing very hard. Kayla blamed me and our beliefs for her father's death and from that day on she tried her best to distance herself from me, the Coesen and her birthright." Vivian turned herself in the chair so that she faced Cianne.

"I knew the night I met Tristan that my daughter had once again deceived me. It angered me, yes; but not for the reason you may think. I was angry not because Tristan was a Middling who received your gift or that he is a Protector who has fallen in love with his ward. I was hurt because Kayla didn't trust me enough to confide in me. To tell me what she saw in your future so that I could have…I don't know, helped maybe. But she didn't trust me." Vivian sighed. "I guess I never gave her reason to trust me." She placed her hands on the table and began rubbing one with the other. "I was Vivian the Sovereign first, and if there was any time left over from my duties, I was a mother." She reached across the table and held out her hand.

Cianne placed her hand in Vivian's.

"The night Tristan saved you I had sent Zeta along because I thought he wouldn't be able to do it. Zeta would save the day and Tristan would decide that being a Protector wasn't for him. But he managed to save you and he did all this knowing that his power wasn't at its full capacity. He didn't once get deterred or show any fear. Our people aren't born fearless. We cry and get scared like everyone else but are soon taught to brave any obstacle with strength and determination. Tristan has all the traits, both the mental and physical strength of a great Protector who has trained years and years to acquire. He already possessed the strength and determination that only was enhanced by the power you gave him."

Vivian smiled at Cianne.

"I've been watching him Cianne. I know he will make a wonderful husband to you, and a loving father. And I am certain he will protect his family better than anyone else can. You know," Vivian paused, "I was in love once." Cianne smiled as she saw Vivian's chest rise and the ends of her mouth curl into a smile. "I was young and full of dreams then. We both were, until our roles were made clear to us. I was soon mated to Gaither and my love never forgave me for choosing duty over him. The day I was married to Gaither," Vivian exhaled, "was the last time I saw him. I tried to convince your mother that duty was more important than love. I admit now that I was wrong."

Cianne could see the pain in her eyes. Vivian lifted her hand to her eye. She took her finger and touched the tear that was forming in the corner. Cianne felt her heart breaking and had no luck fighting her tears back.

"You are my only grandchild of my only child, Cianne. It may not be apparent to you but I love you very much. I have waited all these years to be a part of your life and I want your life to be full and filled with the love that your mother and I could never hold on to. So, when I say that I have resigned myself already, I mean to say that I will support and protect you. We will deal with the consequences, whatever they are, together."

"Thank you," Cianne breathed. Her cheeks wet with tears. She gave Vivian's hand a gentle squeeze. Vivian leaned closer and gently patted Cianne's face with a napkin.

"It's not as if you needed my permission," Vivian said, smiling.

"But I did," Cianne said, sobbing. "You…you're my grandmother." Cianne held her hand up, motioning to Tristan that she was fine.

"So now that we have that settled, I think I'll retire to my room," Vivian stood. She gave Cianne a kiss on the cheek and embraced her tightly before leaving her on the patio.

Cianne sat on the patio wondering about what kind of life Vivian had. She wondered what her life would be like without Tristan. Even when she didn't have him, when he was just an infatuation of hers, she had her dreams in which she had him. She couldn't imagine life without him. Cianne could see that

Vivian had a strong love and duty to her people, but to sacrifice everything she could have had…

Cianne knew she couldn't do the same. She would never give up Tristan or her child. Never. She looked down at her little bump. "I'm not sure how everything is going to turn out but I promise that we will always put you first," Cianne told her baby. She smoothed her hand over her belly.

The baby moved as if motivated by her touch.

Just then Cianne realized she had to think of a way to get Tristan to propose to her again. She slowly got to her feet then walked down to the pool house and made up some excuse about being tired and needing to go home to get some rest. Tristan seemed a bit worried at first but relaxed when she informed him that it was normal for pregnant women to feel tired often. He kissed her, a little too passionately she thought, then he let her go.

Blushing, Cianne said goodbye to Zeta after Tristan agreed to give her a few hours alone to rest.

The market wasn't crowded at all when Cianne picked up some things she needed for the dinner she planned to prepare for Tristan tonight. She felt good about her decision to tell Vivian. Not even the dirty look she was getting from the cashier was going to bother her today.

Besides, she'd gotten use to the sneers and stare downs since being with Tristan. He was somewhat of a celebrity to the girls of West Hills and the surrounding cities so whoever had his heart had their wrath. It wasn't a surprise that the cashier who had attended West Hills High with them was giving her dirty looks.

"You think having a baby will keep him around," the cashier said, so low Cianne barely heard her.

Her name tag said Regina but Cianne knew her as Reggie. She looked up to see two eyes cutting her into little pieces. Tristan and Regina had a moment during sophomore year. A moment was the way he described it, that happened during one of Tristan and Bianca's off periods. Even though Tristan never committed to any of the girls he hooked up with, he never lied to them. His honesty, charisma and god-like looks solidified their unyielding devotion to him.

Well that, and the *personal* attention he bestowed on them made him legendary.

Usually, Cianne would have ignored Reggie and just paid for her purchase. But today she was feeling a little salty. She reached into her purse and took out her wallet. She pulled out a credit card and handed it to Reggie.

Reggie looked at the card dismissively at first glance, but did an instant double take. She looked at Cianne and hissed, "You can't use this card." She placed the card down in front of Cianne rather than handing it to her.

"Oh," Cianne opened her purse again. Sounding naïve she said, "I'm sorry. I thought this was the new card with my name on it." She pulled out her wallet and slid another card halfway out. "Sorry, I know I have one in here that doesn't have his name on it." After going through a few more cards that actually were hers but she pretended weren't, she pulled out one of her credit cards.

Regina took the card, processed the transaction and again placed the card on the ledge for Cianne to pick up. Cianne loaded her bagged groceries in the cart and began to push it but stopped. She looked back at Regina.

"I almost forgot Reggie, is your address still the same?"

"Yeah," she snapped, "Why?"

"Tranae will need to know where to send your wedding invitation." Cianne turned back around and began pushing the cart to the exit. "Have a great day, Reggie."

Today was going so well that Cianne wasn't going to let it be spoiled by anyone. She tipped the young boy who rushed over to load her bags in her car and drove home with a smile on her face.

Cianne called Tranae, and when her best friend arrived, she laid out her plan to get Tristan to propose, again. They prepared dinner while Cianne told her the gist of it. She and Tristan would eat first. After dinner, she would begin a conversation about their future, then at some point she would somehow encourage him to pop the question.

It's that simple, she thought.

Then… Tada, she's engaged, queue the choir.

"Where's your dad going to be tonight?" Tranae asked.

"I'm not sure but I think he has a girlfriend," Cianne said.

Tranae grinned. "You're kidding."

"Nope," Cianne said. "But I think he feels weird about it though, because he hasn't come out and told me yet." Cianne put the front burner of the stove on low heat. "I don't know," she said then shrugged. "Anyway, he doesn't come home at least three nights a week now."

"Well," Tranae said, "I guess ole dude had to get out there sometime." Tranae played with the skin from the chopped onion. She looked into space for several long minutes.

"What's wrong?" Cianne asked.

Tranae would have normally made several more comments about her father dating again. Some would have even been funny, but Tranae didn't jump at the opportunity. Something was definitely wrong.

Tranae gave her a crooked smile. "Everything is changing so fast. With Brian going away and Tristan and you having a baby and going lord knows where, I feel that we are going to lose each other in all of this." She paused. "It's been Tranae and Cianne for so long, I don't know if I'm ready for it to just be Tranae."

Cianne walked around the table and sat next to Tranae, who turned around in the chair to face her. "We are never going to be those friends who call every three years and still claim that we are besties. We are always going to be close, Tranae. There are things going on right now that I haven't been able to tell you about, but I swear as soon as I can I will. You are my only sister." Cianne hugged her tightly then held her at arm's length. "And, the godmother to my little girl."

Tranae sang out a powerful high-pitched scream. "Really?" she asked with disbelief, "I am?"

"Tristan is going to be so mad at me. We were supposed to ask you and Brian over a formal type dinner or something. He has it all planned, so you need to act surprised when—"

"I will," Tranae said, cutting Cianne off. "You know I'm a good actress. Oh my god, I'm a godmother." She fanned her tears.

Cianne managed to calm Tranae and finish cooking before eight o'clock. She left Tristan over five hours ago and he still hadn't arrived. He probably had some things to do, she figured. So Cianne, with Tranae's help, put dinner in some containers and set them in the refrigerator. After talking over some baby names and eating a few pieces of bread to ease her hunger she was feeling a little tired, so she told Tranae she was going to take a nap before Tristan got there. Tranae offered to stay while she slept but Cianne, feeling more and more like her old self again, told her friend there was no need.

Thanks to Dr. Garrison, she was able to decline the offer and she felt comfortable as she locked the door when Tranae left.

Cianne managed to get her shoes off before crawling onto the bed. Her eyes closed and opened slowly as she thought of a time not long ago, when she could stay up until 3 a.m. then wake up at six. Her eyes closed again and sleep took over.

Across town

Music rose from the basement like smoke from a fire and it was just as unforgiving. It filled every room in the modest sized home of Mr. and Mrs. Carter. Several times today, Mr. Carter had to beat the floor with a broom, signaling for his son to turn down that damn music.

Beating the floor with the broomstick was done so much over the course of the day that he could tap the exact indentation in the floor without even looking. It was a routine that both Mr. Carter and his wife were usually unconscious of except for today. Today was different. It was June 28th, the first day of an overdue yet well-deserved vacation for the aging repairman.

Mrs. Carter got up off the sofa again and this time she yelled down the basement steps. She informed her son that if he didn't turn that damn music down that she would turn the electricity in the basement off. It didn't happen right away but eventually the music was turned down. Not off, like the Carters would have liked, but low enough for them to comfortably concentrate on the rest of the movie they had been straining to hear.

Mrs. Carter, a five foot something sweet woman, looked at her watch when she heard the basement door open and voices come from the hallway. It was a quarter to nine and her son's female friend was leaving.

She hated those nasty fast girls her sons dealt with. Mrs. Carter wondered if this fast girl was coming back, like she had every night this week. She really hated fast girls but that seemed to be the way most of them were these days.

The two elder Carters sat on their sofa and gave each other a look as the girl said goodbye to their youngest son. The back door shut and they heard his heavy footsteps going back down the basement stairs.

A half hour later, before going off to bed, Mrs. Carter called down the basement to her son. "Goodnight Nicklaus," she screamed over the music. He yelled goodnight and she shut the basement door. She joined her husband in their bedroom on the third floor where she fell asleep and didn't wake up until she heard loud shrill screams coming from downstairs.

When she and Mr. Carter ran down the steps they almost knocked down that fast little girl Nick had been entertaining earlier. She was crying uncontrollably, and only a few words were decipherable through her sobs.

Basement and Nick was all they could make out.

Mrs. Carter was so upset that she was awakened for this nonsense again that she called 911 this time. She wasn't going to go through this again. Her son needed help and this time she was going to make sure he got it. She looked at the time that was displayed on the wall clock in the kitchen.

It was 1:30 a.m.

Mr. Carter started down the basement stairs to see what the girl, probably high off pot, was screaming about. As he slowly made his way down the stairs he prayed that Nick hadn't hit this girl too.

It was just a few years ago that they had to smooth over the incident with a girl he met at a nightclub who accused him of raping and beating her. For some unknown reason, his son always seemed to choose the wrong type of girl.

When Nick was accepted to Kennecott University he thought his son would finally find a nice mature girl. They didn't expect trouble to find their boy there, but it had. Nick was kicked out because of a fight with a VIP.

He isn't a bad kid, Mr. Carter thought as he stepped off the last step. His son just had bad luck, that's all. He stopped short as he took in the scene.

"My God." Mr. Carter gasped, then covered his mouth with his hand.

His baby boy was lying half on his bed, half on the floor. Stumbling forward, Mr. Carter braced himself on the edge of his son's mattress. He quickly retracted his hand when he felt the sticky wet fluid between his fingers. He lifted his hand to his face and stared at the blood with wide watery eyes. The sound of his scream was heard throughout the Carter home.

He didn't notice that the music was no longer playing.

Chapter Nine

Cianne slowly woke to the muffled sound of a car horn blaring somewhere outside. She placed her arm over her closed eyes. It was a failed attempt to block out the sun's light so she could go back to sleep. But once the light of day hit her eyes there was no way she would get back to sleep. She sighed.

Dinner, she thought as she quickly sat up.

"Ouch," she grimaced. Cianne moved her hand to the side of her round belly. Sitting straight up that fast tugged at something. Cianne felt for the baby.

Her little package moved as if to say, 'I'm alright mommy.'

"Sorry sweetie," Cianne said in a low voice.

"Moved too fast again?" Tristan's voice came from one of the corners in her room.

Cianne looked over toward the familiar but exhausted sound of Tristan's voice. He was seated in her desk chair. His long legs were stretched out in front of him and his upper body sort of leaned to the side with his head resting on the tip of the chair's headrest. Clearly, he was way too big for her chair.

Tristan stood slowly and stretched. The sound of his bones creaking under his clothing made Cianne wince. He walked over to the bed and sat next to her. He gently laid his head on her chest at the same time he propped up the pillows behind her so she could lay back.

"What time did you get here?" Cianne asked. She caressed the nape of his neck.

"I don't know, about three-thirty a.m.," he groaned. Tristan placed his hand on her stomach. The baby kicked several times, her way of greeting her father when he touched Cianne's belly.

Cianne glanced at her clock. It was only a little after eight in the morning. "It's still early. You can go back to sleep," she said as she slid from under him and off the bed.

Tristan moaned as he reached for her to come back.

Cianne backed away from his reach causing him to plop down face first on the bed in a very dramatic fashion.

"Why didn't you just lie in bed with me?" she asked.

"I didn't want to make you uncomfortable." Tristan turned face up on the bed. He put his hands behind his head and looked over to Cianne, who was standing near her doorway. "I'm up," he said. Lust flickered in his eyes and over his face but dissolved almost immediately. "All I need is a shower." He reached for Cianne. "But first I want to hold my girls."

It had been weeks since they were intimate and Cianne could see him fighting his urges from time to time. She tilted her head as her eyes focused on his extended arm and hand.

"Oh yeah," he said. Tristan turned his arm in the air as he looked at it. "I had sort of an accident." He reached for her again.

"An accident?" She frowned.

Cianne moved to her bed to get a closer look at the bandage. It was wrapped around his entire left hand and wrist. His fingers and thumb were the only parts exposed. The bandage was white except for a blood trail that ran from his pointer finger to a few centimeters away from center of his wrist.

Cianne sat down on the bed. She grimaced as she took his bandaged hand in hers. "Have you had it looked at yet?"

"No," he said, as he turned his bandaged wrist and pulled her close. "It doesn't hurt but if you want, I will."

"I want," she said.

Tristan propped himself up on his arm and leaned his head on his palm. Cianne mimicked him.

"I noticed you cooked for me." He smiled "her smile".

"I did," she said then grinned. Cianne pulled her bottom lip in her mouth and began to nibble on it.

"What's the occasion?" Tristan asked. He played with the hair that fell over her shoulder between them.

Cianne looked at him nervously before sitting up and scooting to the edge of the bed. Tristan did the same. She looked into his eyes. "Do you think you could love me for the rest of your life?"

Tristan traced his thumb over her lips. "You are the only woman I'll ever love, Cianne. Your face is the only face I want to wake to. I will never desire any woman's touch, taste, or scent the way I do yours. I will not only love you my entire life," he said as he stared at her intensely, "my death will change nothing."

"I want to be your wife." She didn't look away.

Tristan smiled. He leaned forward and kissed her passionately but pulled away suddenly and looked at her with an exaggerated curious look. "Why do you want to marry me?" he asked playfully.

"Alright," she said. He wanted this to be uncomfortable for her. "I know what life was like wanting you from a distance. Now that I have you I don't ever want to be without you again. You are the only man I'll ever love."

Tristan pulled her into a gentle kiss. When they separated, he had the black ring box he offered her a few weeks ago between them. Cianne's eyes went from the box then to him, with an inquiring look.

"Brian called me and asked if I had spoken to you. When I said "no", he quickly blew me off. Then I saw that you had cooked one of my favorite meals Celia makes for me only on special occasions. Also, Tranae called your cell phone over ten times last night. You left it in the kitchen. So, I thought I'd better be prepared," he said, smiling, "just in case."

He opened the box.

Cianne couldn't find the air she needed to breathe, let alone speak. The ring, her ring, was…breathtaking. Sparkling inside the box was a platinum band with a baguette style setting, and in its center, was a very large emerald cut diamond.

"Like it?" he asked.

"It's amazing," Cianne said when she found her voice. "I love it." She told him just as the tears started to run down her cheeks. "How did you…" She looked up at him. "Did you pick this out yourself?"

"Brian helped," he said. Tristan got out of bed and went down on one knee. He took the ring from the box and lifted her left hand. "Cianne Baxter, will you marry me and make me the happiest man on the planet?"

"Yes. Yes. Yes." Cianne wrapped her arms around his neck and kissed him again and again as she said yes over and over again. Eventually he slid the flawless ring on her finger.

Cianne glanced at her engagement ring again, then to Tranae who was very impressed with the ring Tristan had chosen. The two were up for hours, talking about the upcoming nuptials and looking over bridal magazines and internet images. The number of bridesmaids, the colors, and the venue were the main topics of discussion.

"I want a small intimate ceremony," Cianne said as she looked at Tranae. "Close friends and relatives only."

"Nope, we should do it up honey. A huge venue with lots of fanfare and everyone we know." Tranae countered. She pointed to a picture of a lavishly decorated hall.

Both Cianne and Tranae looked up from the magazine when they heard the doorbell.

"I'll get it," Tranae said as she jumped up.

◉

Tristan took a shower, redressed in his clothing from the previous night, and was lying peacefully on Cianne's bed when he heard the doorbell. He processed Cianne's emotions and found no immediate reason to get up until he heard the distinctive voice of Detective Malone.

Tristan begrudgingly rolled out of bed and walked down the stairs.

"Ah, there you are Mr. Bertram. I have been looking for you," Det. Malone said, standing in the doorway.

Tristan stepped down the remaining four steps and walked over to the door. He stood next to Tranae, who was holding the door open. Cianne stuck her head out of the kitchen. When she saw it was the detective she came out of the kitchen and into view.

"Should I ask why?" Tristan asked, putting his hands in his pockets.

Malone noticed Tristan's bandaged hand. "What's wrong with your hand there?" the detective asked.

"Just a little cut," Tristan said, downplaying his injury. He lifted his hand in the air and turned it around for the detective to see. "What can I do for you?"

Cianne walked over to Tristan and he took hold of her hand. She locked her fingers with his. The detective's eye caught the sparkle from her engagement ring while Cianne looked at him.

Malone raised his eyes to meet Tristan's again. "Nicklaus Carter was found dead in his parent's home in Cedar Creek last night. Where were you last night between 9 p.m. and 2 a.m.?"

Tristan looked at the detective and gave him a devilish grin. "Doing my best to be a good citizen," Tristan said calmly.

Cianne squeezed his hand tightly. *"What's going on Tristan?"*

"I want you to relax Ci." He looked down at her. He could feel the emotions swelling inside her. He placed a kiss on her forehead. *"Calm down and don't worry."*

"Ready when you are," Tristan told Malone.

Malone turned partially around and motioned for two officers. Tristan dropped Cianne's hand and moved her behind him. He looked at Tranae, who was watching everything with a panicked look in her eyes.

'Tranae," Tristan said calmly. "Tranae," he said again and waited until a confused Tranae looked at him. "Could you watch over Cianne for me? I'll be back." He looked at his watch on his free wrist. It was 11 a.m. "Before two p.m."

Cianne pulled at Tristan's arm as he turned his back to the two officers and allowed them to put the cuff on one of his wrists. Tranae nodded as she put her arms around Cianne.

"Congratulations," Det. Malone said, looking at Cianne. Cianne looked from Tristan to Malone. "On your engagement," he said as he pointed to her ring.

Tristan watched as Cianne looked at her finger. He saw the light glistening off the engagement ring as the officer cuffed his other hand.

"Thank you," Cianne said, politely.

Tristan allowed the officers to turn him around and lead him past Malone and outside.

"Ms. Baxter," Malone said, "I have a few questions for you. Would you mind coming down to the station also?"

Tristan instantly turned around and in a swift movement was back on the porch where Malone still stood outside of the door. The officers, both taken aback by the speed in which he moved, hustled up the walkway and onto the steps. They grabbed Tristan by the arms and shoulders. Tristan felt Cianne's alarm and her face clearly showed it when he looked at her.

Tristan forced himself to relax. "I don't think that making my pregnant fiancé come to a police station is a good idea."

Malone turned to look at Tristan as he stood frozen in place a few feet away. The detective frowned as he noticed his officers struggling to move Tristan, who refused to budge. Both of the officers were in pretty good shape but still they could not get Tristan down the stairs and in the police cruiser.

"I guess you're right," he said casually. "A police station is no place for a beautiful pregnant woman such as yourself, Ms. Baxter," Malone said to Cianne but kept his eyes on Tristan.

Tristan backed away, slowly at first; then he turned around and walked to the police cruiser with little assistance from the officers. He got into the police car without incident and sat quietly as Malone said a few words to Cianne and Tranae.

Tristan looked at Cianne through the window. *"Don't worry,"* He smiled her smile. *"I love you."* He faced forward as the cruiser pulled off and disappeared down the street.

Not that it mattered to him, but Malone had sat Tristan in his office instead of one of the interrogation rooms. He preferred the gray/white abysmal look of the interrogation room. Here, in the cop's office, he felt like he was on a job interview.

"So how long do I have?" Malone flipped his pencil around and tapped it on his desk with every half turn.

Tristan glanced down at his watch. "I'd guess…maybe an hour."

Malone looked at the time displayed on his computer monitor. "So then, are you going to tell me where you were between 9 p.m. and 2 a.m.?"

Tristan looked at Malone for a few minutes. "I respectfully choose not to. Am I your only suspect for both murders?" Tristan was relaxed but not overconfident as he sat in the chair across from Malone.

"The truth," Malone said then smiled, "Yup."

He liked Tristan, had since their second meeting. He enjoyed the beating Tristan had given Nick and JC. He liked the stuff Tristan was made of, so he didn't have a problem with being completely honest with the kid; something he had never done with any other suspect.

"You happen to fit the description of the man seen around the building before JC's murder. No one was seen coming or leaving Nicklaus's home."

"I can see why I would be a suspect," Tristan admitted. "But that description line is so arbitrary. I and over a million guys are lumped into the description you're going on."

"These guys are responsible for kidnapping your fiancé, trying to kill her, and you. And let's not forget they tried to extort a very large sum of money from you. A million other guys don't have the connection you have," Malone informed him.

"And with all this, my client would not be ignorant enough to risk his promising future and a life with his beautiful fiancé to settle some insane score," a charismatic voice interjected.

Tristan turned in the chair to see a well-dressed gentleman standing in the doorway of Malone's office, with both hands in his pockets. He was tall, with hair that was dirty blond; his face was devilishly handsome and his eyes were the palest gray Tristan had ever seen. The man looked like a Scandinavian god from a comic book.

Tristan had never seen him before but that meant nothing. His father was always searching for the best of the best and this guy gave the impression he was indeed the "best". Even though the lawyer looked about late-thirties/mid-forties,

Tristan found himself wondering if Cianne would find him attractive.

He shook the thought out of his mind.

Tristan watched as Malone looked at his computer screen, most likely noting the time. The lawyer's sudden arrival was unexpected.

Tristan scrutinized the lawyer. Everything about him screamed confidence—his custom suit, polished shoes, and the beautiful watch that hung from his wrist. The look in his eyes seemed easy going but Tristan suspected that the man was cunning.

The savvy lawyer walked into the office and extended his hand for Malone to shake. A few seconds passed before Malone shook the hand that was presented to him.

"I'm Kenneth Langley, attorney for Mr. Bertram," the man said. He released Malone's hand then turned to Tristan. "Mr. Bertram, Det. Malone has not charged you with any crime so we are free to leave."

Malone tapped the pencil in his hand on his desk. "Not quite an hour," Det. Malone said as he raised his brow.

"I'm sure you'll make up for it the next time," Tristan said. He stood.

"Next time? Is that an admission of guilt?" Malone stood as well.

Tristan walked through his office door behind Langley but stopped and looked over his shoulder. "Not at all," he said. *Just a prediction*, he thought. He knew Nick wasn't bright enough to pull off a kidnapping for ransom all by himself. Couple that with the fact that neither Nick nor JC was the voice he heard in the field that night. *A third body will be added to the detective's workload.*

"Maybe I'll get a confession next time." Det. Malone said with a grin.

"Unlikely." Tristan turned to see Langley waiting by the elevator and joined him.

Tristan nor Langley spoke as they rode the elevator to the lobby. There was a luxury SUV waiting for them when they exited the building. Langley opened the back door for Tristan. Once Tristan was inside the vehicle, Langley slid in beside him, and the driver pulled into traffic. Langley remained silent so Tristan tilted his head back and tried to take a quick nap before dealing with his father.

When the vehicle came to a stop, Tristan slowly opened his eyes. He looked out of the open car door and what he saw wasn't his house; he was in Vivian's driveway. He saw Langley standing in front of the mansion's door waiting for him.

"Okay," Tristan said. He got out of the vehicle and joined Langley at the door.

Langley lowered his head in what Tristan thought was a bow, then turned and opened the front door to the house. That was when Tristan noticed the mark on Langley's neck. If he wanted to put it into words, he would have to say it looked like a piece of a pie, the upper left piece. It was in the exact same place as Cianne's birthmark, only it was missing three pieces of the pie and a thin outer ring.

"You're an Arkean," Tristan said with amazement.

"I am," Langley replied.

Tristan stared at him, taking in the paleness of Langley's skin, his light gray eyes, and fine blond hair. "But you're white," Tristan said bluntly.

Langley raised a brow then said calmly, "It would appear so."

He slightly raised his hand, offering Tristan the lead over the threshold. Tristan stepped inside.

"Soahn Vivian is in the kitchen," Langley told him.

Tristan watched Langley walk in the opposite direction he was to go. He stood there for a moment, still perplexed about Langley and his birthmark, before walking toward the kitchen.

Vivian was seated at the table when Tristan stepped into the kitchen. Her hands were gloved and she looked to be cutting thorns from long-stemmed roses and placing them in a clear blue vase.

He scanned the kitchen as he walked over to Vivian. Tristan scanned every room he entered. Taking mental notes of his surroundings and any potential threats were second nature now. Comfortable that no immediate threats were present, he walked over and stood a few feet from the chair Vivian sat in and waited for her to speak.

"Would you like something to drink?"

When he shook his head no, Vivian motioned for him to sit. He did.

"Cianne called."

Tristan was a little nervous and he was sure it showed. He had been reading the Annals and he now knew the Coesen regarded Vivian as their queen. He lowered his gaze, careful not to look at Vivian and he knew now not to speak unless he was spoken to.

"Is your hand alright?" she asked. Her voice held no hint of anger or emotion at all. "We could have a doctor look at it."

"I…I'm…it's fine, Soahn," he said looking at her. Tristan lowered his gaze when she looked back at him.

Vivian smiled. "So, you must have read the part of the Annals that refers to me and my ancestors. That doesn't mean you need to bow or treat me any different than you have been. I do not practice many of the old ways. I prefer to be respected rather than feared. I am regarded as royalty, but all that bowing 'red carpet' nonsense is a bit dated. I actually liked your, as Cianne would say, *spicy attitude*. It's refreshing." Vivian focused her gaze back on her roses. "It seems you have caught the attention of a Detective Malone. How much does he know?"

"He knows nothing regarding the Coesen, or anything else." Tristan said, looking her in the eyes. "I know that as a Protector I need to be tactful. I would never tell anyone or do anything that would reveal us…" he said. "I mean the Coesen," Tristan amended.

"You are now, one of *the* Coesen, Tristan," Vivian said to him with a smile. "So, that's that then. I will not bring the subject up again. Langley is my attorney, and brother. He will handle any other situations that should arise in reference to this matter. Cianne and I both feel that it isn't necessary to involve your family's attorney regarding said matter and Langley is very good at what he does." Vivian smiled. "The other reason I wanted you here was to talk to you about Cianne."

Tristan's brows furrowed. He glanced at the exit then began to rub his hands over his thighs.

"There's nothing wrong with her. I just want to tell you face to face that I am very pleased that my granddaughter has chosen you as her mate. I also would like you to..." She paused and looked up at him. "To look at me as family, if you can."

Tristan stood up slowly, as to not frighten her. He walked the few steps to close the space between them and motioned for her hand. When she gave it, he gently pulled Vivian to her feet and hugged her like one would hug a family member instead of a Queen.

Tranae picked up the warm glass of milk that sat untouched in front of Cianne and poured it slowly into the sink. She turned the faucet on and rinsed the milk away. Tranae pinched the bridge of her nose as she looked over to the refrigerator and groaned with disgust, then she looked to Cianne.

Cianne returned the disgusted look.

"The baby needs the calcium," Tranae sneered. She opened the refrigerator and poured more cold milk into the glass.

Cianne stood up. Not knowing what was going on with Tristan was driving her crazy. She slowly made her way into the sitting room. Sitting near the end of the sofa, she laid her head on the armrest. Pulling her feet up to her side and placed them on the middle cushion.

She wished she could take that day back all those months ago. If she would have just gone to Houston and told Tristan about the pregnancy, maybe Nick and his friends would have given up that stupid idea to kidnap her. Nick and JC would still be alive, and wedding plans, Protectors and her long-lost family would be their only concerns.

If only she hadn't gone to Nick's dorm room that day long ago.

Tranae came into the sitting room and sat crossed legged on the floor. Her head touched the same cushion Cianne's head rested on. "Do you think Tristan did it?" Tranae asked.

Cianne closed her eyes. She hated that she asked herself the very same question. "I don't know," she answered. "And I don't want to ask him."

"It's not like he would tell you the truth. Why would he tell the mother of his child that he may have…" she said, then swallowed, "beaten the bastards who kidnapped her to death. But all is well now, he'd tell you, and I'm not a crazed maniac or nothing."

"You think he's a crazed maniac?" Cianne asked in a low voice.

Tranae shook her head frantically. "No…I didn't mean it like that," Tranae told her. She shrugged. "I'm just saying that if I were him, I wouldn't be too quick to tell you something like that."

"He wouldn't lie to me," Cianne said in the same saddened tone. She sighed. "That's why I haven't asked him about it. I don't want to know because if he did and I knew…" She took a deep breath. "I don't know how I would feel about it."

"They were going to kill you, Cianne. Remember that. If it was me and Brian was killing those fuckers, I would give him my blessing."

Cianne couldn't believe what she was hearing. "And if he got caught and sent to jail before he could ever hold your baby in his arms…" Cianne looked Tranae in the eyes. "Then would you give him your blessing?"

"Well, if you put it like that," Tranae said. She put her forehead on Cianne's. "I…"

Before Tranae could say another word, she and Cianne heard the front door open then close. They both looked up to see Tristan standing in the entryway of the sitting room.

Tranae smiled and stood up. "That was fast!"

Cianne, on the other hand, had a very worried look on her face. Tristan leaned against the frame of the entryway.

"I hope you ladies weren't speaking ill of me," he said.

Tranae kissed Cianne on the forehead. "Not possible Mr. Perfect," Tranae said as she started toward him. She looked back to Cianne. "Call me later so we can discuss the wedding plans." She hugged Tristan. "Make sure she drinks that glass of milk that's in the fridge. She needs more calcium."

"If you couldn't get her to drink it, how do you fathom I will be able to get her to do it? I'm putty in her hands," he confessed.

"Man up, Tristan," she whispered, "just put your foot down." Tranae winked at him before leaving.

Tristan stood there for a moment looking at Cianne as she looked at him. His smile had faded and he looked serious for the moment. He was standing over her, and lifting her in his arms before she even registered that he had moved. He sat on the sofa with her cradled in his arms, all in a blink of an eye.

"You're getting faster," she said, as she put her arm around his neck and laid her head on his shoulder.

"A little." He kissed her lips, but Cianne didn't respond. Tristan pulled back and looked at her, puzzled that she hadn't responded to his kiss.

"I'm worried," she admitted.

"You have no reason to be," he said. Tristan smiled as he moved his hand up and down her back. "Now kiss me or I will sing to the baby for a straight hour."

Cianne looked into his blue eyes for a few seconds before bringing her hand up to touch his face. He leaned in and kissed her again. This time she responded, although her thoughts were everywhere at once. But his touch had the power to make all things right. She would trust in him; if he said there was nothing to worry about, then there was nothing to worry about.

Chapter Ten

The mall was never her favorite place and now Cianne just ached all over whenever anyone mentioned the word mall. Malls took so much out of her mentally. It was the second week of July and everyone knew that meant people crowding the malls to get away from the summer heat. That meant finding parking, all the walking, and let's not forget all the people she had to dodge to keep her precious cargo safe. Plus, the smells, a barrage of overpowering scents assaulting her too sensitive, so pregnant nose.

Without any manner of escape other than actually leaving, Cianne endured.

Tranae crossed in front of Cianne and headed for the third and hopefully final Maternity/Baby store they'd visit today. Cianne sighed but Tranae grabbed her hand and pulled her inside. The store was upscale like the rest in this particular mall. The unisex designs *were* refreshing. Not one commercial character did she see in the entire place.

"Looks like we saved the best for last," Tranae said as she headed for the back of the store.

Cianne was in agreement and relieved. This did seem like the best store for baby gear. Baby shopping was much more intricate than she originally thought and God help her, she was so ready to give up and leave the mall.

She thought it to be an easy process of going out and getting a couple of bottles, some tees, and a few blankets. But *no*, it wasn't that easy. Shopping for a baby was more complicated than a Millennium Prize Math Problem.

Well, it wasn't that bad but she'd read over a dozen articles on which bottles to get. With colic, toxic chemicals in the plastic bottles, and the argument of glass versus plastic, one had to be a scientist. Not to mention the nipples. They were a whole other subject.

"These are tees made of all natural fibers. Let's get them." Tranae held them out.

Cianne nodded her head in agreement.

"Which do you want, monkeys, giraffes, polar bears, or turtles? I like the monkeys and the giraffes."

Cianne held out her hand. "Monkeys are good."

"What am I saying?" Tranae beamed. "We have unlimited funds. We can get both."

She watched as Tranae grabbed several items with both animals and handed them to her. "We don't have unlimited funds." Cianne straightened the items she held.

"Can I help you?" A tall woman with a killer figure asked as she moved toward them.

Tranae stepped around Cianne. "Yes," Tranae said, "can you show us more items with these cute little monkeys and giraffes?"

"I'll be glad to help you." The woman motioned for Tranae and Cianne to follow her as she sashayed to the rear of the large store.

Cianne decided not to follow. Instead she found a bench near a fitting room and had a seat. Tranae was in her element. Shopping was her gift. Cianne enjoyed shopping too, but she had to be in the mood and she wasn't in the mood.

Her thoughts about shopping were cut short when an odd feeling overtook her. Cianne raised her head and looked around the store. She got the sense she was being watched but no one other than a little girl, her pregnant mother, and a store clerk, was within her line of sight. She glared out into the mall. People moved about but no one stood out.

Vibrations and the soothing ring tone of her phone pulled Cianne's attention to her purse.

"Ci," Tristan said over the line, "felt a little weird, thought I should call."

"Just overwhelmed," she told him, "that's all."

Tristan said nothing for a few long seconds then said, "Let me speak to Zeta please."

Cianne stood and went to the entrance of the store. Zeta sat on the second-floor railing, drinking a smoothie and ignoring a group of boys who were trying very hard to get her attention. When she saw Cianne, she jumped down from the rail with the grace of a ballerina and strolled over to her. Cianne held the phone out for her to take.

Zeta took the phone then took two steps away from Cianne and spoke so low into the cell phone that no one other than God and a Protector could hear what she was saying. After a minute, with a smile and a shrug, Zeta handed the cell phone back to Cianne with her fingerless gloved right hand.

"Everything ok?" Cianne asked Tristan.

"Just told her not to let you over-exert yourself," he said, "and to have some fun, of course. It's her day off."

Cianne smiled as the boys ogling Zeta stepped out of the way so she could once again take her position on the railing.

"Still feel like you're being watched?" Tristan asked.

Creepy much? Cianne sighed. "Do you feel *everything* I feel?"

"Only when you're distressed my love," he said.

Cianne turned around and strolled back down the hallway. She stopped in her tracks and sighed but started for her destination again. Her mall experience earlier didn't go too well and she wanted to see Tristan, and even if that meant sitting in during his studies then so be it.

The hallway led to a small alcove that had a door on either side. Cianne took a breath and tried to calm her nerves. It wasn't as if she'd never been to this side of the house before. She'd come here a few times since Tristan started his training.

Hanging out with him while he sparred was hard at times. Watching the way his long muscular limbs flexed when strained sent electricity all through her. The way he always looked calm even when she knew he was being pushed to his limit made her anxious to touch his sore muscles. The way his body glistened with the sheer covering of sweat was disturbingly delicious.

Watching Tristan without touching him was indeed hard but she could control her desires, she had to whenever he was near.

But his mental training was something altogether different. It wasn't a visual feast like his physical training. It was more like school in many ways. It was held in the library of the manor. The room was comfy even with the floor to ceiling wall-to-wall shelves.

Cianne had never met the owner of this beautiful mansion, a Coesen named Langley. She could tell by the way his home was furnished that he was into history and luxury. She knew nothing else about the man other than Vivian trusted him enough to stay in his home and to safeguard her private Annals, books in which were recorded her personal and Coesen history.

Cianne took another breath before reaching for the doorknob to the library. Her reluctance wasn't due to the fact that it reminded her of school, she loved school. It was because she wanted nothing to do with Coesen history. Cianne had no desire to be a part of this world other than having a personal relationship with her grandmother. She wanted none of their rules or politics. But she would support Tristan and his fascination with this world they had been thrown into.

Cianne pulled the door open. Tristan, who was sitting on one of the sofas and already looking her way, stood when he saw her. He smiled as he made his way over to her, and kissed her lips gently while he pulled her into the room.

"Where's Vivian?"

Tristan looked back at her then he tilted his head toward a door located on the far right of the room.

"Have you eaten today?" she asked.

Cianne knew that Tristan could go days without eating. Most Protectors could, without suffering the way she and most humans would from the lack of nourishment, but she still wanted him to eat.

Tristan sat her down then sat next to her. He gave her a knowing grin before pulling an energy bar from his pocket and waving it from side to side. "I asked Zeta to bring me one of the huge chicken burritos they sell at the mall. I thought you were going home to rest. I could have gone with you to the mall if I knew you wanted to come to the session today."

Cianne almost rolled her eyes but was able to catch herself. "I'm not here for any session," she told him. "Tranae dropped us off here after our shopping expedition." Cianne still didn't drive too many places alone now.

Tristan smirked, his self-confidence shining through his bright eyes like a beacon. "So, you've come to see me then."

She loved that about him. His confidence was endearing. "Do I have to have a reason to be here?"

"No, you do not," Vivian said as she strolled into the room. "It's nice to have you drop in today Za..." Vivian discarded the name before it came completely out. "Cianne."

Cianne stiffened when Vivian approached but when her grandmother leaned over and embraced her, she relaxed. Although they'd become a bit closer over the weeks, it was still so new. She didn't remember the feel of her mother in her arms and wondered then if this, holding Vivian, felt anything like it. The thought made her give Vivian a squeeze before they parted.

"Shall we get started?" Vivian said as she smoothed her hand over her tightly pulled back hair. She sat on a sofa that was in front of them. "Let us review what you've read."

Tristan picked his tablet up from the table and typed in a password. He touched a few buttons then lifted his head. "There was a reference about half-breeds or Breeds," he glanced at Cianne then back to Vivian. "I'd like to know more."

Though his expression was blank, Cianne knew the subject interested him more than any other. He told her about Langley, assuming the Coesen was a half-breed. Then there was the subject of their child. Cianne wondered if Vivian knew how conflicted Tristan was with Coesen law concerning Breed. But like him, she suspected Vivian hid her personal feelings and would tell him what he wanted to know no matter how the information was received.

Just to prove it, Vivian began her lesson right away, before Cianne could interject or dismiss herself.

"Even though we are human our DNA has been altered a great deal. These alterations are what set us apart and allow us our abilities…abilities that can be very dangerous if unleashed on the outside population, so we have to govern ourselves. Half-breeds or *Breed*, are the offspring of a Coesen and a Middling. It is rare that the two will conceive these days and if conception is achieved the pregnancies will almost always end in a miscarriage.

"The small few who survive are often born with no ability or birthmark. The fear among our people is that because Breed are often born without the mark or abilities, they can mix with Middlings and may pass the dormant gene on until it manifests in later generations, which will ultimately be our ruin. Governing ourselves is a challenge but we manage." Vivian crossed her legs. "The concept of governing a Breed who decides to live under Middling law was…well it was among other things…troublesome for The Council. So, the conception of half-breeds was deemed a crime."

Cianne touched her belly as a cold chill washed over her skin. Tristan placed his hands over hers. Instantly she felt his warmth but her anxiety was still present. She wanted to know what the punishment was.

Tristan knew as soon as the question left his lips that bringing up the Breed might be a mistake but he needed to know. Besides, Vivian's unorthodox method of teaching was more disciplined than any other instructor he ever had. He was given the Annals, and after reading a volume he was to come to Vivian to discuss it.

He had one chance to review with her before moving to the next volume. In the latest volume he studied, there were a few sentences that told of the half-breed or Breed. Because the Annals only hinted at the topic, he wanted to know more. He worried that he might not get another chance to have Vivian explain it.

"What's the punishment?" Cianne almost whispered.

Vivian sighed but each of them knew she would answer. Tristan knew that Vivian wanted Cianne to know all of Coesen history, even if it upset her.

"The Coesen and the offspring were put to death."

Cianne choked on Vivian's words. "You killed innocent children to keep your secret?"

Vivian's face paled and her lips tightened but only for a moment. "For centuries, the Council thought their deaths were justifiable. If one child were to live, it could mean trouble for the Coesen and the unsuspecting world."

Vivian's matter of fact tone was rubbing Cianne the wrong way; Tristan could sense the array of emotions inside her clawing for dibs. He watched as Cianne bit back a comment, then she closed her eyes. It was an attempt to relax, he figured.

"You said for centuries the Council thought it was justified to put them to death. Do they still feel that way?" Cianne managed to ask without sounding angry.

Vivian preened with pride, probably at Cianne's display of restraining her emotions during this difficult discussion "About nineteen years ago the law was revised," Vivian told them.

Tristan raised a brow. The timeframe was too coincidental.

"I implemented a new way of dealing with the Breed that doesn't impede their civil liberties," Vivian gave a halfhearted smile.

Tristan could sense Vivian's desire to share more but since Cianne didn't plan on coming over to the "dark side" she wasn't privy to certain information.

He scooted to the edge of his seat, and asked the burning question. "So, some of these Breed are born with abilities even though they only carry some of the genetic makeup of a Coesen?"

Vivian smiled but didn't answer for a moment, causing Tristan to shift in his seat. He didn't intend to reveal his reasoning for his inquiries, but with his last question it was clear. When he looked to Cianne, she seemed uninterested, like she hadn't heard him.

With a tilt of her head and a sweet smile that could bring the hardest man to his knees, Vivian spoke. "There is one sitting beside you. Cianne's father was not a Coesen. Again, you have to realize that a very long time ago we did, for a short time, have to breed with Middlings. In those times, the Coesen were genetically closer to the Source. The children were born with the mark and their abilities developed. Some of those children were great Coesen and their descendants are revered. But, times have changed. The Breed of today aren't as gifted. Even some Coesen are born with no ability but they still bear the mark and can produce offspring who always have the mark and may develop abilities.

"As I've said, most of the Breed do not survive the pregnancy. Some who do, expire during the first few months of life. Any survivors are closely monitored but steps are taken. To encourage and allow cross-breeding now, without consequences, would endanger our race. The Council can never allow our people to be compromised no matter the consequence."

"Why nineteen years ago?" Cianne asked.

He thought she'd be fuming by now but she was calm. "Your mother," Tristan absently answered.

Vivian confirmed with a nod. "I always detested the law as a young woman, even though my particular bloodline was the purest until…" She raised a brow, then cleared her throat. "I could never allow my only child and heir to be hurt or stripped of her abilities. However," Vivian said, looking Cianne in the eye, "there was an exception that predated you. You see, my Arkean ancestors were harsh rulers and they felt the old laws were what kept our people safe and hidden. But even with their archaic way of thinking, Fagan, my forefather and the last male Sovereign of the Arkean tribe, accepted a tri-bred child in his home and raised the child as his own.

"Of course, there was opposition from the elders and Council but Fagan would hear none of it. He loved the child instantly and in Fagan's eyes, Tomas was a Coesen. He felt that if Tomas wanted to live as one he would be accepted and as such he was bound by our laws and protected by them. Tomas mated a Coesen and although there were some genetic abnormalities, his heirs eventually were born with the birthmark, and were given the title of Child of Jai for their matriarch. Langley is a Child of Jai, and his forbearers were indispensable and I treasure them as family."

Cianne's emotions were all over the place. Tristan was sensing a variation of emotions that he couldn't quite pin down. Was she upset, hurt? Had she heard that their baby girl may not survive?

He tried to focus on just one thread of her emotions but it proved useless. Of course, she'd be upset. He placed his hand over her shoulder, pulled her to him, and lay his head on hers.

"You do not have to worry about the baby," Vivian said. Her voice was softer than usual. "The child will be fine."

Both Tristan and Cianne looked up at her.

"How do you know that for certain?" Cianne asked.

Tristan hated the sadness in her voice.

Vivian simply stood without saying a word. She walked over to Cianne and dropped to one knee. Somehow Tristan sensed that Vivian had never dropped to her knees for anyone. He held his hand out to help her up but she waved him off.

"Because, her parents are strong, survivors. She will be fine."

Tristan felt Cianne relax, somewhat. "If they don't have the mark, how do you find these children?"

"Finding a breed is very difficult, because yes, they don't often bear our birthmark anymore." Vivian stood. She walked over to one of the large bookshelves and brushed her fingers over some of the books as she strode alongside the shelves. She stopped and her finger traced the spine of one of the larger books. She pulled it free. "Most of them emit no energy or force that would suggest they are indeed Breed. But we do have ways to find them."

Vivian smoothed her hand over her hair again. "We are woven throughout the world, working and living among Middlings. Our scientists know what to look for so whenever a pregnant woman is treated in any modern hospital in the world all her medical information including blood work is placed in an electronic file. We have access to all that information and if we see signs that point to a possible Breed conception, we follow up. If the Coesen parent is smart, he or she will keep the child off the grid, so we use other ways to find them." She handed Tristan the book and took a few steps back.

"It can be a long process but we usually find them before their twelfth year. In this book, you will find a current glossary of abilities. All Coesen must register his or her abilities with the exception of The Council of Four with CARD, the Coesen Ability Registration Department. The ability registry is public knowledge within the Coesen." She walked to the door she'd originally entered through. "We'll end the session here," she said as she disappeared through the door.

Cianne moved closer to Tristan to look at the large book. The cover was dark brown leather, with no title. She pulled the cover open and looked at the first page. Her eyes moved over the page for several seconds.

"It's not in English," Cianne said as she looked at him. "Will you be able to read it?"

Tristan knew she could read and speak Coesen even if she refused to acknowledge or use it. He figured her ability to understand the spoken language was instant because he could understand it. But gaining an understanding of the written language had proved difficult for him. Tristan had studied for four days and nights without sleep until finally one day it made sense. That day, he realized Cianne was reading one of the books without the key Vivian supplied him.

"I can read it," Tristan said, handing it to her. He got to his feet and walked to the door that Vivian went through and knocked. When he was told to enter, he did. "Excuse me, may I speak with you?" he asked Vivian before lowering his head.

Vivian sat at a large desk. She looked up from some paperwork she seemed to be reading and said, "Yes?"

Ask her, he told himself. *Ask her.*

"I would like your sponsorship to enter the Maatii."

Tristan watched her expression closely and took comfort in the fact that she didn't seem surprised by his request, which meant she may have at least considered it. Either that or she was the emotionless shell of a woman Joseph so often said she was. Well, Joseph didn't really refer to her as a "shell of a woman". Joseph's words were that Vivian was a "heartless, emotionless bitch" to be exact.

"Understand that if you fail, it will not matter to anyone that you haven't reached your full potential." Vivian twisted in the chair until she faced the desktop computer and typed as she spoke, "I expected you to ask to participate, but that you've asked me to sponsor you…" She smiled then said, "You and the three you are teamed with will not get a redo and if you fail you will never be a Royal Guard. You will also be the one your team and everyone else will blame regardless of who costs your team the victory. Are you prepared for that?"

Tristan walked over to the massive desk that almost filled the room. "I won't fail," he told her.

"Fail in what?"

Tristan whipped his head around to see Cianne standing in the doorway. He wasn't quite sure how to answer.

"The Maatii," Vivian said without hesitation. "It's a tournament of sorts that Coesen participate in to gain Royal Guard status."

Tristan went to Cianne. He shook his head from side to side as he felt Cianne's trepidation pulse through him. "I can't be killed," he said, trying to calm her, "the tournament is held in a dreamlike state." He took her hands in his and brought them to his lips.

Cianne ignored his gesture and leaned her head to the side to see around him. She was seeking confirmation from Vivian.

Tristan turned to look at Vivian as well. Maybe he could give her a signal to not give too much information.

"It's true. If you die in the game you just wake up but…" Vivian let her gaze fall back to the computer screen.

She wasn't paying his subtle eye blinks any mind. He was screwed.

"The pain you experience if injured will feel very real. I hear it can be quite excruciating."

"Why would you want to do this?" Cianne shook his hands. "You don't have to prove yourself to them."

"Buttercup," Tristan said, touching her face, "I'm not trying to prove myself to them. I want to prove myself to you." He traced her bottom lip with his thumb, hoping she'd melt under his touch like she often did.

Cianne closed her eyes and her lip trembled under his touch causing her to swallow her protest. She melted, which meant he had a chance at winning this one.

"When my team finishes this test, you will know that I am capable of protecting you and our baby no matter what comes at us. That the Source was right to choose me and only me to protect you."

Cianne gripped his wrist and pulled his hand away from her face and placed it at his side. "I don't need you to prove anything to me Tristan. You know I don't want this for us. I don't want any of it. I know you're fascinated with being a part of this…this world, but it's not all kings and queens and dragons. They judge, sentence, and kill to keep secrets. Is this the life you want for us…for our baby?"

"All governments do whatever is necessary to keep their secrets, Ci." He touched her belly. "Even religious organizations have done the same. No matter what we choose to believe or where we choose to involve ourselves, we are still subject to laws, persecution, and/or the prosecution of others." He spread his arms out. "And yes, I do want this, but you're wrong." He touched her face again. "I've never believed that this is a fairy tale. It's just that I know in my heart that this is where I belong." He fell silent, thinking of what he wanted to say. What he wanted to tell her. Then he knew. "But if you ask me, I will turn my back on the training, the studying, and everything Coesen."

For her happiness he would do anything, give up everything.

"Before you deny him the honor, Cianne, know that all Royal Guards have to complete the Maatii. As you already know, Tristan has decided to live by our laws. And you've decided that you are going to allow Tristan to remain your

Protector, whereby we will have to amend some laws. Being so, he will need to take on the Maatii challenge. The decision lies with you, again. But, even if you decide to strip him of his position, another Protector will still be assigned to your family. Even if you aren't a part of…" she said, spreading her arms and flashing a faint smile, "this lifestyle. Because Princess, you are still, like it or not, a Royal, and your family will still need protection. It's time you realize that it doesn't matter if you are half in or all out, you are who you are and there's nothing that can change that."

Vivian was siding with him. Tristan had turned to look at her when she started talking, and he could have sworn Vivian smiled at him. It wouldn't be the first time she'd given him a genuine smile but...

Half shocked and half proud for coaxing a smile and support from Vivian, he turned back to Cianne. She gazed up at him with worry behind her radiant eyes. He wished he could read minds. It was torture not knowing what was going on in that beautiful head of hers. Feeling her emotions was frustrating and even more so because he would never know the reasons for her moods unless she shared. Lately, it seemed she didn't feel like sharing.

"There's no way he can die doing this?" Cianne asked.

"As I mentioned, the pain of a wound will feel very real for the competitors but no, he cannot die." Vivian gave Cianne a sympathetic look.

Tristan saw Cianne softening on the idea of him competing. Vivian must have noticed it as well because she pounced.

"Then it's settled," Vivian said as she typed, "you have my nomination, which means you will be representing the Royal Arkean family. I have randomly chosen your team as well. You have a week from today to ready yourself."

Tristan knew by her tone that she was dismissing them. "I thank you," he said, bowing his head. He turned a defeated-looking Cianne toward the door and placed his hand on the small of her back to escort her out.

"Oh, and Tristan," Vivian called after him.

He looked over his shoulder.

"You have up until the day before the Maatii to change your mind and attempt it at a later date."

She was offering him the chance to wait until Cianne's powers were unbound. His response was a smile.

"You will go forward then?"

He nodded.

"Although you are at a disadvantage, I trust you know what is expected of you."

"I do, Soahn" he said with another bow of his head.

Chapter Eleven

A week later

Tristan sat inside the same spacious office he stood in when he requested Vivian's endorsement for the Maatii. The office was eerily quiet and the urge to decorate the space was pressing at him. With only five pieces of furniture–a monstrous desk and chair, along with two other chairs in the center of the room, plus a large bookcase, the space was a minimalist's dream. The room was bleak compared to the opulent library and the rest of the mansion.

His attention was fixed on Vivian, who sat behind the desk. She was writing on a piece of stationary that had a rendition of the Arkean insignia on the letterhead.

Tristan patiently sat in one of the chairs in front of her desk for over fifteen minutes and neither he nor Vivian spoke a word. He wasn't feeling anxious or anything but he was wondering how the Maatii would begin. He only knew what he read, which was very little; an alternate plain of existence, three tasks to complete, and all within the time allotted. Oh yeah, and the possibility of pain.

Other than those things, he knew nothing. Neither Vivian nor Zeta offered any information about it and Tristan knew better to ask them.

A light knock on the door drew him from his thoughts.

"Please come in Demetri," Vivian said without looking up.

Tristan watched over his shoulder as the knob slowly turned and the door eased open. He saw a long foot step over the threshold first. The leg in which it was attached slid through, then the rest of Demetri appeared. Tristan had to raise his head to see the rest of the tall thin man who crossed the room with long effortless strides and was now standing beside him. His face suggested he was a young man, barely thirty but the age lines that pinched at the corner of his eyes told another story.

Tristan thought the man tall before but with him standing so close, Tristan felt that labeling the man as tall was simply not accurate enough. He found himself wondering if all Demetri's clothing was custom made.

"Let's begin," Vivian said.

Tristan just turned his head to meet Vivian's gaze when he felt a pair hands grip his shoulders. A low hum or vibration began to come from Demetri, or was it coming from Demetri's hands? Was it a hum or was it a vibration?

Tristan couldn't tell but he tried to remain calm. To be honest he wasn't able to tell much of anything at the moment. His lids felt so heavy he could barely keep them open.

No, must stay awake, he told himself as he pried his eyes open. He saw Vivian raise her brow just as sleep threatened him again.

"I think he's fighting me," Demetri grumbled.

Vivian sounded amused as she looked at Demetri and said, "Really, how odd." Her flat monotone voice returned as her gaze once again turned to Tristan, "you must relax."

The Maatii
The Village

Tristan heard his name through the haze. At least that's what it sounded like, his name. Yeah, it was his name because he heard someone say it again. The voice speaking sounded familiar but the words sounded distorted, mangled.

He tried to force his eyes open.

"Tristan," the voice said again.

The process of getting his eyes open took longer than it should have, which made him wonder exactly how long he was out of it. When he managed to pry them open, his head rocked from one side to the other.

"Tristan, you must relax."

"His mind is very strong." A male voice echoed around him though he saw no one.

Tristan tried to block the voices and fought to push the fog from his vision. Slowly the office began to come into view again. The bare walls seemed to surround him like a cage. His gaze shot to the large desk, then to the familiar face that sat behind it. Just as their eyes met his breaths increased and his heart began to race. Something was…

"Relax son," Vivian said again.

Son, Tristan grasped onto that one word and calmed his breathing.

"Good," Vivian said in a soothing tone, "There are a few things I must tell you before you begin. Do you understand me, are my words clear?"

With his vision once again perfect, Tristan sat up in the chair and nodded as he looked around the room where only he and Vivian sat. Hadn't he heard a male's voice?

"Good, it sometimes takes a while to get your bearings. With you fighting Demetri's pull, which no one has ever been able to do, he had to use more power." She shook her head and smiled. "Well anyway, let's begin. Maatii means to act as one. You and three others who have been brought here must navigate a number of obstacles to reach three orbs. Each of you must lay a hand on the orb in each challenge at the same time," Vivian explained. "Once each of you has touched the orb, that challenge will end and the next will begin. Your team will have six days to complete the Maatii. You can be injured in the Maatii. Your brain will react as if you were actually injured, which means the pain is real. Any of you can also die, though this death is not a physical death, it will end the challenge and you and your team will fail the Maatii." She waited for his response to see if he understood.

Not trusting his voice yet he nodded again.

"The Maatii is a challenge of strength, resolve, and intellect. As your sponsor, I am allowed to give you one piece of advice." Vivian looked at him but said nothing for a long time. "My advice to you is that you need to use the strongest weapon you have. To find the orbs, follow the light." With that she disappeared and he was left alone.

"Strongest weapon?"

Shaking his head, Tristan rose to his feet and walked to the only door and pulled it open. The library was not what was on the other side of the door. A breathtaking view that appeared before him shamed all the beautiful places he ever traveled to. He stepped through the door into a lush forest of trees. In the air, he saw a floating mass of land that resembled the terrain of an island paradise. Above that was another floating land mass with a large mountain. They looked like land-steps.

Tristan's attention fell on three doors that looked out of place and the three men stepping through them. Each looked as if they were in their late teens/early twenties, same as Tristan. Each wore a black mock neck body suit. On the left side of their collar was the symbol of a tribe. He assumed that was the tribe each man represented.

Tristan held his arms up to look over his own suit. The fabric was smooth, light and covered half his fingers, all of his palm and wrist. His feet were covered as well and there was some kind of sole that protected his feet and toes. In sum, he and the rest of the team were dressed like modern ninjas. Only they had no weapons.

What did Vivian mean, Use my strongest weapon?

Tristan looked up, noticed that all eyes were on him, and was the first to move away from his door. Following his lead all three men stepped forward as well. When they did, each of the doors disappeared.

Two of the men stood at his left. The one closest to him was the Bode, identified by their insignia on the left side of his collar. He was about 5'6" in height with dark skin and eyes, short hair and the build of a trained fighter. His lips were full but spread tight. Overall, the Bode looked unfriendly and menacing with a slice of lemon.

To the Bode's right was the Gedgi, according to the insignia on the left side of his collar. He was tall, slender, and looked to be all muscle. His skin was the color of cinnamon and his eyes, a soft brown with thick dark lashes. They were the kind of lashes women would pay for. With a head full of tiny silky chestnut curls, he could easily pass for a Disney star. He didn't smile as he looked at Tristan and the others but he wasn't frowning.

To Tristan's left was the Quende. He couldn't see his insignia but there was only one tribe left. He was about the same height as Tristan, light golden skin, a strong jaw, and thickly lashed brown eyes with a slight epicanthic fold. His hair was closely cut and even though no smile graced his face, the dimples on each cheek were very noticeable. He had broad shoulders and looked as if he'd been training all his life.

"I'm Jacobi," the Gedgi said. He peered up at the sky then to the group.

The Bode went down on his haunches. "No need to give our names," he said moving his hands over the ground. "Just call us by our tribe's mark."

Unfriendly, just as Tristan thought.

"I agree," the Quende said. He looked around, then his attention was on Tristan again. He gazed at Tristan blatantly, sizing him up perhaps, and then turned his gaze to the forest. "We should get to it."

He clearly wasn't friendly either.

Each of them looked at a light up above the trees at the same time. The beam of light that seemed to be coming out of the trees to touch the heavens was bright and hard to miss.

"Follow the light," one of them said.

Tristan hadn't matched their voices to their faces yet but he soon would.

They all moved forward into the dense forest. It seemed as if they'd walked forever before the trees began to space out. Eventually they saw the border of a village. Using the trees as cover, they searched for their target.

"Do any of you see anyone?" Jacobi whispered.

Tristan shook his head as he knelt behind a tree and rubbed dirt on his hands. The others must not have seen anyone or the orb either because the Bode began to climb the tree he'd been standing under.

As Tristan stood, the Bode dropped back on the ground and everyone huddled around him. Tristan figured that someone would take the lead and he could tell from the moment he laid eyes on the Bode, that he would be making a play.

"It's dead center of that village, about a mile or so in. I don't see any locals though, just a bunch of huts," the Bode said.

Tristan was squatting, listening to them but at the same time he was taking in his surroundings. There were no birds chirping or flying. No insects bugging them or buzzing around. No sounds of nature at all.

Jacobi frowned. "I'm sure something's guarding it."

"We have to take them by surprise," the Bode said. He moved his gaze to each of them. "Disarm the first one you engage and get your hands on a weapon. We'll fight our way to the orb."

The plan was absurd. There was no way this was going to be that easy but there was no use speaking up right now. The way they looked at him earlier suggested that they saw him as an outsider, not that it bothered him, because he was. Besides, he needed to know what they were up against and as bad as running in blind was plain idiotic, it was the fastest way.

Hopefully they wouldn't lose their dream-state heads. Plus, he also wanted to know his team better, so…why not find out more in the heat of battle?

But…

"Did anyone notice there are no animals here, no insects, no birds?" Tristan asked as he looked at each of them.

"So, what if there isn't," the Bode sneered.

Tristan swung his gaze to their "leader". "So, I'm betting there are no children here either." Each of them gave him a look that said "and your point is". "It means that these guys are warriors. They don't hunt. They probably don't sleep or need rest if they don't eat. They don't tend to wives or children or chores. There will be no taking them by surprise."

"Relax," the Bode said. "You just follow us and we'll get you to the orb safe and sound. Just stick close to someone."

The three Coesen stood and began heading toward the village. Jacobi, the Gedgi, looked back at Tristan, who hadn't moved.

Tristan stood, silently cursed, then followed them. He looked up at the sky. If the sun here moved like their sun, then four hours had passed already. Also, something inside him was telling him that four hours had passed. He reminded himself that they were a team as he increased his stride to catch up.

Things played out just as Tristan thought they would. The seven-foot hairless coal black warriors were not surprised. Built for combat, with fierce black eyes and no fear, they were waiting. The Warriors met the Protectors with such force and sheer numbers that his team barely made it a hundred feet into the village before retreating. It was a miracle that they all made it out of there alive. Now the four of them were back in the forest licking their wounds.

"Hold still," Jacobi told the Quende. He pulled at the arrow sticking out of the back of the Quende's left shoulder.

Jacobi, injured as well, had a long gash down his arm that had been bleeding out until he tied it off.

"Just pull it out," the Quende grunted. He squirmed as Jacobi attempted to pull the arrow free for the third time.

The Bode walked several paces then turned around and walked back to where he started just do pace the steps out again. He'd been pacing since their retreat ten minutes ago. His forehead glistened in the sun as the blood from his head wound blended with his sweat.

Tristan looked up at the sun. He felt no heat coming from it and wondered if the sun here was just an illusion or was it his body that maintained itself at a comfortable temperature. He knew at some point his body would naturally regulate his temperature to always keep him comfortable. He would hardly ever overheat or be too cold unless in extreme weather and even then, it would take time for him to be affected. He just thought it would happen after Cianne's abilities were unbound. He wasn't sure which factor was keeping his body cooled just right but he was thankful.

The Bode huffed.

Not taking the defeat well.

"Attend your wounds; we need to get to that orb," the Bode said.

The Quende growled with a curse. He said he wanted to remove the arrow himself but Jacobi insisted on doing it, telling the Quende that he would do more damage by pulling it out at an angle and that it would be better if one of them did it.

The Bode didn't volunteer and Tristan didn't either, figuring no one would want his help, so that left Jacobi. Seeing how Jacobi struggled with the task now, knowing that the guy was extremely strong and that removing the arrow would be simple for either of them, Tristan wondered if Jacobi was just a little freaked about doing it.

Maybe the blood bothered Jacobi. *Probably not.* Or maybe it was because the Quende was in pain that caused

Jacobi to stall in just ripping the arrow free. *Maybe*. Whatever the reason, Jacobi was still trying to remove the damn arrow.

Jacobi lowered his head and sighed before looking away from his task at hand and spoke. "Why haven't they come after us yet?

Tristan stood. He walked over to where Jacobi, the gentle Gedgi, was performing what should have been a simple extraction, yet seemed to border on heart surgery. "Because they don't fear us," Tristan said.

He scooted Jacobi aside and squatted down next to the Quende, who was watching him with crazed eyes. Tristan gently placed his hand on the ball of the Quende's shoulder and inspected how deep the arrow went. He let his fingers glide over and under the wound. The other Coesen were frozen in place as they watched.

"It's between the bones," Tristan informed the Quende. Then without warning, Tristan gripped the Quende's shoulder and pushed the arrow through with his inspecting hand. Tristan snapped the arrow head off then pulled the wood out from the back. He moved so fast that the Quende hadn't finished howling another curse before Tristan was tying a piece of torn cloth around the wound.

"Thanks," the Quende hissed. He extended his hand from his good arm. "My name's Oloyede."

Tristan took the hand offered. "No problem, name's Tristan." He sat down on the large fallen tree trunk next to the Quende and pulled at the torn fabric around his neck where his insignia once was. One of the warriors had attempted to play slice and dice with him. The cuts weren't too deep but he had to remove the collar that bore his sponsor's insignia because the fabric was rubbing against them.

"If you aren't a pet, then what the hell are you?" Jacobi demanded. He stood over Tristan with his eyes virtually popping out of his head.

The Quende and the Bode followed Jacobi's gaze with their eyes. Tristan slid his hand over the skin behind his left ear that was absent of a Coesen brand. A brand they all now knew he didn't have.

"A fucking Breed," the Bode accused. He readied a staff he'd taken from one of the warriors.

With lightning speed, Tristan got to his feet with a blade in each hand and faced off with the Bode. "I'm not a Breed but what if I was?" he growled.

"Look," Jacobi said, eyes still fixed on Tristan.

On Tristan's suit over his heart, a new golden Arkean symbol appeared, replacing the insignia that was once on his collar. The Bode frowned but looked equally confused and angry.

Oloyede got to his feet. "Cut the shit. I don't care what he is. He's here, so The Council trusts him. And I shouldn't have to mention that he bears the Royal insignia. I mean shit, the fact that it gets torn off and reappears pretty much says our Sovereign has his back." He cut his eyes at the Bode. "Plus, he tried to warn us about going in that village all gung ho. He moves fast and fights just as good as we do and saved your ass in there, if I remember correctly. And in case you forgot, he's a part of our team. He dies, we all fail." Oloyede stepped between Tristan and the Bode. "So, if you want to give up, kill yourself, or we can work as a team, because I'm not going to let you raise a hand against him."

The Bode gave both of them a hard stare before lowering the staff and turning his back to them.

Jacobi, clearly entertained by what was going on, walked over and extended his hand with a smile. "I'm Jacobi," he introduced himself again.

Tristan tucked one of the blades in the holster that had appeared on his back after he stole them, and shook Jacobi's hand. "I know." He then looked at Oloyede. "We're six hours in," Tristan said, "I have an idea."

The Bode angrily stalked back toward the others. "What," he said, pointing at Tristan, "we're supposed to listen to him now?"

Jacobi squatted. No one noticed he had an ax until he embedded it into the tree trunk in front of him. "The guy does carry the seal of approval so…" He patted his chest where Tristan's new insignia had appeared.

"This is comical," the Bode laughed.

"Were you not with us thirty minutes ago?" Oloyede said to the Bode as he threw the arrowhead that Tristan had removed from his shoulder in no particular direction. "We just got our asses handed to us. I'm all for listening to any plan right now."

The plan, Tristan explained, was to draw as many of the warriors out of the village that they could, so they'd have less opposition when they made a run for the orb. How to draw them out was up for debate but in the end, they decided on three forms of distractions.

It took a few hours for them to prepare.

"The village is one big sphere so you guys have to pan out on the far side. Once you've heard the signal start setting the fires then get as close as you can to the orb."

"What about you?" Jacobi asked. He was finishing up making the last of the torches. Starting fires without matches was a basic survival skill that all Protectors had to learn, but Jacobi was the most skilled at it. "You'll be farther away from the orb than we are."

The Warriors had several advantages. Earlier Tristan noticed that there were no animals, no sounds of running water, not many sounds at all. Tristan wanted to strip them of their advantage, their numbers, by using loud noises to draw them out of the village. Separating them would work in his team's favor. The Warriors' vision seemed to be normal and while he couldn't be certain, even the best vision was useless if smoke was a factor. And with the fire, he hoped to instill panic if possible.

Tristan tested one of the ropes they secured around a tree to use it like a battering ram. His task was to swing the tree back and let gravity take over so that it fell into a larger tree to create a loud thudding sound. They made several of these contraptions, all lined up next to each other, so Tristan could have them going off in rapid succession.

"Once I've started a third cycle of battering, I will head for the orb, whether they've taken the bait or not. One thing I do know is that they aren't as fast as we are. We know the basic layout of the village from our first encounter so I will be able to navigate through to the orb quickly. Plus, it's not like you'll be doing nothing while waiting for me to join you. Believe me, you'll be busy enough."

The Bode secured the staff he liberated from one of the Warriors on his back. "It's time," he said as he grabbed several unlit torches."

Oloyede and Jacobi nodded and secured their weapons as well.

"Get as close to the orb as you can. Make them come to you," Tristan said as they walked away.

Oloyede looked over his shoulder and gave Tristan one last glance before breaking into a full speed run with the others. Tristan had seen that look before. It was the "don't fuck this up" look. His lips curved into a half smile.

Tristan pushed back the heavy tree, straining two more steps, then let go. He knew the extra steps may cause the swinging tree to knock down the tree it was going to connect with but it was the last go-round. He deduced from the smell that the fires were already started in the village and he had no use for the battering ram or base tree anymore.

He was already sprinting to the village when he heard the tree falling. He was right about the warrior's curiosity. More had come out to investigate than he had thought would.

Just yards away from the village now, he could see the red flames and black smoke rising from the huts. He wasn't sure why they even had huts but at the moment he didn't care. All he was concerned with was team victory.

He slowed as he got further into the village, passing huts and warriors engulfed in flames. In front of him, suspended in air and surrounded by a heavenly glow a few hundred feet away, was the orb. His heart almost drummed through his chest with excitement.

He scanned his surroundings. It was utter chaos. Bodies falling, grunts of combat, sounds of metal clashing. He inhaled the scent of battle and rolled his shoulders. This was what he was meant for.

Each of his teammates had fought their way close to the orb; Jacobi was the closest. Engaged with three warriors in hand to hand combat, he was dealing with the odds well enough but…

Where is his weapon?

Oloyede was mere feet away from Jacobi, throwing one of the warriors into several other advancing ones. The Bode was the furthest away. With his staff in hand, he was surrounded. For every warrior the Bode crumpled, another joined the party.

Without a thought, Tristan unsheathed the two double edged blades he'd also liberated during their first campaign and took off to where he was needed the most. Sliding between two warriors, he sliced the backs of their knees, tearing through muscle and tendon before he was even noticed.

The two warriors dropped to their knees in agony but the pain they felt was only for a second, time enough for Tristan to turn and drive the blades in the front of their throats. He pushed to his feet in a fluid motion, standing next to the Bode. Tristan knew there was no time for either thanks or looks of hate; whatever the Bode felt would have to wait. More warriors were coming back to the village from his diversion in the forest so they had to get to the orb.

"Killing comes easy for you," the Bode said as he kicked a warrior in the knee. The Bode flinched at the sound of the warrior's bone breaking.

"We're not here to play, we're here to win!" Tristan yelled out. "Kill or wound to cripple, do whatever it takes to get them off your ass so we can get to the orb." He buried a blade in a falling warrior's temple and used his foot to push the body free of his weapon.

As Tristan swung around he saw that one of the warriors had Jacobi by the neck and another was about to run a machete through his chest. Tristan threw one of his blades at the warrior with the machete. Moving faster than the eye could see, Tristan got behind the warrior who held Jacobi's neck and twisted *his* neck just as his flying blade entered the warrior who held the spear.

Both of the Warriors slumped to the ground.

At the same time, Oloyede and the Bode were slicing their way to the orb. Jacobi and Tristan started doing the same when an arrow whizzed by Tristan's face, barely missing him, and would have hit him if he hadn't have heard its approach. He was unable to avoid another arrow that was shot at the same time as the first. It landed in his already injured thigh, knocking him to the ground.

As a roar left Tristan's mouth, the pain was nothing compared to the anger he felt. His team was surrounding the orb and he was only a few feet away. He attempted to stand but a foot struck the right side of his jaw, whipping his head to the side. Spit and blood sprayed from his mouth. Ears ringing, Tristan tried to shake the sting off as he drove his blade into the warrior's knee. At the same time, Oloyede kicked the Warrior in the chest, driving him back a few feet.

Jacobi was shouting something, counting down probably.

Oloyede grabbed Tristan's arm, pulling him to his feet. With Tristan in tow, Oloyede ran with unnatural speed to the orb. On one, all four of them slammed their palms down on the orb at the same time.

The Vortex
Stage Two

Everything around him was illuminated in a comforting white glow, making it difficult to see anything. Tristan's wound on his thigh, no longer searing with pain, felt renewed as if it had never been sliced open then pierced with an arrow only moments before. Overall, he felt a deadly calm. The feeling was so comforting, so appealing, he never wanted to leave.

"You never have to," a lovely feminine voice sang out.

Tristan looked around but couldn't see anyone. The air, if that's what it was, had a salacious scent to it. It reminded him of heat, passion, and forbidden sex.

Am I floating?

"I shouldn't be here," he said.

"I can give you all you desire, my love," the voice moaned.

He felt soft hands slowly moving up his legs. When fingers teased his thighs, Tristan's body trembled. He wanted the hands all over him. He wanted more.

"I want to give you more, to pleasure you," she said.

Her voice was more seductive than her touch. He found himself craving both equally.

"Please don't deny me," she pouted.

"Deny you?" He tensed. No, he needed more. The female used her nails to playfully claw at his inner thigh. So, close. He needed her hand closer, on him. He tried to reach out to her.

"I can't move. Where am I?"

She pouted then purred with delight. "Right where you should be, my stallion."

As Tristan felt her climbing up his body, hers began to take form. Her skin was a soft sable color and in the white light, gave off a mesmerizing glow. Her eyes, dark with kohl black liner around them that was drawn out to her temples, looked hungry and they were fixed on him. Her lips, oh God, were full, succulent, and as red as blood. He could think of several places on his body he would love to see and feel them on.

"You only need ask and I will place them anywhere and everywhere you desire," she said leaning down and kissing the tip of his ear.

Tristan moaned. The pleasure of her touch, her lips on his skin, was unbearable. He didn't want to live another second if he couldn't have her under him. He hardened for her. The need to be inside her was so intense that it was painful.

"Tell me you want me. Beg me to take you to the height of ecstasy," she whispered in his ear. "Ask me to make love to you and I will, forever."

Forever. Forever, he said to himself over and over again.

Tristan took her by the wrist. He was relieved that he was able to move. He pulled her hands from him, causing her bare breast to press against his shirtless chest. She was naked and so was he. The revelation did nothing but infuriate him. He squeezed her wrist so tightly, a normal woman would have screamed for release. She, this creature, only smiled as she ground against him.

"Release me," he demanded.

"I'd rather not," she whined. "You, I like."

"Now," he insisted.

She seductively pulled her bottom lip into her mouth with her teeth. "If you insist."

Just like that, Tristan found himself standing in an open field. Oloyede, Jacobi and the Bode stood in front of him.

Jacobi raised his hands in front of his face and turned them front to back. He touched his chest then dropped to his knees on the grassy earth he stood on.

"Where in the hell were we just now?" the Bode asked. He let the tips of his fingers brush across his head where the skin was split open when they fought in the village. No deep gash and no blood.

Tristan looked them over then turned his attention to himself. Just like the others, his wounds were healed and his suit was repaired. No, better than repaired. It was as if it had never been damaged. And on the left side of his collar the gold Arkean insignia sparkled.

He moved his hands to his back and pulled out the twin blades, the ones he'd taken from the warriors in the village. The others also had their stolen weapons.

Oloyede looked over the machete he held in his hands. "A Phantom's lair, but now I think this is the next Challenge," he said as he placed the weapon in the holster on his hip.

"How much time do you think the Phantoms ate up?" Jacobi asked. Still on his knees, he stared up at the others.

As soon as he posed the question the answer flashed in their minds.

"About eight," the Bode said.

Tristan noticed that the Bode seemed more on edge than the others. Maybe his experience with the Phantoms was more upsetting than his own.

Oloyede looked up, prompting Tristan to search the sky for the beacon. The orb's glow reached out into the sky to the west. Tristan couldn't judge the exact distance but he knew it wasn't close.

"We better get moving," Oloyede told them. He led the way and the others fell in step.

Tristan brought up the rear. His mind was restless but his awareness of his surroundings was keen as he kept pace with his team. He hadn't learned about Phantoms and the fact that he spent over eight hours with a naked one was…unsettling, to say the least.

"You alright? You haven't said a single word in almost six hours."

Tristan didn't realize that Oloyede was walking beside him until he spoke. It seemed the Phantom had affected him enough to zap his focus.

"I'm fine," he gritted out, never making eye contact.

When Oloyede didn't leave him to his own thoughts Tristan gave the guy a sideways look. He didn't expect the Quende to be the first to spark up a conversation with him. Actually, he didn't expect conversation from any of them unless it was related to their end goal. Well, except for Jacobi. He was uncharacteristically approachable and friendly for a Coesen, yet it was Oloyede who decided to chip at the ice first.

Interesting, he thought. "Thank you for getting me to the orb back there."

"If we're going to complete this thing we have to do it as a team." Oloyede bent and picked up a long blade of grass.

His movements were so graceful it seemed that he didn't even break his stride though, Tristan noticed.

Oloyede placed the blade of grass in his mouth and gently tugged. "So," he began, "I was wondering...if you aren't a pet—"

The ice broke.

"First," Tristan interrupted, "What's a pet?" Being curious himself, he figured he would get some information too.

Oloyede grimaced. "I don't want you to get offended."

Tristan raised a brow.

Oloyede shrugged. "A pet is a Child of Jai," he said. "They are a particular breed of Coesen who are descendants of a forced mating of a Coesen named Jai and a Middling a long time ago; after mating with Middlings were forbidden."

"That doesn't explain why you all think I'm one of these Children of Jai?"

Oloyede twisted the grass in his mouth. "Well, because even though they breed with other Coesen, some with the darkest skin you'll ever see, they are still born with fair skin and light eyes. Hence..." He waved a hand at Tristan. "Child of Jai. Some say a vindictive Coesen who didn't want them to ever be fully accepted by the four tribes cursed the bloodline so they could never produce dark-skinned offspring."

"So, because they look white and I'm white, that must be the only explanation of why I'm here?"

Oloyede shrugged then nodded.

"Hate to break it to you but I'm not a Pet," Tristan said. He shrugged as well.

"Clearly," Oloyede spit the grass out.

"And you knew this, why?"

"You bear no birthmark. See, Jai's never told her bastard child who the Coesen were. When she died, her child lived as a Middling, with no mark or abilities. That child mated with a Middling. When she passed on and the parents died, somehow Jai's grandchild was returned to the Coesen. The child grew and mated with a Coesen and their children bore the birthmark even though his mother didn't." Oloyede shrugged. "Which means you must be Breed."

Clearly, I'm not a pet, well not the type of pet you're talking about." Tristan grinned.

The grass beneath their feet started thinning out an hour or so back. Now the terrain was a mixture of grass and rock.

Tristan thought about Langley. He had a birthmark on his neck. "So why are they called pets?"

"Because when Jai's grandchild was given to one of the Arkean Sovereign, instead of killing the child like our law decreed, he adopted him as his own," Oloyede explained. "Some call them pets. So…you feel like sharing?"

"Neither of my parents are Coesen, which means I am not breed."

Oloyede's eyes grew bigger as he stared at Tristan. The graceful stride he exhibited minutes before faltered, and the poor guy tripped over a large rock sticking out of the ground.

Tristan gave him a moment to take in that information before continuing. "But I am a Protector. From what I learned, I was nine when I went through the cycling. I almost died but my Coesen's mother helped me through it. Because I'm not a Coesen she kept me a secret. I eventually met my Coesen and began my training a few months ago."

"A few months ago!" Jacobi blurted out with shock. Though he walked ahead of Tristan and Oloyede, he was apparently paying close attention to their discussion. "That doesn't explain how you got the Golden Insignia of the Sovereign." He strained his neck as he looked back at Tristan. Jacobi slowed his stride to allow Tristan and Oloyede to catch up. "I've heard of it talked about but never knew of a Protector having the golden insignia. I don't know anyone who knows someone who has ever worn it before."

Tristan felt a surge of pride but didn't show it. "I just asked her to sponsor me and she agreed. I don't know anything about a Golden Insignia. As I said, I just started training."

"It's a big deal," Oloyede said.

Tristan couldn't tell if his tone suggested frustration or admiration.

Jacobi sighed. "You know her personally?"

Tristan nodded, but his brow furrowed in confusion.

"One of those, hey Jacobi?" the Bode sneered from in front of them. He hadn't slowed but due to their heightened hearing he was still in the loop.

Tristan and Oloyede stopped. Tristan looked at Jacobi who also stopped but just shrugged with a smile. When Tristan turned to Oloyede, the Quende avoided his gaze then started walking again.

Tristan frowned. "One of what?" he asked.

"He's a Sovereign-ite." the Bode chuckled.

Tristan caught up with Oloyede. Jacobi stayed a few steps behind them. "He just has a crush," Oloyede told Tristan. "A lot of the guys find Sovereign Harper…" He paused as if trying to find the right wording then said, "attractive."

"She's hot," Jacobi emphasized the "t".

Tristan couldn't decide if he wanted to cry out in laughter or scream out in horror. A part of him thought of Vivian like a mother-in-law, headmaster type figure. Plus, it always angered him how some of his friends complimented his *own* mother's beauty, so much so that Brian was the only friend he allowed in his house when his parents were home. He trusted his mom but he'd seen and read enough about hot moms to know shit happens.

But not on his watch.

Vivian was an authority figure, someone you should fear, so he never really looked at her in *that* way. With that, he brought to mind images of her. It then dawned on him how truly beautiful the woman really was. Then the picture of Vivian was replaced with images of Cianne. He saw her face, her lips, and those curves that always filled him with need. Laughter brought him back to the now.

"A Sovereign-ite for sure," Oloyede called out.

"I do not see her that way," Tristan said angrily, showing emotion for the first time during the Maatii.

"No? That smile on your face seconds ago says otherwise." Oloyede laughed.

Tristan shot him a look that said, "KILL", in all caps.

With his hands raised in defense and bent over from laughter, Oloyede attempted to apologize but couldn't seem to find his words. After laughing until he couldn't breathe, he was finally able to choke out his apologies while moving forward again. He tripped over another boulder but Tristan grabbed his arm and righted him before he hit the ground.

Oloyede was still laughing and now the Bode and Jacobi had joined in. With a disgusted sigh, Tristan released Oloyede's arm, allowing the giggling fool to fall to the rough ground. To his dismay, his treatment of Oloyede caused Jacobi and the Bode to laugh more. The side-splitting snorts and air-sucking hoots seem to go on and on.

Tristan saw a large body of water to his right so he decided to slow down to give them time to recover, being as it was so damn funny. Eventually they began to quiet. Oloyede held his side as he tried to get to his feet and yes, he was still somehow laughing a little after the others stopped.

Tristan let out a small chuckle. He knew now why the Quende's dimples were so deep, but to look at Oloyede you would never guess a fierce fighter, and yes—he was fierce, could be so jovial.

For several miles, Tristan refused to acknowledge Oloyede. At one point the Quende asked him why he was so offended; that Sovereign Harper was indeed such a seasoned hottie that any man in his right mind would consider her so.

All but Tristan would consider her in that way, and he wouldn't get into the reasons for that. He didn't feel inclined to share that part of his life with any of them for now.

"Man," Jacobi whined, "I could use a bacon cheeseburger right now...extra bacon."

The Bode gave a snort then asked, "Was that what the Phantom offered you, food?"

Tristan wanted to know what the others were offered but didn't feel comfortable enough to ask.

"I was offered more than a cheeseburger," Jacobi said with a grin. "I was in a room with a huge buffet of all my favorite foods. There was every gaming console you can think of with all the games I love and some I've never even seen before. A gaming recliner sat in front of the biggest screen I've ever seen. I was in fricking heaven." The Gedgi's grin widened when he finished speaking.

The Bode snorted again. "That's what you desire, food and toys? How old are you?"

It was clear to Tristan then. Jacobi was just a kid. Tristan turned his head and looked the kid over. How hadn't he noticed the innocent face, the lack of knowledge in his "doe in the headlights" eyes?

"I'm sixteen," Jacobi said as he lifted his chin, "and I resisted it all, didn't I?"

He had.

"What did you see?" Jacobi challenged.

The question was for the Bode but he ignored it and kept walking.

"I was shown a healthy child," Oloyede offered. "My wife is pregnant and she has been going through a lot of complications. I saw her give birth in our home and it was problem-free. The baby was beautiful. Looked just like me…well the Asian part of my bloodline was evident in the eyes."

Tristan knew that early in Coesen history, before mating Middlings was forbidden, the original Four had taken a number of brides. Some were of different ethnicities.

"A healthy baby and wife is what I want more than life itself." Oloyede's words came out soft and pained.

To resist that must have been very hard, Tristan thought as he looked at Oloyede. If Vivian hadn't assured him and Cianne that the baby would be fine, he may have had the same desire. A desire he wasn't sure he could turn from no matter how false it felt.

"I pray to the Source that you have it," Tristan said, breaking the silence.

No one seemed to notice that they'd stopped walking.

"I do too," Jacobi said.

The Bode, who looked as pained as Oloyede, nodded in agreement. They stood in silence for a moment then began walking again, side by side.

Oloyede glanced over at Tristan. "What did they offer you, Tristan?"

Tristan didn't see any harm in sharing this. "A female," he said then cleared his throat. "I was offered a naked female." He felt all eyes on him and for the first time in a long time he felt a tinge of embarrassment. "I'm abstaining…so…"

"Hard huh?" Jacobi asked. The Gedgi's innocence was shining through again.

"No," Tristan said without hesitation. "She was beautiful and her touch was painfully arousing but she wasn't mine."

"You must have some woman if you didn't give in," the Bode said.

Tristan eyed the Bode, whose gaze was set ahead of them but his mind seemed further away. Tristan wondered what the warrior desired most and was about to ask when he heard Jacobi gasp in awe.

In front of them was a large mountain which peak looked as if it touched the sky. The light from the orb seemed to come from inside the mountain's center.

Within an hour, they reached the base.

"Looks like we're going to be climbing," the Bode said as he reached up with his right hand and pulled himself up. He glanced at Tristan and Oloyede who stood together. "I'll go first," he said, "I'm a pretty good climber." He scaled the mountain with little to no effort.

"Jacobi, won't you go next," Tristan said. That way if the kid slipped, Oloyede or Tristan could possibly catch him. For some reason, he felt protective of the kid now that he knew he was so young.

Oloyede gave Tristan a nod, a silent understanding passed between the two.

Jacobi hesitated before finding a ridge his fingers could grip then he began climbing.

Oloyede let Jacobi get a good distance up before reaching for the same small ridge. "I'm next," he said, following the Gedgi's path.

Tristan gave the area around him one more thorough scan then he looked up. The Bode was definitely a good climber. Good was an understatement. He was fast as well, and was almost to the top.

Tristan made his way up the mountain. He moved swiftly at an angle, slowing so he and Oloyede flanked underneath Jacobi on either side. Tristan decided to take the rear for the same reason the Bode took the lead. He was good at climbing but he was even better at fighting. He would strike down any threat that followed while the Bode could take down any threats at the top.

When Tristan pulled himself up onto the ledge he knew it wasn't the top but he stopped because his team had. Standing, he looked around. Without asking, he knew this was where they were supposed to be. He glanced at his teammates and understood that they knew as well.

In front of them, crafted into the side of the mountain, were four gigantic arches.

"We are to separate," Oloyede said. "Everyone ready?"

They all gave a nod. Jacobi even smiled. The boy was obviously enjoying himself. Tristan realized then that this must be like one big life-size video game for the teen. The idea made Tristan like the kid even more. Jacobi wasn't afraid, he was excited.

Tristan watched as Jacobi entered one of the archways first. The Bode chose next. Oloyede made eye contact with Tristan, a silent good luck maybe, then looked forward and ducked into the archway in front of him.

He moved his hands over the hilts of his daggers. The weapons were still with him. Satisfied, he scanned the area around him again then entered the only archway left.

Tristan assumed the center would look like an ancient temple with beautiful statues and hieroglyphs. Instead it was just a hollowed out dark cave. The average person would not be able to see their hand in front of them in the blackness that surrounded him but Tristan had no problem seeing inside the dark abyss.

Even though he wasn't at full potential he suspected his eyesight and hearing couldn't get any better.

Tristan listened intently. He heard his teammates' breathing and footfalls but it appeared that no others lurked inside the caves. Also, the sound of moving water was further ahead. He wondered then if the others had run into any obstacles because so far, he hadn't.

He picked up speed as the scent of salt water wafted in the air. After running a few hundred feet more he slowed to a jog. When he saw the light at the end he began to walk. Ahead a wall of water covered the exit.

The closer he came to the wall of water, his exit, the ground under his feet became more slippery. It was covered with a thin layer of water that caused it to look like black glass. Water sprinkled on him as he stepped toward the exit.

Slowly, Tristan walked through the curtain of water. Standing on a small ledge, he looked out over the wide expanse. Sticking from the ledge he stood on was a metal pole that looked about 700 feet long. Just beyond and somewhat under the pole, maybe 100 ft. or so, was the illuminated orb floating in the air.

Presto.

Tristan exhaled and took in his surroundings again. It looked as if he were inside a large volcano but instead of a simmering pool of lava, underneath the orb was a vortex of swirling water that looked breathtaking as well as deadly. Directly across from him was the Bode, standing on a ledge similar to the one he stood on. Oloyede stood on a ledge to his left and Jacobi was just walking through his water curtain opening to his right. It seemed as if they were all the same distance apart. If you were to draw a line from him to Oloyede then from Jacobi to the Bode, the lines would make a perfect cross.

"Walking across these poles isn't going to be easy." The Bode was bent over the ledge, running his hand over his pole.

Tristan heard him clearly over the rushing water.

In unison, they each stepped forward. Tristan's right foot slid forward as soon as it touched the pole, causing him to lift it and back away. Trying again and doing his best to balance himself, Tristan eased onto the pole as slowly as he could.

One step, two steps, three steps.

Crossing the pole was going to take some time but it was going to be a piece of cake, he thought, until he felt the pole move. It wasn't a jolt of movement at first. It just felt like a barely noticeable vibration.

"Brace yourselves." Tristan said right before the pole jerked under his feet. In the fraction of a second of warning, he managed to crouch down and grab the pole with both hands. He glanced around at his teammates.

Oloyede had held on and was in the process of hoisting himself back to his feet on the slowly retracting pole. The Bode also hung on. Sitting, he was getting to his feet. Jacobi, on the other hand, was hanging from the pole with one hand. He lost his footing but he managed to grab hold of the wet slick pole.

"Can you go the rest of the way with your hands?" the Bode called to Jacobi.

Jacobi attempted to reach up with his dangling arm, but an earsplitting howl came from his mouth. "I can't," he said, catching his breath. "I hit my arm when I fell. I think my arm is broken."

There was no way Jacobi would survive if he fell into the unrelenting vortex that swirled beneath them. And even if he did survive, where did the vortex let out? They would fail the challenge and that was something that Tristan couldn't allow. Failure was not an option.

"I'm slipping," Jacobi yelled.

Tristan didn't think. He rarely did when things became dire. He just went on auto pilot, trusting his inner self or spirit to guide him. His spirit always got him through the tough plays on the football field. It always brought him out of the vicious fights he rarely instigated but always won, granted never unscathed. He depended on an "act now" method of survival whenever he was in a tight spot and he never let himself down.

Tristan pushed off, launching himself from his pole, and aimed for Jacobi's. Jumping to another pole at the distance they were was madness he knew, but it was unavoidable. They had nothing to lose; if he failed they would be no worse off than if Jacobi simply fell into the Vortex. But if he succeeded…

He soared through the air like a gymnast, his body perfectly angled with a small arch in his back. Extending one hand out at an upward slant, Tristan grabbed hold of Jacobi's pole. With his other hand, he caught Jacobi's arm just as the kid's grip slipped.

Oloyede laughed, and the Bode cursed a string of profanity at him that was in both English and Coesen but the words didn't have any heat to them.

Easily raising Jacobi by his wrist, Tristan hauled him up so that their eyes met. "I need both my hands so you have to hold onto my neck. Can you hold on?" Tristan asked him. Jacobi nodded so Tristan slung him around saying, "Scoot to my back."

Jacobi used his legs to secure himself to Tristan. Then, when Tristan let go of Jacobi's good arm, Jacobi snaked it around Tristan's shoulder and around the front of his neck.

The pole was still retracting and was doing so faster than it had seconds ago. Jacobi fisted the fabric over Tristan's left shoulder to secure himself.

Once Jacobi was on his back, Tristan had use of both his hands to grip the pole while his legs dangled. He placed one hand in front of the other and began crossing the pole. When he got into a steady rhythm he moved quicker, because not only was the pole retracting faster but the extra weight on the pole was causing it to bow. The other team members were moving faster as well as if they sensed the urgency.

The pole began to rock.

"I don't think it was meant to hold two of us. Good thing I didn't eat this morning." Jacobi sounded somewhat excited by their ordeal.

But Tristan heard a small tinge of worry in his voice.

Moving closer to the edge of the pole, Tristan chanced a look at Oloyede and then the Bode. They were still inching forward.

When Oloyede's eyes met Tristan's, he must have seen the urgency.

"Bode, we have to move faster," Oloyede yelled over the rushing sound of the water. With that, each of them moved at a more hurried pace, careful not to slip.

"Damn it," Tristan called out. The further they got to the end of the pole the more it seemed to loosen from the rock securing it. "Hold on." He moved faster to the edge. His two teammates matched his pace. As Tristan approached the end, he heard loud screeching sounds—the pole was working free from the rock wall that encased it.

Tristan also heard the faint sounds of rocks falling free into the vortex below. He and Jacobi looked down at the same time, both dreading the pain of drowning that waited if they were to fall.

Tristan stopped. "We're not going to make it like this," he said to Jacob. "I'll get us to the orb but you have to trust me."

Jacobi half-heartedly chuckled. "No choice really."

Tristan began swinging them back and forth. With each swing came a pull on the pole, causing more rocks to dislodge. Gaining speed by moving back and forth, by the fifth swing forward, Tristan felt more confident. The Bode and Oloyede had reached the ends of their poles and were staring at them. On the sixth swing back Tristan yelled to them, "Wait!" in the Coesen language. The moment his hands released the pole, it broke free of the wall, the tip grazing Jacobi's back before toppling down into the vortex.

At the same time, Tristan and Jacobi shot up in the air feet first, well above the level of all the poles and high above the orb. As gravity began to take over, Tristan told Jacobi to let go of his back and neck as they angled backward, head first. He grabbed the kid by the wrist and angled them forward. With the orb in his sight, Tristan calculated and counted in his head... 1 2 3 4 5...

"Jump!" Tristan yelled to his teammates.

Oloyede and the Bode jumped at the same time. All hands stretched for the orb that floated beneath them.

The Pride
Final Stage

Tristan stood on the edge of a planet, or that's what it looked like to him. It reminded him of the stories during Christopher Columbus' time that told of the world being flat. The literal edge of a world was under his feet.

He stood on a mixture of dry and green grass. Above him were two Suns and a blue sky that seemed closer to him than a sky should be. He leaned forward over the edge, and saw part of the massive land mass that he and his teammates had just been on, the mountain with the water vortex.

Below the vortex plane, he could see the first plane with the Warriors. The village land mass was just as big as the vortex land mass, but unlike the vortex plane where half its surface was visible, he could only see a little more than a fraction of the village land's surface.

"It's like looking down at a set of land-steps, from the top of a staircase," Oloyede said.

Tristan turned his head from the heavenly sight to look at Oloyede when he heard his voice. Beside Oloyede was the Bode, glaring down at the spectacle. Tristan didn't see Jacobi so he turned to his left but Jacobi wasn't there either. Panic pricked at him.

Did the kid fall behind?

Jacobi must be still in play because they were still inside the Maatii.

Tristan stepped closer to the edge. He could jump and return to the Vortex to see what kept Jacobi, leaving the others here to wait for them. He gazed at the distance between this plateau and the one beneath, that was the Vortex.

Would a jump from this height kill me? He thought. but realized it didn't matter. Without the kid, they could not go any further.

"Careful," a familiar voice said from behind him, "You might fall and ruin our chances for victory."

Tristan whirled around to see Jacobi rubbing his injured shoulder. They walked toward each other. Just two feet away, Tristan extended his hand but Jacobi dropped to one knee and lowered his head.

"Because of you, I made it to this third challenge. You have my gratitude and my trust from this moment on."

Tristan's brows arched and he tilted his head in confusion. He looked at his extended hand that was between them, then dropped it to his side. Feeling awkward, he turned to look at the others. Oloyede smiled and the Bode, who always seemed a hair trigger away from exploding with anger, curiously disguised what may have been a grin and shrugged. Tristan turned his attention back to Jacobi, who was still kneeling.

Oloyede walked up and slapped Tristan on his back. "Just touch his shoulder so we can get moving," he said as he walked by. His voice was laced with amusement.

"Uh…anytime," Tristan said as he laid his hand on Jacobi's shoulder. The kid stood and moved so Tristan could pass. Tristan noticed the sparkle in the kid's eyes but said nothing. The kneeling thing was strange and he didn't want to question it or things might just get weirder. Tristan followed behind Oloyede and the Bode, allowing a few feet of distance. "Does anyone know how much time has passed? I can't seem to tell anymore."

Bringing up the rear, Jacobi answered quickly, "I'm getting nothing."

Tristan turned his head to see Jacobi, who was right behind him, virtually on his heels. Tristan's brows creased for a moment. The kid smiled at him. Tristan shook his head then faced forward again.

"It's pure genius," the Bode said. "It will drive us mad not knowing how much time we have left."

"Yeah," Tristan looked at the sun. Thank the heavens his body, like all Protectors, naturally regulated his temperature to a comfortable degree no matter the climate. "Total genius," he admitted.

They walked for what seemed like an eternity in the direction of the light the orb released into the sky. None of them knew exactly how long it would take to reach it, but they continued. The Suns above them stayed in the same position it had been in from the moment they arrived. He didn't like that they were flying blind, in a sense.

Of course, it was a way to break them. Then there was the other issue.

Tristan hadn't mentioned it because he didn't know if it he was the only one who felt it. He looked around the savanna-like grasslands that surrounded them. The grass was as high as his waist and what little trees scattering the area were small and spaced out, no more than a few were bunched together.

They saw large animals such as impalas, buffaloes, and wildebeests as they walked. Small bodies of water marked every few miles. As calm as this plane of existence seemed, Tristan felt more on edge than he had on the other two, and he had no doubt that they were being hunted.

"You sense it too?" the Bode asked. He pulled his staff from his back slowly as he kept his pace beside Tristan.

Tristan nodded. "Yup, my Spidey sense is firing away."

Just as the last word left his mouth something came at him, moving so fast that he barely had time to react. The force with which it hit him drove Tristan a few feet away and laid him flat. He could hear yelling around him but whatever had attacked him was so large that it was literally crushing the life from him.

Tristan took a deep breath and heaved the beast off him with a growl. With no time to rest or recover, he got to his feet and pulled the blades that he barely had time to ready, out of the animal's body. After a quick inspection, Tristan realized he was looking at the biggest lion he ever laid eyes on.

Frowning, he spun on his heels. Another lion was attacking. He was prepared to help the others with the second lion when the animal next to him moved its paw. The lion was still alive.

Tristan couldn't allow it to get up. He quickly looked to where he figured the animal's heart would be. A wound was already there from one of his blades, so he stabbed his blade in the area once more and the beast stilled. When he turned to see where the others were, the second lion was dead as well and Jacobi was sprinting toward him.

Jacobi stopped beside him. "You alright?" he asked as he stared at Tristan.

Tristan scanned the area thoroughly. His muscles relaxed and he pushed away the soreness that threatened him. "Fine," he said, "you?"

"I'm good." Jacobi relaxed but when he looked at the lion he visibly tensed again. "My god," was all he could say in reaction.

Tristan watched Jacobi stare at the lion with amazement. "The others?" he asked. He bent and wiped the blood from his daggers on the grass as he waited for an answer. "Jacobi…the others?" he repeated when Jacobi didn't answer.

"We're good," Oloyede said, walking up.

Tristan holstered his daggers and looked at the Bode, who nodded.

"This thing looks like it weighs a half ton and it's got to be more than eleven feet long, longer probably." Jacobi couldn't mask the excitement in his tone. "Look at its head. It's bigger than a freaking smart car."

Not as big but…

"We can't stay here," the Bode said, suspiciously eyeing their surroundings. He sounded more uneasy than Tristan felt. "These two are probably nomads. There are no females lurking around so these were probably excluded from the pride when they became adults. The pride lionesses will be smaller than these two but they'll be faster and more vicious."

Jacobi smiled, "Faster," he said with admiration.

Oloyede looked at the beam of light in the sky. His gaze traveled the beam of light downward. They'd been walking for some time, getting closer to the orb and the mountain that had two large caves, one above the other. Both caves had enormous slabs of rock that looked like steps leading up to them. The orb's light was coming from an opening at the top of the mountain.

"It figures," Oloyede whispered as he looked around.

"Where the hell are they?" Tristan reached behind his shoulder and touched the hilt of one of his twin blades.

"I don't know," the Bode said. Among them, he seemed to have the most knowledge regarding big cat behavior. "Hunting maybe," he said.

"Maybe not," Jacobi said, looking around.

Ahead, about a hundred feet between them and the clearing was rock steps. All around, twenty or so lionesses had snuck up on them and were getting in place, creating a circle with them enclosed in it.

"Run for the mountain!" the Bode yelled. "Don't let them close us in."

Jacobi led the team. Closest to the mountain, he darted through a wide gap that wasn't yet closed by the lionesses. Oloyede followed him. Tristan and the Bode bolted, neck and neck, squeezing between two of the huge beasts.

The Coesen and Tristan were clearly faster than the lionesses but as they hurtled past, one of the beasts swiped out at them with her huge paw. Sharp claws raked at the Bode, slicing into the flesh covering his leg and thigh, breaking his stride. The Bode cried out in pain as his leg lifted behind him. Falling forward, he hit the ground hard and his body rolled and skidded to a stop ahead of Tristan.

Slowing, Tristan beat the lioness to Bode and scooped him up and practically dragged him to the stone steps. From a distance, the steps had seemed lower but now he could see that the top of the steps was a lot higher than he originally thought. The first cave was about fifteen feet high.

Great.

The lionesses were fast on the Bode's and Tristan's heels. With no time to climb and help the Bode to safety, Tristan practically threw him up to Jacobi who was lying flat on the top of the first step and reaching for them.

When the Bode was pulled to safety, Tristan unsheathed his daggers and turned to face the lionesses that were fast approaching. When one of the big cats opened its mouth to grab him, he leaned back out of its reach, then lunged forward, slicing at the cat's exposed neck.

At the same time, Jacobi managed to pull the Bode up three more of the steps to the first cave, and Oloyede dropped down from the step above to fight alongside Tristan. Several big cats approached.

A loud roar ripped through the air, sending a shiver through Tristan.

"It's coming from inside the cave," Jacobi said. He quickly leaned the Bode against a rock wall and turned to face the lion that was coming out of the cave.

"We have to move," Bode called out.

"Too late for that," Jacobi readied his machete. He placed himself between the lion and the Bode.

The lion took three paces then pounced. Jacobi moved to the right and swung the machete to his left, cutting through the lion's mane and slicing into its shoulder. The blade was caught in the beast's bone.

Jacobi let go of the machete and quickly ducked the lion's paw, then dug his foot into the ground and ripped his weapon free. As he freed his machete, he spun, piercing the beast's eye. The lion wailed in agony, moving several big paces back.

Oloyede glanced up and saw the huge lion Jacobi faced. He turned back in time to slice at another attacking lioness as she swung her paw, removing two of its toes and beating the animal back. The lioness lost its footing so Oloyede rushed forward, knocking off the ledge and onto the ground below. He glanced at the lionesses below then climb up to reach his teammates.

"Tristan," Oloyede called, as he climbed the rock steps to help Jacobi. As he was pulling himself up onto the fourth step, the one Jacobi and the Bode were on, Tristan passed him.

Tristan stood in front of the Bode, covered from head to toe in blood. He once again scooped up his injured teammate, threw him over his back, and climbed up three more stone slab steps. Laying the Bode against another wall, he quickly scanned above and below.

Oloyede was working his way up the stairs when another lioness attacked him. He looked uninjured, and by his movements seemed fresh for the fight. Meanwhile, Jacobi was still fighting the lion on the fourth step, in front of the cave.

Tristan turned to the Bode, pulled the staff from the Bode's holster, and placed it in his hands. He squatted and inspected the Bode's wound, which was wrapped tightly with a piece of his shredded pant leg. "Will you be alright?" Tristan stood. He anxiously peered down at the battle. Jacobi and Oloyede, who made quick work of the lioness he faced, were fighting the beast together.

"I'll be fine, go!"

"Try to stay awake." Tristan jumped down the one step, rolling to his feet then jumping down another. By the time Tristan reached the pair, Jacobi was kicking a lioness that was stalking up the steps toward him. Oloyede was dodging the lion's massive paws, no doubt looking for a kill shot.

Standing above the fray, with the tips of his blades down, Tristan jumped. He landed on the lion's back, driving his blades deep into the animal's flesh.

"You have to get away from that cave!" the Bode yelled down to them.

Oloyede pulled Jacobi away from the ledge, placing the kid behind him just as a lioness tried to take his head with her huge mouth. At the same time, Oloyede rose up and kicked another lioness on the nose hard enough to knock it to the step below. Then he, Jacobi, and Tristan sprinted up the stairs to join their injured teammate.

With a moment to breathe, Oloyede stood on the edge of the step, waiting for another attack. Jacobi went to the Bode and checked his thigh. And Tristan climbed the remaining eight steps and peered inside the larger cave at the top. With no immediate threat apparent, he quickly returned to his team.

"Can you walk?" Tristan asked the Bode, but kept his eyes on Oloyede.

"I'll try," the Bode grunted.

Jacobi shook his head "It's broken and he's bleeding out."

Tristan nodded. He walked over to the steps and glanced down. One of the lionesses dragged the lion he killed down the steps and out of the way.

Oloyede looked over at them and yelled, "Round two."

Tristan pulled a claw from his side. Blood trickled from the wound but it wasn't that bad. When he cut off the lioness' toe it prevented her from causing more damage. He looked over to the Bode who was alert but growing pale. He turned his gaze to Oloyede then to Jacobi. Both of them looked weary.

They were stuck on the same rock step for so long defending themselves from the big cats, that they were exhausted. No one could determine how long they were on the step or how much time had passed. The sun never moved from its position in the sky.

An hour, three, or twenty, could have passed. All Tristan knew was that they couldn't keep going at this challenge the way they had. The lionesses would rest, attack in stages, then rest again, giving them hardly any time to rest themselves. They'd done the same song and dance for survival too many times and no headway was being made.

Tristan got to his feet, dropping the claw as he stood. Oloyede and Jacobi stood as well, looking to him as if they were awaiting his instruction.

"We can't just stay here fighting off these damn things. The Bode is going to bleed to death and we'll never be Royal Guards," Tristan said. He didn't mention the pain the guy must be feeling.

"He'll die sooner if we move him," Jacobi said.

They killed one of the males and several females so far but there was about a dozen left. Some sat under the scattered trees for shade, some paced back and forth, keeping an eye on their next meal of course, them.

Oloyede went to the edge of the step. He looked out at the lionesses below then kneeled and looked over his long blade. The weapon held true during each battle. A truly unique blade with its intricate handle and unusual glowing markings that were of no language they'd ever seen.

"I agree with Tristan," Oloyede said then sighed. "We are never going to stop the cycle these lions have us on before time runs out or we're all dead. We have to do something."

Jacobi agreed with a halfhearted nod.

"If we can't get you to the orb then we bring the orb to you," Tristan said to the Bode. His determination was unyielding and everyone heard it in his voice. Jacobi stood straight, as if Tristan's words had revived him.

The Bode literally laughed.

Oloyede just stared out at the Lions like he hadn't heard what Tristan proposed.

The Bode continued to laugh hysterically.

"You think it'll work?" Oloyede spoke so quietly that only they could have heard him. He looked totally defeated. "No one has ever attempted this. And how are you going to bring it here," he asked, extending his arms in front of him, "without touching it?"

"He's going to carry it back in something." Jacobi grinned. "But someone will have to stay here with our injured brother and someone will have to go with you," he said as he turned to Tristan.

Tristan rubbed his hand over his face. He was just as frustrated as Oloyede and the Bode. He needed this just as much as they did. "Look, we lose this if he can't touch the orb. We lose this if we try to fight it out with them," he said, motioning to the beasts. "If more than two of them could fit on the steps at one time, we would have died hours ago. I won't give up now. We can't give up now."

"Thank you for trying to keep me in play," the Bode said, trying to stand.

Jacobi was at the Bode's side immediately, pushing his shoulder down so he couldn't get up. Tristan was at his other side. The Bode turned to Tristan, extending his hand. Tristan grabbed his hand at the wrist, the customary way the Coesen shook hands as the Bode spoke in the Coesen language.

"My name is Shane and I truly believe you can lead us to victory." His tone was more relaxed than it had been their entire time together.

Tristan replied in the Coesen language. "We will all be victorious, Shane."

"The Alpha, a male lion, he's most likely up in that cave," Shane said.

Oloyede raised his head to look at the second cave above them then turned back to watch the lionesses below.

Jacobi smiled then shrugged. "I'm in."

They all looked over at Oloyede who continued to watch the pride.

Shane winced as he looked at Jacobi and Tristan. "He's going to be much bigger than these here and I'm betting he's guarding the orb. He won't be happy when you take it," Shane grunted out.

Tristan rubbed his neck. "So, no matter who goes with me or who stays with Shane, either way it's not going to be a walk in the park."

Oloyede secured his blade to his back. "Jacobi seems to know more about helping Shane with his wounds, so I'll face the alpha with you."

"I'll keep us alive until you both return," Jacobi said self-assuredly.

Tristan knew the kid was more than capable, and his confidence was a plus. He made his way to the large stone step above them with Oloyede following close behind. He looked back at Jacobi and Shane before he began hiking himself up the steps.

Tristan and Oloyede remained silent as they entered the dark cave. Tristan hummed with anticipation as they trekked forward. A part of him, a part he kept hidden from the world, relished danger and a good fight. He had no problem killing those warriors in the village but would have been more satisfied if he could have inflicted more suffering upon them for keeping him from his goal.

His goal right now, was to face and defeat the biggest adversary he'd ever encountered.

With a devilish grin, he slowly moved forward.

About thirty feet in, Tristan raised his fist for Oloyede to stop then pointed down. Scattered on the floor in front of them were the bones of animals that had been brought to the alpha. The place was filled with them.

It took time but eventually they were able to maze through them all. Soon the light from the orb began to light the way for them. Following its glare, the pair finally saw the alpha.

Saying it was bigger than the lionesses was a grave understatement. The lion was beyond huge. It was titanic, with a full black mane with golden highlights that was meant to intimidate. If they wound up in his mouth, Tristan doubted the thing would even have to chew them before swallowing.

The lion, aware of them, roared and the entire mountain shook as if the earth was seperating beneath it. Tristan looked over at Oloyede who was crouched and ready to strike. With his eyes narrowed and his daggers in hand, Tristan attacked.

Outside the cave, Jacobi and Shane were engaged in a battle with a lioness. Shane swung his staff just as the lioness jumped at him. The staff landed on the side of her face driving her head sideways. Jacobi swung his ax at the same time, slicing the lioness' leg open. She bellowed with pain but continued with her attack until she heard the loud roar of the king of the pride. The animal jumped down the steps, clearly fearful of the alpha lion.

Stunned by the roar themselves, Jacobi and Shane tried to brace themselves as the mountain trembled. His strength depleted and no longer able to hold up his staff, Shane dropped it to the ground with a grunt. Out of the corner of his eye, Jacobi saw Shane rest back against the rock wall he sat against, but he was transfixed with the movements of the lionesses below.

A few females went into the cave under them.

"They're probably scared of him," Shane suggested.

"Yeah," Jacobi said, "I can see that."

The remaining lionesses who didn't go inside the cave moved far away from the mountain but they could still be seen.

"A stay of execution, I suppose," Jacobi said, as he kneeled next to Shane and checked his makeshift bandages.

Tristan and Oloyede fought together with speed and diligence as if they had been a team for years. When Oloyede ducked the mammoth paw and enormous claws, Tristan struck. If

Tristan was turning out of the way, avoiding the charging beast, Oloyede attacked. Their moves were graceful and effective, but with every hit the beast took, it only seemed to grow angrier.

"Check the orb," Tristan called to Oloyede, who was standing beside him. Tristan darted to his left, carving a piece of flesh from the lion's front leg. Another roar rocked the foundation of the mountain.

The lion surged forward, Tristan in his sights, allowing Oloyede to move away.

Oloyede ran to the floating orb. Its pearl glow was bright but not painfully so. He waved his hand under the orb, feeling for the invisible line that he believed held it but he felt nothing. But the orb did dip a fraction. He knew this meant it could be moved from whatever force that was holding it. He just needed something to use so as not to touch it.

Tristan hit the rock wall hard. His left hand was gripped around the beast's top right canine and his right hand gripped the animal's lower left canine, preventing it from swallowing him. His muscles strained as he used all his strength to hold the lion back so he wouldn't be crushed. His legs strained as well, as one foot was flat on the wall behind him and the other planted on the ground, bent for support.

At a stalemate, both Tristan and the beast pushed with all their might, neither relinquishing to the other.

But something flashed in Tristan mind, some piece of knowledge from one of his viewings of a show on "Animal Planet", something about a lion's jaw. With a vicious tug of his hands in opposite directions, he twisted the animal's jaws and felt bones grind together as he heard a harsh crack. An ear-splitting howl, part roar, shook the cave. Releasing the lion's canines, Tristan dodged a falling boulder. The beast fell as rocks and dust rained down on it.

Oloyede dodged several large rocks, and when one threatened to fall on the orb, Tristan watched him launch himself in the air to intersect it, nudging the rock in another direction.

Tristan pushed to his feet. In front of him, the lion lay motionless, apparently gravely injured by the rock fall. The only reason he knew it lived was because of its labored breathing. Tristan approached the animal through a cloud of swirling dust, with his blades out but pointed downward.

Dropping one of his blades, Tristan raised the other with both hands on the hilt as he stood over the beast. With all his strength, he embedded his dagger into the animal's fleshy neck and yanked downward, cutting clear through the lion's throat. Turning on his heels, he backed up several feet. Holding his dagger pointing out, he sprinted forward, heading straight for the lion's heart.

Jacobi covered Shane with his body as rocks and dust fell all around them. When the rocks stopped falling, he used his hand to shield his eyes as he tried to see through the dust storm. He made out two figures jumping down the steps above them.

"They're back," Jacobi whispered. "They're back!" he said again, this time yelling it. He moved away from Shane and they both looked at Tristan and Oloyede as they leapt from the step above them.

Tristan and Oloyede dropped to their knees in front of their teammates, their friends. Each of them moved into a circle formation without being prompted. The orb, wrapped in the king of the pride's skin, sat in the center. Oloyede held it down, careful not to touch the orb itself, or it would float away.

They all looked at each other. Tristan felt connected to them, this trio of Guardian's he fought alongside. "See you on the other side," Tristan said then smiled.

"The other side." Oloyede smiled.

"The other side," Jacobi whispered.

Shane only nodded. His face was pale and he seemed as if he was barely able to keep his eyes open.

Tristan grabbed Shane's wrist.

Oloyede let some of the lion's skin fall from the orb, using a small piece of skin to shield his other hand to hold the orb in place. "On three," he said, looking at each of them.

One…

Two…

Three.

Tristan placed his and Shane's hand on the orb at the same time.

His aches and pains were gone. The smell of blood and the stickiness he felt all over his body was also gone.

A drum…someone was beating drums and water was rushing through pipes.

Slowly, Tristan pried his eyes open. The light of the sun had imprinted on his lids so when he opened his eyes, everything was bathed in a bright glow.

He was once again in the large office, sitting in the chair he was sitting in before the Maatii. Tristan felt a hand lifting off his shoulder. He turned and looked up to see a figure drenched in bright light.

Demetri?

Yes, Demetri is his name.

Tristan heard someone swallow. A woman, he deduced from the delicate sound. He closed his eyes and covered his ears trying to shut out the light and all the sounds that were amplified around him.

"Just focus, you can control it."

God, was she using a damn bullhorn?

Tristan moaned but he concentrated. It took longer to tune down the sounds than it did to adjust his sight. Once his hearing was at a normal level Tristan turned his attention to

Vivian. Oddly, she had an enormous smile on her face. It was rare that she smiled and even rarer that it was meant for him.

His head was still a bit foggy but he remembered touching the last orb. "You're pleased that we completed the challenge?" Tristan asked, not recognizing his jagged voice.

He rubbed the back of his neck.

Vivian stood. Still smiling, she walked around the enormous desk. At the same time, Demetri left the room. When Vivian sat in the seat next to Tristan, Demetri returned and was handing her what looked like a glass of water. She took the glass and offered it to Tristan.

He lifted the glass to his mouth and drank. When he pulled the glass away, he frowned.

Not water.

"It will help with the dizziness you're experiencing," Vivian said. Her voice sounded different, lighter; she sounded happy.

Tristan arched his brow then slowly put the glass to his mouth again and drank. Once he got the sugary sweet drink down, she spoke.

"Tristan," Vivian said, still smiling, "you have more than pleased me. Your team broke two records. You, yourself, have started a new record as well."

Tristan sat up in the chair, stunned. He was just hoping to finish in the allotted time. Breaking records wasn't on his mind.

"What records?" he asked. His tone and demeanor revealed none of the excitement he felt.

A veil of pride covered Vivian's face for a moment.

He would not let his emotions rule him in response to her rare display of emotion. She rarely fell victim to her emotions but this was a momentous occasion.

"You are given six days, a total of one hundred forty-four hours, to complete the Maatii. Usually, when a team succeeds, they do so in a five-day-plus time frame. The first to finish in a record time of eighty hours was Cassius and his team.

Whodai and his team accomplished the task in seventy-six hours."

She took the glass from Tristan and handed it back to Demetri.

"Your team has managed to complete the Maatii in less than seventy-one hours. The second record you shattered was with the warrior battle. Yours was the first to strategize to beat the warriors of the village. And you Tristan, you alone are the only one to slay a Pride Lion King."

Tristan tried to soak it all in, but before he could, Vivian spoke again.

"Now, it's time for your brand." Vivian turned to Demetri who opened the door.

Standing outside of the door was a girl. Her face was round, her nose a button and her long straight pink and black hair was pulled into a high ponytail. As she walked into the room she smiled, revealing a set of silver braces with pink and black bands. Her skirt was denim and the t-shirt she wore had the word Bubble-lishous splayed across her chest.

"This is Keera. Give her you right hand."

"Hi," Keera said as she bounced to his side.

Tristan held out his right hand and Keera took it.

Keera took hold of Tristan's arm. "You're cute."

"Keera," Vivian's tone was all warning and no fun.

Keera scrunched her face in protest. "Well he is, Auntie," she said as she used her finger to caress the back of his hand. "I hear you rocked the Maatii," she said to him. "Cool."

Tristan laughed. "Thanks."

She tilted her head. "For saying you're cute or telling you that you rock?"

He was about to answer her when a stinging sensation began to radiate through his hand. It wasn't exactly painful but it was certainly irritating enough to cause his back teeth to ache. But the ache was forgotten when he noticed what was happening to his hand.

A shield with two flaming blades on each side of it appeared in the center of the back of his hand. Around the shield and between the flaming blades each of the Coesen tribal names were spelled out in script. At his wrist, three small white stars symbolizing the three tasks appeared, evenly spaced out. The center tip of each star stretched, widened, and broke into several white streams that circled his arm but came together just under his bicep. As the markings continued up his arm the stinging became a burn.

Tristan winced as the burning image rounded his shoulder. He watched as his shirt sleeve burned away to reveal the image of a majestic lion's head on his shoulder. The lion's mane continued, to overflow slightly onto his chest, back, and neck. The brand on his hand was in a gray outline. The stars and the lion's mane were a luminescent white but were lined and defined in the same gray ink that also seemed to glow.

Keera grinned. "You likey?"

Tristan raised his arm, twisting it around to inspect it thoroughly. After a minute, he looked at Keera. "I love it."

"Glad I could be of service," Keera said then bowed her head. She straightened then turned to Vivian, "Can I stay Auntie Viv, just for a couple of days?"

"Keera, you know you cannot. But…" Vivian teased the word out, "I will allow you to stay for dinner so you can meet your cousin Cianne."

The girl's eyes lit up. "Cool," she sang.

"Come then," Vivian stood. "Let's go plan dinner." She placed her arm around the girl's shoulder. They walked to the door.

"Keera, you're cute too," Tristan said, then winked.

Vivian shook her head but Keera squealed with pride.

"Don't let that go to your thirteen-year-old head," Vivian said as they walked into the library.

Alone in the office now, Tristan looked over his arm again. His Royal Guard brand was like none he'd seen before. All the Royal Guard brands he'd seen were all the same and stopped at the wrist. Only record breakers like Cassius and Whodai had a star to signify the record they broke. He had three. Tristan was also pretty sure he was the only Royal Guard with a sleeve brand. It would be a permanent reminder to him and all Coesen who saw it, that he had accomplished greatness.

What was even better, he wouldn't have to explain the beautiful artwork to his mother because only Coesen could see it. Well, and he saw it, but only because he was a Protector.

As he sat in the chair, mesmerized by Keera's work, he wondered if his teammates' brands were as impressive as his.

Then, in that moment, it finally sank in that they had succeeded. Not only did they succeed, they triumphed. Tristan finally smiled.

SHEA SWAIN

The Presence of your Company

Is Requested

At the
Engagement Celebration

For
Tristan Patrick Bertram
&
Cianne Baxter

Saturday the thirty-first of July two
thousand and ten
Time: 2pm
At
Tranquil Hills Country Club
8120 McGriegle Rd.
Phoenix, Arizona
Dinner and Dancing

Chapter Twelve

It was cool in the room, extremely pleasant, but Cianne still felt warm. She wore a long thin-strapped dress that matched her eyes and designed to complement all her curves perfectly, even her recently acquired ones.

She was now twenty-four weeks pregnant by the calendar, but Dr. Reginald said that she was measuring at twenty-nine weeks. This was totally normal she was told. The point was that Cianne looked pregnant and had for some time now.

That fact didn't bother her. She enjoyed being pregnant but she was feeling a little self-conscious about being at her own engagement party with a bun already in the oven. She smoothed her hand over her belly as she avoided stares by lowering her eyes to look at the champagne glass in front of her.

"It only matters what we think," Tristan whispered in her ear.

Cianne leaned into the soft caress of his breath and closed her eyes. He kissed her temple and reached for her hand under the table. They interlocked their fingers.

"You believe that, don't you?" she whispered back.

Tristan, who had turned his head to regard her father, turned his gaze back to her.

His eyes reflected only love. So much love that Cianne knew that no one's opinion mattered to her but his. She smiled before he kissed her lips.

"To the happy couple," Joseph said.

His voice rang out from the side of the room where the microphone was placed and over the large hall that comfortably seated over two hundred of their family, friends and some people she didn't know.

Joseph then lifted his champagne glass in the air, prompting the rest of the room to do the same. Cianne lifted her glass of apple juice.

A chorus of voices repeated, "to the happy couple", then the sound of the glasses clanging, filled the room.

"I love you." Cianne mouthed the words to her father.

"I love you too, Buttercup," he said into the microphone.

The main course had been served and the toasting was done. Cianne felt happy and relieved. Happy for all the obvious reasons and relieved that everything was winding down. It had gone beautifully.

She looked around the large hall feeling self-conscious again as she watched people get up and go to the dance floor when the music started. She looked at Tristan who was watching the dance floor.

"Would you like to dance?" Cianne tilted her head toward him.

"I'm good," he said, shaking his head.

Cianne found Tranae on the dance floor among a mass of people. She and Brian were together, dancing and laughing. Actually, most everyone was either already up and dancing or they were talking to someone.

Cianne glanced around the room once more. *Bingo*, she thought. "Zeta looks a little lonely," Cianne said. "I bet she would like to dance."

"We dance all the time." Tristan laughed.

"You spar all the time, that's not the same." Cianne gave his shoulder a nudge.

Tristan stood and bent over Cianne and kissed her forehead. "Will you be ok here by yourself?" he asked. He was holding the back of her chair now and talking to her with the side of his face pressed against hers.

"I think I will be fine," Cianne assured him. She watched Tristan walk off, then looked around at two of the twelve security guards who were in the hall. They were provided by the Country Club; it was standard for high rollers she figured. Not to mention all the supernatural protection that was provided as well, due to this event also doubled as her "coming out" party.

There were Coesen spread throughout the hall as well. Vivian officially announced Cianne to the Coesen world just after Tristan completed the Maatii.

"It was time," Vivian told her after she appeared on Coesen News Today, CNT for short.

To Cianne's surprise, Vivian invited the news anchors to cover the engagement party.

The network even requested a private interview with her and Tristan before the party. Cianne reluctantly agreed; the interview was short and the questions asked weren't too bad. Plus, the network planned to air it at a later date.

Tristan, of course, was his charismatic self and had both interviewers eating out of his hands. By the end of the interview, the female anchor was referring to him as the White Lion Prince.

Tristan looked over at Cianne. He gave her a smile as he made his way to Zeta. She watched as Zeta, who looked stunning in her midnight blue dress, refused at first, then with a little convincing, agreed to dance with him.

Tristan was a wonderful dancer. *Of course, he would be,* she laughed to herself.

Cianne sat for a few minutes watching everyone dancing and having fun when the number one symptom of late pregnancy called to her. She slid out of her chair and disappeared unseen into the hallway.

She waddled down the elegant hallway to the just as fancy restrooms. She'd been a few times already so she didn't need to follow the signs. She knew the way.

When Cianne was done, she stood in the hallway thinking of the walk back to the ballroom. It didn't seem that long when she was coming from the opposite end. She suddenly felt tired so she sat on one of the strategically placed benches that lined the long beautiful lobby. She planned to rest a bit before returning to the ballroom.

She leaned back against the wall and closed her eyes.

"I can go get someone for you, if you need help."

Cianne opened her eyes. A boy about the age of thirteen, or maybe a little older, was standing over her. "No," she said, sitting up. "I'm fine. I just needed a little rest. All this fussing over me can be a bit taxing."

The boy looked at her for a moment before speaking again. "I can sit here with you if you want," he offered, "just to make sure you're ok."

Cianne smiled at him. "That would be nice," she said. She scooted over, offering him a seat beside her. He sat down but allowed a lot of space between them. Cianne looked over at him when she noticed him watching her. He was very handsome, with dirty blonde hair and flawless skin. Cianne thought it was nice that pimples hadn't made a full assault on his handsome face yet. She'd been lucky too. The curse of puberty totally bypassed her.

The thing that stood out about the boy the most though was his vibrant greenish-blue eyes. Cianne always thought green eyes were ok as far as eye color went. She adored brown and blue eyes. But this kid's eyes were amazing.

"You have really nice eyes," she said, still staring into them.

"Thank you," he said, looking away. "Yours are nicer. They remind me of my mother's eyes."

Cianne blushed. She wasn't sure why, but the conversation seemed a little intimate. "Are you and your parents here with the Baxter party, the Bertram party, or the other party?" she asked him. The other party being the Coesen party.

"I'm not here with my parents." He looked at her again. "I could walk you back to the ballroom if you like. You shouldn't really be out walking alone in your condition."

Cianne thought it funny that she was being lectured by a child. She laughed. "How old are you?"

He thought before answering the question. "Old enough," he said with a grin. "And smart enough to know that you need help."

Cianne touched his hand that was resting on the bench between them. "I didn't mean anything by questioning your age. I was just thinking that you may know more about pregnancy than I do. Do you have any little brothers or sisters?"

"My parents and my brother are dead," he said, looking straight into her eyes.

If he felt sad about the loss of his family, Cianne couldn't tell.

There was an awkward moment of silence. She didn't know what to say. Thank goodness she heard Tristan calling to her from down the hall.

"Cianne," Tristan jogged over to the bench, his tone laced with relief. "I wish you would have let me know you needed to use the restroom."

"Why? Were you going to carry me?" she grimaced.

"I could have," he said. Tristan looked at the boy sitting next to her. Then he saw that Cianne was touching the boy's hand.

The boy saw Tristan looking at their connected hands too before he quickly moved his hand from under hers.

Cianne looked at the boy, then to Tristan. *"You're intimidating him."*

The boy frowned, seeming a bit confused.

"I didn't mean to." Tristan took a step back.

Cianne patted the boy's leg before trying to stand. Both Tristan and the boy assisted her. Cianne balanced herself and looked at her new friend. "Thank you…" she said to him, asking his name.

"Turner," the boy offered.

"Tristan, this handsome young man is Turner. He wanted to make sure I was alright."

"Thank you for watching over my girls for me," Tristan said.

Turner just gave Tristan a barely-there smile. Then the boy nodded at Cianne before walking down the hall away from them and the engagement party.

"I think he has a crush," Tristan said, turning Cianne toward him.

"He was just being helpful." Cianne smoothed Tristan's suit jacket. "Do I sense a hint of jealousy, Lion Prince?"

"Maybe," he said. "But a kiss may ease my mind. Yeah," he said, "that would do it."

Cianne stood on her toes. Tristan pushed her shoulders down so her feet were flat again. He then leaned down and kissed her.

Tristan held her steady when he pulled away from the kiss. "If you are up to it, I have some friends I'd like you to meet."

Cianne slowly opened her eyes. "Anything," she said then smiled dreamily as she touched her bottom lip.

He loved that he affected her the way he did, still. Her touch was just as intoxicating to him.

Tristan held her close as they walked into the hall. He led her through the crowded dance floor as guests parted to allow them passage to the tables that lined the other half of the great room. Three men stood as they approached, and Tristan couldn't help moving faster.

He made sure Cianne was steady on her feet before rushing the men. The four of them laughed and clapped each other's backs before one of the men noticed Cianne.

Tristan turned, took her hand, and eased her to his side. "This is Cianne, my fiancé."

He laughed when Jacobi pushed Oloyede out of his way and took Cianne's hand and kissed it.

"Amazing… You're even more amazing close-up," Jacobi said.

Tristan was pushing Jacobi away when Cianne blushed with a smile, then turned her head to gaze at him, exposing her birthmark.

Tristan bit back a curse when he saw each of his friends, and everyone who remained seated at the table react with shock as their eyes went wide. Seconds later, everyone who could see the mark went to one knee, including Shane, Oloyede, and Jacobi.

The women did a low curtsy. All heads were down.

"Totally not necessary," Cianne said in her practiced noble voice.

Tristan could tell she'd been practicing.

"Please everyone," she added, as she motioned for them to stand.

Heads began to lift but the group still seemed tense. The music in the hall had stopped, and Tristan could sense Cianne's concern. She was now looking around the hall to a number of guests looking their way.

Some of the Coesen, who were further away and didn't know why the guests in front of them were bowing, looked unsure as if they didn't know if they should bow as well.

Tristan moved forward and took Oloyede and Shane by the arm. He lifted them to a standing position. Cianne leaned down and touched Jacobi's arm and motioned for him to stand.

"Please everyone, just relax," Tristan said.

"Everyone," Vivian spoke into the microphone. "My granddaughter and her fiancé prefer this affair to be a non-formal one. They wish for everyone to just enjoy themselves and celebrate their good fortune of having found one another. So, rise please," she said as she lifted her hands at her side, "and have fun."

Slowly, everyone who was bowing began to rise, but the guests still seemed to be unsure of what to do next. Then Vivian cued the band. The music began to play again and the guests started to once again have fun though a small handful, Coesen and Middlings, continued to stare.

"Hello," Cianne said to Jacobi.

Tristan turned from looking at Vivian back to the people in front of him. Jacobi seemed in a panic as his gaze took in Cianne's beautiful face.

"You didn't say she was… That your girl...woman, that she was our princess," Shane mumbled.

"I didn't know how you all would take it," Tristan admitted, rubbing the back of his neck. Why on earth he was embarrassed he didn't know. "I'm still not sure how you guys will take it."

"You were worried about our reaction?" Oloyede asked, frowning.

"Amazing," Jacobi whispered again.

"Stop staring," Tristan barked, but in a hushed tone. He pushed at the kid's shoulder to get his attention.

Jacobi blinked, then looked at Tristan. His expression of fascination quickly turned to embarrassment.

Tristan looked at Cianne and lifted a finger for her to excuse them, then moved off to the side, motioning for his three friends to join him. Once they had some space between them and Cianne he spoke low.

"Look, I know the laws, and we are breaking several by being together. I just didn't know if you three would accept us. You're all Coesen," Tristan said. He knew then that he cared what these men thought of him when not many people's opinions mattered to him.

It was obvious that Jacobi was totally enamored with Cianne. Tristan could have told the kid that she was Satan in the flesh and he would most likely have been onboard. Shane was still frowning, and Oloyede…his face was unreadable.

Without a word, Oloyede turned his back on Tristan and went to the table where he was seated.

Tristan shifted from one foot to the other, then lowered his head. He wished that Oloyede would understand but he couldn't ask him to accept his relationship with Cianne. He had no right to ask any of them to accept him. They were Coesen, and now Royal Guards, raised and sworn to uphold their laws.

"This is Maia, my wife," Oloyede said.

Tristan looked up to see the lovely honey eyes that belonged to Maia.

"Maia, this is Tristan. He is my brother in arms."

Maia leaned forward and gave Tristan a hug. "I've heard so many good things about you. It's finally nice to put a face to the name."

"It's nice to meet you as well, Maia." Tristan motioned for Cianne to join him. He took her gently by her hand and arm. "This is Cianne, the reason I breathe."

Maia tried to bow again but Cianne caught her arm. "It's nice to meet you, Maia." To Oloyede she said, "Thank you for taking care of Tristan during the Maatii." She looked at Shane and Jacobi, "Thank you all."

Shane stepped forward. "He was the one who took care of us." He lowered his head then quickly looked up at Cianne. "I am Shane."

"Nice to meet you, Shane," she smiled.

Tristan and Cianne sat at his friends' table for over an hour talking. Maia and Cianne discovered that their due dates were only weeks apart, only Maia had no idea what she was having. He later introduced Brian, Tranae and some of his school friends to his new friends and was happy when everyone got along wonderfully. None of their Middling friends questioned the way the Coesen reacted to Cianne. Every Middling at their school was fed the same story his parents were, the truth. Cianne was from a royal family who had just recently found her.

"Wait...I thought your name was Zaria," Jacobi said, confused.

Cianne and Tristan shared a smile. "It was, but my mother changed it to Cianne shortly after I was born." She took Jacobi by the arm and stepped into his side. Giving Tristan a wink and excusing herself to the others, she said to Jacobi, "Now...Tristan has been speaking of you so highly that you have gained the interest of my grandmother, Sovereign Harper. She is dying to meet the young warrior who saved his team from a monstrously large lion."

When Jacobi looked back at them, Tristan noticed his cheeks were inflamed.

Chapter Thirteen

Cianne reached her out and moved her open hand around the space beside her. When she didn't feel Tristan's body next to hers in the large bed, she opened her eyes and lifted her head slightly off the soft pillow.

Once her eyes confirmed what her hand knew she closed them and laid her head back down. Tristan was up already, yet he hadn't come to bed until four in the morning. He, Brian, Shane, Jacobi and Oloyede had decided to have their own little after-party.

She rolled over on her back and looked up at the ceiling. "Time to get up, I suppose," she sighed. Cianne got out of bed, went into the bathroom, and turned on the shower.

Cianne held onto the railing as she walked down the unfamiliar staircase. It felt a little unusual being in the mansion so early, or sleeping here for that matter. The truth was she never really thought of staying the night with Vivian before last night. It was just where everyone had seemed to converge for drinks after the engagement party.

Tristan and his crew had several drinks, so Vivian insisted they all stay the night.

The house was cool even though it was the first of August. It was a big house, the kind of house that had lots of furnishings but wasn't overly crowded. Even with all its nice décor the house still didn't feel like a home to Cianne. It didn't feel lived-in.

She walked toward the kitchen slowly, looking to her left and then to her right, hoping she would see Vivian or Tristan. But she didn't see either of them or anyone else when she entered the kitchen. What she did see was a large basket of muffins sitting on an island countertop.

Cianne took a blueberry muffin from the basket and grabbed a paper napkin from the basket next to it.

Feeling that she would be a bit more comfortable outside, Cianne made her way to the patio. Once she opened the patio doors she felt the warm breeze of August hit her. She closed her eyes and exhaled before stepping onto the patio, then closed the door behind her. She looked to the pool house where Tristan normally trained.

"Good morning."

Cianne turned around. Someone was sitting at one of the long patio tables behind a half wall of potted trees. She stepped on the terrace and walked around the wall. His back was to her, but she knew it was Whodai. He wore a white tee shirt that clung to his chiseled torso and a pair of khaki shorts. His skin was a smooth dark silk but the Bode mark was clearly visible. As she moved closer to him he turned his head slightly, giving her a view of his profile.

"Good morning," Cianne said. The fingers on her free hand felt the hemline of the summer dress she wore. It was shorter than she liked but Vivian had picked it out, which meant that it was appropriate to be seen in it, she guessed.

Whodai turned in his chair. He gave her a once-over then a smile of approval. Cianne slowly walked over to the table. His eyes were fixed on her as she walked.

"Do you mind if I sit with you?" she asked.

"I'd be honored," he said, standing. Whodai pulled out a chair next to him. The chair was actually closer to him than she wanted to sit but she sat down in it anyway.

His gaze released her when she sat. "Orange juice?" He lifted a large glass pitcher that sat in the center of the table.

"Yes please." Cianne brushed a few strands of hair from her face. She placed her napkin on the table in front of her and the muffin on top of it. "Thank you." She took the orange juice he handed her.

"Those are better warm and with a little butter." He motioned to the muffin.

Cianne looked at her muffin. "It sounds better but I really don't know where everything is here, or how to use them. Viv…" She didn't really know how she should refer to Vivian when talking to other Coesen. Should she use her name or should she say grandma? Cianne didn't know, and Vivian hadn't said. "Everything is usually done for me when I visit." She looked up at him as she fiddled with the corner of the napkin.

Whodai had a beautiful smile; she knew that he came from a wealthy family and that he was widely admired, but she liked that he didn't seem arrogant.

Speaking of arrogant, she thought, *where is Tristan?*

As soon as the thought came to her, she saw two figures moving out of the corner of her eye. She looked down to the pool house/sparring room again. There in the room, in full combat mode, were Tristan and Zeta.

"Congratulations," Whodai said.

Cianne looked back to Whodai, who was watching her watch Tristan. "Thank you."

"So, when is the big day?"

"April 16th," she picked at her muffin.

"I can warm that for you." Whodai leaned over and slowly reached for the muffin.

She quickly covered the top of the muffin. "Oh, no thank you. It's fine." He straightened up. Cianne picked a small piece off her muffin and put it in her mouth.

Whodai leaned back but continued to look at her. Feeling his eyes, Cianne looked over to him again.

"I don't mean to stare," he said. "It's just, for years all I saw was a picture of you when you were a young girl. To be here with you right now is such an honor. You're all grown up and so very beautiful."

Cianne looked down at her muffin, her cheeks flushed.

Whodai cleared his throat. "Forgive me if I've made you feel uncomfortable." He tilted his head to see her eyes better. "You are very shy for someone so lovely. That's rare."

She smiled but still avoided looking at him. "Thank you," Cianne said.

He laughed, causing her to smile bigger. "So," he said, "how was it growing up…" he asked then paused, "normal?"

"Confusing," she admitted. She took a sip of her drink to wash down the dry muffin.

"How so?" he asked.

"It was lonely not knowing what was wrong with me, and having to make sure that no one got too close so they wouldn't see the real me." Cianne took another sip of juice, and placed the glass softly on the table.

Whodai seemed to think about what she said for a moment. "I see," he said.

Cianne continued to pick at her muffin. "What was it like growing up as a Coesen?"

"It can be wonderful for those who choose to accept their roles." She gave him a confused look. He continued, "I chose to live in the Coesen world." Cianne was still confused. "I will explain," he said. "We are a very affluent society. We have locations around the globe that are completely inhabited by *our* people. They are small cities inside of large cities if you will, that has every comfort a Middling city has offer. So, in truth we choose the level of involvement we would like to have outside our Coesen world. There are some of us who have decided to have little to no dealings with Middling people. Some prefer to split their lives between the two worlds. Then there are some who want a normal life and choose to live like

Middlings. But those who do will always at some point need the Coesen."

Cianne looked away. Her mother was one of those who wanted a normal life and who wanted her to have the same, or at least up until she was eighteen. Cianne looked at her muffin and pushed it away. She was no longer hungry.

"Allow me to warm that for you."

His words came out normal but to Cianne the words sounded slow and drawn out. A sudden wave of dizziness rolled over her. She touched the right side of her head as it began to ache.

"Are you alright?" Whodai asked. He got up, squatted down next to her chair, and placed his hand on her forehead.

"Yes, tired I guess," Cianne closed her eyes. "I think I need to lie down for a while." With his help, she got to her feet.

"I can help you to your room," he offered.

Again, his words sounded distorted and drawn out to Cianne. Her head felt as if someone was squeezing it. By far this was the worst headache she'd had in recent memory. Cianne hadn't suffered a headache in so long she forgot how painful they were. She braced herself for the vision that would come. She stood with one arm supported by Whodai and one hand on the table. A few seconds went by and nothing… no vision.

"*Ci?*" Tristan transferred.

"*Bug…that's all,*" she told him.

For a moment, she was scared she was getting a vision and that feeling signaled Tristan. She really needed to work on her fear. Though he seemed to sense some of her anxiety at times, she was relieved it was mainly her fear that he felt. If he had to endure all of her emotions, she feared he'd never leave her side.

Cianne looked at Whodai, who studied her intently.

"No," she panted, "I can manage." Cianne suddenly felt cold. Her head still ached but she was no longer dizzy. She pushed gently off the table and tried to balance on her own two feet.

Whodai stood close by, still holding her arm.

She gave him a nod and he released his hold. Cianne made her way to the patio doors then turned back. "I've enjoyed your company." She managed a smile, then pulled the door open and made her way to the bedroom she was occupying.

Whodai pushed the chair Cianne had been sitting in under the table with his foot. He would have liked more time with her but he knew that the opportunity to speak with her would present itself again. He just didn't know how soon that would be.

He casually walked down the steps toward the pool house. He had been watching Tristan from the patio before Cianne joined him. He wanted to see what the abomination had learned. Interesting enough, the Middling wasn't half bad. In truth, Whodai had to admit to himself that Tristan was better than some of the more seasoned Royal guards.

He would only admit that to himself though.

Tristan the Maatii record breaker. What a joke, he fumed. The Watige Cato or White Lion was what they were calling him now, his so-called friends.

The sheep. How easily they accepted the Middling, Whodai sneered.

He was not so easily swayed. Tristan would not have his allegiance unless he had no choice in the matter. When duty demanded it of him he would have to be the perfect subject. Until then, he would show Tristan who was the best.

Whodai followed the path and was now standing in the doorway of the pool house. Zeta stopped what she was doing and acknowledge him with a bow of her head.

Tristan met his eyes for a moment then turned his attention back to Zeta.

Whodai dismissed Zeta with a wave of his hand. As for Tristan, Whodai didn't expect a bow or even an acknowledgment, but he wanted to show the "White Lion" a thing or two. Actually, he needed to. Every cell in his body demanded it.

"Would you like a little competition?" Whodai asked.

Zeta gave Tristan a look that told him to decline the request. But she must have seen the spark in his eyes because she turned to Whodai and said, "We were actually just finishing up here."

"I wasn't asking you." Whodai said arrogantly. "I was speaking to him." He looked at Tristan.

Zeta lowered her head in submission.

"Maybe some other time," Tristan said. He imitated Whodai's hand dismissal with a sigh. He didn't care for Whodai's attitude and desperately wanted to put him in his place because obviously, no one ever had. Except, Zeta was his mentor and she clearly wasn't comfortable with Whodai's offer. "I was actually headed back inside." Tristan looked at Zeta. "I'll see you in a bit." He started toward the doorway but stopped just as Whodai put his hand up to block his way.

"Believe me," Whodai said with a smirk, "It won't take long."

Tristan backed up some to give Whodai space to enter the room. "Fine," he said. He saw the apprehension in Zeta's eyes but that didn't deter him. What harm could it do? He would spar for a few minutes and then go check on Cianne. He knew she was adjusting to their connection and he was trying not to push or irritate her, but he didn't buy her bug excuse.

Whodai stepped into the room. Both men gave the other a nod to indicate their readiness. Whodai confidently came toward Tristan, who began to strike. Whodai successfully blocked Tristan's first strike and every one after that.

With every blow Tristan threw, Whodai deflected it and subsequently struck back with a powerful blow of his own that landed true. The first few blows that Tristan took stung and each blow that followed seemed to connect with more force and intent, resulting in more pain.

He's too fast, Tristan thought as Whodai's fist connected with the side of his rib cage. His body rose from the floor and shook with the impact. Tristan dropped to one knee. He held his side with one hand as he looked up at Whodai, who stood over him.

"You see," Whodai said, "even with our dear princess on your arm, you are still just a Middling."

Tristan knew that control of one's own thoughts was a vital part of a Protector's training. Allowing Whodai to get under his skin was not an option. He had excellent control of his mind and his body. He was told his skills compared to those of a Protector in their third year of training, and that it was a compliment no Coesen's Protector had ever gotten from any instructor.

He was told that he was remarkable and awe-inspiring, a glorious anomaly. Yeah, he added the glorious, but hey...

Tristan relaxed then flashed to his feet and in the air. He lifted his left leg and connected a solid kick to Whodai's side. Whodai locked Tristan's ankle under his arm but before he could strike, Tristan quickly lifted his free leg up and kneed Whodai under his chin. A tooth chattering crack was heard.

A stunned faced Whodai dropped Tristan's leg and fell back hard on the mat.

Tristan glanced at Zeta for his instructor's approval, but she looked horrified. Confused, he focused on Whodai.

Whodai got to his feet with blinding speed. The combination of blows he threw was so fast that Tristan would never really know how many there were. If Tristan had to put a number to how many hits he sustained he would say about six before the finishing blow knocked him out of the pool house and onto the pool chairs that were ten feet away.

Tristan lay dazed, but managed to lift his head. His back was on the ground and one of his legs dangled over a pool chair. Whodai walked toward him with a look on his face that would chill the devil.

"Lord Whodai," Zeta called out, "S'il vous plait nes pas." She sounded scared. "Notre reine ne serait pas heureux si cette lecon devait se poursuivre."

Whodai stopped and slowly turned to look back at her. Tristan could still see his profile and the grin that spread across Whodai's face.

"Calme-toi mon petit," Whodai told her.

Tristan, who was trying to push himself up, held his hand to his chest and grunted. He felt a stab of pain that increased when he moved.

Whodai crouched down next to Tristan and spoke low enough that only Tristan could hear him. "You are out of your element here in my world." Whodai gestured to their surroundings. "I'd stick to terrorizing college boys if I were you." Whodai stood. He smiled before walking away.

Tristan grimaced as Zeta helped him to his feet. His chest felt like he'd been hit with Thor's hammer. "He doesn't like me much, huh," Tristan said, then winced.

"It's more complicated than that." Zeta helped Tristan sit on the lawn chair she had taken off his leg. She sat down on another chair next to him. "I don't like speaking of things that do not involve me," she said, looking uncomfortable, "but I feel you should know what the complications are. It is not just that you are a Middling. It is not even that you are a Protector who is marrying your ward."

"Then what is it?" Tristan's voice was strained. Christ, it even hurt to breathe let alone talk.

"It is a tradition of ours that has lasted through the ages. We call it the Tandot."

"I didn't read anything about a Thandiot," Tristan grunted out.

"Tan-dot," Zeta spoke the word slower. "There will be no reference of it in any of the standard Annals. The Tandot is a competition of sorts. Early on, a Guardian had his pick of the females. But the hand of each royal heir became a coveted prize. The Four decided that suitors had to prove themselves. Of course, the Arkean heirs were most prized, being as that heir would eventually become Sovereign.

"Over the years the, Tandot process has been perfected with the leaps and bounds of technology. Parents can choose to have their children tested at age five. They are given an array of medical tests and everything is considered. The potential suitor's appearance, health, intellect, and lineage are all scrutinized. Only the best can proceed with the physical testing. Each suitor then prepares for the final stage, which is combat."

"So, what you are trying to say is," Tristan said, "that Whodai won Cianne."

"At the age of sixteen, Whodai beat out all other suitors. None of them were younger than the age of eighteen." Zeta allowed Tristan a moment to absorb what she had just told him. "Tristan, you should stay away from him. I have seen firsthand what he is capable of when he feels he has been disrespected or mocked."

"I've done nothing to disrespect him. If anything, he has gone out of his way to disrespect me." Tristan moved to get to his feet and again felt a sharp pain in his chest. He grunted but continued to push himself to stand. "Whodai isn't just a Protector then," he surmised. "He's a Coesen who won Cianne's hand in marriage by winning a competition. That's just super."

"He isn't just any Coesen. Whodai is the son of Eldra, leader of the Bode tribe and one of the Four." Zeta stood and reached out to try and help Tristan. "...and he isn't a Protector."

Tristan stopped and gazed at her for a moment. "Even better." He waved off her offer to help. Zeta walked with him toward the house. Tristan's eyebrows crinkled. "Then what is his power?"

"His ability, Saik, is similar to that of a Protector. He has speed and strength just as we do, only he seems to be stronger and faster." Zeta reached out for Tristan's arm again as they climbed the few steps to the door. He again refused.

"I didn't read anything in the Annals about Royal Eldra having a son." Tristan climbed the steps a little slower than he usually would have.

Zeta looked confused by the question. "Oh right," she said. "Coesen children are taught our history, we don't often choose to read the Annals unless required. The only offspring who are chronicled in the Annals are the ones who will succeed their parents as head of the family. Raya, Whodai's older sister, will inherit Eldra's title."

"I hope she's nicer than her brother." He moved out the way when Zeta stepped in front of him to get the door.

"I have only met her once; she was pleasant." Zeta answered not realizing he was being facetious.

Tristan gave her a little laugh but calmed when he realized she wasn't getting it. "So why is Whodai here? Does he want to formally call me out?" Tristan walked into the great room, followed by Zeta. She closed the door behind her. Tristan leaned on the back of a chair.

Zeta looked at him, her eyes glossed over.

Does Whodai scare her that badly? Or is she upset about me being hurt? And lord he was hurting more than he wanted to admit.

"I need to take a look at you." Zeta took Tristan's right arm and lifted it over her head and helped him to the other side of the house where her room was located. She opened her door and helped him to an ottoman at the foot of her bed.

Tristan waited while Zeta went into one of three doors that lined the walls of the large room. The room wasn't really what he expected Zeta's room to look like. The walls were white with red stripes or red with white stripes, depending on how one looked at it. The bed was covered with white lace sheets and red and pink pillows. In a corner sat a television on a white bookcase unit. Girly décor filled the room. Posters of shirtless male movie stars and musicians stared back at him.

"Nice poster." Tristan motioned to the back of the door they'd entered the room through. A picture of a shirtless rap artist turned rocker, with his jeans unbuttoned and his happy trail exposed, faced them.

"O…k," Zeta said. But she looked embarrassed. She kneeled next to the ottoman. "Lift your shirt," she ordered.

Zeta watched Tristan slowly lift his shirt. She looked at the large dark purple bruise darkening on the skin over his ribs. She met his eyes briefly as she extended her hands to feel for any damage under the skin, but she hesitated.

Then she touched him and her blood boiled and her head fuzzed at the contact.

"It's that bad?" he asked, looking at her.

Zeta looked up at him, her eyes wide. "No," she whispered, trying to find her voice. *Get hold of yourself,* she repeated in her head. When she slowed her heartbeat, she looked back at the bruise and cleared her throat. "It could have been worse. You need to take care of yourself. We are not the perfect machines we like to think we are. Our bodies have a breaking point, Tristan. We need to rest, mend, and nourish it like any other living thing."

She lifted her hands again. It wasn't as if she didn't touch his skin on a regular basis, she reminded herself. She touched him all the time. But would that be considered touching him or was it hitting him?

Hitting wasn't the same as feeling the warmth of his skin on her fingertips. Or the tingling charge her body felt when his chest rose and fell with every breath. Zeta placed her hands gently on his skin again. Her eyes closed and she relished every second, then she shook off the pleasure. She applied a little pressure as she moved her hands slowly from his chest to the middle of his back. She took longer than what was needed.

"How many?" he grunted.

"Two," she answered, pulling her hands away. Zeta wiped the bruise and the area around it with a piece of gauze that was wet with alcohol. "This cream should help a bit with the discomfort." She squeezed some white cream into her hand and applied the cream to the bruised area. Then she took an ace bandage from her kit. Every time she rolled the bandage around his back, her body moved in a little closer to his chest. Wanting nothing more than to place her lips to those tight pecs of his, she tried to quiet her desire. Eventually she managed to cover part of his chest and stomach with the bandage.

"You never told me why Whodai is here." Tristan lowered his shirt and arms when the bandage was secure.

She took a deep breath. "He is here to formally concede to your union with Cianne. Whodai met with our Sovereign this morning to give his blessing."

"Why would we need his blessing?"

"If he had chosen, he could have requested a duel for her hand while you are in your current state, not being at your full potential. You would have surely lost." She got to her feet. "You should be grateful he conceded. The fight would have been to the death."

"Remind me to thank him the next time I see him," Tristan said sarcastically. He stood. "Thank you for wrapping me up, little one." He winked.

Zeta blushed. It never occurred to her that might speak French fluently. *Why wouldn't he, he understands Coesen dialect as well,* she conceded.

Tristan walked toward the door but turned back, "Hey, any news about what the Four are going to do about me and Cianne yet? I mean, is there going to be a falling out over our wedding?"

"So far, everyone who knows she exists is just rejoicing the coming of our Halo. No one will make a charge right now, because for the first time in over a hundred and fifty years, the four tribes are united as one again and it's all because of Cianne's coming." Zeta watched his expression change from concern to a smile. The butterflies wrestled in her stomach.

Stop, she thought to herself, *stop.*

"Thanks again for the first aid," he said, "and for saving my butt." Tristan walked out of her room.

"You're welcome," she said under her breath. She fell back on her bed and looked up at her ceiling.

I am a despicable person.

Tristan made his way up what seemed to him, an endless spiral staircase. He weighed the degree of discomfort he could bear before taking each step at a normal pace. It wasn't too bad with the bandage on.

After what felt like a climb to the fifth floor, Tristan came to the second-floor bedroom. Cianne lay on the bed. The dress she wore was short, barely covering her upper thigh. His body came to life immediately as he walked over to the bed and stood over her.

Her eyes were open but unfocused.

"Cianne," he said softly.

She didn't move, just stared straight ahead. Tristan backed away from her and looked in the direction she was looking. There was nothing there other than a large wooden wardrobe. He stepped back in front of her line of sight.

She still didn't blink so Tristan lightly touched her face with his fingertips and she focused on him.

"Hey there handsome," she said as she smiled up at him. Cianne lifted up on one arm and moved over on the bed so he could sit. "I just had the worst headache I've ever had."

"What were you just doing?"

"Uh, I guess I may have fallen asleep. Why, was I talking or something?" Cianne covered her stomach with her hand protectively as he sat next down.

"Not really. Any dreams?" Tristan asked. He kissed her on the head.

"None," she said, tugging on his shoulder. Tristan grimaced. "Ah, Zeta was a little rough with you today. I'll ask her to take it a little easier on you." Cianne laughed.

"You laugh but for someone so small she packs a powerful punch." Tristan positioned himself slowly so he was lying next to her. He scooted down so that he was lightly resting his head on her belly. "How's my little girl doing?"

He spoke into her stomach. He felt a nudge where his hand rubbed. Then a number of nudges under his head came one after the other. "Cianne," he said, "I have something to tell you." He wanted to tell her about Whodai winning the Tandot, and about his stakeouts and what he'd been doing the past few weeks. He wanted to tell her everything.

When she didn't answer, he looked up even though her breathing told him she had fallen asleep. With a smile, he lowered his head next to her stomach again.

"Settle down sweetie, mommy is sleeping." The nudging stopped and Tristan got comfortable.

His gaze fell on the nightstand on the other side of the bed. A black leather briefcase sat on top of it. Inside of it was a pair of custom daggers.

The blackest of black twin, double serrated blades, were 17 inches and made of a unique metal. The blade flowed seamlessly, thickening into the guard and hilt. The head of a white lion with its mane flowing out and around the Halo symbol that all Guardians were branded with finished the design.

The daggers had been specially made and given to him by Oloyede, Jacobi, and Shane.

Last night, after the engagement party, they'd brought the after-party back here. Well into the morning they drank, talked, laughed and to Tristan's surprise, pledged their allegiance.

Yes...his friends dropped to one knee after offering him the daggers. With heads bowed and right arms bent over the top of their head, every man had vowed to protect him with their lives. Each of them would die to protect their prince.

Once they stood, Tristan didn't hesitate to do the same even though they protested. But he insisted. Just as they had, he dropped to his knee. After the night died down, Tristan and Shane had sat beside a passed-out Jacobi and a sleeping Oloyede.

Shane lifted a beer to his mouth, took a swallow, them looked over at him. "I was tempted with my brother," he said solemnly. "You see, we were Sentry guards together. He died two years ago during a raid on a Dregan hideout. You know the last thing he told me as I held him in my hands as he bled out?" He paused. "He said, 'See you on the other side.'"

Tristan was speechless.

Shane placed his hand on Tristan's leg. "Why did you say that when you put my hand on the orb?"

Tristan shook his head. "I don't know. We'd been through so much I guess I didn't want to say goodbye," he told him.

Shane smiled. "Brothers don't say goodbye," his said and his smile widened.

Tristan's eyes fluttered as he looked at the case. He raked his gaze over his woman who lay beside him, thinking he was the happiest man alive. He fell asleep soon after.

Chapter Fourteen

Brian lifted the glass up to his lip and paused. "Who-what broke two of your ribs?" he asked before taking a drink from his glass.

"Whodai, and yeah he broke two of my ribs." Tristan placed the menu down on the table. The waitress hadn't returned for their order yet and he sipped the remaining watered-down cola from his glass. Tristan looked around the crowded sports bar. "Why do we come here all the time? Can't we find another place with good food that isn't always so crowded?"

"We come here for the nachos and hot wings. For those, the service and the crowds are do-able. Besides Bar-None is our spot." Brian placed his empty glass back on the table just as the waitress came into sight.

"Sorry guys, we're very busy. What can I get you?"

"It's ok Kim," Brian said, reading her name tag, "Two Grande nachos, and a large order of atomic wings."

"I'll get that started for you and I'll be right back with two refills." She walked away with a bounce and a big smile.

"What's his problem and tell me again why you didn't beat that ass?" Brian watched a family pass their table. He waved at the little boy and the kid waved back.

"I guess he doesn't think I'm good enough for Cianne." Tristan figured a half truth was better than a full lie. "And the truth is, the guy handled me," he admitted. Tristan never had to admit losing a fight before. By all accounts he and Whodai didn't actually fight but it was clear who the victor would have been if it came to that.

"Wow," Brian said in disbelief. He didn't dwell on it though. "So, Cianne is some kind of princess? Does that mean you guys will be moving to Zamunda?" He laughed, moving his hand from the table as the waitress filled their drinks before walking away.

"Real funny…you probably been holding on to that Eddie Murphy joke all day," Tristan smirked. "But yeah, I guess she is," Tristan said, "but I don't think we're moving to Zamunda anytime soon."

"Good, because I don't have time to look over new applicants for your job. My laundry is very important to me and you do it so well." Brian chuckled. They laughed. "Were you even going to even tell me about getting questioned by the police again?"

"Nothing to tell really," Tristan said, "It's not that big a deal." Tristan looked up at the tall redhead named Kim who was standing over them. She placed a steaming plate of atomic wings in the middle of the table. Another woman, dressed exactly like Kim, walked up and handed her the nachos one at a time. She placed one in front of each of them.

"It's a pretty big deal, Tristan. I know your parents are freaked, and Cianne…what did she say about it?"

"Is there anything else I can get you?" Kim asked. The question sounded more seductive than helpful.

"Thank you, this is fine," Tristan said looking up at her. The girl smiled, showing a good number of her white teeth as she walked away.

Brian shook his head. "Anyway," he said.

"My parents don't know much because I'm not using our family lawyer. All they know is that the suspected kidnappers were found dead. They are out of town so much and so busy that they haven't got the time to bother with local news. As for Cianne," Tristan said shrugging, "she hasn't shown any interest in the matter. We haven't actually talked about it." He lifted a nacho that had meat sauce and chives on it. He dipped it into his sour cream and placed it into his mouth.

"She isn't interested? You would think she would be, being as you have been questioned twice," Brian said.

Tristan's expression grew serious. "I was going to talk to her about it but then I realized that it wasn't necessary. She's been through enough."

Brian looked up from his plate. "I've thought about if it were Tranae that all this had happened to. I would have the urge to bust a head or two. That being said, I wouldn't want to trade a life with the woman I love and my child for an 8 x 12 cell that I share with a dude nicknamed Yule Log." Brian giggled. "A dude doesn't get that nickname because he liked the chocolate cake people make on Christmas."

"Why?" Tristan asked, laughing. "Why do you always say stuff like that?" Tristan dropped the chili covered nacho back onto his plate. "I can't eat with an image like that in my head. What…do you save all your nasty comments for when people are eating?"

"What you imagine in your head has nothing to do with me." Brian smiled. "But if you're not going to eat that…" He pulled Tristan's plate over to his side of the table.

"Knock yourself out." Tristan sat back. He wiped his hand with a napkin. "So how does it feel to be a Bobcat?"

Brian looked up from his plate and sat back. His mood seemed to change with the question. "It feels good but it would feel a lot better if we were going together like we planned," Brian said sullenly.

"Life was a lot simpler when we were thirteen."

"Yeah and who would have thought that Cianne Baxter would have given you the time of day?" Brian sort of smiled. "And look at you two now. Getting married and got a baby on the way." Brian wiped his hands with a napkin and placed it on his half-eaten nachos. He looked around at the people in the restaurant.

"You've always been a step ahead of everyone, Tristan. With sports you excelled, as a student, and a friend too. I always thought you were so lucky and that everything came easy for you. Women fall at your feet, men want to be you, and to top it off you're richer than sin." Brian looked at Tristan. "But it wasn't long before I realized that with all your luck, talent, and that huge silver spoon you have stuck up your ass, that whoever picks who gets what, when we are created, couldn't have given it to a better person. What I mean is, you could have been a total tool and you aren't, and that comes from inside."

"Is there anything else I can get for you guys?" the waitress asked, breaking their man moment. Brian and Tristan looked up at the same time.

"I think we're good." Tristan took the bill she handed him.

"Alright, I'll leave that with you, and take your time," she said. She turned to walk away but turned back. "My friend and I were wondering if…" she started, "if you two would like to go out later. You know and hang out."

"I'm sorry—" Tristan started.

"Maybe Friday or Saturday then," she quickly said, before he could finish his refusal.

"He's engaged to be married. That's what he's trying so politely to say," Brian spoke up.

"To the gorgeous brunette with the dazzling eyes?" she asked.

"That's the one," Tristan smiled at her.

She stepped closer to the table. "My friend would really like to get to know you," she said to Brian. Then she looked over to a very attractive blonde who was watching them from an entryway. "And I don't care if you don't. It could be our secret," she said to Tristan.

Brian raised his brows. "Wow," he said with a chuckle. "If you don't respect yourself at least respect—"

"Sorry, we can't," Tristan broke in. "We're both very devoted."

"Pity," she said, her lower lip pushed out. She looked at Tristan for a second longer before walking away.

"Wow, it's like that? What happened to the nice waitress we had ten minutes ago?" Brian laughed.

"That was her," Tristan said, laughing. "Did you see the way that blonde looked at you?" Tristan frowned. "Better not make eye contact."

"Stop playing." Brian reached for the bill. "I got this one."

Tristan firmly held on to it. "I got it. Besides you need to be more frugal now that you are going off to TSU."

"You got a point." Brian retracted his hand. "Don't leave too much of a tip, you might send the wrong message." He pulled his keys out of his pocket and pushed the remote starter that was attached to his keychain.

It felt airless when they stepped outside. The heat rose from every surface in waves. Brian visibly looked uncomfortably hot but he stood in between their cars anyway as if he wanted to say something.

Brian leaned on his car. He quickly moved when the heat from the metal singed his arm. He cursed the car. "So how are Cianne and the baby doing?" Brian rubbed his hot skin.

"You know Cianne isn't one to really complain. Most of the time I'm left guessing." Tristan opened his door and leaned over the driver's seat to start his engine.

"Did she say anything about Tranae?"

Tristan winced. "Not yet but when she does, you'll know." He looked down.

A few days after the engagement party Tranae decided that she and Brian weren't going to work out.

Tristan put his hands in his pockets and played with some loose change he had forgotten about. "I can't tell you to not stress it because I know I would be." Tristan put his hand on Brian's shoulder. "If you're able, try to give her a little space to adjust to everything."

Tristan knew that he wouldn't be able to follow the advice he had just given Brian. If he were Brian, he would find a way to make Tranae talk to him. Camp out in front of her house if he had to. He saw it in a movie a long time ago. It took almost the entire summer for the kid in the movie to get the girl to fold.

But time was what Brian didn't have, he only had a week. Only a week to change Tranae's mind and convince her that a long-distance relationship could work.

Brian shook his head, acknowledging Tristan's advice before opening his car door. "I'll try." His face appeared uncharacteristically stressed.

A rush of cool air hit them which made Brian smile. He seated himself behind the wheel of his car and shut the door. Brian rolled his window down only an inch, to allow as little cool air to escape as he could. "I uh," he said, "guess I'll see you Saturday."

"Cianne and I will be there." Tristan tried to sound enthusiastic. "What day you heading out again?" he asked.

"Tuesday, remember?"

"Right," Tristan rubbed his neck. It was Thursday, August 5th. That left only four days with his best friend.

Tristan wanted to mention that Cianne was working on getting Tranae to come to Brian's off to college party but he didn't want to get Brian's hopes up.

"I told you these would be the best ribs you ever tasted," Dr. Garrison said. He picked up a piece of meaty rib and bit into it. The meat pulled effortlessly from the bone. A little too easily, he had to reach up to catch a falling piece.

Cianne had eaten good ribs before but nothing like these. As soon as she smelled them when Dr. Garrison brought them into the office, she knew she was going to like them. The sauce was a perfect complement but somewhat messier than she would have liked.

"Is this why you don't get sauce on your ribs?" She lifted her hands that were coated with the tasty thick sticky sauce.

"I just like to eat it the way old southerners used to. Some of those sauces can take away from the actual flavor of the meat." He pushed more napkins across the coffee table toward her. "So, we have a few more minutes, what else would you like to talk about?"

They had talked about almost everything and the things she shouldn't talk about, she did anyway—changing key details and putting a Middling spin on everything of course. It was getting easier to censor things now.

There *was* something she wanted to discuss.

Cianne looked to the ring that dangled on the long chain she wore. Even though she never admitted it, she did think about him from time to time. She looked over to Dr. Garrison who was looking at her and probably wondering what she was thinking.

Over the last few weeks they had become…well friends. He was being paid, but she actually liked talking to him. Cianne thought about the first time she met him and how the word "therapist" kept flashing in her head over and over. A therapist was what he was, she told herself as the word seemed to flash in her head every time her eyes blinked. After that first day, the word never appeared to her again.

"My father," she said faintly. She wiped her hands with a wet nap and closed the food container that now held only bones.

"Is there something going on with Joseph that you don't feel comfortable discussing with him?" Dr. Garrison wiped his hands and sat back in his chair. He tossed the wet nap on the food container.

"Well no," she started, "but since you brought him up, I think my dad has a secret girlfriend." Cianne sprung back on the chair with a bounce. "I think he isn't sure how I would react to her so he hasn't brought her around."

"How would you react?"

"I would love it. I've been telling him to date for years," she said then frowned, "but I think he feels like he's betraying my mother's memory or something like that."

"Well if you're fine with it then just ask him. He may just tell you." Dr. Garrison shrugged.

"I'll wait until he's ready," she said. "Joseph isn't the father I was referring to." She cleared her throat. "I have been thinking of my bio-dad lately." She swallowed hard. "I was wondering if it is silly to want to find out who he was. I mean, I think he may be dead. Everyone refers to him in past tense, but I just want to find out about him." Cianne took a breath. "I feel like I should know who he was if I'm going to move forward."

"I see," Dr. Garrison said, "though, I can't really give you my opinion if I don't know all the circumstances."

Cianne rolled her eyes, thinking of how to explain. "Ok, the story I was told is that my bio-dad had done some bad things and when my mother found out she feared for her safety and mine. She ran with me, so I've never seen so much as a picture."

"These bad things, did your mother happen to tell you what they were? Could he be a danger to you?"

"My mother said very little about him. I think that she loved him so much that she couldn't handle talking about him." Cianne grunted. The baby was in a position that made her uncomfortable so she gently pushed on her belly. The baby moved so she relaxed.

When she looked back at the doctor, he looked sad for such a brief moment that she dismissed it.

"Do you have any information about him?" he asked.

"She left a diary," Cianne said. "It mentioned he had a relative that I think would be good to start with."

Dr. Garrison tapped his fingers on the arm of the chair. "How do you think this… looking for your bio-dad…" he said, mimicking the word she used for her birth father, "how do you think this would affect Joseph?"

"I don't know really, but isn't it my choice if I want to look for him?" Cianne asked.

"Ultimately," he told her. "Have you discussed this with Tristan yet?"

"Not yet. He's been really busy lately." Cianne bit her bottom lip.

"Maybe you should wait then. There is so much going on right now with you and your family. Wait to look for him and if you should decide to take up this venture after the baby is here, then I will help you locate him." Dr. Garrison looked at his watch.

"Sounds like a plan," she agreed. "I have waited this long, I guess I can wait a few more months."

Cianne knew that when Dr. Garrison looked at his watch it meant they only had a few minutes left before his next patient arrived. She began collecting her trash.

"I can clean this up," he said. "You need to be going if you are going to make it to your soon to be mother-in-law's in time."

"I almost forgot," she said, as she tried to get to her feet.

Mrs. Bertram was very excited about Tristan's upcoming birthday. She was so excited that she wanted to start planning the party now, even though his birthday was September 3rd, almost a month away. In truth Cianne was just as excited.

Dr. Garrison rushed over to her. "Let me help you up."

When the doctor touched her, the baby let loose a light flurry of kicks, like she did with Tristan's touch. Cianne laughed. It seemed the baby liked Dr. Garrison.

"Thank you." Cianne got to her feet with his assistance. She grabbed her shoulder bag and they walked to the door together. "I will see you Tuesday."

"Tuesday," he said then smiled as he held the door for her. "Drive safe."

"Have a nice weekend," Cianne said as she hurried down the hallway.

Chapter Fifteen

"**Well** young one, how are you feeling?" Dr. Reginald stood over the sink with her hands dripping wet. She reached over to the paper towel dispenser and grabbed a few towels to dry her hands.

"Other than the fact that I'm always uncomfortable now and that I'm finding it hard to get in a good position to sleep at night? My breasts are leaking, and I have really bad heartburn, but I'm fine," Cianne said.

She sat on the exam table with her legs apart to make room for her belly, her belly that looked as if she was hiding a large ball under her shirt rather than a baby.

Dr. Reginald rubbed her hands together to warm them. She then walked over to Cianne and lifted her shirt and began rubbing her partially warmed hands over Cianne's belly. Suddenly the baby kicked hard against her hands.

"She really doesn't care for me much," the doctor laughed.

"It's not that she doesn't like you," Cianne said, "it just seems like she only prefers people I know well to touch my belly."

Dr. Reginald gave her a confused look. Cianne looked at Tranae, who was sitting on a chair watching them, then back at the doctor.

"I've been noticing the difference. When she hears people or I am touched by people she seems to like, she nudges me, like soft kicks. If she isn't familiar with the person's voice or touch, she kicks hard and sometimes I think she balls up," Cianne explained. "I know it sounds crazy."

"Not at all," the doctor said. "Being as she is a special baby, it makes a lot of sense. She's perceptive." She picked up the fetal heart monitor that lay on the counter. She placed the monitor on Cianne's belly and listened.

The sound of a strong heartbeat filled the room. The doctor left the monitor on Cianne's belly for a minute before removing it. She took the paper out of the monitor and looked at it.

"Her heart beat sounds strong." Dr. Reginald placed the monitor back on the counter. "Are you eating ok?"

Cianne giggled. "Whatever isn't tied down."

"Just make sure you don't skip any meals. Don't worry about gaining too much weight, you will fit back in those jeans shortly after you give birth." Dr. Reginald sat down on a stool and rolled it over to the exam table. She lifted Cianne's pants leg and felt around her ankles. "Try eating smaller meals several times a day and that will help with your heartburn. In reference to your breasts, try these pads." She opened a drawer and handed Cianne some samples. "You can find these at any pharmacy. Are you still determined to have the baby in the hospital? You know we have been delivering our babies for decades the old-fashioned way."

"I would feel safer in the hospital," Cianne said.

"If that's what you want, I will make the necessary preparations." Dr. Reginald looked over at the large calendar on the wall that showed it was October 7th then turned back to Cianne. "You are thirty-four weeks so you're going to need plenty of rest in the next few weeks and keep off your feet if you can."

"I can try," Cianne said. She grimaced.

"I want to see you in two weeks. If you start having contractions that are consistent, about ten minutes apart, call me." The doctor stood up and walked to the door and pulled it open. "If you like, I can have an escort show you around the birthing center at the hospital."

"That sounds great." Cianne stepped down off the exam table.

"I'll be back with some information for you and then you are all set to go." The doctor left the room.

"Thanks for coming with me today, Tranae," Cianne smiled.

"I have been waiting for you to ask me," Tranae told her. "And just so you know, I don't mind being backup buddy when Tristan can't make it."

The doctor came back in and handed Cianne a pamphlet. "See you in a few," she said with a smile.

Tranae picked up Cianne's purse and they walked out the exam room and down a small hallway. The waiting room was full of patients and Cianne wondered how many of the women here were Coesen. She waved to the secretary before she and Tranae left out of the office's main doors.

"I guess we should be on our way then," Tranae said. She helped Cianne down a few brick stairs. They walked through the maze of cars to get to theirs.

"You know you are supposed to be loyal to me, not to Tristan. You are my best friend not his." Cianne got in the back seat of her car. She pulled the seat belt out and wrapped it around her, making sure the bottom belt was under her belly.

"I was asked to drive you somewhere and that's what I am going to do." Tranae started the engine.

"Are you going to tell me where?"

"It's a secret and don't start whining. You should be happy to do this considering that party you and his mother threw for him last month." Tranae fastened her seatbelt. "Now sit back and enjoy the ride."

Cianne laid her head back and closed her eyes. The party *was* a little too much. It was held at the Plaza, one of the hottest clubs in the Midwest. Tristan was somewhat surprised, or more like embarrassed, but he accepted it and tried to enjoy himself. Brian even showed up though it was uncomfortable for him and Tranae to be in the same space.

"Thank you for being my friend," Cianne said as Tranae pulled out into traffic.

It had been a hard two months for Tranae. Cianne knew Brian's departure was tough on both of them. After he left for the University, Tranae didn't want to see anyone for the first few days. She would answer Cianne's phone calls but would only speak to her long enough to tell her she was ok. Cianne felt so bad. She and Tristan were the ones who set them up in the first place.

Cianne decided that she wouldn't think about it now. She was going to close her eyes and listen to the sounds of traffic moving around her.

Tranae turned to look at Cianne in the back seat. "Did you sleep the entire forty minutes?"

Cianne opened her eyes slowly. She put her hand on her forehead. "I guess I did."

"We're here." Tranae opened the car door and got out of the vehicle.

Cianne opened her door but had a harder time sliding out of the car. "Where is here?" Cianne asked as she smoothed her long skirt down.

"Follow me," Tranae said, leading the way.

"Is it some kind of an event today?" Cianne stopped and looked around the parking lot that was completely filled with vehicles. "How did you get a parking space at all, and so close?"

"Come on, we're going to be late." Tranae took Cianne by the hand and led the way.

They walked on a long sidewalk that led to a large area filled with chairs facing a beautiful water feature. In front of the chairs and the fountain was a long red ribbon stretched out between two large columns. Cianne searched the crowd for Tristan.

"C'mon, he's over here." Tranae said as they moved through the crowd until they reached one of several large tents. Under the tents were long tables containing lots of food.

"Thank you for getting my package here safely." Tristan kissed Tranae on the cheek.

Cianne looked to the man of her dreams. She lifted her chin and Tristan kissed her. Not the long kiss that she was hoping for but a light kiss, appropriate for being in public.

"Now that you are here we can get started."

Tristan led Cianne to a row of seats that were placed behind the ribbon and in between the large columns. On the other side of the ribbon were rows of seating that faced them. Tranae, who was sitting in the front row on the opposite side of the ribbon waved to Cianne. Cianne smiled but was completely confused.

"What's going on?" Cianne asked.

"Just a few more minutes," Tristan promised.

The seats filled very quickly, leaving a good amount of people standing. Cianne looked at the full figured attractive woman who sat next to her. The woman sat a cute little girl around the age of three on her lap.

"Hello," Cianne said as she waved to the little girl.

The woman smiled at Cianne. Her little girl didn't speak but instead tried to touch Cianne's hair but the woman pulled her down on her lap and lifted a finger to her lips. The woman then pointed to a man who was standing in front of the microphone. Beside him, Tristan stood.

"Hello everyone, my name is Kevin Ford and I would like to thank you all for coming out and supporting this lovely place we have graciously been blessed with. I'm not really a speech giving person but it seems our benefactor isn't much of a public speaker either. I drew the short straw."

Some people in the crowd laughed. Cianne was still confused.

"It's true. I am standing here because I actually drew the short straw five minutes ago." The crowd erupted in laughter when the man pulled a tiny straw from his pocket. The man laughed a little too before clearing his throat. "Alright," he said. "Earlier this year my wife and I lost our brother, Peter Walters. He was a good kid who for some reason, made a bad decision. That decision ultimately led to his death." He paused briefly. "When we received the news of his death and the circumstances surrounding it from the police, my wife and I were devastated."

How sad, Cianne thought as she tried to remember why the name seemed familiar.

"The police described him as a thug or street kid, not the quiet smart kid who studied hard and was the first in our family to go to college. He was just another statistic to them, and I am ashamed to say we…" he said, looking at the woman sitting beside Cianne, "we were beginning to believe that maybe we didn't know him as well as we thought we did. That was until we got a call from this man, Tristan Bertram." He gestured to Tristan.

Cook? Cianne sucked in a breath. She covered her mouth as she glared at the woman beside her. The woman placed her hand on Cianne's leg as she offered her a sweet smile. Cianne looked to Tristan, who gave her a sympatric smile.

"A week after my brother died we got a call stating he wanted to see us, said he had something important to tell us about our brother. When he came to our home that first day, we could not have ever imagined what he would bring to our lives. You see, Tristan did something that he didn't have to do. He felt that we should know that Pete died saving his fiancé's life. That in the end, even though Pete made a bad decision, he was man enough to try to fix it." He paused again as he glanced at Cianne, seemingly holding in his emotions. "So today I would like to thank Tristan Bertram for the wonderful gift he gave my family. He gave the Pete we loved back to us and a beautiful park in place of the rundown school where he lost his life. This place will be known from this day on as the Peter Walters Memorial Park."

If the man at the microphone didn't say this was the place she would have never guessed. Cianne felt a thickness in her throat as she looked around the park. This was the place she had been held and where Peter died for her.

She instinctively clapped with the crowd as her eyes filled with tears.

The crowd continued to clap as Tristan stepped up to the microphone. He briefly hugged the man before speaking.

"I just wanted to thank the community for its patience and the opportunity to build something that I hope will benefit everyone in some way." Tristan looked to Cianne and said, "If my beautiful fiancé, Mrs. Ford, and little Wanda would come up and help us cut the ribbon please."

He walked over and reached for Cianne's hand. She wiped her tears away with her fingers and allowed Tristan to help her to her feet. She wasn't sure who, but someone handed them an oversized pair of scissors. They all put their hands on the scissors and cut the red ribbon.

"The Peter Walters Memorial Park is now open to the public," Tristan sang out.

People slowly walked along the winding paved sidewalks, enjoying the park grounds and taking in all its beauty. Freshly planted trees stood all around them. Bushes and planted flowers completed the green landscape. But the man-made pond that was located in the center of the park sparked the most interest from the guests.

With large decorative boulders and a lovely water feature in the center, it clearly was a beautiful sight. Along the borders of the pond were large iron benches for relaxing, the perfect place to enjoy a long novel or to cuddle with a special someone.

Cianne couldn't take her eyes off the pond.

"It's a beautiful day."

Cianne looked over to see Cook's sister and his niece sitting down beside her on the bench.

"I am so glad the weather cooperated," the woman said.

"It *is* a nice day," Cianne said in agreement. The little girl, Wanda, wiggled and struggled to be free of her mother's arms.

"I should have introduced myself sooner but the crowd kind of took the opportunity. I'm Stacy Ford," she said. The woman extended one hand while holding the toddler tight with the other. "And this little bucket of energy is Wanda."

"It's nice to meet you Stacy, I'm Cianne." Cianne took her hand. "Nice to meet you also, Wanda." Cianne presented her hand to the child.

Wanda stopped squirming and reached both arms out for Cianne.

"May I?" Cianne asked Stacy as she reached for Wanda.

The toddler didn't wait for her mother to release her. She took advantage of her mother's one hand hold and managed to squeeze free. Wanda fell into Cianne's hands.

"Sorry, she's a little hyper," Stacy smiled.

"She's perfect," Cianne said looking at the child. The little girl stood on the bench as Cianne held her around the waist. Wanda put one arm around Cianne's neck and one hand on her belly. She looked into her angel face to see Wanda's large innocent eyes looking back at her. "How old is she?"

"She is two going on thirty. How far along are you?"

"Thirty-four weeks."

Wanda played in Cianne's hair with one hand, singing the word "baby" with every stroke of her other hand on Cianne's belly. The baby inside of Cianne moved beneath Wanda's hand. This caught the girl's attention. She pulled her hand from Cianne's hair and began rubbing Cianne's belly in small circles with both her hands.

Cianne looked out over the pond. Her mind raced, looking for the right thing to say to Cook's sister. What could she say?

"It's hard to believe that an old abandoned school use to stand here. And over there," Stacy pointed, "was a run-down abandoned apartment development."

Cianne looked over to the open space that was now a large playground off in the distance.

"That's one of three playgrounds," she said proudly. Stacy looked at Cianne's tormented face and sighed. "How are you doing?" she asked compassionately.

Cianne looked away from Stacy's gaze. Tears filled her eyes and began to roll down her cheeks as she sat quietly. Wanda continued to rub her belly.

"If there was any way I could have known what he, JC and Nick was up too, I…" Stacy stopped.

"Do you need me?"

Tristan stood talking with Stacy's husband and Mr. Bertram a good distance away. Cianne couldn't see his face but she saw him looking in her direction.

"Always, but I'm good." Cianne sniffed and wiped her tears away. Her attention went back to Stacy. "Peter is the only reason I am sitting here today." She wiped more tears from her face with the help of Wanda.

"No cry," Wanda pleaded.

"He cared for me. He brought me home cooked meals and prenatal vitamins for my baby. Peter tried to help me escape, and that's why he isn't here with you and your family." Cianne felt a sadness she hadn't felt since she looked into Peter's lifeless eyes as he lay on the cold floor of that school.

"I'd like to think he's here still. Watching us and keeping us safe," Stacy smiled. Her face looked sad but at the same time happy. "When I think back to all those days he came by my house for dinner... Peter would eat, and then he'd ask for extras to take back to school with him. At least that's what he'd told us. I should have known something was wrong. He was visiting way too much." Stacey cleared her throat. "Well," she said, "Let's not make this a sad day." She looked over at her daughter who was now leaning into Cianne and dozing off on her belly. "She likes you. Wanda never lets anyone really touch her, other than family, uh and Tristan."

"She's a beautiful little princess." Cianne continued to rub little Wanda's back.

"You know, he was very worried about how you would react to being here again. He loves you so much." Stacy looked over to Cianne and smiled. "And he is totally devoted to you. I can't tell you how many times my husband and I heard him say he was engaged," she said, laughing. "He is really a wonderful person, doing all this for us."

"He is amazing." Cianne smiled.

"We are totally indebted to Tristan, taking care of all the funeral arrangements and being there," Wanda said. "Believing in my husband like he did… No one would have taken a chance like that with someone they didn't know. We are so very grateful for him."

Cianne sat mesmerized as she listened to Stacy tell her about Tristan. He kept all of this a secret just to surprise her. And it was a good surprise, because she had no idea that Tristan had even contacted Peter's family.

"Wanda's asleep," Tristan said.

Neither of them had heard him approaching and both women looked up. Stacy smiled.

"She's taken an interest in Cianne," Stacy said.

"Let me take her to Nana for you." Tristan lifted the toddler off Cianne.

Wanda cried and began to reach for Cianne until she saw it was Tristan who was lifting her up. She wrapped her tiny arms around Tristan's neck and lowered her head on his chest and closed her eyes.

"I'll be right back," he told them.

"Hey sweetie," Cianne's father called to her.

Cianne turned her head around to see her father walking over to her. He wasn't alone. Alongside of him was a woman. He motioned for Cianne not to stand.

"Hi daddy," Cianne said, beaming. "So, you knew about all this and kept it a secret?"

"Well…" He smiled.

"Yeah, you're good at keeping secrets." Cianne twisted her smile. Her father did the same. Cianne then looked at the woman next to him.

"This is Alex," Joseph introduced.

Alex put her hand out. Cianne stood up with the speed of a woman who was not carrying a large ball of baby inside her. She reached out and hugged Alex. They embraced each other.

"I have been waiting patiently to meet you," Cianne said, releasing her.

"See Alex, I told you she would like to meet you. There was nothing to be afraid of." He took Alex's hand in his.

"It's nice to meet you too, Cianne." Alex smiled with relief.

Cianne introduced Alex and her father to Stacy. The three struck up a conversation that Cianne tried to be a part of but she just couldn't stay focused. "Excuse me," she said eventually.

She made her way to the pond. She sat on a large rock and leaned back; looking over her shoulder she watched the water glisten in the sun. She loved the way water moved.

"You're a vision sitting there," Tristan said. He walked over to her and laid his hand on her leg. "How is my Nadia doing?"

"Nadia?" Cianne eyebrows wrinkled.

"You don't like it?" He sat beside to her.

"Don't know, where did you get that name?"

"**I** got it from the Annals. It was the name of an Arkean princess from your blood clan. It means hope." Tristan rubbed her leg as he looked at Cianne. She seemed a million miles away to him. "Is something wrong?"

Cianne looked at him. "This," she said, sighing. She looked all around. "This is so beautiful. I understand why you wanted it to be a surprise. I don't think I would have been able to see this place again, the way it was." Cianne placed her hand on his. "But how did you come up with this idea?"

"When I visited Stacy and Kevin to give my condolences, I had to drive by this place. They actually live a few blocks from here. After the funeral, they invited me to their home again. After speaking with Kevin for a while, I quickly realized Peter's motivation to do what he did. Kevin was laid off several months previously from his construction job and Stacy was struggling trying to make ends meet with her job. Their home is nice enough inside but the neighborhood isn't the kind of place they had envisioned raising a family in."

The laughter of children playing distracted them both. They looked in the direction from which it came. Several children were running in the grass with small multi-colored windmills. Tristan smiled, anticipating the day when his baby would be running with other children at the park.

"Kevin and Stacy's neighbors and friends were very kind and seemed like good people; they welcomed me instantly," he continued. "So, as I drove home that night, I thought of you raising Nadia alone with no help and having no park for her to play in or a safe place to live. So, I came by a few days later and proposed a sort of solution to some of the things I could help with. They liked the plan and I set it in motion. This is the first wave of changes we plan to bring to this neighborhood," Tristan said smiling.

After he finished speaking, Tristan and Cianne both sat watching the way the water moved. They didn't say too much to each other. He loved that they were the kind of couple that could just sit and enjoy each other without too many words. They were content with just being. Everyone else seemed to be enjoying themselves as well. Even Tranae looked as if she was having a good time.

They sat there until they heard a person clearing their throat behind them. They both turned around at the same time to see Tristan's parents standing a few feet away.

"We have to get on our way, son. We have to be in Houston early tomorrow." Mr. Bertram smiled.

"*So...that's where your gorgeous smile came from,*" Cianne transferred.

Tristan raised his brow at Cianne as he stood then lifted her to her feet. She probably hadn't seen his father smile too often.

"I wanted to tell you before leaving how nice this turned out, and what a success your first solo project has been. I am very proud of you," Lesley Bertram said. "I can't wait to see the rest of your plans." He put his hand out to shake his son's hand.

Tristan took his father by the hand and then leaned in toward him. The hug was brief but meant a lot to Tristan. When they released, they both sort of backed away. Tristan felt a sense of accomplishment that he never felt from getting good grades, or being the best at everything. This was a moment he never really thought would happen. His father seemed proud of him.

"Thank you, Mr. Bertram, this park will mean a lot to the people living here." Cianne hugged him.

Mr. Bertram's arms wrapped around Cianne's waist but he looked over her shoulder at Tristan, probing his face. Tristan shrugged. Once her hold around his neck loosened, Mr. Bertram held her hands in his.

"Although I can't say I mind being hugged by my beautiful daughter to be, I am curious to know what I've done to deserve this one?" Mr. Bertram asked.

"Allowing Tristan to do all of this," she said with a smile.

Mr. Bertram looked around Cianne to Tristan again who looked a little puzzled, then enlightened.

"I think Tristan has something to tell you." Mr. Bertram kissed her on the cheek.

"See you later, sweetie," Mrs. Bertram said, kissing her on the cheek as well.

Tristan took a confused Cianne by the hand. He led her to an empty bench and sat her down.

"I didn't need my father to finance this project, Ci." Tristan explained. "Or any other project, although I may want to partner with him sometime in the future. I funded and oversaw the park project myself. Now the rebuilding of the neighborhood will be a joint project between me and the city but most of the money will come from my side."

Cianne still looked at him blankly.

"I don't need any money from my father. Yes, my parents are wealthy, separate and as a whole, but I myself am pretty well off too."

"Enough to do all of this?" she questioned.

"My grandfather was Patrick Arlington." Tristan paused when he saw that she recognized the name. Of course, she would, everyone knew of his grandfather. Patrick Arlington was one of the richest men, if not *the* richest man in the world. "He was my best friend and I was his only beneficiary."

Cianne took a moment to let the information sink in. Tristan was a billionaire or possibly richer than that. "I won't have a problem signing a prenuptial agreement," she said the first thing that came to her mind.

He looked at her. The edges of his lips curled into a smile. "I wouldn't allow it. All of what I have is nothing if I don't have you to share it with. And if I ever lost you, I would be so devastated that money would have no meaning to me." Tristan kissed her hand. "So, if the day comes that you decide you don't love me anymore and you want to part ways, then you and Nadia deserve half if not more of what I have. But know that what you leave me with, I will use every cent to try and win you back."

"I will never leave you, Tristan."

"Good," he said. Then he kissed her the way she wanted to be kissed earlier.

As the evening came to an end, Cianne found Tranae under a tree talking on her phone. She hung back a little, not wanting to interrupt the call. Tristan, who spent most of his time at this function with her, had to eventually go off and talk business with Kevin and a few others.

Cianne liked Kevin, Stacy and little Wanda. So, when Stacy asked her and Tristan to dinner on Sunday, Cianne agreed.

"How you holding up?" Tranae asked as she walked up beside her.

Cianne whipped her head around to find Tranae watching her. "My feet are killing me and my back is beginning to ache," she admitted. She looked at Tranae's eyes. They looked puffy with a hint of redness to them.

"Stay here then. I'll get the car," Tranae said, turning away from Cianne's wondering stare. "You sit down."

Tranae walked off toward the front of the park where they had parked.

Cianne sat down on a bench, knowing that as soon as she sat down her feet would thank her, but when she stood up again the pain would be worse than before. It was another wonderful symptom of pregnancy that she could do without. She grimaced as she moved her foot inside her shoe.

Even walking a few feet to the car is going to be painful, she thought, and was about to stand until she saw Tristan standing next to her. Again, she hadn't heard him coming.

"Tranae sent me. I never considered how hard all this may be on you and Nadia." He scooped her up in his arms, cradling her. Cianne swung her arms around his neck. He touched his forehead to hers. *"I'm going to run you a nice bath and rub the soreness from your feet tonight."*

"I think I am going to stay home tonight, Tristan," Cianne told him.

She loved sleeping in Tristan's bed but recently she was having trouble sleeping. The urge to be with him had become increasingly nerve-wracking, seeing as they agreed that it would be better to wait until after the baby was born to be intimate again.

The connection between them was growing every day and Cianne felt that if they were intimate and she lost control again, she may unknowingly do something to risk the baby's safety or his. He agreed reluctantly, accepting that her abilities were totally unpredictable right now.

The other reason she didn't want to sleep in his bed was because Tristan was a touchy-feely sleeper. He was one of those people who held you tight and didn't let go until he woke up. Her body heat had increased during her pregnancy. Coupled with his body heat, his bed was now a sauna instead of a comfortable bed like it had been at one point.

"Alright," he said.

Cianne knew that he wouldn't argue with her even though he preferred for her to sleep at his house. And even though there hadn't been any security issues, Cianne knew that Tristan wouldn't let her stay anywhere without him, which made her feel safer than the president.

Tristan walked effortlessly toward the waiting car as if he was carrying five pounds instead of a hundred and thirty. His breathing didn't quicken and his pace was steady. Once there, he gently placed her in the backseat of the car, helping her with the seatbelt and kissing her before closing the door.

"Good night Tranae and thank you for coming."

"No problem, Tristan." Tranae started the engine after Tristan tapped the roof.

The ride home was virtually quiet except for the sound of breakup music playing. The theme of the music told Cianne it was best not to ask any questions because when Tranae was ready she would unburden her heart.

Getting home took less time than getting there, Cianne thought as the car pulled onto one of two empty parking pads next to her house.

Tranae turned off the engine and walked around the car to help Cianne out. Taking on some of Cianne's weight, Tranae helped her to her front door. Once the door was opened Cianne braced herself on the frame.

"I can make it from here," Cianne told her friend. She knew Tranae wasn't in any mood for anything other than a long candle-lit bath and streaming music.

Tranae walked down the porch steps. When she reached the last step, she turned back to Cianne, who was waiting to see her get to her door safely.

"Have you ever thought of looking into the future? You know, just to see if you and Tristan are still a couple?" Tranae looked up at her with doe-like eyes.

"No. To be honest Tranae, I think that looking at the future is redundant. I mean if you believe in fate, then it's no point, everything is already written. If you believe in contingency or chance, anything can happen. Every little decision we make can change the direction of our lives. So, regarding the future, I choose to live life in the now versus watching it play out in my head," Cianne half-smiled with a shrug.

Tranae sort of smiled back before turning and walking across the street to her brightly lit house. Cianne watched her friend open the door and go in before she walked through her door and locked it.

She took a long shower and put on her night clothes. Before going to bed she placed a clean blanket and pillow on the sofa in the basement for Tristan, who thought she didn't know he slept there when she stayed home—just because he left before she woke.

Chapter Sixteen

Sunday, October 10th

The two-story townhouse was a little over 800 square feet total. The two bedrooms, one bath residence had a 9x7 L-shaped kitchen that contained a single piece of off-white linoleum flooring, the kind of flooring that seemed to attract stains. A small round table with four metal chairs was placed in a small carpeted dining area. As you entered the front door you were in a square 14x14 foot living room that didn't seem big enough to hold a sofa, loveseat, a matching chair, and a small entertainment center but it did.

This was the home of Kevin and Stacy Ford and their little tyke Wanda. It didn't matter how big or small it was because to watch them, to see how they interacted with one another, Tristan knew that they were happy in spite of the cramped conditions.

"Would you like something more to drink?" Stacy called from the kitchen as she poured Cianne another glass of tea.

"No thank you Stacy," Tristan said. He lifted his glass to let her see that he was still working on what he had. Tristan glanced over at Cianne who was sitting at the dining room table a few feet away. He winked.

"I like them." Cianne gave him a little smile.

"I knew you would."

Tristan looked at Kevin, who was explaining to him the dynamics of a television show that happened to be playing in the background. The brief exchange with Cianne hadn't diverted him much; he was able to catch up with the plot with no problem.

◉

"I really enjoyed the chicken parmesan, Stacy." Cianne flipped through one of the photo albums that Stacy pulled out.

"I can give you the recipe if you like," Stacy offered. "That is Peter when he was at camp. He was twelve." She pointed to a picture of a skinny kid with glasses that seemed to cover his entire face.

"He was a little guy," Cianne said, looking up from the album at Stacy.

"Yeah, he didn't start bulking up until a year after this was taken." Stacy looked at Cianne and smiled.

A silent notification went off in Cianne's head. "May I use your bathroom again?" Cianne asked.

"I remember those days." Stacy waved her hand.

Cianne rose from her seat and walked behind the sofa Tristan and Kevin were seated on to get to the steps that led to the second floor. As she walked up the stairs the phone rang.

When Cianne came back down the stairs a few minutes later, both men were on their feet, Tristan near the front door and Kevin in the kitchen, behind the only dividing wall on the first floor with Stacy.

Tristan looked at her, not a look that would suggest something was wrong, but a calm look with just a hint of a smile. Calm would normally not worry her, but in Tristan's case, a quiet calm accompanied with a slight smile was a precursor. What would he need to be that calm about? The look was the kind that a demolition specialist gave right before blowing up a building.

The look Tristan was giving her was one she had seen twice before. The first was when Tristan and Nick met for the first time. The second, was that day in the police station when Tristan attacked Nick and his friend.

Why can't I feel his fear like he feels mine?

If she could, then maybe the composed look he was flashing her as she walked over to him wouldn't have looked so frightening?

"Kevin wants me to meet a friend of his," Tristan said casually. He gave her a quick peck on the lips. "Will you be ok if I leave for a few minutes?"

What kind of friend is this, who can't come and knock on the door and be welcome in the Ford's home?

"I'll be fine," was all she said as she gave a half-smile.

Stacy followed Kevin out of the kitchen. Cianne thought the expression she saw on Stacy's face might have been fear or worry, but Stacy quickly replaced it with a smile.

"All set?" Kevin asked Tristan.

Tristan nodded and turned toward Kevin as he opened the front door. Cianne heard Kevin lock the door from the outside a few seconds later.

"Would you like a piece of coffeecake, Cianne?" Stacy turned and disappeared back into the kitchen.

It was a short trip. They didn't even leave the housing complex, but the large scope of the community was bigger than Tristan originally thought. Kevin and Tristan waited in the car in silence for ten minutes before two figures stepped out of the space between two rows of townhomes.

"That's them right there." Kevin pointed.

Tristan looked out of the car window and into the shadows that surrounded two figures a good distance away. He opened the passenger side door of the old Accord and stepped out onto the concrete. Kevin did the same. Tristan followed Kevin on a dirt path that was barely lit by the badly spaced lights attached to the sides of the townhouses. The two dark figures slowly approached them and stopped just a few steps away.

Tristan quickly sized them up. The taller and older of the two was dressed in fine clothes and nice dress shoes. He was a big guy, a little taller than Tristan and a lot heavier. He wore one piece of jewelry, a ring on his pinky finger that didn't quite blend with the rest of his expensive attire. The firearm that he unsuccessfully tried to conceal inside a shoulder holster under his jacket raised a red flag.

Tristan hoped this guy was smarter than he looked.

The shorter, younger of the two was just a boy. He dressed like most teenagers did. It was a phase Tristan was happy to say he never went through. The baseball caps and jeans still had price tags, something Tristan still didn't understand. The dim street light gleamed off the large diamonds in one of the youngster's ears as he moved around anxiously. He seemed like a kid who tried to work hard at looking threatening, but he didn't and wasn't. Although, a wannabe gangster is often times more dangerous than the real thing.

"This is Lo," Kevin told Tristan as he glanced at the larger of the two. Then he looked to the kid and said, "And this is Maddox. He has some information for you."

"Mad-dog, man," Maddox said. "My name is Mad-dog, jeesh."

Tristan figured the boy was about fifteen years of age.

"Why you tryna put me out there like that?" Maddox complained. Every word he spoke was accented with an exaggerated facial expression and hand movements. "I don't want this…" Mad-dog said, giving Tristan a suspicious look, "*man* knowing my government and shit."

Maddox seemed a little on edge.

Kevin stepped forward, prompting Mad-dog to take three quick steps back before the man named Lo placed a hand firmly on the kid's shoulder.

"Don't forget who you're talking to boy." Lo said in a low husky voice as he glanced at Kevin. He looked back to Mad-dog. "Now, I want you to tell this man," he said, glancing at Tristan, "everything you told Peanut."

Mad-dog slightly cowered. "I uh, I don't mean no disrespect Key. I mean Kevin," Mad-dog said sheepishly. Lo dropped his hand and the kid seemed to relax, a bit. He swallowed hard and began. "Back on May 14th I was over on Mayfield and Denton Avenue over in Grayson. I was trying to get at this chick so I went to her job. She works at this food spot that got the best oxtails in the city." He looked up, realizing by their faces that no one cared about those details. "So, when I was sitting in the joint waiting for her shift to end, I saw Pete and that fool Jason. They were with two other dudes I didn't know. I stepped to 'em; you know to say hi to my man Pete and shit. So, I get to the table and I say 'what up' and Pete looks at me all nervous and shit, like I was busting up something vital. Then he looks across the table to the other two dudes before saying hi, like he needed permission."

"What happened after that?" Kevin asked.

"He said 'hi'. I took it that he was handling some business so I dipped with the cutie," Mad-dog said.

"Is there anything you can tell me about the other guys he was sitting with?" Tristan asked.

Mad-dog looked at Tristan with his lips turned up. He looked away as if he wasn't going to answer that question.

"The man asked you a question, boy," Lo hissed, "and if I have to remind you of your manners toward my cousin's guest again…" Lo laughed, a husky threatening kind of chuckle.

Mad-dog straightened up instantly and looked at Tristan. "Yeah," he looked up as if he was thinking for a moment, "the white dude he was wit, had short hair like a soldier. He had a tat on his neck too, wires or some shit like that. And he was some kind of rent-a-cop." Mad-dog looked at Lo, "That's all I know." Lo looked at Tristan as if asking if he was finished questioning the teen.

"Thank you," Tristan said, to both of them.

Mad-dog waited for Lo to nod before turning away. He took a few steps then stopped and turned to face them again. "I think he worked for a school or something," he said. The boy's tone and grammar were different now, normal and without all the street flavoring. "Campus Security was stitched on the pocket of his uniform."

M. Patton, was the name that flashed in Tristan's mind. It was the name of the security guard who broke up his fight with Nick and JC a few months before the kidnapping.

"I hope that helps you find your man," Lo said, in the same husky voice. He looked Tristan over again, raising an eyebrow, and a smile slowly formed on his face as if he knew not to judge a book by its cover. "Don't be a stranger, Key," he said, as he turned to walk in the direction Mad-dog had gone.

"So," Tristan said as he sat in the passenger seat of the car and turned to Kevin. "You are the Key in KeyLo?" The word KEYLO happened to be spray painted on the sides of buildings and other surfaces here and all around the city. Tristan even noticed the tag on the side of a bus in West Hills once.

"I was young and stupid. I saw little to no future for myself so I decided that I would make one. It wasn't until I met Stacy that I realized I could go at it differently." Kevin pulled in front of his townhouse.

"How does Lo feel about the redevelopment that's in the works? Won't it mess with his money?" Tristan knew that this was a drug infested area and that it had nothing to offer kids like Mad-dog—Maddox. He wanted to change that, and he couldn't wait until Kevin and his family moved into their new house.

"He won't be a problem," Kevin said confidently. Somehow Tristan knew Kevin meant it.

Being tired was something she learned to accept. What she didn't understand was how Tristan was running around like the energizer bunny. After leaving Kevin and Stacy's he just dropped her off and got her settled before leaving again.

She didn't ask any questions about where he and Kevin went or what they did in the half an hour they were gone. Again, she was afraid of what he might tell her.

Cianne rolled over in her bed. On her nightstand sat her Mother's diaries. They had sat on her nightstand for months without Cianne so much as flipping through a page or two. She stared at the leather books for five minutes.

Her mother was on her mind lately. The fact that her mother would never see her baby or get to know the Tristan she loved, the older Tristan, hurt Cianne. She lay on her side with her hands under her face. Sadness filled her as she closed her eyes.

When Cianne opened them, she did so slowly, and a familiar blinding bright light encircled her. As before, when the light faded and she could focus, Cianne was standing in a recognizable room. It was the living room downstairs in her house—the house she lived in currently, but all the furniture was different. It was different but she recognized it all because it was the furniture from their old house. Her parents brought it to this house when they moved in, and when her mother passed away her father replaced all the furniture.

"I was wondering if you were going to return." A low voice came from behind Cianne.

She twirled around with a smile on her face. She recognized the soft voice at once. Her mother was lying on their colorful sofa with a light blanket on her feet and a book in her hand. She and her mother had cuddled on that sofa so many times when she was a little girl. Cianne remembered tracing the patterns with her finger as she fell asleep in her mother's arms while they watched television after dinner on the nights her father worked late.

"I'm not really sure how it works yet." Cianne smiled.

"Cianne!" Kayla reached for Cianne. "You're pregnant!"

Cianne didn't note that her mother used her current name as she walked toward her until her very large belly was close enough to touch. "I'm thirty-five weeks," Cianne said, smiling.

Kayla placed the book down on the table and rubbed her belly gently, making large circles with her hands. Cianne felt a burst of joy as her mother smiled and spoke to the baby. This was something that she would never have guessed possible a year ago. Her mother who had been gone for ten years was touching her baby belly.

"Mom," Cianne kneeled. Surprisingly she was able to get to her knees with no discomfort or pain, like she wasn't being weighed down by an anvil.

Kayla touched her face.

"I'm in love with him, Tristan." Cianne took her mother's hands in hers. "He is everything to me. I never imagined being whole again when you left me. And I never thought that I could ever have this but you gave me someone who loves me and that I love." The tears ran freely from Cianne's eyes. "We are going to be a family soon. When you left me, I thought that I would just exist until it was my turn to die. He showed me that I deserve more. He loves me just the way I am."

Kayla sobbed as Cianne hugged her tightly. Her baby was having a baby, and little Tristan Bertram was the father. Even though she saw some of his future when she touched him just a few weeks ago, she didn't see a baby.

Actually, the vision she saw ended with the conception of love between Cianne and Tristan, the day they first spoke to each other at school. That's how she knew where to move, from the image of Tristan in his high school letterman's jacket.

She hadn't seen past that.

Kayla was overwhelmed with the unknown now. Cianne was happy and that's what every mother hoped for but was that happiness going to last? Life and love were so unpredictable. She had to see…

Kayla had to see what would happen to her daughter. Maybe she could see Cianne's future now, maybe Kayla could use the baby to see.

She held Cianne tight and closed her eyes.

Cianne held her mother close. She missed feeling her and smelling her; she missed seeing her. She took in a deep breath of her mother's scent and hoped that she could remember it when this moment was gone. She inhaled deeply again before slowly separating from the embrace.

"Mom…" Cianne said. Kayla's face was pale and her eyes were open wide. "Is everything ok?"

A line of blood ran from Kayla's nose. Her mother lifted her hand to her nose and smeared the blood across her face. Cianne got a tissue from the table and handed it to her.

Kayla's eyes were teary. "Everything is fine baby, I'm just so happy for you. I hoped for your happiness."

"You didn't know I would love him?" Cianne asked.

"No baby. I could only feel the love in him. I felt that his love was genuine and unconditional. I am so happy that it all worked out."

It suddenly dawned on Cianne that she was in her own living room. Her younger self could walk in on them or even worse, her father could. At this point he was still in the dark about The Coesen. "Where is dad and little me, what day is it?"

"Let's see, it's about one in the afternoon and the date is May 20th. You are at school and dad is at work. Later you will be going to the mall with Tranae and her mom," Kayla said, smiling. "Your first playdate with the kids across the street."

Cianne felt as if someone grabbed her heart and started squeezing. She looked at her mother, who didn't look sick. Maybe tired, but not sick, considering what day this was.

"Mom, today…" Cianne cried out as she was yanked back. "Nooooooo,"

Cianne sat up in her bed, back in her bedroom. Her heart raced as she held the sheets clutched in her hands.

She didn't get to say goodbye. She'd briefly gone back to the last day of her mother's life and she didn't get to say goodbye.

Cianne balled up in the fetal position and just cried. Tonight, she was grateful that Tristan couldn't feel her sadness…because she wanted to just be alone right now.

Chapter Seventeen

October 11th, Monday
9 a.m.

"**W**hen can you be here?" Vivian used her shoulder to press the cell phone to her ear as she chopped onions into little cubes for her omelet.

She knew that Cassius would want to finish his task before returning to her. He invested six months already and was close to annihilating a long-time opposing faction but she needed him. He was the best.

"We can be there tomorrow, by 8 a.m. What are the details?" Cassius was ready to serve his ward and dear friend without complaint.

"A sentry called a few minutes ago." Vivian stopped chopping and wiped her hands with a towel. "It seems he has been getting a number of calls from Curtis Willard."

"Hmm," Cassius said.

Vivian heard a little sigh behind his acknowledgment. This was because Curtis Willard was a Coesen who was out of his mind.

"Curtis Willard is notorious for reporting unsubstantiated information. He is known as a quack, Vivian."

"I realize this Cassius, and the sentry in charge of taking reports for this region usually takes Curtis's reports and files them..."

"But this time?" Cassius asked.

"This time, Curtis Willard mentioned Dr. Garrison, Cianne's therapist. It seems that Curtis is a janitor in Dr. Garrison's office building. He seems to think that Dr. Garrison is different."

"What does he mean by...different, other than that personal issue I advised you about."

"Willard is saying that he would get a feeling or sense the things that Garrison had done. He said that the sins of the doctor were open to him whenever he focused on him hard enough. He said THE-RAPIST flashed before his eyes whenever he looked at the man. Now, he claims that he senses nothing when he focuses on the doctor, nothing at all." Vivian knew that Curtis had lost most of his mind but he was still a Coesen and he still had an ability that could be trusted.

"So, what do you think?"

"I think it is worth looking into," Vivian said into the receiver.

Cassius sighed again. "May I speak freely?" Cassius asked.

"You may always speak your mind Cassius, you know this."

"I don't understand why she was allowed treatment by this...this person anyway. He is a sick individual and should be locked away forever. We should have taken care of him when we became aware of his problem and our Halo should have never been exposed to that freak." Cassius' voice raised an octave, making his irritation clear to Vivian.

"Cassius, you know our laws. We are to stay impartial, and most of all keep out of, if not limit our influence in, Middling affairs. His sexual appetite, or crimes, is not our concern. What should concern us is that he is highly respected in his profession and is the best in his field. We needed the best for Cianne and it seems that he has done his job. She is doing better than she was before the kidnapping, according to Joseph and Tristan," she said then paused, "remember our laws Cassius."

"I didn't mean to let my personal feelings—" Cassius started, sounded regretful.

"This is top priority, Cassius. I need to know what is different about the doctor."

"I will treat it as such."

Vivian disconnected the call and placed her cell phone on the counter. She hoped that this would end up being nothing. That Cassius would find that Dr. Garrison may have just miraculously changed. But she knew better—even if he had changed in some way, Curtis should still see something. Everyone emits energy and unconscious thoughts.

Whatever the case, Cassius would find out what was going on so he could get back to his mission.

Minutes to midnight.

It only took Raul twenty minutes to get the information Tristan needed, but almost twenty-four hours to call Tristan back on the burner phone he purchased at the convenience store the night before after finding out what Mad-dog told him.

Raul was an old acquaintance of Tristan's from a private school in Europe they both attended, and he was a very good hacker. All you needed was his personal number, which only a select few had, a throwaway cell phone, also known as a burner, and his fee.

The fee varied according to the level of illegality. If you wanted something as simple as a locker next to a girl you had a crush on, the fee would be a few hundred or so. If you wanted personal information the fee jumped a great deal. The locker change was worth the money and so was the address for M. Patton, a single, thirty-two-year-old, campus security guard for Kennecott University.

He parked a mile away from Patton's house, grabbed a flashlight from under his passenger seat; his vision clarity was excellent but fluctuated at times, tonight being one of those times.

Tristan walked in the shadows to get there; it was dark at 218 Druid Lane. With no apparent movement inside Tristan could only assume that Patton was either asleep or not home.

Tristan didn't really have a plan. What he wanted first and foremost was to prove that this guy was involved, that this Patton was the ringleader. Nick and JC meant nothing.

Someone had come up with the plan to kidnap and extort money for Cianne. Someone shot Zeta and then went to the school and killed Peter with the intent to kill Cianne. Nick and JC could never be confused for thinkers, and the plan was pretty good and might have worked if it wasn't for them having worst luck in the world—kidnapping a Coesen.

Tristan walked to the rear of the house and stepped inside the rundown yard of a shabby one-story ranch-style home. The fence was hardly standing as Tristan quietly ducked through a missing section of it. The dirt patched back yard had a shell of a flatbed truck leaned against a towering tree that shaded the way to the back door of the house. Tristan stood by the tree for a few seconds as he looked into the quiet house through what looked like a kitchen window.

He stood still as he looked around. Nothing moved in the darkness and only a street lamp gave off light but it was quite a distance away. Tristan looked at the window again. It was cracked open.

He should have invested in an air conditioner, Tristan thought as he crept under the window, again sticking to the shadows. Once underneath it, he jumped up with ease and pulled himself up on the brick window ledge. The screen was missing, so Tristan carefully raised the window with his gloved hands and leaned his head inside to make a quick assessment of the area.

The house was quiet so Tristan slipped inside, being careful not to disturb anything that may make noise. It was very dark but it took no time for Tristan's eyes to adjust. He stood still and listened for any signs of Patton being home. He only heard a low humming sound, like the sound of an old refrigerator or ceiling fan. It didn't matter what the sound was now. He was already inside.

First, I need to make sure he is the one.

Tristan was just about to move when he heard a muffled sound. He froze in place and listened. Hearing nothing, he walked slowly through the kitchen and turned a little corner into what was the large living room. He stared into the darkness but for some reason he was having a hard time seeing. He reached inside his pants pocket for the small flashlight but didn't pull it out. Tristan rested his hand on it, not quite sure he wanted to give himself away just yet. It wasn't until he heard the muffled sound again that he took it out.

This time he knew exactly what it was. There was no mistaking the sound. It was low and sounded almost like a cough, but it was someone clearly asking for help. Tristan stood still in the archway between the kitchen and the living room with the tiny flashlight, still turned off but in his hand.

"Why is it that people find themselves compelled to investigate a noise or a sound in the dark unknown?" an unfamiliar voice asked.

Tristan took a few steps back, his head whipping from side to side, struggling to see who was speaking to him and from what direction. He had the light but still didn't want to turn it on. If he used the light he would be able to clearly see the person who asked for help and the person who had spoken to him but they would be able to see him too. He couldn't even tell what direction the voice had come from so he couldn't use the glare of the light to mask himself.

He did know one thing—it wasn't Patton's voice that he just heard.

"You can still leave," the voice said.

Tristan didn't recognize the voice at all. He stood still, moving only his eyes. He bent his arm that held the flashlight up so that it was very close to his temple, but he didn't turn it on just yet.

"Patton?" Tristan said.

"I know you know that I am not Patton, or were you just trying to confirm if Patton is here? I assure you, he is here and is currently in stable condition," the voice said calmly.

Tristan heard another low grunt. A sign of confirmation from the stranger that Patton still lived?

"You can still leave now, Tristan. No harm no foul," the voice said plainly.

This person knows me.

Tristan stepped forward slowly into the darkness but only got a few inches into the room before he felt something. He could move his arms, head, and legs but something prevented him from moving forward, though he didn't feel any hands on him.

Tristan pushed the button on the flashlight. Almost simultaneously, the flashlight was somehow ripped from his hand. But Tristan saw what was hidden by the dark before he himself hit the floor.

A man not much older than him stood about thirty feet away. The man's left hand was raised in front of him toward Tristan, poised in the universal hand signal for stop. The stranger's right arm was raised straight up and above his head.

Tristan had quickly glanced up as a muffled cry came from above. He stumbled back and to the floor as he saw what he knew was Patton, rigid and fixed to the ceiling. In that moment and for the first time in his life Tristan felt the fear of death rush over him as the stranger caught the flashlight in his left hand and the room went dark.

October 12th

10:00 a.m.

Thor's damn hammer did a job on him. At least that was the way he felt after being handled for the second time by a Coesen. This time Tristan's head was the target and not his ribs. And the pain only got worse as he sat up and threw his legs over the edge of his bed. His elbows rested on his knees as he rubbed his hanging head repeatedly.

Tristan remembered being at Patton's house the night before, and someone else was there too, another Coesen. He could only remember the tiny flashlight leaving his hand, seeing a flash of someone else and then Patton, and then everything going dark.

Wait a minute…

He looked around. It was his bedroom he was in but he didn't have the faintest idea of how he got there.

Tristan stood, but was unable to maintain his balance. He flopped back down on his bed…hard. He let his upper body go limp and fall to the bed as well, grunting only when his head came in contact with his mattress. He felt as if he partied for seven days straight but only he couldn't remember the good parts. Something told him there were no good parts to last night.

Was that last night?

Tristan opened his eyes again. He began feeling his jean pockets for his cell phone. He sighed with relief when he felt it in his side pocket. He checked the date and time before he dialed Cianne's number.

Tristan kept the conversation short. He had no explanation for why he didn't call her last night and he wasn't going to tell her what happened. The good thing was Cianne wasn't upset and she didn't seem too worried.

Apparently, she spoke to Martha earlier in the morning. Martha apparently looked in on him and told her that he was asleep. Cianne had an appointment with Dr. Garrison this morning, another one he was going to miss. So, he told her he would see her after he got himself together.

Tristan needed to talk to Vivian. He was sure a Coesen was responsible for the deaths of Nick, JC, and now most likely Patton. He needed to know if Vivian had ordered their executions and if she had, why wouldn't she have given him that order.

He stood up slowly this time. He would clean up then…

My truck, he thought, *shit*. He needed to have it picked up before the police found the body and canvased the area.

11:45 a.m.

It's worse than we imagined," Cassius said. His voice sounded grim and anxious as he walked from the bedroom of Dr. Garrison's condo and into the living room his team just finished searching.

"There are photos here. Surveillance photos of Cianne, Tristan, and even you. More of Cianne than anyone else, even photos of the engagement party. I had Stella talk to the doorman. He says there is a young man coming and going from the doctor's apartment, a young man in his early twenties. What are your orders?"

Vivian paced the length of the room several times before sitting on the sofa. "Where's the doctor?"

"He left an hour ago. It took us all that time to locate the safe and open it," Cassius admitted.

"And the young man, where is he?"

"The doorman said that he was seen by the night doorman leaving out around 8 pm last night and there is no notation of him returning to the building," Cassius said.

"Gather all you can and I will call you back. Cianne sees Dr. Garrison today." Vivian looked up as Tristan walked into the room. "I will call you back." She placed the phone on the table in front of her. "Tristan, good. You're here."

"Did you order their murders?" Tristan got straight to the point. The queen/subject roles were not happening right now. He was still not feeling himself and it kind of pissed him off a little.

"Excuse me?"

"I went to Patton's house last night."

Vivian gave him a confused look.

"Patton, the brains behind Cianne's kidnapping," he explained, "but when I got there, there was another Coesen in the house." Tristan stood over an empty chair across from where Vivian sat. He gripped the back of the chair. "Why didn't you tell me you sent him to kill those assholes, and why didn't you trust me to do it?'

Vivian's face went pale. She looked at Tristan, and her mouth moved like she wanted to say something but she closed it. She opened it again, "What did he look like?"

Tristan's brows rose but he didn't answer the question.

"What did he look like?" Vivian asked slower.

"He looked like he was in his mid-twenties, a little taller. He had an average build I guess. Blond hair and sort of a strong jawline and chin."

"What color were his eyes?"

"I really didn't get a chance to gaze into them," he said sarcastically.

"Could they have been greenish-blue; did they resemble Cianne's?"

Tristan thought about the question. "They could have. I don't know. All I know is this guy was powerful. He must have knocked me out only I can't remember him doing it. Then I wake up in my own bed and my truck is parked in my garage. This guy knew where I lived, where I slept, and my alarm codes. What's going on?"

Tristan saw Vivian's mind connecting the dots that he himself couldn't do.

She lifted her hand and motioned for him to wait. Vivian picked up her cell phone and dialed.

"Cassius, bring me the doctor." She spoke urgently. "The young man that lives with him may be responsible for the murders of the boys who kidnapped Cianne." Vivian let Cassius respond. "I don't know but we can't chance it." She paused again. "I'm not sure. It could be a Coesen. Bring the doctor. We know his whereabouts. He will know where to find the boy."

"What the hell is going on?" Tristan demanded.

"Doctor," the secretary said over the intercom. "It's 12:05, I'm off to lunch," she hummed. She was the secretary for several of the doctors on the first floor, but over the last few months she became quite taken with Dr, Garrison. "Would you like to join me?"

"No thank you, Karen. I have a lot to do, maybe tomorrow."

"Ok," she sounded disappointed. "I will be back in an hour then."

"Alright Karen," Dr. Garrison said. "Enjoy your lunch."

Dr. Garrison looked at his watch. He had about a half hour before his next patient. He placed the folder he was looking over in his drawer. He logged on to his computer and was about to play a game of poker when he noticed a woman standing with her back to him in his office.

"Hello," he said, standing. "Are you lost?"

The woman turned around slowly.

Dr. Garrison slowly stumbled back into his chair.

"I may be," she said, sounding confused. She walked closer to his desk, rubbing frantically on something small in her hands. "I didn't think it would work. I figured I could do it too. It seems I can, but I guess I got a little lost along the way."

"Kayla…can it, be you?" Dr. Garrison slowly walked around his desk. He reached out his hands to touch the beautiful woman who just appeared in his office but she took a few steps back. Dr. Garrison seemed to look offended at first then realized the problem. He smiled then he closed his eyes.

Kayla looked at the older gentleman as he approached her. He knew her name. When he walked toward her she backed away. Now he was standing in front of her with his eyes closed.

She wondered if she should leave, then she suddenly felt a wave of heat come from the man. He stood still as ripples of heat floated in the air similar to heat rising from a hot tar-covered road on a scorching summer day.

Kayla backed up a few more steps as she watched what was happening right in front of her. She wouldn't have believed it if she hadn't seen it with her own two eyes. One moment an older man who was graying around his hairline was standing in front of her.

Now, she couldn't catch her breath because in place of the older man stood her Caleb, as young as he was the day she last saw him. He stood there as handsome as she remembered. His eyes, a memorable blue-green, just as his daughter's, stared lovingly at her.

"Caleb!" she rushed into his arms. He held her tight as he showered her face with kisses. She wanted to hold onto him like this forever, but she pulled away after only a few seconds. He tried to pull her back but Kayla resisted. "What, how did you…?"

"I can take the form and sound like anyone, remember. It hurts like hell to do but it's one of the ways I've been able to keep the Guard from knowing I'm alive all these years," Caleb said smiling, "and the only way to get close to our daughter."

"So, you've met Cianne?" Kayla asked.

"I see her regularly. Of course, it is when I take the form of her therapist, whom you just saw. I've also spoken to her in the form of my fifteen-year-old self at her engagement party," Caleb admitted, "but never as you see me now, in my true form."

Kayla forgot Caleb could do such a thing. Maybe it was best that she didn't remember, for his safety. *Safety,* she thought. "Does Vivian know you're here?" Kayla asked. Panic strained her voice.

"I suspect she still thinks I am dead," Caleb said. He held her shoulders and began to pull her to him.

"I need you to listen to me, Caleb." She stretched out her arms, pushing him back. "Something terrible is going to happen."

"Let me just look at you for a moment."

"Please Caleb, there isn't much time and I don't know how long I have here!"

"Just tell me how you are here, first. Have you seen Cianne yet? Kayla, she is beautiful, she looks like the both of us. She will be here shortly." He rambled on with excitement.

She pulled him over to the sofa and they both sat down.

Kayla smiled. "I've seen her. She has been visiting me," she said quietly.

Caleb took her hand, and his smile all but disappeared.

"I'm not really here, Caleb. Cianne has the ability to time weave, just as I do. She comes to me in my time, where I am still alive. She is eight in my time. I am using all the strength I have to be here now with you, because your daughter needs us. I've signed my death warrant in ink by coming here but I had to try and prevent what is going to happen. What's the date?"

He looked confused. "It's October 12th."

Kayla covered her mouth with her hand. "The time?" she mumbled.

"Ten after twelve," he said looking at his watch.

"Time weaving is so unpredictable but it seems that I found you here, of all the places you could have been, and at the right time. Thank goodness you gave me this." Kayla opened her hand to reveal the wedding ring he gave her, the ring that Cianne now wears around her neck. "It brought me straight to you, and to think I thought the idea of putting our blood in the rings was so gross." Kayla placed the ring back on her finger. "You have to hurry. Listen to me carefully, Caleb. Today, a short time from now, something is going to change our daughter's life, something that she will never recover from. I need you to do whatever you can to prevent it from taking place."

"What is it?" Caleb asked anxiously.

"I'm not sure how or why but I saw a glimpse of his life when I touched him as a child. I knew he loved her. I didn't look further and now everything that I've done to get them together may be the undoing of all life. When she loses him, it will change her: she will destroy all life on this planet." Kayla took a deep breath. "Tristan is going to die today, at or around 1 pm. You can't let that happen. I can only assume it was the baby I saw the future through when she visited me this night, in my time. From what I have seen, everything changes with Tristan's death. He is her connection to her humanity and without that connection she will never again love anything or anyone else as long as she lives. His death will create a darkness within her that she will spread throughout the world."

"Where do I go?" he asked.

"It's close to my old house, Roland Road and Ridgeview Park Lane. You need to leave now." Kayla leaned in and barely kissed his lips. "I love you, always." She felt herself fading away, here in this time, and there, in her own time.

◉

Caleb touched his lips with his finger. He was about to leave just as the office door flew open.

Cassius looked completely taken aback as he peered at Caleb from across the room. He hesitated but it only took a half of a second to recover.

"I was expecting to see Dr. Garrison, but you will do."

"I was just on my way out old man," Caleb winked.

He dug down deep for the power he so rarely used, to get to the location Kayla gave him but nothing happened.

Cassius stepped forward into the office. His Guards followed but Caleb only focused on the one who looked strained and a bit sweaty. This man must be the reason he couldn't use his mental abilities. He heard of the Cleoma, a Coesen who had the power to zap another's ability but he never saw one in person before.

"Seems you've found the one Coesen who can affect some of my abilities. Alright," Caleb looked at the watch on his wrist again. It was 12:20 p.m. "If you proceed, I will be forced to kill you *and* your toy soldiers."

"You will be the one dying today," Cassius said, "and this time I will make sure you're dead."

12:35 pm

"Call Cianne," Tristan commanded his in-car Bluetooth. The radio cut off, allowing the sound of the ringing phone to come from his SUV's speakers. He applied more pressure to the accelerator with his right foot, passing several cars stopped at the red light he'd just run.

A man in a sedan beeped his horn, slamming on his brakes and yelling a curse as his vehicle spun in the intersection.

"Hey, you," Cianne's voice sang out through the speakers.

"Where are you now?" he asked impatiently. His tires screeched as he made a sharp right turn.

"We're at the light at Roland Road and Ridgeview, by the park," she said.

"I want you to turn around and go back home. Don't open the doors for anyone."

"Tristan, what's wrong? Why don't you want me to go to my appointment with Dr. Garrison?"

Another car horn screamed at him. "Ci, I will explain everything. Just go to your house and wait for me. I should get there a few minutes after you."

"Alright," Cianne said.

"Can you turn around daddy?" she asked.

Joseph Baxter looked in his rearview mirror at Cianne who sat in the backseat and gave her a worried look.

She held the phone to her ear and was about to disconnect when she screamed, "Dad, look out!"

Cianne saw the car coming straight at them but it was too late to act. She heard Tristan yelling her name and the echoes of metal colliding through his speakers as well as all around her when the car hit hers. So, she hugged her stomach and lowered her head.

She wasn't certain how long she was out or if she lost consciousness at all. She slowly raised her head from the back seat and looked at her father. He moaned but didn't open his eyes. She then looked at her stomach. Cianne relaxed a little when she felt the baby move but she knew that she needed to get out of the car because her baby was in danger.

Voices were all around her, but nothing was making any sense. She was dizzy and her head ached. Cianne's hand instinctively went to her head where it hurt the most. She slowly rubbed a gash then looked at the blood that was on her fingers.

"Miss, can you move?" a man was yelling at her.

In slow motion, or at least it felt like slow motion, Cianne looked over to her right and through the shattered window next to her. She rubbed her head a few more times before she could focus on the man who was pushing and tugging at her door.

"Can you move miss?" He asked again.

Cianne looked at him and shook her head. The man tugged at the door repeatedly and was able to pull it partially open. Cianne unhooked her seatbelt and began pushing at the door while the gentleman pulled. She looked at him just as the man was about to speak, but instead of speaking he suddenly fell to the ground. He was looking past her and his face was twisted with fear. The man lifted his hands in self-defense as he pushed away from the car with his feet.

"Hey," Cianne managed to say. "Hey." She continued to push at the door.

Just as she got the door open she heard the loudest sound she had ever heard in her life. The unfamiliar sound vibrated through her, causing her heart skip a beat and her ears to ring. As Cianne whipped her head around, blood and pieces of flesh sprayed all over her body. She gasped with disbelief as screams rose all around her. She blinked several times as she tried to wipe the blood from her eyes to focus on her father's body that was now slumped over the center console of the car and partially onto the passenger seat.

Cianne's breathing became rapid. She pushed at the jammed door once more before it creaked open. Stepping out of the car she weakly cried, "Daddy."

"Daddy?" She limped around the rear of the wreckage to get to the driver side door. "Daddy," she sobbed as she reached out, but didn't touch him.

Cianne took no notice of the people hiding behind cars and poles, screaming for her to run. She didn't notice the warm clear liquid that was slowly running down her legs now. She didn't hear Tristan who was screaming her name over and over again in her head.

All she could think about was her father and how he was smiling at her a few minutes ago; and now he was slumped over like a sack of dirty laundry while pieces of his brain dripped from her hair. Cianne didn't even notice the gun that was trained on her the entire time it took her to get to the driver's side door of her father's car.

"Look at me you whore. I want the last thing you see to be my face."

Cianne stopped pulling at the driver's side door. Sobbing uncontrollably, she turned around with her eyes wide and wild. The gun was what she saw first. Then she saw who was pointing it at her from about a foot away. Her tears and the blood made it hard for her to see clearly but she knew who it was.

Bianca and Cianne looked into each other's eyes for a moment before Bianca's gaze dropped to Cianne's large belly. The hatred in her eyes filmed over with tears.

"It's true then!" she screamed. "You're pregnant. Is it his? Is that Tristan's baby in you?" Bianca held the gun with both hands as she wiggled it between them.

Cianne didn't respond.

"Answer me you bitch!" she demanded angrily.

Cianne closed her eyes, as if dismissing her.

Bianca screamed and pulled the trigger. The bullet burned through Cianne's flesh and its force knocked her back into the mangled car behind her. The force in which she hit the car bounced her forward to her knees. Bianca watched Cianne use her hands to stop from falling onto her stomach.

Sitting back on her knees, Cianne looked up at Bianca.

Bianca felt no sympathy as she put pressure on the trigger. The second bullet hit Cianne, knocking her to her butt. The car prevented her from falling completely back. Her body rested on the front tire of her father's car.

Bianca gritted her teeth then cried out as she pulled the trigger four more times. It took a moment for her to realize it wasn't Cianne she was unloading into anymore. She let her hand that held the gun fall to her side as she stepped forward.

"No," she whispered with disbelief at first. "How..." She inched closer. "No!" she screamed. "How did he?" She looked up and around, trying to make sense of what she was seeing but nothing could explain it.

Bianca rushed forward then stopped when she stood over him. "No," she breathed out.

Tristan was on his knees. He used his body to completely cover Cianne. His chin rested on Cianne's head and his arms were wrapped around her.

Bianca touched his head and in doing so, caused his body to slowly slide sideways. He fell back, almost landing on her feet, but she jumped out of the way. Blood spilled from his mouth and his face fell to the side with his vacant eyes focused at her.

"NO!" Bianca screamed again. But this scream was louder and more blood curdling than the ones before. "I have nothing," she said. She put the gun to her temple and pulled the trigger.

The few people who witnessed the entire scene unfold in front of their eyes that afternoon could not agree where Tristan had come from. No one saw him jump from the moving truck that crashed into a palm tree, nor did they see him running at a speed that no man could possibly run, to shield the pregnant woman whom none of them had lifted a finger to help.

Mr. and Mrs. Bertram sat in a corner of the waiting area located on the second floor of Wingate University Hospital. Everyone stood when they entered only minutes before. It was Mr. Bertram who announced to everyone that Tristan didn't survive his injuries. Mrs. Bertram sobbed louder, her face buried in his chest, when her husband made the announcement.

Now Lesley held his sedated wife in his arms as she stared at the patterns on the carpet beneath their feet. He had to be strong. He couldn't break down just yet. He had to be his wife's support, her rock. He had to be strong for Cianne. So, he waited just like everyone else for news about the only link they had left to their only child.

Vivian stood gazing out of the large windows that looked out over the parking lot. She looked at the puke green chair that she had just got up from. She walked over to another chair but decided she didn't want to sit.

Feeling useless, she went back to the window, not knowing what she should do. *What can I do?* She wondered helplessly, desperately trying to come up with something.

Vivian looked over at Mr. and Mrs. Bertram. She'd only known them for a brief time. She liked them and felt honored that they would be family soon. Now they would be connected for life by tragedy. Her heart ached for them because Vivian knew what it felt like to lose a child.

Vivian glanced at Zeta. Her eyes spoke volumes to all who looked into them. She stood at the edge of the waiting area. Three other guards were posted nearby. Though they were on duty, Vivian suspected that her safety wasn't on the Zeta's mind.

Vivian walked over to her young Guard. "Do you need some time alone?" Vivian asked.

Zeta looked up. She stood straight when she saw Vivian standing in front of her. "No, Sovereign," she replied.

Vivian knew just by looking into her glossy eyes that she was lying.

"You spent a lot of time with him. It's alright if you need some time, Zeta. I am well protected here," Vivian told her.

It was true. The hospital was a Coesen facility. Forty percent of the staff were Coesen. Vivian would be safe.

"I'd rather stay," Zeta said in a hushed tone.

Vivian touched her shoulder and Zeta lowered her head slightly then raised it again.

"Have they said anything yet?"

Vivian turned around to see Tranae. Her eyes were bloodshot red and puffy. Tranae's parents and brother sat in the waiting area as well. Brian's family was on the way. They said he was told something happened but no one told him about Tristan's passing.

"Not yet," Vivian answered.

Vivian watched Tranae go back to her family with her head lowered.

Cianne was in surgery for thirty minutes now and there was no update yet on her condition or the baby's. A team of Coesen was caring for her but that didn't ease Vivian's mind at all. She walked back to her little corner of the room and sat down. She put her head in her hands.

Get a hold of yourself Vivian, she told herself. *This is the problem with mourning,* she thought to herself. Mourning is a selfish emotion. The thought of not seeing her granddaughter alive again ripped her apart. *But what about the dead?* she thought. They will never see anything ever again, never eat another bite, or smell another flower.

Or in Tristan's case, will never hold his child. That was if the child...

Vivian was the first to see the doctor. She stood up and all but ran toward him. The doctor looked at her and then he glanced over to the corner where the Bertrams were seated. Mr. Bertram stood, but didn't move when the doctor lifted his hand.

The doctor was asking for a moment alone with her.

Mr. Bertram sat back down and the doctor escorted Vivian out of earshot but still in view of everyone. He turned her so his back was to the onlookers.

"Sovereign Harper," he whispered, "the delivery went smoothly considering the circumstances."

Vivian looked at him with terror-filled eyes. She didn't think she heard him clearly.

"You were able to save both Cianne and the baby?" Vivian's hands were clasped together tightly in front of her; her shoulders rose as she waited for his response.

He cupped her hands with his own. "Cianne managed to deliver naturally without incident, but…"

"But what, is there something wrong with the baby?"

"No," he said, "well yes…but it isn't life threatening. One of the babies did sustain a wound in the leg. But the bullet went clean through without damaging anything."

"One of the babies?" she asked, confused.

He managed a small smile. "The boy was delivered first, then the girl came shortly after."

The doctor, being a Coesen along with the rest of the staff in the operating room, knew how momentous this birth was to Vivian and the Arkean tribe. Not only had there not been a male child born to her bloodline in a very long time, there hadn't been more than one child born of a single pregnancy to her line either. In fact, no twins were born to any Coesen bloodline in all their history.

"Twins." Vivian whispered, "And one is a boy?" Vivian covered her mouth. Then she asked, "Cianne…how is Cianne?"

"We've managed to keep her stable long enough to deliver the babies. Well, in truth I am not sure if it was us who kept her stable, but we now have a problem." The doctor looked scared. "It doesn't look good."

"Are you saying she will not survive this?" She looked him in the eyes.

"Cianne is so very different from us."

"Of course, she is different. That is why *you* are operating and not a Middling."

"I mean to say that she is not what we anticipated. You see, we can use and respond to medications the same way regular people do but in Cianne's case none of what we are giving her is working properly." The doctor hesitated before continuing. "She seems to be in a great deal of pain now the babies have been delivered and no drug we have is working on her.

"I honestly don't know how she is surviving this. A bullet went through her hand and is lodged in her right shoulder. Another entered her chest. And then there's the one that went clear through the baby's thigh, but we recovered that. We need to operate but she will not survive it without medication and anesthesia, and she will not survive if we do nothing. As I said before, I don't know how she is still with us, or how long she will last." He looked down. "There's really nothing we can do."

"Find me the best Phantom in this region," Vivian said. "You are going to operate."

Vivian stayed behind while everyone else went to see the babies. She sent two guards to go as well. She didn't share any news about Cianne's condition to anyone. She wanted to exhaust all her options before giving up.

Sitting alone for the first time since this all began, she couldn't hold back her tears any longer. *The Phantom has to work*, she thought, and if not, she would try something else. They were Coesen. Nothing was impossible. With all the power they possessed, there had to be someone who could help.

"Sovereign," Zeta said, her voice unsteady. She touched Vivian on the shoulder.

Vivian looked at Zeta, who was looking toward the elevator. Vivian followed her gaze and saw the two people who walked out of it. When she saw Cassius, everything came back to her. She forgot about the mission when she got the call from Officer Perkins telling her Cianne was attacked. She forgot about Dr. Garrison and the young man. Even Cassius had slipped her mind.

It didn't matter now because Cassius was walking toward her.

Vivian stood slowly. She narrowed her eyes as she looked at Cassius. Something about him didn't look right. He wasn't moving his legs as he came toward her. The person with him followed close behind, hidden. When she was able to see him, the young man, she couldn't help gawking at him. She moved toward them.

He…he looked exactly like Caleb. *An exact copy of Caleb*, she thought.

As they came closer Vivian backed up and Zeta and the remaining Guards quickly stepped in between her and the oncoming pair.

"What did you do to him?" Vivian asked, shielded by the Guards and Zeta. *Cassius isn't walking*. He was actually floating a few inches off the ground. His eyes were open but he didn't seem to be conscious.

"I am only going to say this once," Caleb said calmly, "I would prefer not to kill any of you but I will if you don't tell me where she is." He looked at Vivian as he spoke. He needed to get to Cianne but he was tired of ducking around corners and avoiding guards. He also didn't have time to be cordial, not that he planned to.

The three Guards stepped forward. Caleb extended his arm and Cassius flew several feet away and fell hard in a chair, in a seated position. Caleb slid under the arm of the first Guard and struck him hard in the lower back with his fist. He then jumped in the air and kicked the second Guard that was to his right in the chest.

Using that Guard's chest as leverage, Caleb pivoted his foot on the Guard's chest and kicked off, flying inches over the head of the Guard head who attacked him first. Standing behind the first Guard now, Caleb kicked him in the back of the leg. When the Guard fell to his knees, Caleb squatted low, turned sideways and hit him with an open-handed forceful blow to the center of his back. He then jumped up and kicked the approaching third Guard a few feet in the air. In all it took less than twenty seconds.

Caleb easily blocked Zeta's attack and grabbed her by the neck. He looked at Vivian, who watched silently. All three Guards lay motionless on the floor. Vivian took a single step toward him. In response, Caleb lifted Zeta by the neck so that her feet dangled free. He looked at Vivian, fury evident in his face.

"Cianne likes this girl, despite the girl's feelings for Tristan. I don't want to harm her or you. Or anyone else," he said looking at the three Guards that lay motionless on the floor. "They will be fine in a few hours. The ones at Dr. Garrison's office are alive as well." He looked back to Vivian, allowing the pain he felt to seep into his eyes and the look on his face to soften.

"I am here to help. Kayla sent me, but your men prevented me from getting there in time."

The words were not spoken, but Vivian heard him clearly. She stepped back and placed her hand over her chest; his ability to project his words in her head shocked her, and their meaning clearly stung.

Caleb sighed the said, "This could have been prevented?"

"Can you help her now?" Vivian asked.

The operating room doors swung open, catching everyone inside off guard. The surgeon and his staff turned in surprise to see Caleb enter the room with Vivian close behind. Cianne lay on the operating table, but her face wasn't visible from the doorway because a nurse was in the way. Many of the staff members surrounding her slowly backed away from the operating table as the two walked toward them.

Caleb was the first to see her face. She was flushed and wet. Her hair was soaked from sweat and from a damp cloth that a nurse was using to dab her forehead with water. He bent next to her and touched her cheek with his fingers.

"She keeps going in and out of consciousness," said the nurse closest to her head.

Caleb looked up at the woman. She looked concerned and scared at the same time.

"Could you unhook her from all these machines please?" Caleb said softly.

The room full of Coesen looked over to Vivian, who stood behind Caleb. Vivian nodded so the nurse began disconnecting her.

"Leave us," Vivian ordered after Cianne was disconnected from all the equipment.

Quickly, they filed out of the room, everyone except Vivian. She closed the doors. "Can you help her?"

Caleb looked over his shoulder at her and then back to Cianne without saying a word. He stood and placed a hand on Cianne's forehead. He looked over his shoulder again and said, "I need you to stand behind me."

Vivian looked a little annoyed by the request but did what he said.

"Closer," Caleb said, as he looked at Cianne.

Vivian cleared her throat as she moved closer until he felt her touching him. Almost immediately, she felt warmer. At first, she thought it was because she was in close proximity to her enemy but that wasn't it. The room became hotter and brighter. It became so hot that Vivian began to perspire, and bright enough that she had to cover her eyes with her hand.

In a matter of seconds her hands weren't enough to protect her eyes from the light. Vivian leaned into Caleb. She rested her forehead on his back to shield her eyes from the light. When it felt like the room couldn't get any hotter or brighter, things began to shake. The shaking was subtle at first, and she heard clinking sounds, like bottles tapping together. Vivian could also hear Zeta and a few other voices outside the room, shouting frantically and banging on the doors.

They must not be able to get in, Vivian thought.

The clinking noise elevated to a clanging sound as the furniture shook harder. Vivian felt arms around her now, holding her tight, covering her. She kept her eyes closed as the clanging sound soon became the sound of smashing glass. The entire room and everything in it began to shake violently as if an earthquake had hit. She felt arms tighten around her then a gush of wind rushed past them, almost knocking them to the floor.

Vivian was just about to scream out 'What was happening' but the light subsided and the rumbling suddenly stopped. She slowly began to remove her hand from her eyes and lifted her head. After her eyes adjusted, she realized she was up close and personal with Caleb Scott. She tried to move her arms but soon realized that Caleb, who was holding her, hadn't released his grip.

Vivian wiggled a little. "Let go of me," she said squirming. "You can release me now."

But he had her locked in a strong hold. When she looked up at him, she gasped. His eyes were stark red with only the pupils retaining their dark tint. He stared vacantly forward. She turned her head as far back as she could to see what he was watching. There was nothing there other than the closed doors and the frantic people shouting to get inside.

Vivian was about to try again, to wiggle free, when something behind Caleb caught her attention. It was Cianne's feet. They seemed to hang in the air, a good inch above the bed. Vivian's gaze climbed Cianne's body; the left leg had a small hole with blood trickling from it. Cianne's arms were at her sides just loosely dangling. A loose hospital gown covered her but blood was soaking through it.

When Vivian saw Cianne's face, her mouth fell open.

Cianne's eyes were red just as Caleb's were and her long hair was raised, floating in the air. Vivian saw Cianne tilt her head to the side then when she looked down at her, their eyes met.

Does she recognize me?

"Tristan?" Cianne spoke. Her voice sounded sweeter and a little softer than Vivian remembered. "I can't feel Tristan," she said, looking directly at Vivian.

Vivian's eyes welled up as she thought again about their loss, and how Cianne would never again see the smile that she loved so much. Vivian didn't know what to say as she looked into Cianne's crimson eyes.

Vivian was speechless, but while she contemplated what she should say to Cianne she noticed a change in Cianne's expression. Cianne's lips began to quiver and then her hands fisted. Her eyes widened, as if she knew. The look on her face changed from concern to shock and horror.

Cianne remembered the shooting. She remembered Tristan covering her and his words.

"You're my first thought when I wake and my last thought when I close my eyes," he had whispered to her as his body shook with each impact.

"TRISTAN!" Cianne cried out, her voice full of agony and pain. As she yelled out, everything that could move, flew outward from her. The surgical lighting behind her burst into flying glass.

Vivian lowered her head again just as the bed flew up and over them, just missing Caleb's head by a few inches. The rectangular windows on the door, and every glass item in the room seemed to explode. Weighted items flew away from Cianne like missiles.

Vivian heard a low grunt come from Caleb and felt a slight squeeze from his arms that were still wrapped around her.

Then there was no sound, nothing. Caleb's arms slowly dropped from her, so Vivian lifted her head. She looked at Caleb. He looked back at her for a moment before dropping to his knees. Vivian attempted to catch him as he fell, but he was too heavy and he continued his slide to the floor. She held him as they dropped to their knees together.

"Go help her," he grunted, as he motioned to Cianne with his head.

Vivian nodded as she jumped to her feet to go to Cianne's side.

Cianne was sitting in a corner with her knees pulled up to her chest and her face hidden from view. Vivian grabbed a sheet from the floor and covered Cianne's trembling body.

"No…no…no…no…no…" Cianne muttered continuously as she rocked back and forth.

Vivian looked up as Zeta and some of the staff rushed into the destroyed room. The look on everyone's face was a mixture of fear and curiosity.

"Oh," a nurse said, as she ran to Caleb. She was the same nurse who spoke to him earlier.

Caleb raised his hand to stop her advancement. The nurse stopped instantly, as if an invisible force was holding her back. Then Caleb took his other hand and slowly moved it to his chest. A long piece of metal, possibly a part of the gurney, had skewered him.

The pole went through his back and out the front of his shoulder. He slowly worked the metal out of his body with no assistance. Caleb dropped it to the floor and the clanging ricocheted through the room. He swayed back and forth a bit before dropping his hand to the floor to brace himself from falling.

The nurse, free to move now, kneeled at his side.

"Don't touch me." he said harshly.

The nurse stood up and backed away.

Caleb touched his chest where he'd been impaled. Blood dripped freely through his fingers as he squeezed the wound until it was fully healed. He was on his feet seconds later and standing over Cianne.

"You need to heal yourself, now that you can." Caleb transferred as he looked down at his daughter.

Cianne stopped murmuring and looked up at the man who spoke to her. She stared into an exact copy of her eyes, as they looked down at her.

To be continued in…
THE DESCENT OF THE HALO
Excerpt Below (Unedited)
Head on over to my website www.SheaSwainWrites.com for
Upcoming Releases,
Character Dream-casting
And sign up for my Newsletter
THANK YOU
and
Please consider leaving a review!

"There were no palaces made of gold. No harmonious chords

sung by Angels standing near the pearly white gates of

Heaven to lead the way.

Heaven wouldn't have me.

Death abandoned me.

Left barely alive, with the darkness, immeasurable time, and

the memories of her and him. Though, as hard I fought the

darkness their faces were blocked from me. As time slowly

crept on, their presence, their warmth, their love, left me.

In the end, I felt nothing but the pain of my loss and the

desire for revenge."

Caleb

Prologue

The Atlantic Ocean
Late summer, circa 1816

The stench of urine and feces combined with perspiration, other body fluids, and filth assailed Jai's senses. It was so terrible that she found it difficult to think of what was happening to them. Or, where they were being taken?

What are they going to do to with us?

All of these questions crossed her mind before she and her ward were thrown down the steep stairs and chained to others whose skin color was like theirs. She even thought about what her people would do when they discovered they were missing.

As hopelessness washed over Jai, she could only think of her ward, Marda, who clung tightly to her. The girl's thin arms were wrapped around her neck so tightly that breathing through the stench had become even more difficult.

Jai gently pulled at Marda's arm so she could take in air. Loosening the girl's grip caused Marda to slide a few inches down Jai's torso, settling more into her lap. Awake now, Marda moaned.

Jai sighed. Even if she could focus, even if she could use her ability, there wasn't much she could do to the pale people who held her and many others with dark skin captive on the water vessel that was carrying them. She was just a neophyte, a novice that no matter how well she knew how to wield her power it wasn't an ability that could save them. In truth, Jai's ability was only enough to secure her future as the first wife to the Prince of her tribe and secured her position of handmaiden to his sister, the Princess Marda, until their joining.

A loud cry rising above the continuous sobbing caused young Marda to squeal and tighten her grip again. *Another has passed*, Jai guessed.

Jai understood their language like it was her own. The ability was a gift most Coesen were capable of. So, she understood the pale man when he came down with a pair of clothed men of color to haul off the one who'd passed. They carried the body up the steep stairs and through an opening, which was the only source of light shining into the sunken room, and tossed the it overboard. None with shackles moved.

The light was the way to freedom but only through death.

Jai looked down at Marda who began to shake and cry uncontrollably. She wrapped her arms around the girl, squeezing a little tighter. "Close your eyes little one," Jai whispered in their tongue.

As Marda closed her eyes, Jai gently stroked her cheek. She may not be able to use her ability to escape but she could take Marda away from this place. Not physically, of course, but to Marda the images in her mind, whimsical and amazing, will be as real as the stench of the floating prison they were in.

Jai closed her eyes and called to her ability and almost instantly young Marda fell silent.

With the girl tucked away in a world of sweet dreams, Jai opened her eyes. She looked around the room at the scared, lost faces that were crammed together so closely that there was little space to extend a limb. Her attention settled on the men who were kept separated and who were chained to one another and shackled to the floor. Her gaze landed on one particular male. He was watching her too.

Why?

She was considered a beauty among her people. Her eyes were dark brown, her black lashes were long, and her dark brows were naturally arched. Her chin and nose were longer and narrow due to her Egyptian ancestry but they blended perfectly with her warm beige skin, salmon colored lips, and her darker than coal hair. And even though she'd only seen sixteen dry seasons, her intelligence matched her beauty.

Jai still wasn't certain that attraction wasn't his motive.

The man watching her slowly bowed his head while maintaining eye contact with her.

He knows what I am.

Did he think she could save them? There would be no saving them, at least not by her anyway.

She studied the man's features—his comely looks, his build which showed his physical strength, and his quiet reserve that spoke of his patience.

A tear rolled down Jai's cheek when she saw the tribal markings on his chest. He was from the small village where Jai and ten other Coesen representatives were sent on behalf of the Quende King, Garwe.

King Garwe had also sent his daughter, Marda, to show how serious he took the Kepe King's proposal. Talks of joining the two tribes had gone on for two full seasons. King Garwe knew the Kepe wanted to merge due to the raiding of villages by pale men that had consumed the coastal lands, but according to their law, the Coesen people were to remain indifferent to the dealings of Middlings.

It was rumored that King Garwe wanted more power. By joining the two tribes he could gain that power. His youngest daughter Marda, whose beauty at eight dry seasons shamed other Coesen, was to be presented as bride to the Kepe King's son.

No one foresaw that the Kepe village would be raided and the Coesen King's daughter would be taken from their lands.

Jai shook her head at the man who bowed, then lowered her head in a modest bow to him. She'd seen the Kepe warriors fight bravely. Most were killed in the quick raid. In some backwards way, Jai considered those who lost their lives to be the fortunate ones.

She let her head fall back against a wooden beam she was leaning against. Somehow, she knew that where they were going, her regal status no longer mattered.

Maiden Hall Plantation
Virginia, Fall of 1816

Marda lifted her head when the wagon stopped. Shaking with fear, she tried not to think of how empty her stomach was as she thought of how far from home she was. She looked up at Jai, who was watching a pale-faced man who stood beside the wagon. He was speaking to a Negro standing next to him. The pale-faced man barked out commands and the Negro just mumbled and nodded, never looking the man in the eyes.

Negro was what the pale-faced people called people with dark skin. She heard them say it many times since her capture. She didn't care for the word. She didn't care for the word Nigger either, another of their words for dark-skinned people. If she had to choose between the names she heard the pale people use for people of color, she preferred colored, but that didn't seem right to her either.

Marda also disliked their way of speaking. Their words sounded harsh, clipped, and forced. Not like her language. Her language sounded like a soothing song. And her people often smiled at one another. Not like this pale man or the others she saw in this land.

Marda eyed the Colored man as he made his way to the wagon where she and four others like her were huddled together. It wasn't long before she felt herself being pulled from Jai's arms and out of the wagon. She tried to tighten her grip around Jai. Marda even clawed at Jai's arms and screamed, but the brown-skinned man yanked her free.

"Simma down here girl," the brown-skinned man said.

Only, Marda kept screaming.

"Ain't nobody gonna hurt ya here, chile. I'm Barkly." He placed her feet on the ground, grabbed her by her arms, and shook her.

Marda looked up at the man's face staring down at her. He had a tired face but his light brown eyes had a gentle look to them. When he let her go, she moved close to him as he helped Jai down from the wagon.

Marda shuffled to Jai's side and grabbed her arm as the brown-skinned man slapped his hand against the wagon. As the wagon pulled away, Marda watched through hooded eyes as the others in the back huddled closer together.

The brown man spoke to her and Jai but Marda just continued to look at the wagon as it rolled further away, down the dirt path. Marda's eyes searched out the pale man who made some kind of trade for them when they were herded off the boat earlier. He sat in the front of the wagon with ropes that were tied around the others' necks in his hands.

The man was called Shaw, and his pale gray eyes peered back at her as he rode away. Marda cringed when she saw his thin lips turned up into a wicked smile. When Marda felt Jai pull her close, she turned away from Shaw's crooked grin.

"Dis place, 'tis new for y'all but all gone be fine." The brown man smiled as he led them through a field of low cut grass. "The misses, she fair to us."

Ahead, there was a small white dwelling with openings for air and a portal for entering. It was the prettiest thing Marda had ever seen but the man didn't stop there. Marda slowed to appreciate the dwelling as they passed but the brown man continued walking and Jai continued to pull her along. So, Marda quietly followed but was rewarded as they traveled through a maze of hedges and colorful flowers.

In the distance, a large white dwelling came into view. Marda exhaled a breathless sigh. In her eight dry seasons, she had never seen anything so grand, so beautiful as the dwelling that stood before her. For the first time since being thrown into this new world, she thought of something other than home.

She wanted to explore every corner.

As they approached, she saw that the sheer size of the dwelling was magnificent. The paint was so white it was blinding. It had so many air openings and tall white beams that seemed to hold the upper level up. Her current thought was where the opening for her to go inside would be in such a place.

Marda was so enthralled that she wasn't paying attention to where she was going so she ran into Jai, who had stopped at a white wooden entry on the ground.

Barkley bent down and tapped two times on the wooden entry. "Barkly here, wit dem girls the Missus asked fer."

Jai and Marda looked at one another then to the entry as it was pushed up and open. Marda felt the urge to back away but relaxed when she felt Jai squeeze her close. A round face woman with a round body popped her head out of the large hole in the ground. She wore a head wrap and was dressed in coverings that made her look like one big mass of fabric.

"Don't just stare at me. C'mon in now," the heavy woman said. She reached for Jai but Jai ripped her hand from the woman's grasp then looked at the man.

"Dey fresh off the boat," Barkly said to the woman. "Don't know our talk much." He pointed to Jai and Marda, then to the heavy woman. "Y'all get on in now."

Jai slowly extended her hand, but held onto Marda tightly with her other. They slowly walked down into the underground space with the round woman's help. When the entry slammed closed above them, they both whipped their heads around.

They were alone with the round woman in a dimly lit room. The woman took Jai by the hand and pulled her over to where light flickered in the room.

"Let me eye ya some," the robust woman said as she stood in front of them. She circled them slowly. Every so often she would touch or move them closer to the light. She inspected them the same way the pale man, Shaw, had. She looked in their mouths and worked her hands through their hair.

"Good," she muttered under her breath. Then she saw the mark behind Jai's ear.

Marda watched as the heavy women licked her thumb then wiped at the mark.

"Hmm," she said when the mark didn't come off. She shrugged. "Seein ya both, I got a mind to guess why Shaw pay fer ya. A fine face don't mean spit if y'all can't learn proper. 'Cause me no never mind if ya can't use words but it gone be hard learning ya'll to." She shook her head. "Don't want ta think what it gonna do to my work load, to learn ya'll and get ya right for Miss Catherine. Goin' be some work fer sure. *Humph*," she rubbed her apron, "well let's get ya' clean."

●

The large sash windows allowed the sunlight to brighten the entire room. Jai and Marda stood next to each other with their heads lowered but stole glances at the objects in the room. There were so many things that neither of them had ever seen before. Things that Marda wanted to touch but she stood still as the heavy woman, who called herself Tempie, talked to a woman they couldn't see clearly because she sat in a chair facing a window with her back to them.

"Scrub 'em real nice Miss Catherine," Tempie said to the woman.

The woman stood and turned around slowly to look at them. Jai somehow knew not to look at the woman. But Marda couldn't help looking at the beautiful pale skinned woman that walked over to them. Her fair hair looked soft and was pulled up and secured with jeweled ivory combs. Not one single hair was out of place. The light beige dress she wore had short sleeves. A brown satin trimming was tied just under her bosom and the sash stretched down in the front of the long narrow sarong all the way to the hem.

Marda watched the woman with wonder and excitement in her eyes. And when the young woman kneeled down in front of her, she looked into the woman's bright green-blue eyes.

"This child is lovely," Catherine said to Tempie. She placed her finger gently under Marda's chin and moved her head from one side to the other.

"Marked befo' dey come miss," Tempie said as Catherine focused on the pie shaped mark behind Marda's left ear.

"And dey ain't speakin' much. Guessin' dats good."

"Why is she clothed in this attire? It hardly fits."

"Young masta Fredrick's old things' all I find dat's small enough. Ain't never had no small girl in the main house befo'. I speck I can fetch some from de field folk."

"No," Catherine said sweetly. "I'll see what I can find in my trunks that you can make use of."

Marda, mesmerized by young Catherine's eyes and beauty, slowly lifted her hand to touch the woman's face. But before she could touch Catherine, Marda screeched when she felt a burning sting on the back of her hand. She jerked her hand away.

The shock of being touched her in anger for the first time was overwhelming. Never had she felt the sting of anyone's aggression. Marda's eyes began to water just as Jai stepped in front of her, giving Tempie a vicious look.

"Tempie!" Catherine yelled as she stood. "You know I don't allow that type of treatment in my home. You will never touch this child in that manner again."

"Miss," Tempie coward, "she was fixin' ta touch you miss."

"Never you mind that Tempie. In this house, you abide by my rules," Catherine said firmly. Tempie backed away and lowered her head. Catherine then kneeled down in front of Marda again. She looked to Jai and spoke.

"Is she your daughter?"

Jai didn't look at Catherine. She just held a cowering Marda close, eyeing Tempie.

Marda could see how the green-eyed woman would think that. She and Jai shared a common Egyptian ancestor and they did indeed resemble each other but Marda's skin was a darker, a soft sable color.

"Dey don't speak like us, miss." Tempie slightly raised her head but quickly lowered it again.

"Well," Catherine said, "I suppose we will have to talk more so they can learn." She looked at Jai and smiled. "I am sorry." She then slowly extended her hand.

Marda, sensing the woman's gentleness, slowly walked around Jai and stood face to face with her. Catherine took Marda's hand and lifted it to the side of her face. Marda felt the woman's soft, warm skin under her hand.

Catherine looked to Jai. "You and your daughter will not be treated unkindly as long as you are in my home." Catherine gently pulled Marda's hand away and cupped it to her chest, then she slowly stood. "Tempie, take them to the kitchen and give them something to eat. They look starved."

Excerpt's End

Dark Bright

Claiming His Angel Book 1
A Paranormal Romance
Prologue Unedited

Gadreel raised his sword of cerulean fire high above his head. He tightened his hands around the hilt as he prepared to strike the final blow. Time passed as he held still above his injured brother as the fighting around them roared to deafening heights.

"Strike down the Fallen," roared Michael from somewhere nearby.

Gadreel looked up. All around him was death.

Simi, he thought as his gaze fell on Gabriel who just took Simi's head with his own sword of fire.

"Erase them from the Heavens," Gabriel cried out as he walked past the rolling head of their brethren with no regard.

Gadreel hands loosened around the hilt of his sword but when Gabriel met his gaze, he tightened his fingers again as he turned to look back down at Dantanian. The fallen angel was weak and wounded at Gadreel's feet.

With one quick swing, Dantanian's head would be separated from his body. Dantanian would be no more.

Why didn't he escape to the desolate place with Lucifer and the others? Did he think his disobedience would be forgiven? Do he and the others not understand that our Father's forgiveness is solely designed for his favored, the humans.

"Finish it, Gadreel," Dantanian said as he coughed. Low light shined through the deep wounds in his chest and side.

Gadreel furrowed his brows as he flared his fingers out then regripped his sword. He'd bested his brother but searching inside himself, he could not find the desire to kill Dantanian. He knew the Fallen were wrong to question their

Lord. They were not fit for the heavens. Yet, Gadreel didn't think death was a suitable sentence.

Isn't my questioning and hesitancy to carry out the orders given to me by my superiors just as unlawful? Is the penalty death?

Gadreel looked around. Headless bodies strewed the once pristine replica of the Garden of Eden landscape. It was once a place of peace and reflection. Now it will forever be marred by death and fratricide.

I can't...

When his weary eyes met Gabriel's, Gadreel saw the questions mounting in his commander's eyes. He saw when Gabriel's gaze hardened with resolve. He actually felt fear ripple through him when Gabriel's lips thinned as he started toward them.

With a hint of a thought, the flame that encompassed Gadreel's sword rescinded. A flick of his hand and a though and the sword disappeared into the ether only to return when he needed it.

Moving as fast as he could, Gadreel whipped his robe out of the way, bent and lifted Dantanian over his shoulder, and made for the Pool of Province.

He risked his very existence as he ran with Dantanian in tow. Gadreel heard the calls to halt his progress. He dodged the expertly aimed daggers and arrows of his brethren who tried to stop him. To his surprise, some of the judged, the Fallen, stepped in front of some of the blows aimed at him and Dantanian.

As Gadreel jumped over the bodies of Fallen and Devoted, he knew that he would never again step foot in the Heavens. That once he jumped into the Pool of Province, a reflective gateway that allowed Angels to observe humans and crossover to the earth, without permission that the ability to cross back over or to any plain from this moment forth will be forever revoked.

"Noooo," Dantanian cried out.

"It is the only way to save you," Gadreel said as he ran up the stairs to the great pool. Something hit his back, causing him to stumble forward. Dantanian's body fell forward, hitting the tepid pool first. Gadreel followed, sighing as the water that wasn't wet covered him from head to toe.

Gadreel didn't have to call out for his wings to expand. His large white feathered wings flared out instinctively to slow his descent from the heavens.

Scanning the sky, Gadreel searched for his brother but what he saw wasn't an Angel soaring through the darkening skies. What he saw was a smoking body tumble rolling toward the earth. Gadreel positioned his wings back to dive but suddenly felt an intense debilitating pain with the movement.

Gadreel cried out as he pumped his smoking wings long enough to see that they were ablaze. There was only one thing to do. He dived toward Dantanian, tucking his wings back. When he slammed into his unconscious brother, Gadreel shook off the pain and extended his burning wings to slow them before slamming into the ocean.

Coming Soon

INVIDIOUS Betrayal
A Dark Paranormal Romance
Excerpt

Prologue

April 8th, 2012

Ian Howl cradled the delicate, unconscious, girl in his arms as he swiftly made his way through the maze of a mansion to get to the garage. Her head rested on his chest and his arms supported her back and legs as he held her close. The swell of her feminine curves against his body felt all too consuming; the warmth of her skin was like a sweet yet biting burn. Tapping down on his ill-placed desires, Ian forced himself to focus on the present: their escape.

He ignored the hulking guard that sat in the security room who called to him as he rushed by. Turning a corner, Ian glanced over his shoulder to see if he was being followed. He hoped for a confrontation-free getaway, but the odds were against them.

Gently, he lowered the arm that cradled the girl's legs so that they slowly slide down his body until he balanced her on the balls of her feet. Holding her close to his chest, he placed his thumb to the security scanner on the wall. He vaguely thought of her bare feet touching the cold floor, but it was something he couldn't help right now. He needed to get her out of there and a chill was the least of his worries.

Three heartbeats later, the door that lead to the massive garage swung open with an air-locked *swoosh* that brought his hope soaring to new heights. They were almost free.

Ian noticed his car was blocked in, so he grabbed a random set of car keys from the wall hook and pressed the door unlock button. The headlights of a beautiful Porsche flashed, but the vehicle was in the rear of the garage and several cars surrounded it. The third set of keys he tried unlocked a luxury sedan that wasn't blocked in and was close to the garage doors.

Ian had eased the girl into the passenger seat of the sedan and was securing the seatbelt around her when he felt a heavy hand on his shoulder.

"Where do you think you're taking that car, kid?"

Ian turned his head around to see Brad... Or was it Brent? He didn't remember the guard's name, but Ian knew the guy was built like a defensive tackle. Striking first would surprise Brad/ Brent. So he grabbed the hand on his shoulder and pulled the guard into his elbow, targeting his large, beefy face. The guard stepped back, holding his gushing nose. Ian spun around; he thrust the base of his palm upward into the man's shocked, bloody, face causing him to stumble back again then fall to the floor. The guard didn't get back up.

"Please," the girl whispered.

Ian whipped his head around to see that she was still unconscious and strapped in the car. Rushing to the driver's side of the commandeered vehicle, he hopped inside and started the engine. The automatic doors to the parking garage opened when the car tripped the underground sensor and they barreled down the path toward the front gate of the property. Luckily there were still party guests inside because usually those sensors only allowed vehicles with an installed security plate placed under the hood to pass through without human intervention.

Again, the underground sensor allowed the vehicle to pass through. The large main gates had opened, but they were not in the clear yet.

Ian didn't floor the gas pedal until he was clear of his uncle's property. He wasn't being followed, but he continued to check the rearview mirror, knowing their absence would soon be reported.

The girl moaned, pulling his gaze from the road.

Her long dark brown hair was matted to her head, practically covering her delicate face, so he brushed some of it away. Bruises covered her body but her dry lips, puffy red eyes, and the darkening hand prints on her throat were the most obvious. She was in bad shape, and Ian feared that the thin sheet wasn't enough to keep her naked body warm.

"Help me," she moaned.

"I'm taking you to a hospital," Ian told her. He fought the bile that rose from his stomach. Disgust and shame assailed him, but right now he couldn't think of his role in what had happened to her. He had to get her medical help, but he didn't know Howard County, Maryland, all that well. The only time he even came to this part of Maryland was when he visited his uncle.

Ian brushed the back of his hand over her bruised cheek and was about to place it back on the steering wheel when her eyes popped open, jarring him a little.

She didn't move right away. She just looked at him with a hollowed gaze as if her mind had to reboot. Then those chestnut-brown orbs changed from confused to feral in a flash. Before he could react, she was screaming, "No hospital! No cops!" over and over as she kicked at him and pushed at the passenger door with her hands. Ian grabbed at her feet, but his hand slipped and she nailed him hard on the side of his head with her foot.

"All right, no hospitals!" Ian yelled her as he slammed his foot on the brake, causing the car to skid along the nearly empty road. The force of the sudden stop propelled her forward and the side of her head collided with the dashboard. Her body went limp.

"Shit!" he yelled as he slammed his hands on the steering wheel. Ian pulled the car off to the side of the road, took his cell phone out, and dialed his father's cell. The phone rang several times, then the voicemail picked up. He listened to his father's commanding voice, but he disconnected before the taped greeting ended.

"Damn it, Dad, this is important!"

Ian glanced up at the rearview mirror, peering out into the quiet darkness, lost in thought. The weight of his cell phone in his hand made him find his focus again. He turned the phone over in his hand twice before shutting off the power. Ian stared at the cell phone in his hand for a long moment as he unconsciously rubbed at a spot under his armpit.

"They will be looking for me, us."

He glanced at the girl then felt under his arm again. As long as she was with him, they would find her.

Available Now

About the Author

Shea is a woman in love with the idea of love so it's no wonder she writes Romance Novels. The East Coast native is a romantic to her core and reads and watches anything with a love story. She especially likes binging on the Hallmark Channel around Christmas time.

She enjoys meeting people and chatting, collecting Barbie dolls, toys, and is addicted to The Sims games. Shea also loves music and has mentioned that she writes better when she has movie scores playing as white noise in the background.

This new and exciting author writes Adult Romance in the sub-genres of Contemporary, New Adult, Paranormal, Sci-Fi, Dark, and Erotica.

Connect with Shea Swain

Website: www.SheaSwainWrites.com
Email: SheaSwainWrites@gmail.com

Coesen Definitions

Words in italics are defined

Coesen: In the *Ilterian* language, the word *Coesen* means the combination of two or more items, particles, or organisms. The Four Originals adopted the term for their classification that defines them as a race of human-hybrids who originated from a single tribe on the continent of Africa. Most are born with birthmarks behind their left ear. Each tribe has a variation of this mark that they are born with. Some *Coesen* are born with an ability. It is present at birth but doesn't manifest until the age of puberty. Most are born with a single ability. A very small percentage are born with two.

Breed: The child of a Coesen and *Middling* coupling. Most of these children do not carry the birthmark of a full blooded Coesen. The law on the books state that Coesen parent and Breed are to be sentenced to death, the human parent's mind is wiped cleaned. 98% of Breed children are born with no abilities but may still carry the birthmark. If they mate a Coesen, their children may or may not have abilities.

Child of Jai or Pet: Jai of the *Arkean* tribe conceived a Breed with a man named Shaw. Even after her descendants couple with only Coesens, each are born with the physical features of a Caucasian.

Middling: Term to define a human with no *Coesen* blood.

Protectors: A Coesen who is chosen by the *Source* and is infused with power during the *transition* stage to keep the Coesen's Ward safe. They sense when their ward is in danger and is able to locate them at all times. These Coesen are stronger and faster than any living entity on earth with exception of one person, *Caleb Scott.* In history only two Middlings have been chosen by the Source. It is believed that Middling aren't capable of surviving the transformation.

Transition: A Coesen abilities become active when they go through puberty. This process is called a Transition.

Transference: When a Coesen is chosen by the Source to be awarded the abilities to become a Protector.

The Halo: A Coesen whose prophecy states will bear a full halo birthmark and have all the abilities known to Coesen.

The Source: What the Coesen refer to the original source of power, *Lette*.

Royals: The bloodlines closely related to the Original Four. Only four generations are referred to as Royals.

Bodai: The Bodai were the original name and leaders of the nation that eventually become known as the Coesen.

Bresi: The Bresi was formed from the original Bodai who decided to opt out of the change when offered power by the *Original Four*. They isolated themselves for a very long time. Eventually they discover *Pythos*. They pray to his cocooned form as a deity.

Four Tribes: *Arkean, Bode, Gedgi, Quende*

CPA: Coesen Protection Agency, the overseeing security and policing branch for Coesen.

Tandot: A competition of strength, intelligence, and endurance, to win the right to mate a Royal. Only those who are considered perfect Coesen specimens are allowed to enter.

Old Age: The time of the gilded age when Coesen were obsessed with wealth, class, and breed. The rich were set apart as elites. Lineage and wealth dictated your place in society. It wasn't until compassion became fashionable that a new way of thinking was adopted and practiced by the Sovereign and most Coesen. Though, with change there is always the few who hold onto the ways of old.

Pula: Curse word, or derogatory name

Maatii: Three round challenge to become a Royal Guard. You cannot die in the dream-like state but you feel all the pain inflicted on you. The challenge is timed.

The Village: The object is to fight your way through a village full of super beings that do not eat, sleep, or feel pain, in order to reach a pearl like sphere that each member needs to touch at the same time.

The Vortex: The object is for each member to cross a wet, slippery metallic pole over a swirling vortex to reach the pearl like sphere that is floating in the center without falling.

The Pride: The object is to get pass the pride of gigantic lions and lioness to reach the pearl-like orb which is guarded by an even bigger, White Lion.

If you should fail these tasks, you must reapply and do trials over…or settle to be a Sentry Guard

Cycling: The process in with a Coesen has been transferred to. These Coesen endures a physical change over a three-day period.

Rotation: Every Protector must enlist in the *Coesen Guard* for a time period of the service. They can choose the branch. The three branches are, the *Royal* (highest), the *Sentry* (detective Branch), or *Guard* (police branch)

Augur: A Coesen who can see the prophecies.

Fasen: Burial ceremony. The body is washed and cleaned by someone close to the deceased. Close family is in attendance when the body is burned. A viewing is held after the body is returned to ashes to show and offer respect to the surviving family.

Soahn: Term for Royal

Potentate: Sovereign's Mate, King.

Rootstone: The power unit of all *Keystones*.

Keystone: An object that denies or allows access to a protected area.

Veilex: A stone that will react to an enemy of the wearer.

Dregan: Coesen who for whatever reason do not agree with Coesen law. Although they consider themselves separate they follow the most important rules which is why they are permitted to live in peace. The name was taken from a Coesen who broke the law a long time ago.

Sodregs: Dregans who care nothing for the laws and break them without care. They are hunted and tried by the *Guard*.

Dardregs: Dregans who practice the *Dark Arts*. They follow no law and most are minions of Dregan, a Coesen Protector from long ago who fell in love with his ward. He eventually killed several Coesen.

Meriotia: Bonding or marriage ceremony that lasts three days.

The first is a celebration or *Gathering*.

The second day is the *Mating and Blooding ritual/wedding*.

The third day is the *Showering* in which gifts and well wishes are given.

Ilterian: The race of *Lette's* people that hail from a planet far from earth.

Ika: A medicine man or woman of the village.

Oracle: The seer or witch that foresees the future.

Jzerect: Black magic, forbidden.

CARD: Stands for Coesen Ability Registration Department, a specialized section of the Royal Guards. Coesen are required to register all abilities to this agency. Information is kept private unless legal, safety, medical, or employment requires to know the information.

Utopian Circus: A circus run by Coesen with Coesen performers.

Inhibitor Chip: A piece of tech that prevents the wearer from using their abilities.

Purist: Coesen who believe the Breed are an abomination.

Kytel: Group who are against Breed and prefer pure bloodlines.

Veris: The only way the Council of Four can meet face to face without fear of being exterminated in one swift move. In a sleep like state, very similar to the Maatii, each of the Four are ushered to a common room in an astral plane by the head of the Four. While in this mental state their physical bodies are vulnerable so they are housed in a secured room watched over by their Protector.

Hasa: A Coesen title of respect, used for someone who is a paternal protector, or progenitor.

Royal Guard: The justice branch concerning royals. They also handle treats, security, and keep the peace. The Sentry Guards report to them and they report to the Council of Four. They wear a brand, centered on the back of their right hand. A black circle surrounded by the beautifully scripted names of each tribe. A set of knives crossed at their hilts, starting at the wrist, while the blades encircled the script. The tips of the blades ended at the base of their middle finger.

Sentry Guard: The detective and policing branch of the Coesen. They investigate cases for their sector and manage the Coesen Guard. They report to the Royal Guards.

Coesen Guard: Policing branch of the Coesen who handle local cases. They report to the Sentry Guards.

Fading: The stage of becoming invisible before teleporting. The fade can be held as long as the necessary before actually teleporting.

Fader: Someone who can camouflage themselves into the objects around them to become invisible.

The Veris: The act of bringing the Four together on another plane of existence to meet and discuss business.

Monad: A single unit or entity. What the Coesen call the being inside Caleb.

Suma(s): Dry season or summer months.

Rising Sun: 1 day.

Abilities

There are different degrees of these power. The more powerful the Coesen the stronger the effects. Some of the abilities are rare. All abilities are not listed.

Siphon: Can recognize, search, draw the power and ability of another Coesen within range without causing the host harm or alarm. The stronger the Sipher, the longer the distance that they can siphon power. This is a very rare ability.

Empati: A Coesen who can sense power and get readings such as how clean your spirit is.

Engron: A Coesen who can accelerate the growth of living organisms or tissue.

Phantom: A Coesen who can enter your mind and make or produce images that seem real to the dreamer. The recipient will feel the effects as if what presented to them is reality.

Wheddler: A Coesen who can influence another with spoken words.

Time Weaver: A Coesen who can travel through to the past. They can witness events but they cannot interfere mostly because they have no form. People of the past will not be able to see or hear these Coesen. Over time only two Coesen were born with the ability to weave into the future. They both had the ability to be seen and heard, giving them the opportunity to change things.

Fyeah: A Coesen who can wield fire. Two types exist. Some can do it through touch and some can do it through thought.

Seer: A Coesen who can see the future.

Sooth or Truth Seer: A Coesen who can hear the ring of truth from words that are spoken.

Markers: A Coesen who can tattoo skin with only a touch.

Cleoma: A Coesen who can render a Coesen's ability void. This Coesen can make it so you cannot use your ability in their presence.

Toma: A Coesen who can see your inner most secrets, the things you even hide yourself. This is not like reading some one's thoughts, it's reading your desires and fears.

Feeler: A Coesen who senses someone's emotions and sometimes intent through objects they've come in contact with. Some Feelers are strong enough to sense the feeling in a room without touching an object.

Brander: A Coesen who can mark another with tattoo like art by touching a person's skin. The mark is permanent and can only be removed by the Brander or someone in that brander's bloodline.

Reader: A Coesen who can sense the abilities in others.
Scanner: A Coesen who can reach into someone's mind to find intent or goals. They can also see past offenses and evil they are guilty of.
Snare: The ability to wipe another's memories
Saik: This ability is similar to that of a Protector. One has speed, advanced hearing, and has great strength.
Senser: A Coesen who can make their target feel pain or pleasure. This ability can kill.

Places

West Hills High School: A school in Arizona.
Ridgeview Park: Local park near Cianne's home where she usually run for exercise.
Valley Estates: Residential middle-class neighborhood
Kennecott University: Educational institution
Dorchester Psychiatric Hospital: Bianca received her treatment
Northridge Hospital: Hospital where Tristan was discovered during the Cycling
John Hopkins Hospital: Real Hospital in Baltimore Maryland
Wingate University Hospital: Hospital where the twins were born.
Ark Manor: Vivian's Canadian Home
Azazel's Gift Shop: New Orleans
Gering Academy: School for Coesen Three locations, Texas, Europe, and Canada with a small location on the Continent of Africa
Hammonds Drugstore: Local old-style pharmacy. Where Tranae works.
The Broken Nail Tavern: Bill's establishment and front for Watkins

The Man Cave: The bar and grill where Tristan goes while on the run

Koves Glenn: California USA. Koves choice in Coesen. Kove Glenn is a community that Vivian set up for Coesen who fall in love with Middlings. The middling must sign a gag order in blood once they are welcomed into community. They know of the power the Coesens wield and must keep it secret. The Coesen is stripped of their abilities. Any offspring must be registered but it is assumed that they will not have any abilities.

Shoppers Row: Shopping district located in Koves Glenn